Pop
Goes the
Weasel

Pop
Goes the
Weasel

A NOVEL BY

JAMES
PATTERSON

DOUBLEDAY DIRECT LARGE PRINT EDITION

LITTLE, BROWN AND COMPANY
BOSTON   NEW YORK   LONDON

This Large Print Edition, prepared especially for Doubleday Direct, Inc., contains the complete, unabridged text of the original Publisher's Edition.

This Large Print Book carries the
Seal of Approval of N.A.V.H.

This is for Suzie and Jack,
and for the millions of Alex Cross readers
who so frequently ask,
Can't you write faster?

Prologue

GEOFFREY SHAFER, dashingly outfitted in a single-breasted blue blazer, white shirt, striped tie, and narrow gray trousers from H. Huntsman & Sons, walked out of his town house at seven-thirty in the morning and climbed into a black Jaguar XJ12.

He backed the Jag slowly out of the driveway, then stepped on the accelerator. The sleek sports car rocketed up to fifty before it reached the stop sign at Connecticut Avenue, in the posh Kalorama section of Washington, D.C.

When Shafer reached the busy intersection, he didn't stop. He floored the accelerator, picking up more speed.

He was doing sixty-five and ached to crash the Jag into the stately fieldstone wall bordering the avenue. He aimed the Jag closer to the wall. He could see the head-on collision, visualize it, feel it all over.

At the last possible second, he tried to avoid the deadly crash. He spun the wheel hard to the left. The sports car fishtailed all the way across the avenue, tires screeching and burning, the smell of rubber thick in the air.

The Jag skidded to a stop, headed the wrong way on the street, the windshield issuing its glossy black stare at a barrage of early oncoming traffic.

Shafer stepped on the accelerator again and headed forward *against* the oncoming traffic. Every car and truck began to honk loud, sustained blasts.

Shafer didn't even try to catch his breath or bearings. He sped along the avenue, gaining speed. He zoomed across Rock Creek Bridge and made a left, then another left onto Rock Creek Parkway.

A tiny scream of pain escaped from his lips. It was involuntary, coming swiftly and unexpectedly. A moment of fear, weakness.

He floored the gas pedal again, and the

engine roared. He was doing seventy, then pressing to eighty. He zigged and zagged around slower-moving sedans, sport-utility vehicles, a soot-covered A&P delivery truck.

Only a few honked now. Other drivers on the parkway were terrified, scared out of their minds.

He exited the Rock Creek Parkway at fifty miles an hour, then he gunned it again.

P Street was even more crowded at that hour than the parkway had been. Washington was just waking up and setting off to work. He could still *see* that inviting stone wall on Connecticut. He shouldn't have stopped. He began searching for another rock-solid object, looking for something to hit very hard.

He was doing eighty miles an hour as he approached Dupont Circle. He shot forward like a ground rocket. Two lines of traffic were backed up at a red light. No way out of this one, he thought. Nowhere to go left or right.

He didn't want to rear-end a dozen cars! That was no way to end this—end his life— by smashing into a commonplace Chevy Caprice, a Honda Accord, a delivery truck.

He swerved violently to the left and veered into the lanes of traffic coming east, coming right at him. He could see the panicked, disbelieving faces behind the dusty, grime-smeared windshields. The horns started to blast, a high-pitched symphony of fear.

He ran the next light and just barely squeezed between an oncoming Jeep and a concrete-mixer truck.

He sped down M Street, then onto Pennsylvania Avenue, and headed toward Washington Circle. The George Washington University Medical Center was up ahead—a perfect ending?

The Metro patrol car appeared out of nowhere, its siren-bullhorn screaming in protest, its rotating beacon glittering, signaling for him to pull over. Shafer slowed down and pulled to the curb.

The cop hurried to Shafer's car, his hand on his holster. He looked frightened and unsure.

"Get out of the car, sir," the cop said in a commanding voice. "Get out of the car right now."

Shafer suddenly felt calm and relaxed. There was no tension left in his body.

"All right. All right. I'm getting out. No problem."

"You know how fast you were going?" the cop asked in an agitated voice, his face flushed a bright red. Shafer noticed that the cop's hand was still on his gun.

Shafer pursed his lips, thought about his answer. "Well—I'd say about thirty, Officer," he finally said. "Maybe a little over the speed limit."

Then he took out an I.D. card and handed it over. "But you can't do anything about it. I'm with the British Embassy. I have *diplomatic immunity.*"

THAT NIGHT, as he was driving home from work, Geoffrey Shafer started to feel that he was losing control again. He was beginning to frighten himself. His whole life had begun to revolve around a fantasy game he played called the Four Horsemen. In the game, he was the player called Death. The game was everything to him, the only part of his life with real meaning.

He sped across town from the British Embassy, all the way to the Petworth district of Northwest. He knew he shouldn't be there, a white man in a spiffy Jaguar. He couldn't help himself, though, any more than he could that morning.

He stopped the car just before he got to Petworth. Shafer took out his laptop and typed a message to the other players, the Horsemen.

FRIENDS,
DEATH IS ON THE LOOSE IN WASHINGTON.
THE GAME IS ON.

He started the Jag again and rode a few more blocks to Petworth. The usual outrageously provocative hookers were already parading up and down Varnum and Webster streets. A song called "Nice and Slow" was playing from a vibrating blue BMW. Ronnie McCall's sweet voice blended into the early evening.

The girls waved to him and showed their large, flat, pert, or flabby breasts. Several wore colorful bustiers with matching hot pants and shiny silver or red platform shoes with pointy heels.

He slowed to a stop beside a small black girl who looked to be around sixteen and had an unusually pretty face. Her legs were long and slender for such a petite body. She wore too much makeup for his taste. Still, she was hard to resist, so why should he?

"Nice car. Jaguar. I like it a lot," she cooed, then smiled and made a sexy little o with her lipsticked mouth. "You're cute, too, mistah."

He smiled back at her. "Jump in, then. Let's go for a test ride. See if it's true love or just infatuation." He glanced around the street quickly. None of the other girls were working this corner.

"A hundred for full-service, sweetie?" she asked as she wiggled her tight little butt inside the Jag. Her perfume smelled like eau de bubble gum, and she seemed to have bathed in it.

"As I said, get into the car. A hundred dollars is petty cash for me."

He knew he shouldn't be picking her up in the Jaguar, but he took her for a joy ride anyway. He couldn't help himself now.

He brought the girl to a small, wooded park in a part of Washington called Shaw. He parked in a thicket of fir trees that hid the car from sight. He looked at the prostitute, and she was even smaller and younger than he had thought.

"How old are you?" he asked.

"How old you want me to be?" she said, and smiled. "Sweetie, I need the money first. You know how it works."

"Yes. But do you?" he asked.

He reached into his pocket and pulled out a switchblade knife. He had it at her throat in an instant.

"Don't hurt me," she whispered. "Just be cool."

"Get out of the car. Slowly. Don't you dare scream. *You* be cool."

Shafer got out with her, staying close, the knife still pressed to the hollow of her throat.

"It's all just a game, darling," he explained. "My name is Death. You're a very lucky girl. I'm the best player of all."

As if to prove it, he stabbed her for the first time.

Book One

THE JANE DOE MURDERS

Chapter 1

THINGS WERE GOING pretty well that day. I was driving a bright-orange school bus through Southeast on a blistering-hot morning in late July, and I was whistling a little Al Green as I drove. I was in the process of picking up sixteen boys from their houses and also two foster homes. Door-to-door bus service. Hard to beat.

Just one week earlier I had returned from Boston and the Mr. Smith murder case. Mr. Smith and a deranged killer named Gary Soneji had both been involved in that one. I needed a rest, and I'd taken the morning off to do something I'd been looking forward to for a change.

My partner, John Sampson, and a twelve-year-old named Errol Mignault sat behind me on the bus. John was wearing Wayfarer shades, black jeans, and a black T-shirt that read ALLIANCE OF CONCERNED MEN. SEND DONATIONS TODAY. He is six-nine, a very solid two hundred fifty pounds. We've been friends since we were ten, when I first moved to D.C.

He, Errol, and I were talking about the boxer Sugar Ray Robinson, almost shouting over the bus's blustery, occasionally misfiring engine. Sampson had his huge arm lightly draped over Errol's shoulders. Proper physical contact is encouraged when dealing with these boys.

Finally, we picked up the last little guy on our list, an eight-year-old who lived in Benning Terrace, a tough project known to some of us as Simple City.

As we left the project, an ugly smear of graffiti told visitors everything they needed to know about the neighborhood. It read YOU ARE NOW LEAVING THE WAR ZONE, AND YOU LIVED TO TELL ABOUT IT.

We were taking the boys out to Lorton Prison in Virginia. They would be visiting their fathers for the afternoon. They were all young, between eight and thirteen. The Alliance transports forty to fifty kids each week to see their fathers and mothers in different prisons. The goal is a lofty one: to bring the crime rate in Washington down by a third.

I'd been out to the prison more times than I cared to remember. I knew the warden at Lorton pretty well. A few years back I'd spent a lifetime there, interviewing Gary Soneji.

Warden Marion Campbell had set up a large room on Level One where the boys met with their fathers. It was a powerful scene, even more emotional than I'd expected. The Alliance spends time training the fathers who want to participate in the program. There are four steps: how to show love; accept fault and responsibility; attain parent-and-child harmony; discover new beginnings.

Ironically, the boys were all trying to look and act tougher than they actually were. I heard one boy say, "You weren't in my life before, why should I listen to you now?" But the fathers were trying to show a softer side.

Sampson and I hadn't made the run to Lorton before. It was our first time, but I was already sure I'd do it again. There was so much raw emotion and hope in the room, so much potential for something good and decent. Even if some of it would never be realized, it showed that an effort was being made, and something positive could come from it.

What struck me most was the bond that still existed between some of the fathers and their young sons. I thought about my own boy, Damon, and how lucky we were. The thing about most of the prisoners in Lorton was that they knew what they had done was wrong; they just didn't know how to stop doing it.

For most of the hour and a half, I just walked around and listened. I was occasionally needed as a psychologist, and I did the best I could on short notice. At one little group, I heard a father say, "Please tell your mother I love her and I miss her like crazy." Then both the prisoner and his son broke into tears and hugged each other fiercely.

Sampson came up to me after we'd been in the prison for an hour or so. He was grinning broadly. His smile, when it comes, is a killer. "Man, I love this. Do-gooder shit is the best."

"Yeah, I'm hooked myself. I'll drive the big orange bus again."

"Think it'll help? Fathers and sons meeting like this?" he asked me.

I looked around the room. "I think today, right now, this is a success for these men and their sons. That's good enough."

Sampson nodded. "The old one-day-at-a-time approach. Works for me, too. I am *flying,* Alex."

So was I, so was I. I'm a sucker for this kind of stuff.

As I drove the young boys home that afternoon, I could see by their faces that they'd had positive experiences with their fathers. The boys weren't nearly as noisy and rambunctious on the way back to D.C. They weren't trying to be so tough. They were just acting like kids.

Almost every one of the boys thanked Sampson and me as he got off the big orange bus. It wasn't necessary. It sure was a lot better than chasing after homicidal maniacs.

The last boy we dropped off was the

eight-year-old from Benning Terrace. He hugged both John and me, and then he started to cry. "I miss my dad," he said before running home.

Chapter 2

THAT NIGHT, Sampson and I were on duty in Southeast. We're senior homicide detectives, and I'm also liaison between the FBI and the D.C. police. We got a call at about half past midnight telling us to go to the area of Washington called Shaw. There'd been a bad homicide.

A lone Metro squad car was at the murder scene, and the neighborhood psychos had turned out in pretty fair numbers.

It looked like a bizarre block party in the middle of hell. Fires were blazing nearby, throwing off sparks in two trash barrels, which made no sense, given the sweltering heat of the night.

The victim was a young woman, probably between fourteen and her late teens, according to the radio report.

She wasn't hard to find. Her nude, mutilated body had been discarded in a clump of briar bushes in a small park less than ten yards off a paved pathway.

As Sampson and I approached the body, a boy shouted at us from the other side of the crime tape: "Yo, yo, she just some street whore!"

I stopped and looked at him. He reminded me of the boys we'd just transported to Lorton Prison. "Dime-a-dozen bitch. Ain't worth your time, or mine, *Deefectives,*" he went on with his disturbing rap.

I walked up to the young wisecracker. "How do you know that? You seen her around?"

The boy backed off. But then he grinned, showing off a gold star on one of his front teeth. "She ain't got no clothes on, an' she layin' on her back. Somebody stick her good. Sure sound like a whore to me."

Sampson eyed the youth, who looked to be around fourteen but might have been even younger. "You know who she is?"

"Hell *no!*" The boy pretended to be insulted. "Don't know no whores, man."

The boy finally swaggered off, looking back at us once or twice and shaking his head. Sampson and I walked on and joined two uniformed cops standing by the body. They were obviously waiting for reinforcements. Apparently, we were it.

"You call Emergency Services?" I asked the uniforms.

"Thirty-five minutes ago and counting," said the older-looking of the two. He was probably in his late twenties, sporting an attempted mustache and trying to look as if he were experienced at scenes like this one.

"That figures." I shook my head. "You find any I.D. anywhere around here?"

"No I.D. We looked around in the bushes. Nothing but the body," said the younger one. "And the body's seen better days." He was perspiring badly and looked a little sick.

I put on latex gloves and bent down over the corpse. She did appear to be in her mid- to late teens. The girl's throat had been slit from ear to ear. Her face was badly slashed. So were the soles of her feet, which seemed odd. She'd been stabbed a dozen or more times in her chest and stomach. I pushed open her legs.

I saw something that made me sick. A metal handle was barely visible between her legs. I was almost sure it was a knife and that it had been driven all the way into her vagina.

Sampson crouched and looked at me. "What are you thinking, Alex? Another one?"

I shook my head, shrugged my shoulders. "Maybe, but she's an addict, John. Tracks on her arms and legs. Probably behind her knees, under her arms. Our boy doesn't usually go after addicts. He practices safe sex. The murder's brutal, though. That fits the style. You see the metal handle?"

Sampson nodded. He didn't miss much. "Clothes," he said. "Where the hell did they go to? We need to find the clothes."

"Somebody in the neighborhood probably stripped them off her already," said the young uniform. There was a lot of disturbance around the body. Several footprints in the dirt. "That's how it goes around here. Nobody seems to care."

"We're here," I said to him. "*We* care. We're here for all the Jane Does."

Chapter 3

GEOFFREY SHAFER was so happy he almost couldn't hide it from his family. He had to keep from laughing out loud as he kissed his wife, Lucy, on the cheek. He caught a whiff of her Chanel No. 5 perfume, then tasted the brittle dryness of her lips as he kissed her again.

They were standing around like statues in the elegant galley hall of the large Georgian house in Kalorama. The children had been summoned to say good-bye to him.

His wife, the former Lucy Rhys-Cousins, was ash-blond, her sparkling green eyes even brighter than the Bulgari and Spark jewelry that she always wore. Slender, still a beauty of sorts at thirty-seven, Lucy had attended Newnham College at Cambridge for two years before they were married. She read useless poetry and literary novels, and spent most of her free time at equally pointless lunches, shopping with her expatriate girlfriends, going to polo matches, or sailing. Occasionally, Shafer sailed with her. He'd been a very good sailor once upon a time.

Lucy had been considered a prize catch, and he supposed that she still would be, for some men. Well, they could have her skinny, bony ass and all the passionless sex they could stomach.

Shafer hoisted up four-year-old twins Tricia and Erica, one in each arm. Two mirror images of their mother. He'd have sold the twins for the price of a postage stamp. He hugged the girls and laughed like the good papa he always pretended to be.

Then he formally shook twelve-year-old Robert's hand. The debate being waged in the house was over whether Robert should be sent back to England for boarding school, perhaps to Winchester, where his grandfather had gone. Shafer gave his son a crisp military salute. Once upon a time, Colonel Geoffrey Shafer had been a soldier. Only Robert seemed to remember that part of his father's life now.

"I'm only going away to London for a few days, and this is *work,* not a holiday. I'm not planning to spend my nights at the Athenaeum or anything like that," he told his family. He was smiling jovially, the way they expected him to be.

"Try to have some fun while you're away, Dad. Have some laughs. God knows, you deserve it," Robert said, talking in the lower-octave man-to-man's voice that he seemed to be adopting lately.

"Bye, Daddy! Bye, Daddy," the twins chorused shrilly, making Shafer want to throw them against the walls.

"Bye, Erica-san. Bye, Tricia-san."

"Remember Orc's Nest," Robert said with sudden urgency. "*Dragon* and *The Duelist.*" Orc's Nest was a store that sold role-playing books and gaming equipment. It was located on Earlham, just off Cambridge Circus in London. *Dragon* and *The Duelist* were currently the two hot-shit British magazines covering role-playing games.

Unfortunately for Robert, Shafer wasn't

actually going to London. He had a much better plan for the weekend. He was going to play his fantasy game right here in Washington.

Chapter 4

HE SPED DUE EAST, rather than toward Washington's Dulles Airport, feeling as if a tremendously burdensome weight had been lifted. God, he hated his perfect English family, and even more, their claustrophobic life here in America.

Shafer's own family back in England had been "perfect" as well. He had two older brothers, and they'd both been excellent students, model youths. His father had been a military attaché, and the family had traveled around the globe until he was twelve, when they'd returned to England and settled in Guildford, about half an hour outside London. Once there, Shafer began to expand on the schoolboy mischief he'd practiced since he was eight. The center of

Guildford contained several historic buildings, and he set out to gleefully deface all of them. He began with the Abbot's Hospital, where his grandmother was dying. He painted obscenities on the walls. Then he moved on to Guildford Castle, Guildhall, the Royal Grammar School, and Guildford Cathedral. He scrawled more obscene words, and splashed large penises in bright colors. He had no idea why he took such joy in ruining beautiful things, but he did. He loved it—and he especially loved not getting caught.

Shafer was eventually sent to school at Rugly, where the pranks continued. Then he attended St. John's College, where he concentrated on philosophy, Japanese, and shagging as many good-looking women as he possibly could. All his friends were mystified when he went into the army at twenty-one. His language skills were excellent, and he was posted to Asia, which was where the mischief rose to a new level and where he began to play the *game of games*.

He stopped at a 7-Eleven in Washington Heights for coffee—three coffees, actually. Black, with four sugars in each. He drank most of one of the cups on his way to the counter.

The Indian cashier gave him a cheeky, suspicious look, and he laughed in the bearded wanker's face.

"Do you really think I'd steal a bloody seventy-five-cent cup of coffee? You pathetic jerkoff. You pitiful wog."

He threw his money on the counter and left before he killed the clerk with his bare hands, which he could do easily enough.

From the 7-Eleven he drove into the Northeast part of Washington, a middle-class section called Eckington. He began to recognize the streets when he was west of Gallaudet University. Most of the structures were two-storied apartments with vinyl siding, either redbrick or a hideous Easter-egg blue that always made him wince.

He stopped in front of one of the redbrick garden apartments on Uhland Terrace, near Second Street. This one had an attached garage. A previous tenant had adorned the brick facade with two white concrete cats.

"Hello, pussies," Shafer said. He felt relieved to be here. He was "cycling up"—that is, getting high, manic. He loved this feeling, couldn't get enough of it. It was time to play the game.

Chapter 5

A RUSTED and taped-up purple and blue taxi was parked inside the two-car garage. Shafer had been using it for about four months. The taxi gave him anonymity, made him almost invisible anywhere he chose to go in D.C. He called it his "Nightmare Machine."

He wedged the Jaguar beside the taxicab, then he jogged upstairs. Once inside the apartment, he switched on the air-conditioning. He drank another sugar-laced coffee.

Then he took his pills, like a good boy. Thorazine and Librium. Benadryl, Xanax, Vicodin. He'd been using the drugs in various combinations for years. It was mostly a trial-and-error process, but he'd learned his lessons well. *Feeling better, Geoffrey? Yes, much better, thank you.*

He tried to read today's *Washington Post,* then an old copy of *Private Eye* magazine, and finally a catalog from DeMask, a rubber and leather fetish wholesaler in Amsterdam, the world's largest. He did two hundred push-ups, then a few hundred sit-ups, impatiently waiting for darkness to fall over Washington.

At quarter to ten, Shafer began to get ready for a big night on the town. He went into the small, barren bathroom, which smelled of cheap cleanser. He stood before the mirror.

He liked what he saw. Very much so. Thick and wavy blond hair that he would never lose. A charismatic, electric smile. Startling blue eyes that had a cinematic quality. Excellent physical shape for a man of forty-four.

He went to work, starting with brown contact lenses. He'd done this so many times, he could almost do it blindfolded. It was a part of his tradecraft. He applied blackface to his face, neck, hands, wrists; thick padding to make his neck seem broader than it was; a dark watch cap to cover every last strand of hair.

He stared hard at himself—and saw a rather convincing-looking black man, especially if the light wasn't too strong. Not bad, not bad at all. It was a good disguise for a night on the town, *especially* if the town was Washington.

So let the games begin. The Four Horsemen.

At ten twenty-five, he went down to the garage again. He carefully circled around the Jaguar and walked to the purple and blue taxicab. He had already begun to lose himself in delicious fantasy.

Shafer reached into his pants pocket and pulled out three unusual-looking dice. They were twenty-sided, the kind used in most fantasy games, or RPGs. They had numerals on them rather than dots.

He held the dice in his left hand, rolling them over and over.

There were explicit rules to the Four Horsemen; everything was supposed to depend on the dice roll. The idea was to come up with an outrageous fantasy, a mindblower. The four players around the world were competing. There had never been a game like this—nothing even came close.

Shafer had already prepared an adventure for himself, but there were alternatives for every event. Much depended on the dice.

That was the main point—anything could happen.

He got into the taxi, started it up. Good Lord, was he ready for this!

Chapter 6

HE HAD A GORGEOUS PLAN mapped out. He would pick up only those few passengers—"fares"—who caught his eye, fired up his imagination to the limit. He wasn't in a hurry. He had all night; he had all weekend. He was on a busman's holiday.

His route had been laid out beforehand. First, he drove to the fashionable Adams-Morgan neighborhood. He watched the busy sidewalks, which seemed one long syncopated rhythm of movement. Bargrazers slouching toward hipness. It seemed that every other restaurant in Adams-Morgan called itself a café. Driving slowly and checking the glittery sights, he passed Café Picasso, Café Lautrec,

La Fourchette Café, Bukom Café, Café Dalbol, Montego Café, Sheba Café.

Around eleven-thirty, on Columbia Road, he slowed the taxicab. His heart began to thump. Something very good was shaping up ahead.

A handsome-looking couple was leaving the popular Chief Ike's Mambo Room. A man and a woman, Hispanic, probably in their late twenties. Sensual beyond belief.

He rolled the dice across the front seat: six, five, four—a total of fifteen. A high count.

Danger! That made sense. A couple was always tricky and risky.

Shafer waited for them to cross the pavement, moving away from the restaurant canopy. *They came right toward him.* How accommodating. He touched the handle of the magnum that he kept under the front seat. He was ready for anything.

As they started to climb into the taxi, he changed his mind. He could do that!

Shafer saw that neither of them was as attractive as he'd thought. The man's cheeks and forehead were slightly mottled; the pomade in his black hair was too thick and greasy. The woman was a few pounds heavier than he liked, plumper than she'd looked from a distance in the flattering streetlights.

"Off duty," he said, and sped away. Both of them gave him the finger.

Shafer laughed out loud. "You're in luck tonight! Fools! Luckiest night of your lives, and you don't even know it."

The incomparable thrill of the fantasy had completely taken hold of him. He'd had total power over the couple. He had control of life and death.

"Death *be* proud," he whispered.

He stopped for more coffee at a Starbucks on Rhode Island Avenue. Nothing like it. He purchased three black coffees and heaped six sugars in each.

An hour later, he was in Southeast. He hadn't stopped for another fare. The streets were crowded to the max with pedestrians. There weren't enough taxis, not even gypsies in this part of Washington.

He regretted having let the Hispanic couple get away. He'd begun to romanticize them in his mind, to visualize them as they'd looked in the streetlight. Remembrance of things past, right? He thought of Proust's monumental opening line: *"For a long time I used to go to bed early."* And so had Shafer—until he discovered the game of games.

Then he saw her—a perfect brown goddess standing right there before him, as if someone had just given him a wonderful present. She was walking by herself, about a block from E Street, moving fast, purposefully. He was instantly high again.

He loved the way she moved, the swivel of her long legs, the exactness of her carriage.

As he came up behind her, she began looking around, checking the street. Looking for a taxi? Could it be? Did she want him?

She had on a light cream suit, a purple silk shirt, high heels. She looked too classy and adult to be going to a club. She appeared to be in control of herself.

He quickly rolled the twenty-sided dice again and held his breath. Counted the numerals. His heart leaped. This was what the Horsemen was all about.

She was waving her hand at him, signaling. *"Taxi!"* she called. "Taxi! Are you free?"

He guided the taxi over to the curb, and

she took three quick, delicate steps toward him. She was wearing shimmery, silken high heels that were just delightful. She was much prettier up close. She was a nine and a half out of ten.

The cab door swung open and blocked his view of her for a second.

Then he saw that she was carrying flowers, and wondered why. Something special tonight? Well, that was certainly true. The flowers were for her own funeral.

"Oh, thank you so much for stopping." She spoke breathlessly as she settled into the taxi. He could tell that she was letting herself relax and feel safe. Her voice was soothing, sweet, down-to-earth and real.

"At your service." Shafer turned and smiled at her. "By the way, I'm Death. You're my fantasy for this weekend."

Chapter 7

MONDAY MORNINGS I usually work the soup kitchen at St. Anthony's in Southeast, where I've been a volunteer for the past half-dozen years. I do the seven-to-nine shift, three days a week.

That morning I felt restless and uneasy. I was still getting over the Mr. Smith case, which had taken me all over the East Coast and to Europe. Maybe I needed a real vacation, a holiday far away from Washington.

I watched the usual lineup of men, women, and children who had no money for food. It was about five deep and went up Twelfth Street to the second corner. It seemed such a pity, so unfair that so many folks still go hungry in Washington, or get fed only once a day.

I had started helping out at the kitchen years before on account of my wife, Maria. She was doing casework as a social worker at St. Anthony's when we first met. Maria was the uncrowned princess of St. Anthony's; everybody loved her, and she loved me. She had been shot, murdered in a drive-by incident not far from the soup kitchen. We'd been married four years and had two small children. The case has never been solved, and that still tortures me. Maybe that's what drives me to solve every case I can, no matter how bad the odds.

At St. Anthony's soup kitchen, I help make sure nobody gets too riled up or causes undue trouble during meals. I'm six-three, around two hundred pounds, and built for peacekeeping, if and when it's necessary. I can usually ward off trouble with a few quiet words and nonthreatening gestures. Most of these people are here to eat, though, not fight or cause trouble.

I also dish out peanut butter and jelly to anyone who wants seconds or even thirds, of the stuff. Jimmy Moore, the Irish American who runs the soup kitchen with much love and just the right amount of discipline, has always believed in the healing power of p.b. and j. Some of the regulars at the kitchen call me "Peanut Butter Man." They've been doing it for years.

"You don't look so good today," said a short ample woman who's been coming to the kitchen for the past year or two. I know her name is Laura, and that she was born in Detroit and has two grown sons. She used to work as a housekeeper on M Street in Georgetown, but the family felt she'd gotten too old for the job and let her go with only a couple weeks' severance and warm words of appreciation.

"You deserve better. You deserve *me*," Laura said, and laughed mischievously. "What do you say?"

"Laura, you're too kind with your compliments," I said, serving up her usual extra dish. "Anyway, you've met Christine. You know I'm already spoken for."

Laura giggled as she hugged herself with both arms. She had a fine, healthy laugh, even under the circumstances. "A young girl has to dream, you know. Nice to see you, as always."

"Same to you, Laura. As always, nice to see you. Enjoy the meal."

"Oh, I do. You can *see* I do."

As I said my cheery hellos and dished out heaped portions of peanut butter, I allowed myself to think about Christine. Laura was probably right; maybe I didn't look so good today. I probably hadn't looked too terrific for a few days.

I remembered a night about two weeks back. I had just finished working a multiple-homicide case in Boston. Christine and I stood on the porch in front of her house out in Mitchellville. I was trying to live my life differently, but it's hard to change. I had a saying I really liked: HEART LEADS HEAD.

I could smell the flowers in the night air, roses and impatiens growing in profusion. I could also smell Gardenia Passion, a favorite perfume that Christine was wearing that night.

She and I had known each other for a year and a half. We'd met during a murder investigation that had ended with the death of her husband. Eventually we began to go out. I was thinking that it had all been leading to this moment on the porch. At least it had in my mind.

I had never seen Christine when she didn't look good to me and make me feel lightheaded. She's tall, almost five-ten, and that's nice. She had a smile that could probably light up half the country. That night, she was wearing tight, faded jeans and a white T-shirt knotted around her waist. Her feet were bare, and her nails were dabbed with red polish. Her beautiful brown eyes were shining.

I reached out and took her into my arms, and suddenly everything seemed right with the world. I forgot all about the terrible case I'd just finished; I forgot about the particularly vicious killer known as Mr. Smith.

I cupped her sweet, kind face gently in my hands. I like to think that nothing scares me anymore, and many things don't, but I guess the more good things you have in your life, the easier it is to experience fear. Christine felt so precious to me—so maybe I was scared.

Heart leads head.

It isn't the way most men act, but I was learning.

"I love you more than I've ever loved anything in my life, Christine. You help me see and feel things in new ways. I love your smile, your way with people—especially kids—your kindness. I love to hold you like this. I love you more than I could say if I stood here and talked for the rest of the night. I love you so much. Will you marry me, Christine?"

She didn't answer right away. I felt her pull back, just a little, and my heart caught. I looked into her eyes, and what I saw was pain and uncertainty. It nearly broke my heart.

"Oh, Alex, Alex," she whispered, and looked as if she might cry. "I can't give you an answer. You just came back from Boston. You were on another horrible, horrible murder case. I can't take that. Your life was in danger again. That terrible madman was in your house. He threatened your family. You can't deny any of that."

I couldn't. It had been a terrifying experience, and I had nearly died. "I won't deny anything you said. But I do love you. I can't deny that, either. I'll quit the police force if that's what it takes."

"No." A softness came into her eyes. She shook her head back and forth. "That would be all wrong. For both of us."

We held each other on the porch, and I knew we were in trouble. I didn't know how to resolve it. I had no idea. Maybe if I left the force, became a full-time therapist again, led a more normal life for Christine and the kids. But could I do that? Could I really quit?

"Ask me again," she whispered. "Ask me again, sometime."

Chapter 8

CHRISTINE AND I had dated since that night, and it just felt right, easy, comfortable, and romantic. It always was that way between us. Still, I wondered if our problem could be fixed. Could she be happy with a homicide detective? Could I stop being one? I didn't know.

I was brought out of my reverie about Christine by the high-pitched, stuttering wail of a siren out on Twelfth Street, just turning off E. I winced when I saw Sampson's black Nissan pull up in front of St. Anthony's.

He turned off the siren on his rooftop but then beeped the car horn, sat on it. I knew he was here for me, probably to take me somewhere I didn't want to go. The horn continued to blare.

"It's your friend John Sampson," Jimmy Moore called out. "You hear him, Alex?"

"I know who it is," I called back to Jimmy. "I'm hoping he goes away."

"Sure doesn't sound like it."

I finally walked outside, crossing through the soup-kitchen line and receiving a few jokey jeers. People I had known for a long time accused me of working half a day, or said that if I didn't like the job, could they have it.

"What's up?" I called to Sampson before I got all the way out to his black sports car.

Sampson's side window came sliding down. I leaned inside the car. "You forget? It's my day off," I reminded him.

"It's Nina Childs," Sampson said in the low, soft voice he used only when he was angry or very serious. He was trying to deaden his facial muscles, to look tough, not emotional, but it wasn't working real well. "Nina's dead, Alex."

I shivered involuntarily. I opened the car door and got in. I didn't even go back to the kitchen to tell Jimmy Moore I was leaving. Sampson jerked the car away from the curbside fast. The siren came on again, but now I almost welcomed the mournful wail. It numbed me.

"What do you know so far?" I asked as we rushed along the intensely bleak streets of Southeast, then crossed the slate-gray Anacostia River.

"She was dumped in a row house, Eighteenth and Garnesville. Jerome Thurman is out there with her. Says she's probably been there since the weekend. Some needle pusher found the body. No clothes or I.D., Alex," Sampson said.

I looked over at him. "So how did they know it was Nina?"

"Uniform guy on the scene recognized her. Knew her from the hospital. Everybody knew Nina."

I shut my eyes, but I saw Nina Childs's face and I opened them again. She had been the eleven-to-seven charge nurse in the E.R. unit at St. Anthony's Hospital, where once I'd run like a tornado, with a dying little boy in my arms. Sampson and I had worked with Nina more times than I could remember. Sampson had also dated Nina for over a year, but then they'd broken it off. She'd married a neighborhood man who worked for the city. They had two kids, two little babies, and Nina had seemed so happy the last time I saw her.

I couldn't believe she was lying dead in a tenement cellar on the wrong side of the Anacostia. She had been abandoned, like one of the Jane Does.

Chapter 9

NINA CHILDS'S BODY had been found in a battered row house in one of the city's most impoverished, destroyed, and dismaying neighborhoods. There was only one patrol car on the scene, and a single rusted and dented EMS van; homicides in Southeast don't attract much attention. A dog was barking somewhere, and it was the only sound on the desolate street.

Sampson and I had to walk past an open-air drug mart on the corner of Eighteenth Street. Mostly young males, but a few children and two women were also gathered there defiantly. The drug marts are everywhere in this part of Southeast. The neighborhood youth activity is the crack trade.

"Daily body pickup, Officers?" said one of the young men. He was wearing black trousers with black suspenders, no shirt, socks, or shoes. He had a prison-yard physique and tattoos everywhere.

"Come to take out the trash?" an older man cackled from behind an unruly patch of salt-and-pepper beard. "Take that muhfuckin' barkin'-all-night dog while you here. Make yourselves useful," he added.

Sampson and I ignored them and continued walking across Eighteenth, then into the boarded-up, three-storied row house straight ahead. A black and white boxer leaned out of a third-floor window, like a lifetime resident, and wouldn't stop barking. Otherwise the building appeared deserted.

The front door had been jimmied a hundred times, so it just swung open for us. The building smelled of fire, garbage, water damage. There was a gaping hole in the ceiling from a burst steam pipe. It was so wrong for Nina to have ended up in this sad, abominable place.

For over a year I had been unofficially investigating unsolved murders in Southeast, many of them Jane Does. My count was well over a hundred, but no one else in the department was willing to agree to that number, or anything close to it. Several of the murdered women were drug abusers or prostitutes. But not Nina.

We carefully descended a circular stairwell that had a shaky, well-worn wooden railing that neither of us would touch. I could see flashlights shining up ahead, and I already had my Maglite turned on.

Nina was deep in the basement of the abandoned building. At least somebody had bothered to tape off the perimeter to protect the crime scene.

I saw Nina's body—and I had to look away.

It wasn't just that she was dead; it was how she'd been killed. I tried to put my mind and eyes somewhere else until I regained some composure.

Jerome Thurman was there with the EMS team. So was a single patrol officer, probably the one who had identified Nina. No M.E. was present. It wasn't unusual for a medical examiner not to show up for homicides in Southeast.

There were dead flowers on the floor near the body. I focused on the flowers, still not able to look at Nina again. It didn't fit with the other Jane Does, but the killer didn't have a strict pattern. That was one of the problems I was having. It might mean that his fantasy was still evolving—and that he hadn't finished making up his gruesome story yet.

I noted shreds of foil and cellophane wrappers lying everywhere on the floor. Rats are attracted to shiny things and often bring them back to their nests. Thick cobwebs weaved from one end of the basement to the other.

I had to look at Nina again. I needed to look closely.

"I'm Detective Alex Cross. Let me take a look at her, please," I finally said to the EMS team, a man and a woman in their twenties. "I'll just be a couple of minutes, then I'll get out of your way."

"The other detectives already released the body," the male EMS worker said. He was rail-thin, with long dirty-blond hair. He didn't bother to look up at me. "Let us finish our job and get the hell out of this cesspool. Whole area is highly infectious—smells like shit."

"Just back away," Sampson barked. "Get up, before I pull your skinny ass up."

The EMS techie cursed, but he stood and backed away from Nina's body. I moved in close, tried to concentrate and be professional, tried to remember specific details I had gathered about the previous Jane Does in Southeast. I was looking for some connection. I wondered if a single predator could possibly be killing so many people. If that was the case, then this would be one of the most savage killing sprees ever.

I took a deep breath and then I knelt over Nina. The rats had been at her, I could see, but the killer had done much worse damage.

It looked to me as if Nina had been beaten to death, with punches and possibly kicks. She might have been struck a hundred times or more. I had rarely seen anyone given this much punishment. Why did it have to happen? She was only thirty-one years old, a mother of two, kind, talented, dedicated to her work at St. Anthony's.

There was a sudden noise, like a rifle-shot, in the building. It reverberated right through the basement walls. The EMS workers jumped.

The rest of us laughed nervously. I knew exactly what the sound was.

"Just rattraps," I said to the EMS team. "Get used to it."

Chapter 10

I WAS AT THE HOMICIDE SCENE for a little over two hours, much longer than I wanted to be there, and I hated every second. I couldn't fix a set pattern for the Jane Doe killings, and Nina Childs's murder didn't help. Why had he struck her so many times and so savagely? What were the flowers doing there? Could this be the work of the same killer?

The way I usually operate at a crime scene is to let the homicide investigation take on an almost aerial view. Everything emanates from the body.

Sampson and I walked the entire crime scene, from the basement to each floor and on up to the roof. Then we walked the neighborhood. Nobody had seen anything unusual, which didn't surprise either of us.

Now came the really bad part. Sampson and I drove from the woeful tenement to Nina's apartment in the Brookland section of Washington, east of Catholic University. I knew I was being sucked in again, but there was nothing I could do about it.

It was a sweltering-hot day, and the sun hammered Washington without mercy. We were both silent and withdrawn during the ride. What we had to do was the worst thing about our job—telling a family about the death of a loved one. I didn't know how I could do it this time.

Nina's building was a well-kept brown-brick apartment house on Monroe Street. Miniature yellow roses were blooming out front in bright-green window boxes. It didn't look as if anything bad should happen to someone who lived here. Everything about the place was so bright and hopeful, just as Nina had been.

I was becoming more and more disturbed and upset about the brutal and obscene murder, and about the fact that it probably wouldn't get a decent investigation from the department, at least not officially. Nana Mama would chalk it up to her conspiracy theories about the white over-lords and their "criminal disinterest" in the people of Southeast. She had often told me that she felt morally superior to white people, that she would never, ever treat them the way they treated the black peo-ple of Washington.

"Nina's sister, Marie, takes care of the kids," Sampson said as we rode down Monroe. "She's a nice girl. Had a drug problem one time, beat it. Nina helped her. The whole family is close-knit. A lot like yours. This is going to be real bad, Alex."

I turned to him. Not surprisingly, he was taking Nina's death even harder than I was. It's unusual for him to show his emotions, though. "I can do it, John. You stay here in the car. I'll go up and talk to the family."

Sampson shook his head and sighed loudly. "Doesn't work that way, sugar."

He snugged the Nissan up to the curb, and we both climbed out. He didn't stop me from coming along to the apartment, so I knew he wanted me there with him. He was right. This was going to be bad.

The Childs apartment took up the first and second floors. The front door was slightly ornate, aluminum. Nina's husband was already at the door. He had on the proletariat uniform of the D.C. Housing Authority, where he worked: mud-stained work boots, blue trousers, a shirt marked DCHA. One of the babies snuggled in his arms, a beautiful girl who looked at me and smiled and cooed.

"Could we come inside for a moment?" Sampson asked.

"It's Nina," the husband said, and started to break down right there in the doorway.

"I'm sorry, William," I spoke softly. "You're right. She's gone. She was found this morning."

William Childs started to sob loudly. He was a powerful-looking workingman, but that didn't matter. He held his bewildered little girl to his chest and tried to control the crying, but he couldn't.

"Oh, God, no. Oh, Nina, Nina baby. How could somebody kill her? How could anybody do that? Oh, Nina, Nina, Nina."

A young, pretty woman came up behind him. She had to be Nina's sister, Marie. She took the baby from her sister's husband, and the little girl began to scream, as if she knew what had happened. I had seen so many families, so many good people, who had lost loved ones on these merciless streets. I knew it would never completely stop, but I felt it ought to get better. It never did.

The sister motioned for us to come inside, and I noticed a hall table on which there were two pocketbooks, as if Nina were still about. The apartment was comfortable looking and neat, with light bamboo and white-cushioned furniture. The whir of a window air conditioner was constant. A Llardo porcelain figure of a nurse stood on an end table.

I was still sorting through details of the homicide scene, trying to connect the murder to the other Jane Does. We learned that Nina had attended a health-care charity dinner on Saturday night. William had been working overtime. The family called the police late Saturday night. Two detectives had shown up, but no one had been able to find Nina until now.

Then I was holding the baby while Nina's sister took the chill off a bottle of formula. It was such a sad and poignant moment, knowing this poor little girl would never see her mother again, never know how truly special her mother had been. It reminded me of my own kids and their mother, and of Christine, who was afraid I would die during some murder investigation like this one.

The older little girl came up to me while I was holding her baby sister. She was two or three at the most. "I got a new hair-style," she said proudly and did a half-turn to show me.

"You did? It's beautiful. Who did those braids for you?"

"My mommy," said the girl.

It was an hour later when Sampson and I finally left the house. We drove away in silence and despair, the same way we'd come. After a couple of blocks, Sampson pulled over in front of a ramshackle neighborhood bodega covered with beer and soda posters.

He gave a deep sigh, put his hands to his face, and then cried. I'd never ever seen John like this before, not in all the years we'd been friends, not even when we were just boys. I reached out and laid a hand on his shoulder, and he didn't move away. Then he told me something he hadn't shared before.

"I loved her, Alex, but I let her get away. I never told her how I felt. We have to get this son of a bitch."

Chapter 11

I SENSED I WAS AT THE START of another homicide mess. I didn't want it, but I couldn't stop the horror. I had to try to do something about the Jane Does. I couldn't just stand by and do nothing.

Although I was assigned to the Seventh District as a senior detective, my job as liaison with the FBI gave me some extra status and also the freedom to occasionally work without too much supervision or interference. My mind was running free, and I'd already made some associations between Nina's murder and at least some of the unsolved killings. First, there had been no identification on the victims at each crime scene. Second, the bodies had frequently been dumped in buildings where they might not be found quickly. Third, not a single witness had seen anyone who might be a suspect. The most we ever got was that there had been traffic, or people out on the street, where one of the bodies had been found. That told me that the killer knew how to blend in, and that he possibly was a black man.

Around six that night, I finally headed home. This was supposed to be my day off. I had things to do there, and I was trying to balance the demands of Job and homelife as best I could. I put on a happy face and headed inside the house.

Damon, Jannie, and Nana were singing "Sit Down, You're Rockin' de Boat" in the kitchen. The show tune was music to my ears and other essential parts of my anatomy. The kids looked happy as could be. There is a lot to be said for the innocence of childhood.

I heard Nana say, "How about 'I Can Tell the World'?" Then the three of them launched into one of the most beautiful spirituals I know. Damon's voice seemed particularly strong to me. I hadn't really noticed that before.

"I feel like I just walked into a story by

Louisa May Alcott," I said, laughing for the first time that long day.

"I take that as a *high* compliment," Nana said. She was somewhere between her late seventies and early eighties now, but not telling—and also not showing—her age.

"Who's Louise Maise Alcott?" Jannie said, and made a lemon-sucking face. She is a healthy little skeptic, though almost never a cynic. In that way, she takes after both her father and her grandmother.

"Look it up tonight, little one. Fifty cents in your pocket for the correct answer," I told her.

"You're on." Jannie grinned. "You can pay me right now if you like."

"Me, too?" Damon asked.

"Of course. You can look up Jane Austen," I said to him. "Now what's with the heavenly harmonizing? I like it very much, by the way. I just want to know what the special occasion is."

"We're just singing while we prepare dinner," Nana said, and stuck up her nose and twinkled her eyes. "You play jazz and the blues on the piano, don't you? We harmonize like angels sometimes. No special reason necessary. Good for the soul, and the soul food, I suppose. Can't hurt."

"Well, don't stop singing on my account," I said, but they had already stopped. Too bad. Something was going on; I'd figured out that much. A musical mystery to be solved in my own house.

"We still on for boxing after dinner?" I asked cautiously. I was feeling a little vulnerable because I didn't want them to turn me down for the boxing lesson that has become a ritual.

"Of course," Damon said, and frowned like I must be out of my mind to even ask such a question.

"Of course. Pshaw. Why wouldn't we be?" Jannie said, and brushed off my silly question with a wave of her hand. "How's Ms. Johnson?" she asked then. "You two talk today?"

"I still want to know what the singing was all about?" I answered Jannie with a question of my own.

"You have valuable information. Well, so do I. Tit for tat," she said. "How do you like that?"

A little later, I decided to call Christine at home. Lately it had seemed more like the way it had been between us before I got involved with the Mr. Smith case. We talked for a while, and then I asked her to go out on Friday.

"Of course. I'd like that, Alex. What should I wear?" she asked.

I hesitated. "Well, I always like what you choose—but wear something special."

She didn't ask why.

Chapter 12

AFTER ONE of Nana's roast-chicken dinners with baked sweet potatoes and homemade bread, I took the kids downstairs for their weekly boxing lesson. Following the Tuesday night fight with the kids, I glanced at my watch and saw that it was already a little past nine.

The doorbell rang a moment later. I set down a terrific book called *The Color of Water* and pushed myself up from my chair in the family room.

"I'll get it. It's probably for me," I called out.

"Maybe it's Christine. You never know," Jannie teased, then darted away into the kitchen. Both of the kids adored Christine, in spite of the fact that she was the principal at their school.

I knew exactly who was out on the porch. I had been expecting four homicide detectives from the First District—Jerome Thurman, Rakeem Powell, Shawn Moore, and Sampson.

Three of the detectives were standing out on the porch. Rosie the cat and I let them inside. Sampson arrived about five minutes later, and we all gathered in the backyard. What we were doing at the house wasn't illegal, but it wouldn't make us a lot of friends in high places in the police department.

We sat on lawn chairs, and I set out beer and low-fat pretzels that two-hundred-seventy-pound Jerome scoffed at. "Beer and low-fat pretzels. Give me a *break,* Alex. You lost your mind? Hey, you having an affair with my wife? You must have got this bad idea from Claudette."

"I bought these especially for you, big man. I'm trying to give your heart a break," I told him, and the others guffawed loudly. We all pick on Jerome.

The five of us had been getting together informally for a couple of weeks. We were beginning to work on the Jane Does, as we called them. Homicide had no official investigation going on; it wasn't trying to link the murders to a serial killer. I'd tried to start one and been turned down by Chief Pittman. He claimed that I hadn't discovered a pattern linking any of the murders, and besides that, he didn't have any extra detectives for duty in Southeast.

"I suppose you've all heard about Nina Childs by now?" Sampson asked the other detectives. All of them had known Nina, and of course Jerome had been at the murder scene with us.

"The good die young." Rakeem Powell frowned severely and shook his head. Rakeem is smart and tough and could go all the way in the department. "Least they do in Southeast." His eyes went cold and hard.

I told them what I knew, especially that Nina had been found with no I.D. I mentioned everything else I had noticed at the tenement crime scene. I also took the occasion to talk some more about the rash of unsolved murders in Southeast. I went over the devastating stats I had compiled, mostly in my free time.

"Statistic like that in Georgetown or the Capitol district, people in this city be enraged. Going ballistic. Be *Washington Post* headlines every day. The president himself be involved. Money no object. National tragedy!" Jerome Thurman railed on and waved his arms around like signal flags.

"Well, we are here to do something about it," I said in a calmer voice. "Money *is* no object with us. Neither is time. Let me tell you what I feel about this killer," I continued. "I think I know a few things about him."

"How'd you come up with the profile?" Shawn Moore asked. "How can you stand thinking about these kinky bastards as much as you do?"

I shrugged. "It's what I do best. I've analyzed all the Jane Does," I said. "It took me weeks working on my own. Just me and the kinky bastard."

"Plus, he studies rodent droppings," said Sampson. "I saw him bagging the little turds. That's his real secret."

I grinned and told them what I had so far. "I think one male is responsible for at least some of the killings. Maybe as many as a dozen murders. I don't think he's a brilliant killer, like Gary Soneji or Mr. Smith, but he's clever enough not to be caught. He's organized, reasonably careful. I don't think we'll find he has any prior record. He probably has a decent job. Maybe even a family. My FBI friends at Quantico agree with that.

"He's almost definitely caught up in an escalating fantasy cycle. I think he's into his fantasies big-time. Maybe he's in the process of becoming someone or something new. He might be forming a new personality for himself. He isn't finished with the killing, not by any means.

"I'll make some educated guesses. He hates his old self, though the people closest to him probably don't realize it. He might be ready to abandon his family, job, any friends he has. At one time he probably had very strong feelings and beliefs about something—law and order, religion, the government—but not anymore. He kills in different ways; there's no set formula. He knows a lot about killing people. He's used different kinds of weapons. He may have traveled overseas. Or maybe he's spent time in Asia. I think it's very possible he's a black man. He's killed several times in Southeast—no one's noticed him."

"Fuck me," Jerome Thurman said to that. "Any *good* news, Alex?"

"One thing, and this is a long shot. But it feels right to me. I think he might be suicidal. It fits the profile I'm working on. He's living dangerously, taking a lot of chances. He might just blow himself up."

"Pop goes the weasel," Sampson said.

That was how we came to name the killer: the Weasel.

Chapter 13

GEOFFREY SHAFER looked forward to
playing the Four Horsemen every Thursday
night from nine until about one in the
morning.

The fantasy game was everything to
him. There were three other master players
around the world. The players were the
Rider on the White Horse, Conqueror; the
Rider on the Red Horse, War; the Rider on
the Black Horse, Famine; and himself, the
Rider on the Pale Horse, Death.

Lucy and the children knew they were
forbidden to disturb him for any reason
once he locked himself into the library on
the second floor. On one wall was his col-
lection of ceremonial daggers, nearly all of
them purchased in Hong Kong and Bang-

kok. Also on the wall was the rowing oar from the year his college team had won the "Bumps." Shafer nearly always won the games he played.

He had been using the Internet to communicate with the other players for years, long before the rest of the world caught on. Conqueror played from the town of Dorking, in Surrey, outside London; Famine traveled back and forth between Bangkok, Sydney, Melbourne, and Manila; and War usually played out of Jamaica, where he had a large estate on the sea. They had been playing Horsemen for seven years.

Rather than becoming repetitive, the fantasy game had expanded itself. It had grown every year, becoming something new and even more challenging. The object was to create the most delicious and unusual fantasy or adventure. Violence was almost always part of the game, but not necessarily murder. Shafer had been the first to claim that his stories weren't fantasies at all, that he lived them in the real world. Now the others would do so as well from time to time. Whether they really lived their fantasies, Shafer couldn't tell. The object was to create the evening's most startling fantasy, to get a rise out of the other players.

At nine o'clock his time, Shafer was on his laptop. So were the others. It was rare for one of them to miss a session, but if he did, he left lengthy messages and sometimes drawings or even photographs of supposed lovers or victims. Films were occasionally used, and the other players then had to decide whether the scenes were stage-acted or cinema verité.

Shafer couldn't imagine missing a chapter of the game himself. Death was by far the most interesting character, the most powerful and original. He had missed important social and embassy affairs just to be available for Thursday nights. He had played when he had pneumonia, and once when he'd had a painful double-hernia operation the day before.

The Four Horsemen was unique in so many ways, but most important was the fact that there was no single gamemaster to outline and control the action of the game. Each of the players had complete autonomy to write and visualize his own story, as long as he played by the roll of

the dice and remained inside the parame-
ters of the character.

In effect, in Horsemen there were four
gamemasters. There was no other fantasy
game like it. It was as gruesome and
shocking as the participants' imaginations
and their skills at presentation brought
them.

Conqueror, Famine, and War had all
signed on.

Shafer began to type.

DEATH HAS TRIUMPHED
AGAIN IN WASHINGTON. LET
ME TELL YOU THE DETAILS,
THEN I'LL LISTEN TO THE
GLORIOUS STORIES, THE
IMAGINATIVE POWER, OF
CONQUEROR, FAMINE, AND
WAR. I LIVE FOR THIS, AS I
KNOW ALL OF YOU DO AS
WELL.

THIS WEEKEND, I DROVE MY
FANTASTIC TAXI, THE
"NIGHTMARE MACHINE,"
ONCE AGAIN. . . . LISTEN TO
THIS. I CAME UPON SEVERAL
CHOICE AND DELECTABLE
VICTIMS, BUT I REJECTED

THEM AS UNWORTHY. THEN I
FOUND MY QUEEN, AND SHE
REMINDED ME OF OUR DAYS
IN BANGKOK AND MANILA.
WHO COULD EVER FORGET
THE BLOOD LUST OF THE
BOXING ARENA? I HELD A
MOCK KICKBOXING MATCH.
GENTLEMEN, I BEAT HER WITH
MY HANDS AND FEET. I AM
SENDING PICTURES.

Chapter 14

SOMETHING WAS UP, and I didn't think I'd like it very much. I arrived at the Seventh District Police Station just before seven-thirty the following morning. I'd been summoned by the powers-that-be to the station, and it was a tough deal. I'd worked until two in the morning trying to get a lead on Nina Childs's murder.

I had a feeling that the day was starting out wrong. I was tense and more uptight than I usually let myself become. I didn't like this early-morning command appearance one bit.

I shook my head, frowned, tried to roll the kinks out of my neck. Finally, I gritted my teeth tightly before opening the mahogany door. Chief of Detectives George

Pittman was lying in wait in his office, which in fact consists of three connecting offices, including a conference room.

The Jefe, as he's called by his many "admirers," had on a boxy gray business suit, an overstarched white shirt, and a silver necktie. His gray-and-white-streaked hair was slicked back. He looked like a banker, and in some ways he is one. As he never tires of saying, he is working with a fixed budget and is always mindful of manpower costs, overtime costs, caseload costs. Apparently, he is an efficient manager, which is why the police commissioner overlooks the fact that he's a bully, bigot, racist, and careerist.

Up on his wall were three large, important-looking pushpin maps. The first showed two consecutive months of rapes, homicides, and assaults in Washington. The second map did the same for residential and commercial burglaries. The third map showed auto thefts. The maps and the *Post* said that crime was down in D.C., but not where I live.

"Do you know why you're here, why I wanted to see you?" Pittman asked point-blank. No socializing or small talk from The

Jefe, no niceties. "Of course you do, Dr. Cross. You're a psychologist. You're supposed to know how the human mind works. I keep forgetting that."

Be cool, be careful, I told myself. I did the thing Chief Pittman least expected: I smiled, then said softly, "No, I really *don't* know. I got a call from your assistant. So I'm here."

Pittman smiled back, as if I'd made a pretty good joke. Then he suddenly raised his voice, and his face and neck turned bright red; his nostrils flared, exposing the bristly hairs in his nose.

One of his hands was clenched into a tight fist, while the other was stretched open. His fingers were as rigid as the pencils sticking up from the leather cup on his desk.

"You're not fooling anybody, Cross, least of all me. I'm fully fucking aware that you're investigating homicides in Southeast that you aren't assigned to—the so-called Jane Does. You're doing this against my explicit orders. Some of those cases have been closed for over a year. *I won't have it*—I won't tolerate your insubordination, your condescending attitude. I know what you're trying to pull. Embarrass the department, specifically embarrass me, curry fucking favor with the mayor, making yourself some kind of folk hero in Southeast in the process."

I hated Pittman's tone and what he was saying, but I learned one trick a long time ago, and it is probably the most important thing to know about politics inside any organization. It's so simple, but it's the key to every petty kingdom, every fiefdom. Knowledge truly is power, it's everything; if you don't have any, pretend you do.

So I told Chief Pittman nothing. I didn't contradict him; I didn't admit to a thing. I did nothing. Me and Mahatma Gandhi.

I let him think that maybe I was investigating old cases in Southeast—but I didn't admit to it. I also let him think that maybe I had some powerful connections with Mayor Monroe and God only knows who else in the City on the Hill. I let him think that maybe I was after his job, or that I might have—God forbid—even loftier aspirations.

"I'm working the homicides assigned to me. Check with the captain. I'm doing my best to close as many cases as I can."

Pittman nodded curtly—*one* nod. His face was still heart-attack red. "All right, I want you to close *this* case, and I want you to close it fast. A tourist was robbed and gunned down on M Street last night," he said. "A well-respected German doctor from Munich. It's front fucking page in today's *Post.* Not to mention the *International Herald Tribune,* and every newspaper in Germany, of course. I want you on *that* murder case, and I want it solved pronto."

"This doctor, he's a white man?" I asked, keeping my expression neutral.

"I told you, he's German."

"I already have a number of open cases in Southeast," I said to Pittman. "A nurse was murdered over the weekend."

He didn't want to hear it. He shook his head—*one* shake. "And now you have an important case in Georgetown. Solve it, Cross. You're to work on nothing else. That's a direct order . . . from The Jefe."

Chapter 15

AS SOON AS CROSS WALKED out of Chief Pittman's inner office, a senior homicide detective named Patsy Hampton slipped in through a side door that led to the attached conference room. Detective Hampton had been instructed by Pittman to listen in on everything, to evaluate the situation from a street cop's perspective, to advise and to counsel.

Hampton didn't like the job, but those were her orders from Pittman. She didn't like Pittman, either. He was wound so tight that if you stuck coal up his ass, in a couple of weeks you'd have a diamond. He was mean and petty and vengeful.

"You see what I'm dealing with here? Cross knows how to push all my buttons.

In the beginning he would lose his temper. Now he just ignores what I say."

"I heard everything," Hampton said. "He's slick, all right." She was going to agree with Chief Pittman, no matter what he said.

Patsy Hampton was an attractive woman, with sandy blond hair cut short, and the most piercing blue eyes this side of Stockholm. She was thirty-one years old, and on a very fast track in the department. At twenty-six, she'd been the youngest homicide detective in Washington. Now she had much loftier goals in mind.

"You're selling yourself short, though. You got to him. I know you did." She told Pittman what he wanted to hear. "He just internalizes it pretty well."

"You're sure he's meeting with those other detectives?" Pittman asked her.

"They've met three times that I know of, always at Cross's house on Fifth Street. I suspect there have been other times. I heard about it through a friend of Detective Thurman."

"But they don't meet while any of them is on duty?"

"No, not to my knowledge. They're careful. They meet on their own time."

Pittman scowled and shook his head. "That's too goddamn bad. It makes it harder to prove anything really damaging."

"From what I've heard, they believe the department is holding back resources that could clear a number of unsolved homicides in Southeast and parts of Northeast. Most of the murders involve black and Hispanic women."

Pittman tensed his jaw and looked away from Hampton. "The numbers that Cross uses are complete bullshit," he said angrily. "They're dogshit. It's all political with him. How much financial resource can we put against the murders of drug addicts and prostitutes in Southeast? It's criminals murdering other criminals. You know how it goes in those black neighborhoods."

Hampton nodded again, still agreeing when she saw the chance. She was afraid she'd lost him, said the wrong thing by speaking the truth. "They think that at least some of the victims were innocent women from their neighborhoods. That E.R. nurse who was killed over the weekend, she was a friend of Cross and Detective John

Sampson. Cross thinks a killer could be loose in Southeast, preying on women."

"A serial killer in the ghetto? Give me a break. We've never had one there. They're rare in any inner city. Why now? Why here? Because Cross wants to find one, that's why."

"Cross and the others would counter that by saying we've never seriously tried to catch this squirrel."

Pittman's small eyes suddenly burned into her skull. "Do you agree with that horseshit, Detective?"

"No, sir. I don't necessarily agree or disagree. I know for a fact that the department doesn't have enough resources anywhere in the city, with the possible exception of Capitol Hill. Now *that's* political, and it's an outrage."

Pittman smiled at her answer. The chief knew she was playing him a little, but he liked her anyway. He liked just being in a room with Patsy Hampton. She was such a doll, such a cutie. "What do you know about Cross, Patsy?"

She sensed that the chief had vented enough. Now he wanted their talk to be more informal. She was certain that he liked her, had a crush on her, but he was too uptight to ever act on his desires, thank God.

"I know Cross has been on the force for just over eight years. He's currently the liaison between the department and the FBI, works with the Violent Criminal Apprehension Program. He's a profiler with a good reputation, from what I hear. Has a Ph.D. in psych from Johns Hopkins. Private practice for three years before he came to us. Widower, two kids, plays the blues on the piano at his house. That enough background? What more do you want to know? I've done my homework. You know me," Hampton said, and finally smiled.

Pittman was smiling now, too. He had small teeth with spaces between them, and always made her think of Eastern European refugees, or maybe Russian gangsters.

Detective Hampton smiled, though. She knew he liked it when she played along with him—as long as he thought she respected him.

"Any other worthwhile observations at this point?" he asked.

You're such a soft, flabby dick, Patsy

Hampton wanted to say, but she just shook her head. "He has some charm. He's well connected in political circles. I can see why you're concerned about him."

"You think Cross is charming?"

"I told you, he's slick. He *is*. People say he looks like the young Muhammad Ali. I think he likes to play the part sometimes: dance like a butterfly, sting like a bee." She laughed again—and so did he.

"We're going to nail Cross," Pittman said. "We'll send him flying back to private practice. Wait and see. You're going to help get it done. You get things done. Right, Detective Hampton? You see the bigger picture. That's what I like about you."

She smiled again. "That's what I like about me, too."

Chapter 16

THE BRITISH EMBASSY is a plain, Federal-style building located at 3100 Massachusetts Avenue. Its immediate neighbors are the vice president's house and the Observatory. The ambassador's residence is a stately Georgian building with tall, flowing white columns; the Chancery is the actual office building.

Geoffrey Shafer sat behind his small mahogany desk at the embassy and stared out onto Massachusetts Avenue. The embassy staff currently counted 415 people—soon to be cut to 414, he was thinking to himself. The staff included defense experts, foreign-policy specialists, trade, public affairs, clerks, and secretaries.

Although the United States and Britain

have an agreement not to spy on each other, Geoffrey Shafer was nonetheless a spy. He was one of eleven men and women from the Security Service, formerly known as MI6, who worked at the embassy in Washington. These eleven in turn ran agents attached to the consulates general in Atlanta, Boston, Chicago, Houston, Los Angeles, New York, and San Francisco.

He was feeling restless as hell today, getting up from his desk frequently, pacing back and forth across the carpet that covered the creaking parquet floors. He made phone calls he didn't need to make, tried to get some work done, thought about how much he despised his job and the everyday details of life.

He was supposed to be working on a truly silly communiqué about the government's absurd ongoing commitment to human rights. The foreign secretary had rather bombastically proclaimed that Britain would support the international condemnation of regimes that violate human rights; support international bodies involved in the cause; and denounce human-rights abuses, *blah, blah, blah,* ad nauseam.

He glanced through a few of the computer games he enjoyed when he was uptight like this—Riven, MechCommander, Unreal, TOCA, Ultimate Soccer Manager. None of them appealed to him right now; nothing did.

He was starting to crash, and he knew the feeling. *I'm going down, and there is only one certain way to stop it: play the Four Horsemen.*

To make matters worse, it was raining and woefully gray-skied outside. The city of Washington, and also the surrounding countryside, looked forlorn and depressing. It sucked. Christ, he was in a bad mood, even for him.

He continued to stare east across Massachusetts Avenue, looking into the trees bordering a park dedicated to the pacifist bullshit artist Kahlil Gibran. He tried to daydream, mostly about fucking various attractive women currently working at the embassy.

He had called his psychiatrist, Boo Cassady, at her home-office, but she was about to start a session and couldn't talk for long. They agreed to meet after work: a nasty quickie at her place before he went home to face Lucy and the sniveling brood.

He didn't dare play Horsemen again tonight. It was too soon after the nurse. But God Almighty, he *wanted* to play. He wished he could take somebody out in some very imaginative way, right there inside the embassy.

He did have one excellent thing to do today—saving it until now—three in the afternoon. He had used the dice already, played a bit of Horsemen, just to help him make a personnel decision.

He had called Sarah Middleton just before lunch and told her they needed to have a chat and could she stop by his office, say at three?

Sarah was obviously tense on the phone and told him she could do it earlier, anytime, at his convenience. "Not busy, then, nothing much to do today?" Shafer asked. Three o'clock would be fine, she answered hastily.

His secretary, the bestial Betty formerly from Belgravia, buzzed him promptly at three. At least he'd finally gotten through to her about punctuality.

Shafer let her buzz him several times, then picked up the phone abruptly, as if she'd interrupted him at something vital to security.

"What is it, Ms. Thomas? I'm extremely busy with this communiqué for the secretary."

"I'm sorry to disturb you, Mr. Shafer, but Ms. Middleton is here. You have a three-o'clock appointment with her, I understand."

"*Hmmm.* Do I? Yes, you're right. Can you ask Sarah to wait? I'll need a few more minutes. I'll buzz when I'm ready to see her."

Shafer smiled contentedly and picked up a copy of *The Red Coat,* the embassy's employee newsletter. He knew Betty hated it when he used Ms. Middleton's Christian name: Sarah.

He fantasized about Sarah for the next few moments. He'd wanted to have a go at Mzzz Middleton from their first interview, but he was too careful for that. God, he hated the bitch. This was going to be such fun.

Shafer watched the rain hammer down on the traffic crossing Massachusetts Avenue for another ten minutes. Finally he snatched up the phone. He couldn't wait a minute longer. "I'll see her now. Send Sarah in."

He fingered his twenty-sided dice. This could be fun, actually. *Terror at the office.*

Chapter 17

THE LOVELY SARAH MIDDLETON entered his office and managed a cordial
look, almost a smile. He felt like a boa con-
strictor eyeing a mouse.

She had naturally curly red hair, a mod-
erately pretty face, a superior figure. Today
she wore a very short suit, a red V-necked
silk blouse, black stockings. It was obvious
to Shafer that she was out to catch a husband in Washington.

Shafer's pulse was beating hard. He was
aroused by her, always had been. He
thought about taking her, and very much
liked that phrase. She didn't look as nervous and unsure of herself as she had recently, so that probably meant she was
really scared and trying not to show it. He

tried his best to think like Sarah. That made it more fun, though he found it a real challenge to be as squirrelly and insecure as she would surely be.

"We certainly needed the rain," Sarah said, and then cringed before the sentence was even finished.

"Sarah, please sit down," he said. He was trying to keep a straight business face. "Personally, I loathe the rain. It's one of the many reasons I've never been stationed in London."

He sighed theatrically behind the rigid tent he'd made with his fingers. He wondered if Sarah noticed the length of his fingers and if she ever thought about how large he was elsewhere. He would bet anything that she did. It was how people's minds worked, though women like Sarah would never admit to it.

She cleared her throat, then put her hands on her knees. The knuckles of her fingers were white. Christ, he was enjoying her obvious discomfort. She looked ready to jump out of her skin. How about out of her tight little skirt and blouse?

He began to stretch the fingers on his right hand, playing his part as dominator to the hilt. "Sarah, I think I have some bad news—quite unfortunate, really, but can't be avoided."

She sat nervously forward in her chair. She really was nicely built up top. He was getting hard now. "What is it, Mr. Shafer? What do you mean? You *think* you have bad news? You do or you don't?"

"We have to let you go. *I* have to let you go. Budget cuts, I'm afraid," he said. "I know you must find this immensely unfair, and unexpected as well. Particularly when you moved halfway across the world from Australia to take this job, and you've been living in Washington for less than six months. Suddenly, the ax falls."

He could tell she was actually fighting back tears. Her lips were trembling. Obviously, she never expected this. She had no idea. She was a reasonably smart and controlled woman, but she couldn't help herself now.

Excellent. He had succeeded in breaking her down. He wished he had a movie camera this minute to record the look on her face and play it back countless times in private.

He saw the very instant that she lost it,

and treasured it. He watched her eyes moisten, saw the large tears roll over her cheeks, streaking her working-girl makeup.

He felt the power, and it was as good as he'd hoped it would be. A small insignificant game, certainly, but a delicious one. He loved being able to instill such shock and pain.

"Poor Sarah. Poor, poor dear," he murmured.

Then Shafer did the cruelest, most unforgivable thing. Also the most outrageous and dangerous. He got up from his desk and came around to comfort her. He stood behind her, pressing himself against her shoulders. He knew it was the last thing she wanted, to be touched by him, to feel that he was aroused.

She stiffened and pulled away from him as if he were on fire. "Bastard," she said, between clenched teeth. "You are a consummate prick!"

Sarah left his office, shaking and in tears, running in that stumbling way women often do in heels. Shafer loved it. The sadistic pleasure, not only of hurting someone but of destroying this innocent woman. He memorized the stunning image for all time. He would play it back, over and over.

Yes, he was a prick. Consummate indeed.

Chapter 18

ROSIE THE CAT was perched on the windowsill, watching me dress for my date with Christine. I envied the simplicity of her life: *Love to eat those mousies, mousies what I love to eat.*

I finally headed downstairs. I was taking the night off from work, and I was more nervous, distracted, and fidgety than I had been in a long time. Nana and the kids knew something was up, but they didn't know what, and it was driving my three favorite busybodies crazy.

"Daddy, tell me what's going on, *please?*" Jannie clasped her hands in prayer and begged.

"I told you no, and no is no. Not even if you get down on your bony little knees," I said, and smiled. "I have a date tonight. It's just a date. That's all you need to know, young lady."

"Is it with Christine?" Jannie asked. "At least you can tell me *that* much."

"*That's* for me to know," I said as I knotted my tie in the mirror beside the stairs. "And *you not* to find out, my overinquisitive girlfriend."

"You're wearing your fancy blue-striped suit, your fancy dancing shoes, that fancy tie you like. You're *so* fancy."

"Do I look good?" I turned and asked my personal clothier. "For my date?"

"You look beautiful, Daddy." My girl beamed, and I knew I could believe her. Her eyes were shiny little mirrors that always told the truth. "You know you do. You know you're handsome as sin."

"That's my girl," I said, and laughed again. *Handsome as sin.* She got that one from Nana, no doubt.

Damon mimicked his sister. "You look beautiful, Daddy. What a little brownnoser. What do you want from Daddy, Jannie?"

"Do I look good?" I turned to Damon.

He rolled his eyes. "You look all right.

How come you're all duded up? You can tell me. Man to man. What's the big deal?"

"Answer the poor children!" Nana finally said.

I looked her way and offered up a wide grin. "Don't use the 'poor children' to try to get your gossip quotient for the day. Well, I'm off," I announced. "I'll be home before sunrise. *Moo-ha-ha-ha.*" I did my favorite monster imitation, and all three of them rolled their eyes.

It was a minute or so before eight, and as I stepped onto the porch, a black Lincoln Town Car pulled up in front of the house. It was right on time, and I didn't want to be late.

"A limousine?" Jannie gasped, and nearly swooned on the front porch. "You're going out in a *limousine?*"

"Alex Cross!" Nana said. "What *is* going on?"

I practically danced down the steps. I got into the waiting car, shut the door, told the driver to go. I waved out the back window and stuck out my tongue as the car smoothly pulled away from our house.

Chapter 19

MY LAST IMAGE was of the three of them—Jannie, Damon, and Nana—all mugging and sticking out their tongues at me. We do have some fabulously good times together, I was thinking as the car headed over to Prince Georges County, where I had once confronted a homicidal twelve-year-old during the halcyon days of the Jack and Jill killers, and where Christine Johnson lived.

I had my mantra all set for tonight: *Heart leads head.* I needed to believe that was so.

"A private car? A limousine?" Christine exclaimed when I picked her up at her house in Mitchellville.

She looked as stunningly beautiful as

I've ever seen her, and that's saying a lot. She wore a long, sleeveless black shift, black satin pumps with straps, and had a floral brocade jacket draped over her arm. The heels made her a little over six feet tall. God, how I loved this woman, everything about her.

We walked to the car and got inside.

"You haven't told me where we're going tonight, Alex. Just that it was fancy. Someplace special."

"Ah, but I've told our driver," I said. I tapped the partition window, and the Town Car moved off into the summer night. Alex the mysterious.

I held Christine's hands as we drove along on the John Hanson Highway, back toward Washington. Her face tilted toward mine, and I kissed her in the cozy darkness. I loved the sweetness of her mouth, her lips, the softness and smoothness of her skin. She was wearing a new perfume that I didn't recognize, and I liked that, too. I kissed the hollow of her throat, then her cheeks, her eyes, her hair. I would have been happy to do just this for the rest of the night.

"It is unbelievably romantic," she finally

said. "It *is* special. You are something else . . . *sugar.*"

We cuddled and hugged all the way into Washington. We talked, but I don't remember the subject. I could feel her breasts rising and falling against me. I was surprised when we arrived at the intersection of Massachusetts and Wisconsin avenues. We were getting close to the surprise.

True to her word, Christine hadn't asked any more questions. Not until the car eased up in front of Washington National Cathedral, and the driver got out and held the door open for us.

"The National Cathedral?" she said. "We're going in here?"

I nodded and stared up at the stunning Gothic masterpiece that I'd admired since I was a boy. The cathedral crowns over fifty acres of lawns and woods and is Washington's highest point, even higher than the Washington Monument. If I remembered correctly, it was the second-largest church in the United States, and possibly the prettiest.

I led the way, and Christine followed me inside. She held my hand lightly. We entered the northwest corner of the nave, which extends nearly a tenth of a mile to the massive altar.

Everything felt special and very beautiful, spiritual, just right. We walked up to a pew under the amazing Space Window at midnave. Everywhere I looked there were priceless stained-glass windows, over two hundred in all.

The light inside was exquisite; I felt blessed. There was a kaleidoscope of changing colors on the walls: reds, warm yellows, cool blues.

"Beautiful, isn't it?" I whispered. "Timeless, sublime, all that good Gothic stuff Henry Adams used to write about."

"Oh, Alex, I think it's the prettiest spot in Washington. The Space Window, the Children's Chapel—I've always loved it here. I told you that, didn't I?" she asked.

"You might have mentioned it once," I said. "Or maybe I just knew it."

We continued walking until we entered the Children's Chapel. It is small, beautiful, and wonderfully intimate. We stood under a stained-glass window that depicts the story of Samuel and David as children.

I turned and looked at Christine, and my heart was beating so loud I was sure she could hear it. Her eyes were sparkling like jewels in the flickering candlelight. The black dress shimmered and seemed to flow over her body.

I knelt on one knee and looked up at her.

"I've loved you since the first time I saw you at the Sojourner Truth School," I whispered, so that only she could hear me. "Except that when I saw you the first time, I had no way of knowing how incredibly special you are on the inside. How wise, how good. I didn't know that I could feel the way I do—whole and complete—whenever I'm with you. I would do anything for you. Or just to be with you for one more moment."

I stopped for the briefest pause and took a deep breath. She held my eyes, didn't pull away.

"I love you so much, and I always will. Will you marry me, Christine?"

She continued to look into my eyes, and I saw such warmth and love, but also humility, which is always a part of who Christine is. It was almost as if she couldn't imagine my loving her.

"Yes, I will. Oh, Alex, I shouldn't have waited until tonight. But this is so perfect, so special, I'm almost glad I did. Yes, I will be your wife."

I took out an antique engagement ring and gently slid it onto Christine's finger. The ring had been my mother's, and I'd kept it since she died, when I was nine. The exact history of the ring was unclear, except that it went back at least four generations in the Cross family and was my one and only heirloom.

We kissed in the glorious Children's Chapel of the National Cathedral, and it was the best moment of my life, never to be forgotten, never to be diminished in any way.

Yes, I will be your wife.

Chapter 20

TEN DAYS HAD PASSED without another fantasy murder, but now a powerful
mood swing had taken hold of Geoffrey
Shafer, and he let himself go with the flow.

He was flying high as a kite—hyper,
manic, bipolar, whatever the doctors
wanted to call his condition. He'd already
taken Ativan, Librium, Valium, and De-
pakote, but the drugs seemed only to fuel
his jets.

That night at around six he pulled the
black Jaguar out of the lot on the north
side of the embassy, passing by the larger-
than-life Winston Churchill statue with its
stubby right hand raised in *V* for Victory, its
left hand holding his trademark cigar.

Eric Clapton played guitar loudly on the

car's CD. He turned up the volume higher, slapping his hands hard on the steering wheel, feeling the rhythm, the beat, the primal urge.

Shafer turned onto Massachusetts Avenue and then stopped at a Starbucks. He hurried in and fixed up three coffees his way. Black as his heart, with six sugars. *Mmm, hmmm.* As usual, he had nearly finished the first before he got to the cash register.

Once he was inside the cockpit of his Jag again, he sipped a second cup at a more leisurely pace. He downed some Benadryl and Nascan. Couldn't hurt; might help. He took out the twenty-sided game dice. He had to play tonight.

Anything twelve or higher would dispatch him directly to Boo Cassady's place for a kinky quickie before he went home to the dreaded family. A seven to eleven was total disaster—straight home to Lucy and the kids. Three, four, five, or six meant he could go to the hideaway for an unscheduled night of high adventure.

"Come three, four, five. Come, baby, come! I need this tonight. Need a fix! I need it!"

He shook the dice for what must have been thirty seconds. He made the suspense last, drew it out. Finally, he released the dice onto the gray-leather car seat. He watched the roll closely.

Jesus, he'd thrown a four! Defied the odds! His brain was on fire. He could play tonight. The dice had spoken; fate had spoken.

He excitedly punched a number on his cell phone. *"Lucy,"* he said, and he was smiling already.

"Glad I caught you at home, darling. . . . Yes, you guessed it, first try. We're completely swamped here again. Can you believe it? I certainly can't. They think they own me, and I suppose they're half right. It's the drug-trafficking rubbish again. I'll be home when I can. Don't wait up, though. Love to the kids. Kisses to everybody. Me, too, darling. I love you, too. You're the best, the most understanding wife alive."

Very well played, Shafer thought as he breathed a sigh of relief. Excellent performance, considering the drugs he'd taken. Shafer disconnected from his wife, whose family money, unfortunately, paid for the town house, the holidays away, even the Jag, and her fashionable Range Rover, of course.

He punched another number on the cell phone.

"Dr. Cassady." He heard her voice almost immediately. She *knew* it was him. He usually called from the car on his way over to see her. They liked to get each other hot and bothered on the phone. Telephone sex as foreplay.

"They've done it to me again," Shafer whined miserably into the phone, but he was smiling again, loving his flair for the overdramatic.

A short silence, then, "You mean they did it to *us,* don't you? There's *no way* you can get away? It's only a bloody job, and one that you detest, Geoff."

"You know I would if I possibly could. I do hate it here, *loathe* every moment. And it's even worse at home, Boo. Jesus, you of all people know that."

He imagined the tight little frown and Boo's pursing her lips. "You sound high, Geoffrey. Are you, dear? Take your pills today?"

"Don't be horrible. Of course I've taken

my medications. I *am* rushed. I *am* high. On the ceiling, as a matter of fact. I'm calling between blasted staff meetings. Oh hell, I miss you, Boo. I want to be inside you, deep inside. I want to do your pussy, your ass, your throat. I'm thinking about it right now. Christ, I'm as hard as a rock here in my government-issue office. Have to beat it down with a stick. *Cane* it. That's how we British handle such things."

She laughed, and he almost changed his mind about standing her up. "Go back to work. I'll be at home, if you finish early," she said. "I could use a little finishing myself."

"I love you, Boo. You're so kind to me."

"I am, and I could probably get into a little caning, too."

He hung up and drove to the hideaway in Eckington. He parked the Jag next to the purple and blue taxi in the garage. He bounded upstairs to change for the game. God, he loved this, his secret life, his nights away from everything and everyone he *loathed*.

He was taking too many chances now, but he didn't care.

Chapter 21

SHAFER WAS TOTALLY PUMPED UP
for a night on the town. The Four Horsemen was on. Anything could happen tonight. Yet he found that he was introspective and pensive. He could flip from manic
to depressive in the blink of an eye.

He watched himself as if he were an ob-
server in a dream. He had been an English
intelligence agent, but now that the Cold
War had ended, there was little use for his
talents. It was only the influence of Lucy's
father that had kept him in his job. Duncan
Cousins had been a general in the army
and now was chairman of a packaged-
goods conglomerate specializing in the
sale of detergents, soaps, and drugstore
perfumes. He liked to call Shafer "the Col-

onel," rubbing in his "rise to mediocrity." The General also loved to talk about the glowing successes of Shafer's two brothers, both of whom had made millions in business.

Shafer shifted his thoughts back to the present. He was doing that a lot lately, fading in and out like a radio with a bad connection. He took a settling breath, then pulled the taxi out of the garage. Moments later, he turned onto Rhode Island Avenue. It was beginning to rain again, a light mist that made the passing traffic lights blurry and impressionistic.

Shafer drifted over to the curb and stopped for a tall, slender black man. He looked like a drug dealer, something Shafer had no use for. Maybe he would just shoot the bastard, then dump the body. That felt good enough for tonight's action. A sleazebag dope dealer whom nobody would miss.

"Airport," the man announced haughtily as he climbed inside the taxi. The inconsiderate bastard shook off rainwater onto the seat. Then he shut the creaking car door behind him and was on his cell phone immediately.

Shafer wasn't going to the airport, and neither was his first passenger of the night. He listened in on the phone call. The man's voice was affected, surprisingly cultured.

"I think I'll just make the nine o'clock, Leonard. It's Delta *on* the hour, right? I picked up a cab, thank the Lord Jesus. Most of them won't stop anywhere near where my poor Moms lives in Northeast. Then along comes this purple and blue absolute wreck of a gypsy cab, and merciful God, it stops for me."

Christ, he'd been identified. Shafer silently cursed his bad luck. That was the way of the game, though: incredible highs and vicious lows. He would have to take this asshole all the way out to National Airport. If he disappeared, it would be connected to a purple and blue cab, an "absolute wreck of a gypsy cab."

Shafer stepped on the accelerator and sped out toward National. The airport was backed up, even at nine in the evening. He cursed under his breath. The rain was heavy and punctuated by rolling thunder and spits of lightning.

He tried to control his building anger, his darkening mood. It took nearly forty minutes to get to the bloody terminal and drop off the passenger. By that time he'd settled back into another fantasy, had another huge mood swing. He was cycling *up* again.

Maybe he should have gone to see Dr. Cassady, after all. He needed more pills, especially Lithium. This was like a carnival ride tonight—up and down, up and down. He wanted to push things as far as he could. He also felt crazed. He was definitely losing control.

Anything could happen when he got like this. That was the thing. He pulled into the queue of taxis waiting to get a fare back to D.C.

As he got closer to the front of the line, there was more thunder. Lightning crackled high above the airport. He could see the prospective victims huddled under a dripping canopy. Flights were undoubtedly being postponed and canceled. He savored the cheap-seat melodrama, the suspense. The victim du jour could be anyone, from a corporate executive to a harried secretary, or maybe even a whole family back from a vacation to Disney World.

But not once did he look directly at the

queue of potential victims as he inched closer and closer. He was almost there. Just two more taxis in front of him. He could see the queue out of the corner of his eye. Finally, he had to snatch a quick peek.

It was a tall male.

He peeked again, couldn't help himself.

A white male, a businessman, stepped off the curb and was climbing inside the taxi. He was cursing to himself, pissed off about the rain.

Shafer looked the man over. He was American, late thirties, full of himself. Investment analyst, maybe, or banker— something like that.

"We can *go*—whenever you're in the mood," the man snapped at him.

"Sorry, sir," Shafer said, and smiled obsequiously into the rearview mirror.

He dropped the dice on the front seat: *six!* His heart began to hammer.

Six meant *immediate action.* But he was still inside National Airport. There was a heavy lineup of traffic and cops, bright lights glittering everywhere. It was too dangerous, even for him.

The dice had spoken. He had no choice. The game was *on* right now.

A sea of red rear lights glowed at him. Cars were everywhere. How could he do this here? Shafer began to perspire heavily.

But he had to do it. That was the point of the game. He had to do it now. Had to murder this asshole right here at the airport.

He swerved into the nearest parking area. This was not good. He sped down a narrow lane. Another bolt of lightning flashed overhead; it seemed to underscore the madness and chaos of the moment.

"Where the *hell* are you going?" the businessman shouted at him. He slammed his palm into the back of the seat. "This isn't the way out, you ass!"

Shafer glared at the business creep in his rearview mirror. He hated him for calling him an ass. The bastard also reminded him of his brothers.

"I'm not going anywhere," he yelled back. "But *you're* going straight to hell!"

The businessman blubbered, "What did you say to me? What did you just say?"

Shafer fired his Smith & Wesson nine-millimeter and hoped no one would hear it above the thunder and honking horns.

He was soaking wet with perspiration, and he was afraid his black face would run and smear. He was expecting to be stopped at any moment. Waiting for policemen to surround the taxi. Bright-red blood was splattered all over the back-seat and window. The businessman was slumped in the corner as if he were asleep. Shafer couldn't see where the bloody bullet had exited the taxi.

He made it out of National before he went completely mad. He drove carefully to Benning Heights in Southeast. He couldn't risk being stopped for speeding. But he was out of his head, not sure he was doing the right thing.

He stopped on a side street, checked out the body, stripped it. He decided to dump the corpse out in the open. He was trying his best not to be predictable.

Then he sped away from the crime scene and headed home.

He'd left no identification on the victim. Nothing but the body.

Just a little surprise—a *John* Doe.

Chapter 22

I GOT HOME from Christine's house at two-thirty in the morning feeling exhilarated, the happiest I'd been in years. I thought about waking Nana and the kids to tell them the news. I wanted to see the surprised looks on their faces. I wished that I had brought Christine home with me, so we could celebrate together.

The phone rang moments after I stepped inside the house. *Oh no,* I thought, *not tonight. Nothing good comes from phone calls at two-thirty* A.M.

I picked up in the living room and heard Sampson's voice on the line. "Sugar?" he whispered.

"Leave me alone," I said. "Try again in the morning. I'm closed for the night."

"No you're not, Alex. Not tonight. Get over to Alabama Avenue, about three blocks east of Dupont Park. A man was found there naked and dead, in the gutter. The guy is white, and there's no I.D. on him."

First thing in the morning, I would tell Nana and the kids about Christine and me. I had to go. The murder scene was a ten-minute ride across the Anacostia River. Sampson was waiting for me on a street corner. So was the John Doe.

And a lively, mean-spirited crowd. A naked white body dumped in this neighborhood had prompted lots of curiosity, almost like seeing a deer walking down Alabama Avenue.

"Casper the Friendly Ghost been *offed*." A heckler contributed his twenty-five cents as Sampson and I stooped down under the yellow plastic crime-scene tape. In the background were rows of dilapidated brick buildings that almost seemed to scream out the names of the lost, the forgotten, the never-had-a-chance.

Stagnant water often pools on the street corners here since the storm drains are hardly ever inspected. I knelt over the

twisted, naked body that was partly im-
mersed in the cesspool. There would be no
tire marks left at the watery scene. I wondered if the killer had thought of that.

I was making mental notes. No need to
write them down; I'd remember everything.
The man had manicured fingernails and
toenails. No calluses showed on either his
hands or his feet. He had no bruises or dis-
tinct disfiguring marks, other than the cruel
gunshot wound that had blown away the
left side of his face.

The body was deeply suntanned, except
where he'd worn swim trunks. A thin, pale
ring ran around his left index finger, where
he'd probably worn a wedding band,
which was missing.

And there was no I.D.—just like the Jane
Does.

Death was clearly the result of the single,
devastating gunshot to the head. Alabama
Avenue was the primary scene—where the
body was found—but I suspected a sec-
ondary homicide scene, where the victim
was actually murdered.

"What do you think?" Sampson
crouched down close beside me. His

knees cracked loudly. "Sonofabitch killer is pissed off about something."

"Really bizarre that he wound up here in Benning Heights. I don't know if he's connected to the Jane Does. But if he is, the killer wanted us to find this one in a hurry. Bodies around here usually get dumped in Fort Dupont Park. He's getting stranger and stranger. And you're right, he's very angry with the world."

My mind was rapidly filling with crime-scene notes, plus the usual stream of homicide-detective questions. Why leave the body in a street gutter? Why not in an abandoned building? Why in Benning Heights? Was the killer black? That still made the most sense to me, but a very low percentage of pattern killers are black.

The sergeant from the Crime Scene Unit came strolling up to Sampson and me. "What do you want from us, Detective?"

I looked back at the naked white body. "Videotape it, photograph it, sketch it," I told him.

"And take some of the trash in the gutter and sidewalk?"

"Take everything. Even if it's soaking wet."

The sergeant frowned. "Everything? All this wet trash? Why?"

Alabama Avenue is hilly, and I could see the Capitol Building brightly illuminated in the distance. It looked like a faraway celestial body, maybe heaven. It got me thinking about the *haves* in Washington, and the *have-nots*.

"Just take everything. It's how I work," I said.

Chapter 23

DETECTIVE PATSY HAMPTON arrived at the chilling homicide scene around 2:15. The Jefe's assistant had called her apartment about an unusual murder in Benning Heights that might relate to the Jane Does. This one was different in some ways, but there were too many similarities for her to ignore.

She watched Alex Cross work the crime scene. She was impressed that he'd come out at this early hour. She was curious about him, had been for a long time. Hampton knew Cross by reputation and had followed a couple of his cases. She had even worked a few weeks on the tragic kidnapping of Maggie Rose Dunne and Michael Goldberg.

So far, she had mixed feelings about Cross. He was personable enough, and more than good-looking. Cross was a tall, strongly put-together man. She felt that he received undeserved special treatment because he was a forensic psychologist. She'd done her homework on Cross.

Hampton understood that she had been assigned to show Cross up, to win, to knock him down a peg. She knew it would be a tough competition, but she also knew that she was the one to do it; she never failed at anything.

She'd already done her own examination of the crime scene. She had stayed on at the scene only because Cross and Sampson had unexpectedly shown up.

She continued to study Cross, watched him walk the homicide scene several times. He was physically imposing, and so was his partner, who had to be at least six-nine. Cross was six-three and weighed maybe two hundred. He appeared younger than his age, which was forty-one. He seemed to be respected by the assisting patrolmen, even by the EMS personnel. He shook a few hands, patted shoulders, occasionally shared a smile with someone working the crime scene.

Hampton figured that was part of his act, though. Everybody had one these days, especially in Washington. Cross's was obviously his charisma and charm.

Hell, she had an act herself. Hers was to appear nonthreatening and "feminine," then perform contrary to the expectations of the males on the force. She usually caught them off guard. As she'd risen in the department, the men had learned that she could be tough. Surprise, surprise. She worked longer hours than anyone else; she was a hell of a lot tougher than the men; and she never socialized with other cops.

But she made one big mistake. She broke into a homicide suspect's car without a warrant, and was caught by another detective, a jealous older male. That was how Pittman got his hooks into her, and now he wouldn't let go.

At around a quarter to three, she walked to her forest-green Explorer, noting that it needed a wash. She already had a few ideas about the dead man in the street. There was no doubt in her mind that she would beat Cross.

Book Two

DEATH RIDES A PALE HORSE

Chapter 24

GEORGE BAYER was Famine among the Four Horsemen. He'd been playing the fantasy game for seven years, and he loved it. At least he had until recently, when Geoffrey Shafer started to go out of control.

Famine was physically unimpressive at around five-eight, a hundred ninety pounds. He was paunchy, balding, wore wire-rim glasses, but he also knew that his appearance was deceiving, and he'd made a living off those who underestimated him. People like Geoffrey Shafer.

He had reread a forty-page dossier on Shafer during his long plane ride from Asia to Washington. The dossier told him everything about Shafer, and also about the character he played, Death. At Dulles Airport he rented a dark-blue Ford sedan, under a false name. He was still detached and introspective during his thirty-minute drive into the city.

But he was also anxious: he was nervous for all of the Horsemen, but especially for himself. He was the one who would have to confront Shafer, and he was worried that Shafer might be going mad, that he might blow up in all of their faces.

George Bayer had been an M man—MI6—and he'd known Shafer in the service. He had come to Washington to check out Shafer firsthand. It was suspected by the other players that Geoffrey might have gone over the edge, that he was no longer playing by the rules and was a grave danger to them all. Since Bayer had once been stationed in Washington, and knew the town, he was the one to go there.

Bayer didn't want to be seen at the British Embassy on Massachusetts Avenue, but he had spoken to a few friends who he knew would keep silent about having been contacted. The news about Shafer was as bad as he'd suspected. He was seeing women outside his marriage, and he wasn't being discreet. There was a psychologist who was also a sex therapist, and he had been observed going over to her place several times a week, often during working hours. It was rumored that he was drinking heavily and possibly taking drugs. Bayer suspected the latter. He and Shafer had been friends and they had done their share of drugs while posted in the Philippines and Thailand. Of course, they were younger and more foolish then— or at least that was true of Bayer.

The D.C. police had recently put in a complaint to the embassy about a reckless-driving incident. Shafer might have been high at the time. His current assignments at the embassy were minimal, and he would have been dismissed, or sent back to England, if it weren't for his wife's father, General Duncan Cousins. What a terrible mess Shafer had made of his life.

But that's not the worst of it, is it, Geoffrey? George Bayer was thinking as he drove into the Northeast section of Washington known as Eckington Place. *There's more, isn't there, dear boy? It's much worse than the embassy thinks. It's probably the biggest scandal in the long history*

*of the Security Service, and you're right at
the heart of it. But of course, so am I.*

Bayer locked the doors of his car as he
pulled up to a traffic light. The area looked
highly suspicious to him, like so much of
Washington these days. What a sad, totally
insane country America had become. What
a perfect refuge for Shafer.

Famine took in the sights on the mean
streets as he continued through the decid-
edly lower-class neighborhood. There was
nothing to compare with this in London.
Row upon row of two-storied redbrick garden apartments, many of them in dreadful
disrepair. Not so much urban decay as urban apathy.

He saw Shafer's lair up ahead and pulled
over to the curb. He knew the exact loca-
tion of the hideaway from the elaborate
fantasy tales Shafer had spun for his fellow
players. He knew the address. Now he
needed to know one more thing: were the
murders that Geoffrey claimed he'd committed fantasies, or were they real? Was he
actually a cold-blooded killer, operating
here in Washington?

Bayer walked to the garage door. It took

him only a moment to pick the lock and let himself in.

He had heard so much about the "Nightmare Machine," the purple and blue taxi that Shafer used for the murders. He was looking at it. The taxi was as real as he was. Now he knew the truth. George Bayer shook his head. Shafer had killed all of those people. This was no longer a game.

Chapter 25

BAYER TRUDGED UPSTAIRS to the hideaway apartment. His arms and legs felt heavy, and he had a slight pain in his chest. His vision was tunneled. He pulled down the dusty blinds and began to look around.

Shafer had boastfully described the garage and taxi several times during the game. He had flaunted the existence of the hideaway and sworn to the other players that it was real and not just some fantasy in a role-playing game. Geoffrey had openly dared them to see it for themselves, and that was why Bayer was in Washington.

Well, Geoffrey, the hideaway is real, he agreed. *You are a stone-cold killer. You weren't bluffing, were you?*

At ten o'clock that night Bayer took Shafer's taxi out. The keys were there, almost as a dare. Was it? He figured he had a night to experience exactly what Shafer had experienced. According to Geoffrey, half the fun of the game was foreplay—checking out the possibilities, seeing the whole game board before you made a move.

From ten o'clock until half past eleven, Bayer explored the streets of D.C., but he didn't pick up a fare. He kept his off-duty sign on. *What a game,* Bayer kept thinking as he drove. *Is this how Geoffrey does it? Is this how he feels when he's prowling the city?*

He was pulled out of his daydream by an old tramp with a crushed hat who wheeled a cart filled with cans and other recyclables right in front of him. He didn't seem to care whether he got run over or not, but Bayer braked hard. That made him think of Shafer. The line between life and death had faded to nothing for Geoffrey, hadn't it?

Bayer cautiously moved on. He drove past a church. The service was over, and a crowd of people was leaving.

He stopped the cab for an attractive

black woman in a blue dress and matching high heels. He needed to see what this must be like for Shafer, for Death. He couldn't resist.

"Thank you so much," the woman said as she slid into the rear of his taxi. She seemed so proper and respectable. He checked her furtively in the mirror. She didn't have much to offer up top. Pretty enough face, though. Long brown legs encased in sheer stockings. He tried to imagine what Shafer might do now, but he couldn't.

Shafer had boasted that he was killing people in the poorer sections of Washington, since nobody cared about them anyway. Bayer suspected he was telling the truth. He knew things about Shafer from when they were in Thailand and the Philippines. He knew Shafer's deepest, darkest secrets.

Bayer drove the attractive and well-spoken black woman to her apartment and was amused when she gave him a sixty-cent tip for the four-dollar ride. Fifteen percent to the penny. He took the money and thanked her graciously.

"An English cabdriver," she said. "That's unusual. Have a nice evening."

He continued to drive until past two in the morning. He drank in the sights, played the dizzying game. And then he had to stop again. Two young girls were hailing for a taxi on the corner. The area was called Shaw, and Howard University was very close according to several signs.

The girls were slender, delectable in stacked heels and shiny clothes that glowed in the dark. One of them wore a microskirt, and he could see the tops of black or navy thigh-highs as he stopped to pick them up. *They must be hookers— Shafer's favorite prey,* Bayer thought to himself.

The second prostitute was even prettier and sexier than the first. She wore white stacked bath sandals, side-striped white athletic pants, a teeny tank top in blue camouflage.

"Where are we going?" Bayer asked as they scampered over to the taxi.

The girl in the microskirt did the talking. "*We're* going to Princeton Place. That's Petworth, darlin'. Then *you're* going away," she said. She tossed her head back and issued a taunting laugh. Bayer snickered to himself. He was beginning to get into this now.

The girls climbed in, and Bayer couldn't resist checking them out in the mirror. The foxy one in the microskirt caught him looking. He felt like a schoolboy, found it intoxicating, didn't avert his eyes from hers.

She casually flipped him the finger. He didn't stop looking. Couldn't. *So this was how it felt to Shafer. This was the game of games.*

He couldn't take his eyes off the girls. His heart was pounding. Microskirt wore a tightly fitted ribbed tank top. Her long fingernails were airbrushed in kiwi and mango colors. She had a pager on her belt. Probably a gun in her handbag.

The other girl smiled shyly in his direction. She seemed more innocent. Was she? A necklace that read BABY GIRL dangled between her young breasts.

If they were going to Petworth, they had to be hooking. They were certainly young and foxy; sixteen, seventeen years old. Bayer could see himself having sex with the girls, and the image was beginning to overpower his imagination. He knew he ought to be careful. This could get completely out of hand. He was playing Shafer's game, wasn't he? And he liked it very much.

"I have a proposition for you," he said to Microskirt.

"All right, darlin'," she said. "Be one hundred for the half. Plus our ride to Petworth. That's my proposition for you."

Chapter 26

SHAFER LIKED TO KNOW when any of the other players traveled, especially if they came to Washington. He had gone to a lot of trouble to hack his way into their computers to keep track of them. Famine had recently bought plane tickets, and now he was here in D.C. Why?

It wasn't hard to follow George Bayer once he got to town. Shafer was still reasonably good at it; he'd had plenty of practice in tracking and surveillance during his years in the Service.

He was disappointed that Famine had decided to "intersect" with his fantasy. Intersection happened occasionally in the game, but it was rare. Both players were supposed to agree beforehand. Famine was clearly breaking the rules. What did he know, or think he knew?

Then Bayer genuinely surprised him. Not only did he visit Shafer's hideaway, but he actually took the taxi for a ride. What the hell was he doing?

At a little past two in the morning, Shafer watched the gypsy cab pick up two young girls in Shaw. Was Bayer copycatting? Was he setting some kind of trap for Shafer? Or was it something else altogether?

Bayer took the girls to S Street, which wasn't far from the pickup point. He followed the girls up the darkened stairs of an aging brownstone, and then they all disappeared inside.

He had a blue anorak thrown over his right arm and Shafer suspected that a pistol was under the coat. Christ! He'd taken two of them. He could have been seen by anyone on the street. The cab could have been spotted.

Shafer parked on the street. He waited and watched. He didn't like being in this part of Shaw, especially without his disguise, and driving the Jaguar. There were some old crumbling brownstones and a couple of boarded-up, graffiti-covered shacks on the street. No one was outside.

He saw a light blink on the top floor and figured that was where Bayer had taken the two girls. Probably their flat.

He watched the brownstone from two until close to four. He couldn't take his eyes away. While he waited, he imagined dozens of scenarios that might have brought Famine here. He wondered if the others were in Washington, too. Or was Famine acting alone? Was he playing the Four Horsemen right now?

Shafer waited and waited for Bayer to come out of the brownstone. But he didn't come down, and Shafer grew more impatient and worried and angry. He fidgeted. His breathing became labored. He had lurid, paranoid fantasies about what Bayer might have done up there. Had he killed the two girls? Taken their identification? Was this a trap? He thought so. What else could it be?

Still no George Bayer.

Shafer couldn't stand it any longer. He climbed out of the Jaguar. He stood on the street and stared up at the windows of the flat. He wondered if he, too, was being watched. He sensed a trap, wondered if he should flee.

Christ, where the hell is Bayer? What game is Famine playing? Was there a back way out of the building? If so, why had he left the taxi as evidence? Evidence! Damn him!

But then he saw Bayer finally leave the building. He quickly crossed S Street, got into the cab, and drove away.

Shafer decided to go upstairs. He jogged over to the building and found the wooden front door unlocked. He hurried up the steep, winding stairs. He had a flashlight in one hand, and turned it on. His semiautomatic was in the other.

Shafer made his way to the fourth floor. He immediately knew which of the two flats was the one. A poster for Mary J. Blige's *What's the 411?* album was on the splintered and scarred door to his right. The girls lived here.

He turned the handle and carefully pushed the door open. He pointed his gun inside, ready.

One of the young girls came out of the bathroom wearing a fluffy black towel on her head, nothing else. She was a hot number with pert little titties. Christ, Famine must have paid for it. What a fool! What a wanker!

"Who the hell are you? What are you doing in here?" the girl shouted angrily.

"I'm Death," he grinned, then announced, "I'm here for you and your pretty friend."

Chapter 27

I HAD GOTTEN HOME from the John Doe murder scene at a little past three-thirty in the morning. I went to bed but set my alarm for six-thirty. I managed to get myself up before the kids went off to school.

"Somebody was out very, very, very late last night." Jannie started her teasing before I had made it all the way downstairs and into the kitchen. I continued down and found her and Damon in the breakfast nook with Nana.

"Somebody sure *looks* like he had a late night," Nana said from her customary cat-bird's seat.

"Somebody's cruising for a bruising," I said to quiet them. "Now, there's something important I need to tell you before you head out to school."

"Watch our manners. Always pay attention in class, even if the teacher's boring. Lead with our left if it ever comes to a fight in the schoolyard," Jannie offered with a wink.

I rolled my eyes. "What I was going to say," I said, "is that you should be especially nice to Mrs. Johnson today. You see, last night Christine said that she'd marry me. I guess that means she's marrying all of us."

At that point, everything became hugging and loud celebrating in the kitchen. The kids got chocolate milk and bacon grease all over me. I'd never seen Nana happier. And I felt exactly the same. Probably even better than they did.

I eventually made it to work that morning. I had made some progress on the John Doe homicide, and early on Tuesday morning, I learned that the man whose body had been dumped on Alabama Avenue was a thirty-four-year-old research analyst named Franklin Odenkirk. He worked at the Library of Congress for the Congressional Research Service.

We didn't release the news to the press, but I did inform Chief Pittman's office as soon as I knew. Pittman would find out anyway.

Once I had a name for the victim, information came quickly, and as it usually is, it was sad. Odenkirk was married and had three small children. He had taken a late flight back from New York, where he'd given a talk at the Rockefeller Institute. The plane landed on time, and he deboarded at National around ten. What happened to him after that was a mystery.

For the remainder of the week, I was busy with the murder case. I visited the Library of Congress and went to the newest structure, the James Madison Building, on Independence Avenue. I talked to nearly a dozen of Frank Odenkirk's coworkers.

They were courteous and cooperative, and I was told repeatedly that Odenkirk, while haughty at times, was generally well liked. He wasn't known to use drugs or drink to excess; wasn't known to gamble, either. He was faithful to his wife. He hadn't been involved in a serious argument at the office for as long as he'd been there.

He was with the Education and Public

Welfare Division and spent long days in the spectacular Main Reading Room. There was no apparent motive for his murder, which was what I had feared. The killing roughly paralleled the Jane Does so far, but of course the chief of detectives didn't want to hear that. There *was* no Jane Doe killer, according to him. Why? Because he didn't want to shift dozens of detectives to Southeast and begin an extensive investigation on the basis of my instincts and gut feelings. I had heard Pittman joke that Southeast wasn't part of *his city.*

Before I left the Madison Building, I was compelled to stop and see the Main Reading Room once again. It was newly renovated, and I hadn't been there since the work had been done.

I sat at a reader's table and stared up at the amazing dome high over my head. Around the room were stained-glass representations of the seals of forty-eight states, along with bronze statues of famous figures, including Michelangelo, Plato, Shakespeare, Edward Gibbon, and Homer. I could imagine poor Frank Odenkirk doing his work here, and it bothered me. Why had he been killed? Had it been the Weasel?

The death was a terrible shock to everyone who had worked with him, and a couple of Odenkirk's coworkers broke down while talking to me about his murder.

I wasn't looking forward to interviewing Mrs. Odenkirk, but I drove out 295 and 210 to Forest Heights late on Friday afternoon. Chris Odenkirk was home with her mother, and also her husband's parents, who had flown in from Briarcliff Manor in Westchester County, New York. They told me the same story as the people at the Library of Congress. No one in the family knew of anyone who might want to harm Frank. He was a loving father, a supportive husband, a thoughtful son and son-in-law.

At the Odenkirk home, I learned that the deceased had been wearing a green seersucker suit when he left home, that his business meeting in New York had run over, and that he had been nearly two hours late getting to La Guardia Airport. He generally took a cab home from the airport in Washington because so many flights arrived late.

Even before I went to the house in Forest

Heights, I had two detectives sent out to the airport. They showed around pictures of Odenkirk, interviewed airline personnel, shopworkers, porters, taxi dispatchers, and cabdrivers.

Around six I went over to the medical examiner's office to hear the results of the autopsy. All the photos and sketches from the crime scene were laid out. The autopsy had run about two and a half hours. Every cavity of Frank Odenkirk's body had been swabbed and scraped, and his brain had been removed.

I talked to the medical examiner while she finished up with Odenkirk at about six-thirty. Her name was Angelina Torres, and I'd known her for years. The two of us had started in our jobs at about the same time. Angelina was a tick under five feet and probably weighed around ninety pounds soaking wet.

"Long day, Alex?" she asked. "You look used and abused."

"Long one for you, too, Angelina. You look good, though. Short, but good."

She nodded, grinned, then stretched her small slight arms up over her head. She let out a low groan that approximated the way I felt, too.

"Any surprises for me?" I asked, after allowing her to stretch in peace and moan her little heart out.

I hadn't expected anything, but she had some news. "One surprise," Angelina said. "He was sodomized after he died. Someone had sex with him, Alex. Our killer seems to swing both ways."

Chapter 28

ON THE DRIVE HOME that evening, I needed a break from the murder case. I thought about Christine, and that was much better, easier on the frontal lobe. I even switched off my beeper. I didn't want any distractions for ten or fifteen minutes.

Even though she hadn't talked about it recently, she still felt my job was too dangerous. The trouble was, she was absolutely right. I sometimes worried about leaving Damon and Jannie alone in the world, and now Christine as well. As I drove along the familiar streets of Southeast near Fifth, I considered whether I could actually leave police work. I'd been thinking about going into private practice and working as a psychologist, but I hadn't done anything to make it happen. It probably meant that I didn't really want to do it.

Nana was sitting on the front porch when I arrived home at around seven-thirty. She looked peeved, an expression of hers that I know all too well. She can still make me feel like I'm nine or ten years old and she's the one with all the answers.

"Where are the kids?" I called out as soon as I opened the car door and climbed out. A fractured Batman and Robin kite was still up in a tree in the yard, and I was annoyed at myself for not getting it down a couple of weeks ago.

"I shackled them to the sink, and they're doing the dishes," Nana said.

"Sorry about missing dinner," I told her.

"Tell that to your children," Nana said, frowning up a storm. She's about as subtle as a hurricane. "You better tell them right now. Your friend Sampson called a little earlier. So did your compatriot Jerome Thurman. There's been more murders, Alex. I used the *plural* noun, just in case you didn't notice. Sampson is waiting for you at the so-called crime scene. Two bodies over in Shaw, near Howard University, of all places. Two more young black girls are dead. It won't stop, will it? It never stops in Southeast."

No, it never does.

Chapter 29

THE HOMICIDE SCENE was an old crumbling brownstone in a bad section of S Street in Shaw. A lot of college kids and also some young professionals live in the up-and-down, mostly middle-class neighborhood. Lately, prostitution has become a problem there. According to Sampson, the two dead girls were both prostitutes who occasionally worked in the neighborhood but mostly turned tricks over in Petworth.

A single squad car and an EMS truck were parked at the homicide scene. A uniformed patrolman was posted on the front stoop, and he seemed intent on keeping intruders out. He was young, baby-faced, with smooth, butterscotch skin. I didn't know him, so I flashed my detective's shield.

"Detective Cross." He grunted. I sensed that he'd heard of me.

"What do we have so far?" I asked before I went inside to trudge up four steep flights. "What do you hear, Officer?"

"Two girls dead upstairs. Both pros, apparently. One of them lived in the building. Murders were called in anonymously. Maybe a neighbor, maybe the pimp. They're sixteen, seventeen, maybe younger. Too bad. They didn't deserve this."

I nodded, took a deep breath, and then quickly climbed up the steep, winding, creaking stairs to the fourth floor. Prostitutes make for difficult police investigations, and I wondered if the Weasel knew that. On average, a hooker out of Petworth might turn a dozen or more tricks a night, and that's a lot of forensic evidence just on her body.

The door to apartment 4A was wide open, and I could see inside. It was an efficiency, with one large room, kitchenette, bath. A fluffy white area rug lay between two daybeds. A lava lamp was undulating green blobs next to several dildos.

Sampson was crouched on the far side of one daybed. He looked like an NBA power forward searching the floor for a missing contact lens.

I walked into a small, untidy room that smelled of incense, peach-blossom fragrance, greasy food. A bright red and yellow McDonald's container of fries was open on the couch.

Dirty clothes covered the chairs: bike shorts, short-shorts, Karl Kani urban clothes. At least a dozen bottles of nail polish and remover, a couple of nail files, and cotton balls lay on the floor. There was a heavy, cloying smell of fruity perfume in the room.

I went around the bed to look at the victims. Two very young women, both naked from the waist down. The Weasel had been here—I could feel it.

The girls were lying one on top of the other, looking like lovers. They looked as if they were having sex on the floor.

One girl wore a blue tank top, the other black lingerie. They both still wore "slides," stacked bath sandals that are popular nowadays. Most of the Jane Does had been left naked, but unlike many of the others, these two would be fairly easy for us to identify.

"No actual I.D. on either girl," Sampson said, without looking up from his work.

"One of them rents the apartment, though," I told him.

He nodded. "Probably pays cash. She's in a cash business."

Sampson was wearing latex rubber gloves, and was bent down close to the two women.

"The killer wore gloves," Sampson said, still without looking up at me. "Don't seem to be fingerprints anywhere. That's what the techie says. First look-through. They both were shot, Alex. Single shot to the forehead."

I was still looking around the room, collecting information, letting the details of the murder scene flow over me. I noticed an array of hair products: Soft Sheen, Care Free Curl, styling gel, several wigs. On top of one of the wigs was a green army garrison cap with stripes, commonly called a cunt cap among military personnel because it's said to be effective for picking up women, especially in the South. There was also a pager.

The girls were young and pretty. They had skinny little legs, small, bony feet, silver toe rings that looked like they'd come from the same shop. Their discarded clothes amounted to insignificant little bundles on the bloodied hardwood floor.

In one corner of the small room, there were vestiges of brief childhoods: a Lotto game, a stuffed blue bear that was threadbare and looked about as old as the girls themselves, a Barbie doll, a Ouija board.

"Take a good look, Alex. It gets weirder and weirder. Our Weasel is starting to freak out."

I sighed and bent down to see what Sampson had discovered. The smaller, and perhaps the younger, of the two girls was lying on top. The girl underneath was on her back. Her glazed brown eyes stared straight up at a broken light fixture in the ceiling, as if she had seen something terrible up there.

The girl on top had been positioned with her face—actually, her mouth—tilted down into the other girl's crotch.

"Killer played real cute games with them

after they were dead," Sampson said. "Move the one on top a little. Lift her head, Alex. You see it?"

I saw it. A completely new m.o. for the Jane Does, at least the ones I knew about. The phrase "stuck on each other" ran through my mind. I wondered if that was the killer's "message." The girl on top was connected to the one underneath—by her tongue.

Sampson sighed and said, "I think her tongue is stapled inside the other girl. I'm pretty sure that's it, Alex. The Weasel stapled them together."

I looked at the two girls and shook my head. "I don't think so. A staple, even a surgical one, would come apart on the tongue's surface. . . . Krazy Glue adhesive would work, though."

Chapter 30

THE KILLER was working faster, so I had to do the same. The two dead girls didn't remain Jane Does for very long. I had their names before the ten-o'clock news that night. I ignored the explicit orders of the chief of detectives and continued to work on the investigation.

Early the next morning, Sampson and I met at Stamford, the high school that Tori Glover and Marion Cardinal had attended. The murdered girls were seventeen and fourteen years old.

The memory of the homicide scene had left me with a queasy, sick feeling that wouldn't go away. I kept thinking, *Christine is right. Get out of this, do something else. It's time.*

The principal at Stamford was a small, frail-looking, red-haired woman named Robin Schwartz. Her resource officer, Nathan Kemp, had gotten together some students who knew the victims, and had set aside a couple of classrooms for Sampson, Jerome Thurman, and me to use for interviews. Jerome would work in one room, Sampson and I in the other.

Summer school was still in session, and Stamford was busy as a mall on a Saturday. We passed the cafeteria on the way to the classrooms, and it was packed, even at ten-thirty. No empty seats anywhere. The room reeked of French fries, the same greasy smell that had been in the girl's apartment.

A few kids were making noise, but they were mostly well behaved. The music of Wu Tang and Jodeci leaked from earphones. The school seemed to be well run and orderly. Between classes a few boys and girls embraced tenderly, with loosely locked pinkies and the gentlest brushes of cheeks.

"These were not bad girls," Nathan Kemp told us as we walked. "I think you'll hear that from the other students. Tori dropped out last semester, but her home-life was the main reason. Marion was an honor student at Stamford. I'm telling you, guys, these were not bad girls."

Sampson, Thurman, and I spent the rest of the afternoon with the kids. We learned that Tori and Marion were popular, all right. They were loyal to their friends, funny, usually fun to be around. Marion was described as "blazing," which meant she was great. Tori was "buggin' sometimes," which meant she could be a little crazy. Most of the kids hadn't known that the girls were tricking in Petworth, but Tori Glover was said to always have money.

One particular interview would stick in my mind for a while. Evita Cardinal was a senior at Stamford, and also a cousin of Marion's. She wore white athletic pants and a purple stretchy top. Her black-rimmed, yellow-tinted sunglasses were propped on top of her head.

She started to cry her eyes out as soon as she sat down across the desk from me.

"I'm real sorry about Marion," I said, and I was. "We just want to catch whoever did this terrible thing. Detective Sampson and I both live nearby in Southeast. My kids go to the Sojourner Truth School."

The girl looked at me. Her eyes were red-rimmed and wary. "You won't catch nobody," she finally said. It was the prevailing attitude in the neighborhood, and it happened to be mostly true. Sampson and I weren't even supposed to be here. I had told my secretary I was out working the murder of Frank Odenkirk. A few other detectives were covering for us.

"How long have Tori and Marion been working in Petworth? Do you know any other girls from school who work over there?"

Evita shook her head. "*Tori* was the one working the street in Petworth. Not Marion. My cousin was a good person. They both were. Marion was my little doggie," Evita said, and the tears came flowing again.

"Marion *was* there with Tori." I told her what I knew to be the truth. "We talked to people who saw her on Princeton Place that night."

The cousin glared at me. "You don't know what you're talkin' about, Mister Detective. You're *wrong*. You ain't got the straight."

"I'm listening to you, Evita. That's why I'm here."

"Marion wasn't there to sell her body or like that. She was just afraid for Tori. She went to *protect* Tori. She never did nothin' bad for money, and I know that for a fact."

The girl started to sob again. "My cousin was a good person, my best girlfriend. She was tryin' to just protect Tori and she got herself killed for it. The police won't do nothin'. You never come back here again after today. Never happen. You don't care about us. We're nothin' to nobody," Evita Cardinal said, and that seemed to say it all.

Chapter 31

WE'RE NOTHIN' TO NOBODY. It was a horrifying and absolutely true statement, and it was at the deepest roots of the Jane Doe investigation, the search for the Weasel. It pretty well summed up George Pittman's cynical philosophy about the inner city. It was also the reason I was feeling tired and numb to the bone by six-thirty that night. I believed that the Jane Doe murders were escalating.

On the other hand, I hadn't seen nearly enough of my own kids for the last few days, so I decided I'd better head home. On the way, I thought about Christine and calmed down immediately. Since the time I was a young boy, I've been having a recurring daydream. I'm standing alone on a cold, barren planet. It's scary, but more than anything, it's lonely and unsettling. Then a woman comes up to me. We begin to hold hands, to embrace, and then everything is all right. That woman was Christine, and I had no idea how she had gotten out of my dreams and into the real world.

Nana, Damon, and Jannie were just leaving the house when I pulled up into the driveway. *What's this?* I wondered.

Wherever they were going, everybody was dolled up and looking especially nice. Nana and Jannie wore their best dresses, and Damon had on a blue suit, white shirt, and tie. Damon almost never wears what he calls his "monkey" or "funeral" suit.

"Where's everybody going?" I said as I climbed out of the old Porsche. "What's going on? You all aren't moving out on me?"

"It's nothing," Damon said, strangely evasive, eyes darting all over the front yard.

"Damon's in the Washington Boys Choir at school!" Jannie proudly blurted out. "He didn't want you to know until he made it for sure. Well, he made it. Damon's a *chorister* now."

Her brother swatted her on the arm. Not hard, but enough to show he wasn't pleased with Jannie for telling his secret.

"Hey!" Jannie said, and put up her dukes like the little semipro boxer that she is becoming under my watchful eye.

"Hey, hey!" I said, and moved in like a big-time referee, like that guy Mills Lane who does the big pro fights. "No prizefighting outside the ring. You know the rules of the fight game. Now what's this about a choir?"

"Damon tried out for the Boys Choir, and he was selected," Nana said, and beamed gloriously as she looked over at Damon. "He did it all by himself."

"You sing, too?" I said, and beamed at him as well. "My, my, my."

"He could be in Boyz Two Men, Daddy. Boyz Two Boyz, maybe. He's smoo-ooth and silky. His voice is pure."

"Is that so, Sister Soul?" I said to my baby girl.

"Zatso," Jannie continued to prattle as she patted Damon on the back. I could tell she was incredibly proud of him. She was his biggest fan, even if he didn't realize it yet. Someday he would.

Damon couldn't hold back a big smile, then he shrugged it off. "No big thing. I sing all right."

"*Thousands* of other boys tried out," Jannie said. "It *is* a big thing, biggest in your small life, brother."

"Hundreds," Damon corrected her. "Only hundreds of kids tried out. I guess I just got lucky."

"*Hundreds* of *thousands!*" Jannie gushed, and scooted away before he swatted her like the little gnat she can be sometimes. "And you were *born* lucky."

"Can I come to the practice?" I asked. "I'll be good. I'll be quiet. I won't embarrass anybody too much."

"If you can spare the time." Nana threw a neat jab. She sure doesn't need any boxing lessons from me. "Your busy work schedule and all. If you can spare the time, come along with us."

"Sure, Dad," said Damon, finally.

So I came along.

Chapter 32

I HAPPILY WALKED the six short blocks to the Sojourner Truth School with Nana and the kids. I wasn't dressed up. They were in their finery, but it didn't matter. There was suddenly a bounce in my step. I took Nana's arm, and she smiled as I tucked her hand into the crook of my arm.

"Now that's better. Seems like old times," I exclaimed.

"You're such a shameless charmer sometimes," Nana said, and laughed out loud. "Ever since you were a little boy like Damon. You certainly can be one when you want to."

"You helped make me what I am, old woman," I confided to her.

"Proud of it, too. And I'm *so* proud of Damon."

We arrived at the Sojourner Truth School and went directly to the small auditorium in back. I wondered if Christine might be there, but she wasn't anywhere to be seen. Then I wondered if she already knew that Damon had made the Boys Choir, if he had told her first. I kind of liked the thought that he might have told her. I wanted them to be close. I knew that Damon and Jannie needed a mother, not just a father and a great-grandmother.

"We're not too good yet," Damon informed me before he left to join the other boys. His face clearly showed the fear and anxiety of possibly being embarrassed. "This is just our second practice. Mr. Dayne says we're horrid as a tubful of castor oil. He's tough as nails, Dad. He makes you stand for an hour straight without moving."

"Mr. Dayne's tougher than you, Daddy, tougher than Mrs. Johnson," Jannie said, and grinned wickedly. "Tough as *nails.*"

I had heard that Nathaniel Dayne was a demanding maestro—nicknamed the "Great Dayne"—and that his choirs were among the finest in the country and that most of the boys were said to profit immensely from the dedicated training and discipline. He was already organizing the boys up on the stage. He was a very broad man of below-average height. I guessed he carried about two hundred fifty pounds on his five-seven frame. He wore a black suit with a black shirt buttoned at the collar, no tie. He started the boys off with a few playful verses of "Three Blind Mice" that didn't sound half bad.

"I'm really happy for Damon. He looks so proud up there," I whispered to Nana and Jannie. "He is a handsome devil, too."

"Mr. Dayne is starting a girls choir in the fall," Jannie loud-whispered in my ear. "You watch. I mean, you *listen* I'll make it."

"Go for it, girl," Nana said, and gave Jannie a hug. She is very good at encouraging others.

Dayne suddenly called out loudly, "Ugh. I hear a *swoop.* I don't want any swoops here, gentlemen. I want clean diction and pure pitch. I want silver and silk. I do not want *swoops.*"

Out of the corner of my eye, I suddenly saw Christine in the hallway. She was watching Dayne and the boys, but then she looked my way. Her face was principal-serious for just a moment. Then she smiled and winked.

I walked over to see her. Be still my heart.

"That's my boy," I said with mock pride as I came up to her. She was dressed in a soft gray pantsuit with a coral-pink blouse. God, I loved seeing her now, being with her, hanging out, doing nothing—the works.

Christine smiled. Actually, she laughed a little at me. "He does everything so damn well." She didn't hold back, no matter what. "I was hoping you might be here, Alex," she whispered. "I was just this very minute missing you like crazy. You know that feeling?"

"Yes, that feeling and I are well acquainted."

We held hands as the choir practiced Bach's "Jesu, Joy of Man's Desiring." Everything felt so right, and it was hard to get used to.

"Sometimes . . . I still have this dream about George being shot and dying," she said as we were standing there. Christine's husband had been murdered in her home, and she had seen him die. It was one of the big reasons she was hesitant about being with me: the fear that I might die in the line of duty, and also the fear that I could bring terror and violence into the house.

"I remember everything about the afternoon I heard Maria was shot. It eases with time, but it never goes away."

Christine knew that. She had figured out the answers to most of her questions, but she liked to talk things through. We were both that way.

"And yet I continue to work here in Southeast. I come to the inner city every day. I could choose a nice school in Maryland or Virginia," she said.

I nodded. "Yes, Christine, you do choose to work here."

"And so do you."

"And so do I."

She held my hand a little tighter. "I guess we were made for each other," she said. "Why fight it."

Chapter 33

EARLY THE NEXT MORNING I was back in the write-up room at the Seventh District Station, working the John Doe homicide. I was the first one in there.

Apparently no one had noticed Frank Odenkirk as he was leaving the airport. His clothing still hadn't been recovered. The M.E. reported that he had definitely been sodomized after he was killed. As I had suspected, there was no semen. The killer had used a condom. Just as with the Jane Does.

The police commissioner was involved in the Odenkirk case and was putting added pressure on the department. It was making everyone angry and a little crazy. Chief Pittman was riding his detectives hard, but the only case he seemed interested in was the Odenkirk killing, especially since a suspect had been arrested in the German tourist murder.

At around eleven that morning, Rakeem Powell stopped by my desk. He bent low and whispered, "Might have something interesting, Alex. Downstairs in the jail, if you've got a minute. Could be a first break on those two murdered girls in Shaw."

The jail was down a set of steep concrete stairs, just past a tight warren of small interrogation rooms, a holding room, and a booking room. All over the ceiling and walls, prisoners had scratched their street names or used black ink from fingerprinting to write the names. This was incredibly dumb of them, since it gave us information for our files.

It's purposely kept dark down in the jail. Each cell is six by five feet, with a metal bed and a combination water fountain/ toilet. Sneakers had been tossed in the hallways outside several of the cells. It's what experienced prisoners do who won't take the laces out of their sneaks. Laces aren't allowed in the jail for safety reasons.

A small-time drug runner and petty thief

named Alfred "Sneak" Streek was seated like the Fresh Prince of D.C. in one of the holding cells. The street punk looked up at me as I entered his cell. A slicky-sick smirk crossed his face.

Sneak was sporting wraparound sunglasses, dusty dreadlocks, and a bright-green and yellow crocheted hat. His white T-shirt had a drawing of Haile Selassie's face and read HEAD HUNTER. RASTAFARIAN.

"You from the D.A.'s office? I *don't think so.* No dealee, no talkee, my man," he said to me. "So get lost."

Rakeem ignored him as he spoke to me. "Sneak claims to have some useful information about the Glover and Cardinal homicides. He would like us to extend him some courtesy in return for what he claims to know. He's jammed up on a charge that he may have broken into an apartment in Shaw. He was caught coming out of a bedroom window with a Sony TV in his arms. Imagine that. Not very Sneaky of him."

"I didn't rob no ticky-tacky apartment. I don't even *watch* TV, my man. And I don't see no assistant district attorney present with the *au-tho-rity* to make a deal."

"Take off your sunglasses," I said to him.

He wouldn't look at me, so I took them off for him. As one well-known street saying goes, his eyes were like tombstones. I could tell at a glance that Sneak wasn't just running drugs anymore; he was using.

I stood across from Sneak in the jail cell and stared him down. He was probably in his early twenties, angry, cynical, lost in space and time. "If you didn't rob the apartment, then why would you be interested in seeing a lawyer from the district attorney's office? That doesn't make too much sense to me, Alfred. Now here's what I'll do for you, and it's a one-time offer, so listen carefully. If I walk out of here, I *don't* come back."

Sneak half-listened to what I was saying.

"If you give us information that directly helps solve the murders of those two young girls, *then* we will help you on the robbery charge. I'll go to the mat myself. If you don't give up the information, then I'm going to leave you in here with Detective Powell and Detective Thurman. You won't get this generous, one-time offer again.

That's another promise, and as these detectives know, I always keep my word."

Sneak still didn't say anything. A glaze was coming over his eyes. He tried to stare *me* down, but I'm usually better at it than the average TV booster.

I finally shrugged a look at Rakeem Powell and Jerome Thurman. "Okay, fine. Gentlemen, we need to know what he knows about those murdered girls in Shaw. He gets nothing from us when you're finished with him. It's possible that he's involved with the homicides himself. He could even be our killer, and we need to solve this thing fast. You treat him that way until we know differently."

I started to leave when suddenly Sneak spoke.

"Back Door, man. He hang at Downing Park. He, Back Door, maybe see who done those girls. That's how he say it at the park. Say he saw the killer. So how you gonna help me?"

I walked out of the cell. "I told you the deal, Alfred. We solve the case, your information helps, I'll help you."

Chapter 34

MAYBE WE WERE CLOSE to something. Two Metro cruisers and two un-
marked sedans pulled up to the fenced-in
entrance of tiny Downing playground in
Shaw. Rakeem Powell and Sampson came
with me to visit with Joe "Back Door"
Booker, a well-known neighborhood men-
ace.

I knew Back Door by sight and spotted
him right away. He was short, no more
than five-seven, goateed, and so good
with a basketball that he sometimes
played in work boots just to show off. He
had on dusty orange construction boots
today. Also a faded black nylon jacket and
black nylon pants that accordioned at the
ankles.

A full-court basketball game was in progress, a fast, high-level game somewhere between college and pro in terms of athletic ability. The court couldn't have been more basic—black macadam, faded white lines, metal backboards, and rims with chain nets.

Players from two or three other teams sat around waiting their turn to play winners. Nylon shorts and pants and the Nike swoosh were everywhere. The court was surrounded by four walls of heavy wire fencing and was known as the cage. Everybody looked up as we arrived, Booker included.

"We got next!" Sampson called out.

The players on and off the court exchanged looks, and a couple of them grinned at Sampson's one-liner. They knew who we were. The steady *thump, thump, thump* of the game ball hadn't stopped.

Back Door was on the court. It wasn't unusual for his team to hold winners for an entire afternoon. He had been in and out of reformatories and prisons since he was fourteen, but he could play ball. He was taunting another player who was on the court in gray suit pants and high-tops, his chest bare. "You suck," said Back Door. "Take those church pants off. I play you in baseball, tennis, bowling, *any* game—you suck. Stop suckin'."

Rakeem Powell blew the silver referee's whistle he always carries. Rakeem works as a soccer ref in his spare time. The whistle is unorthodox, but it gets attention in noisy places. The game stopped.

The three of us walked up to Booker, who was standing near the foul circle in front of one basket. Sampson and I towered over him, but so did most of the players. It didn't matter; he was still the best ballplayer out there. He could probably beat Sampson and me if we played him two on one.

"Awhh, leave the brother alone. He didn't do nothin'," one of the other, taller men complained in a deep voice. He had prison-style tattoos all over his back and arms. "He was here playin' ball, man."

"Door been here *all day,*" said somebody else. "Door been here for days. Hasn't lost *a game* in days!"

Several of the young men laughed at the playground humor. Sampson turned to the biggest man on the court. "Shut the hell up. Stop dribbling that rock, too. Two young sisters been murdered. That's why we're here. This is no game with us."

The dribbler shut up and picked up the game ball. The yard became strangely quiet. We could hear a jump rope striking the sidewalk in a fast rhythm. Three little girls playing just outside the cage were singsonging, *"Little Miss Pinky dressed in blue, died last night at half past two."* It was a jump-rope rhyme, and sadly true around here.

I put my arm around Booker's shoulder and walked him away from his friends.

Sampson continued to do the talking. "Booker, this is going to be so fast and easy you and your friends will be laughing your asses off about it before we're back in our cars."

"Yeah, uh-huh," said Joseph Booker, trying to be cool in the extreme heat of Sampson's and my glare.

"I'm serious as a heart attack, little man. You saw something that can help us with the murder of Tori Glover and Marion Cardinal. Simple as that. You talk, and we walk right back out of here."

Booker glared up at Sampson as if he were staring down the sun. "I didn't see shit. Like Luki say, I been here for days. I never lose to these sorry chumps."

I held up my hand, palm out, inches from his squashed moonpie face.

"I'm on a stopwatch here, Booker, so please don't interrupt my flow. I promise you, two minutes and we're out of here. Now here's what's in it for you. One, we go away, and you gentlemen finish your game. Two, detectives Powell and Sampson will owe you one. Three, a hundred dollars now for your time and trouble.

"The clock is ticking," I said. "*Tick, tick, tick.* Easy money."

He finally nodded and held out his hand. "I seen those two girls get picked up. Around two, three in the mornin' on E Street. I *didn't* see no driver, nobody's face or nothin'. Too dark, man. But he was driving a cab. Look like purple and blue gypsy. Somethin' like that. Girls get into the back of the cab, drive off."

"Is that it?" I asked him. "I don't want to have to come back here later. Break up your game again."

Booker considered what I'd said, then

spoke again. "Cabdriver a white man. Seen his arm stickin' out the side window. Ain't no white boys drivin' the night shift in Shaw, least none I seen."

I nodded, waited a bit, then smiled at the other players. "Gentlemen, as you were. Play ball."

Thump, thump, thump.

Swish.

Booker could really play ball.

Chapter 35

THE NEW PIECES of information gave us something to run with. We'd done an incredible amount of thankless street work, and something had finally paid off. We had the color of the gypsy cab that had picked up the girls around the time of the murders. The fact that the driver was white was the best lead we had so far.

Sampson and I drove to my house rather than back to the station. It would be easier to work on the new leads from Fifth Street. It took me about five minutes to come up with more information from a contact at the Taxi Commission. No fleets operating in D.C. currently had purple and blue cabs. That probably meant the car was an illegal gypsy, as Booker had said. I learned that a company called Vanity Cabs had once used purple and blue cars, but Vanity had been out of business since '95. The Taxi Commission rep said that half a dozen or so of the old cars might still be on the street. Originally the fleet had been fifteen cars, which wasn't that many even if all of them were still around, which was highly doubtful.

Sampson called all the cab companies that regularly did business in Southeast, especially around Shaw. According to their records, there were only three white drivers who had been on duty that night.

We were working in the kitchen. Sampson was on the phone and I was using the computer. Nana had fixed fresh coffee and also set out fruit and half a pecan pie.

Rakeem Powell called the house at around 4:15. I picked up. "Alex, Pittman's watchdog is sniffing around here something fierce. Fred Cook wants to know what you and Sampson are working on this afternoon. Jerome told him the Odenkirk murder."

I nodded and said, "If the murders in Southeast are connected in any way, that's the truth."

"One more thing," Rakeem said before he let me go. "I checked with Motor Vehicles. Might be something good for us. A purple gypsy got a summons for running a stop sign around one in the morning over in Eckington, near the university, Second Street. Maybe that's where our boy lives."

I clapped my hands and congratulated Rakeem. Our long hours working the Jane Doe cases were finally beginning to pay off.

Maybe we were about to catch the Weasel.

Chapter 36

HE HAD BEEN much more careful lately. The visit to Washington by George Bayer—Famine—had been a warning, a shot over his head, and Shafer had taken it seriously. The other players could be as dangerous as he was. It was *they* who had taught *him* how to kill, not the other way round. Famine, Conqueror, and War were not to be underestimated, especially if he wanted to win the game.

The day after Famine's visit, the others had informed him that Bayer had come to Washington, that he was being watched. He supposed that was his *second* warning. His activity had frightened them, and now they were retaliating. It was all part of the game.

After work that night, he headed to the hideaway in Eckington. He spotted what looked like a half-dozen or so policemen canvassing the street.

He immediately suspected the other Horsemen. They had turned him in, after all. Or were they playing a mind game with him? What were the cops doing here?

He parked the Jaguar several blocks away, then headed toward the hideaway and garage on foot. He had to check this out. He had on a pin-striped suit, city shirt, and tie. He knew he looked respectable enough. He carried a leather briefcase and definitely looked like a businessman coming home late.

Two African-American policemen were doing door-to-door questioning on Uhland Terrace. This wasn't good—the police were less than five blocks from the hideaway.

Why were they here? His brain was reeling, adrenaline rushing through his nervous system like a flash flood. Maybe this had nothing to do with him, but he couldn't be too careful. He definitely suspected the other players, especially George Bayer.

But why? Was this the way they planned to end the game, by bringing him down?

When the two policemen up ahead disappeared down a side street off Uhland, Shafer decided to stop at one of the brownstones where they'd been asking questions. It was a small risk, but he needed to know what was happening. A couple of old men were seated on the stoop. An ancient radio played an Orioles baseball game.

"They ask you about some kind of trouble in the neighborhood?" Shafer asked the men in as casual a tone as he could manage. "They stopped me up the block."

One of the men just stared at him, terminally pissed off, but the other one nodded and spoke up. "Sure did, mister. Lookin' for a cab, purple and blue gypsy. Connected to some killings, they say. Though I don't recall seeing any purple ones lately. Used to be a cab company called Vanity. You remember, Earle? They had the purple people-eaters."

"That was some years ago," the other man said, nodding. "They went belly up."

"I guess they were Metro police. Never showed me any I.D., though," Shafer said, and shrugged. He was being careful to speak with an American accent, which he was good at imitating.

"Detectives Cross and Sampson," the more talkative of the two men volunteered their names. "Detective Cross showed me his badge. It was the real deal."

"Oh, I'm sure it was," Shafer said, and saluted the two old men. "Good to see the police in the neighborhood, actually."

"You got that right."

"Have a nice night."

"Yeah, you, too."

Shafer circled back to his car and drove to the embassy. He went straight to his office, where he felt safe and protected. He calmed himself, then turned on his computer and did a thorough search on D.C. detectives named Cross and Sampson. He found more than he had hoped for, especially on Detective Cross.

He thought about how the new developments might change the game. Then he sent out a message to the other Horsemen. He told them about Cross and Sampson, adding that the detectives had decided to "play the game." So naturally, he had plans for them, too.

Chapter 37

ZACHARY SCOTT TAYLOR is a thorough, analytical, and very hard-nosed reporter on the *Washington Post*. I respect the hell out of him. His relentless cynicism and skepticism are a little too much for me to take on a daily basis; otherwise, we might be even closer friends. But we have a good relationship, and I trust him more than I do most journalists.

I met him that night at the Irish Times, on F Street, near Union Station. The restaurant-bar is in an anachronistic, stand-alone brick building surrounded by modern office structures. Zachary called it "a dumpy little toilet of a bar, a perfect place for us to meet."

In the time-honored tradition of Washington, I have occasionally been one of his "trusted sources," and I was about to tell him something important. I hoped he would agree, and would convince his editors at the *Post* about the story.

"How're Master Damon and Ms. Jannie?" Zachary asked as he sat across from me in a darkened corner, under an old photo of a stern-looking man in a black top hat. Zachary is tall, gaunt, and thin, and resembles the man in the old photo a little bit. He always talks too fast, so that the words all run into one another: *How're-MasterDamonandMs.Jannie?* There was just a hint of Virginia softening his accent.

The waitress eventually came over to our table. He ordered black coffee and I had the same.

"Two coffees?" she asked, to make sure she'd heard us right.

"Two of your very *finest* coffees," Zachary said.

"This isn't Starbucks, y'know," she said.

I smiled at the waitress's brio, then at what Zachary had said—his first words to me. I'd probably mentioned my kids' names to him once, but he had an encyclopedic memory for all kinds of disparate information.

"You should go get yourself a couple of kids, Zachary," I told him, smiling broadly.

He glanced up at an ancient whirring ceiling fan that looked as if it might suddenly spin out of the ceiling. It seemed a nice metaphor for modern life in America, an aging infrastructure threatening to spin out of control.

"Don't have a wife yet, Alex. Still looking for the right woman," said Zachary.

"Well, okay then, get yourself a wife first, then get a couple of kids. Might take the edge off your neuroses."

The waitress placed steaming cups of black coffee in front of us. "Will that be *all?*" she said. She shook her head, then left us.

"Maybe I don't want the edge taken off my rather stunning neurotic behavior. Maybe I believe that's what makes me such a damn fine reporter, and without it my work would be pedestrian shit, and then I'd be nothing in the eyes of Don Graham and company."

I sipped the day- or two-day-old coffee.

"Except that if you had a couple of kids, you could never be nothing."

Zachary squinted one eye shut and smacked the left side of his lips. He was a very animated thinker.

"Except if the kids didn't love or even like me very much."

"And you don't consider yourself lovable? But actually you are, Zachary. Trust me. You're just fine. Your kids would adore the hell out of you, and you would adore them. You'd have a mutual adoration society."

He finally laughed and clapped his hands loudly. We usually laugh a good bit when we're together.

"So will you marry me and have my children?" He grinned at me over the top of his steaming cup. "This is a pickup joint, after all. Singles from the Bureau of Labor Statistics and the Government Printing Office come here, hoping to bed staffers from Kennedy's or Glenn's."

"It's the best offer I've had all day. Who called this meeting, anyway? Why are we here at this dive, drinking really bad coffee?"

Taylor slurped his. "Coffee's fairly

strong, isn't it? That's something to be thankful for. What's up, Alex?"

"You interested in another Pulitzer?" I asked him.

He pretended to think it over, but his eyes lit up. "Well, I might be. You see, I need to balance the look of my mantelpiece. One of my dates told me that. Never did see the young woman again. She worked for Gingrich, as a matter of fact."

For the next forty-five minutes or so, I told Zachary exactly what I thought was up. I told him about the 114 unsolved murders in Southeast and parts of Northeast D.C. I detailed the contrasting investigations of the cases of Frank Odenkirk and the German tourist in Georgetown, and those of the black teenagers Tori Glover and Marion Cardinal. I filled him in on the chief of detectives, his proclivities and his biases, or at least my perception of them. I even admitted that I disliked Pittman intensely, and Zachary knows I'm not that way about too many folks who don't murder for a living.

He shook his head back and forth, back and forth, while I talked, and didn't stop when I was finished. "Not that I doubt any of what you're saying, but do you have any documentation?'' he asked.

''You're such a stickler for details,'' I said. ''Reporters are such wusses when you come right down to it.''

I reached down under my seat and lifted up two thick manila folders. His eyes brightened.

''This should help with the story. Copies of sixty-seven of the unsolved homicide reports. Also a copy of the Glover and Cardinal investigation. Note the number of detectives assigned to each. Check the case hours logged. You'll see a huge discrepancy. That's all I could get my hands on—but the other reports exist.''

''Why would this be happening, this malicious neglect?'' he asked me.

I nodded at the wisdom of his question. ''I'll give you the most cynical reason,'' I said. ''Some Metro cops like to refer to Southeast as 'self-cleaning ovens.' That sound like the beginnings of malicious neglect to you? Some victims in Southeast are called NHIs—that's 'No Humans Involved.' The latter is a phrase used by Chief Pittman.''

Zachary quickly leafed through the reports. Then he shook my hand. "I'm going home to my lonely abode, made bearable only by my single Pulitzer. I have all these fascinating police files on NHIs to read, then hopefully a chilling news exposé to write. We'll see. As always, it's been a party, Alex. My best to Damon, Jannie, Nana Mama. I'd like to meet them one day. Put some faces with the names."

"Come to the next Washington Boys Choir performance," I said. "All our faces will be there. Damon is a *chorister.*"

Chapter 38

I WORKED THAT NIGHT until eight-thirty, and then I drove to Kinkead's in Foggy Bottom to meet up with Christine. Kinkead's is one of our favorite restaurants and also an excellent place to listen to jazz and snuggle up to each other.

I sat at the bar and enjoyed the sounds of Hilton Felton and Ephrain Woolfolk until Christine arrived, coming from an event at school. She was right on time, though. She is punctual. Very considerate. Perfect in almost every way, at least in my eyes. *Yes, I will be your wife.*

"You hungry? Want to go to a table?" I asked after we had hugged as if we'd been separated for many years and thousands of miles.

"Let's just sit here at the bar for a few minutes. You mind?" she asked. Her breath smelled slightly of spearmint. Her face was so soft and smooth that I *had* to lightly cup it in both my hands.

"Nothing I'd rather do in the whole wide world," I said.

Christine ordered a Harvey's Bristol Cream and I had a mug of beer, and we talked as the music flowed over, around, and right through our bodies. It had been a long day, and I needed this.

"I've been waiting for this all day long. I couldn't wait. Am I being too corny and romantic again?" I said, and grinned.

"Not for me. Never too corny, never too romantic. That won't happen, Alex." Christine smiled. I loved to see her like this. Her eyes twinkled and danced. I sometimes get lost in her eyes, fall into the deep pools, all that good stuff that people yearn for but few seem to get nowadays, which is sad.

She stared back, and my fingers lightly caressed her cheek. Then I held her under her chin. "Stardust" was playing. It's one of my favorite songs, even under ordinary circumstances. I wondered if Hilton and

Ephrain were playing the tune for us, and when I looked at him, Hilton gave me a sly wink.

We moved closer together and danced in place. I could feel her heart beating, feel it right up against my chest. We must have stayed like that for ten or fifteen minutes. No one at the bar seemed to notice; no one bothered us, offered to refill our drinks or escort us to our table. I guess they understood.

"I really like Kinkead's," Christine whispered. "But you know what? I'd rather be home with you tonight. Someplace a little more private. I'll make you eggs, whatever you'd like. Is that all right? Do you mind?"

"No, I don't mind at all. That's a perfect idea. Let's go."

I paid our bar bill and made my regrets about the dinner reservation. Then we went to Christine's.

"We'll start with dessert," she said, and smiled wickedly. I liked that about her, too.

Chapter 39

I HAD BEEN WAITING a long time to be in love again, but this was worth it and then some. I grabbed hold of Christine as soon as we were inside her house. My hands began to trace her waist, her hips; they played over her breasts, her shoulders, then touched the delicate bones of her face. We liked to do this slowly, no need to rush. I kissed her lips, then gently scratched her back and shoulders. I pulled her closer, closer.

"You have the gentlest touch," she whispered against my cheek. "I could do this all night. Be just like this. You want some wine? Anything? I'll give you anything I have."

"I love you," I told her, still lovingly

scratching her lower back. "We *will* do this forever. I have no doubt of it."

"I love you so much," she said, then I heard her breath softly catch. "So please try to be careful, Alex. At work."

"Okay, I will. But not tonight," I said.

Christine smiled. "Not tonight. Tonight you can live dangerously. We both will. You *are* handsome, and debonair for a policeman."

"Or even for an international jewel thief."

I swept her up and carried her down the hallway to the bedroom. "Mmm. Strong, too," she said. She flicked on a hall lamp as we passed. It was just enough light to see where we were going.

"How about a trip somewhere?" I said. "I need to get away."

"That sounds good. Yes—before school starts. Anywhere. Take me away from all this."

Her room smelled of fresh flowers. There were pink and red roses on the nightstand. She has a passion for flowers and gardening.

"You planned this all along, didn't you?" I said. "You *did.* This is entrapment. You sly girl."

"I was thinking about it all day," she confessed, and sighed contentedly. "I thought about being with you all day, in my office, in the hallways, the schoolyard, and then in my car on the way to the restaurant. I've been having erotic daydreams about you all day."

"I hope I can live up to them."

"You will. No doubt about it."

I took off her black silk blouse in one sweeping motion. I put my mouth to a breast, pulling at it through her demi-bra. She was wearing a brushed leather skirt, and I didn't take it off, just slowly pushed it up. I knelt and kissed her ankles, the tops of her feet, then slowly came up her long legs. She massaged my neck, my back and shoulders.

"You *are* dangerous tonight," she said. "That's a good thing."

"Sexual healing."

"Mmm, please. Heal me all over, Doctor."

She bit down hard into my shoulder, then even harder into the side of my neck. We were both breathing fast. She moved against me, then opened her legs for me. I moved inside her. She felt incredibly warm.

The bedsprings began to sing, and the headboard rocked into the wall.

She pushed her hair to one side, behind an ear. I love the way she does that.

"You feel so good. Oh, Alex, don't stop, don't stop, don't stop," she whispered.

I did as I was told and loved every moment, every movement we made together, and I even wondered for a second if we had made a baby.

Chapter 40

MUCH LATER THAT NIGHT, we rustled up some eggs with Vidalia onions and cheddar and mozzarella cheeses, and opened a nice bottle of Pinot Noir. Then I started a fire in August, with the air conditioner turned up high.

We sat in front of the fire, laughed and talked, and planned a quick trip away from Washington. We settled on Bermuda, and Christine asked if we could bring Nana and the kids. I felt as if my life were changing fast, going to a new, good place. If only I could get lucky and catch the Weasel somehow. That could be the perfect ending to my career with the Metro police.

I went home to Fifth Street late, and got in just before three. I didn't want Damon and Jannie to wake in the morning and not find me there. I was up by eight o'clock the next morning, bounding downstairs to the delectable smells of fresh coffee and Nana's world-famous sticky buns.

The terrible twosome were just about ready to dash off to the Sojourner Truth School, where they were taking morning advanced classes. They looked like a pair of shiny angels. I didn't get to feel this good very often, so I was going all the way with it.

"How was your date last night, Daddy?" Jannie said, making her biggest goo-goo eyes at me.

"Who said I had a big date?" I made room for her on my knee. She ate a bite of the humongous sweet bun Nana had set on my plate.

"Let's just say a little birdie told me," she chirped.

"Uh-huh. Little birdie makes good sticky buns," I said. "My date was pretty good. How was yours? You had a date, right? Didn't sit home alone, did you?"

"Your date was *pretty* good? You came home with the milkman." Jannie laughed out loud. Damon was giggling, too. She can get us all going when she wants to; she's been that way since she was a baby.

"Jannie Cross," Nana said, but she let it go. There was no use trying to make Jannie act like a typical seven-year-old at this point. She was too bright, too outspoken, too full of life and fun. Besides, we have a philosophy as a family: He or she who laughs, lasts.

"How come you two don't live together first?" Jannie asked. "That's what they all do in the movies and on TV."

I found myself grinning and starting to frown at the same time. "Don't get me going on the silly stuff they do on TV and in the movies, little girl. They always get it wrong. Christine and I are going to get married soon, and *then* we'll all live together."

"You *asked* her?" they all exclaimed.

"I did."

"And she said yes?"

"Why do you all look so surprised? Of course she said yes. Who could resist being a part of this family?"

"Hooray!" Jannie whooped loudly. I could tell she meant it from the bottom of her little heart.

"Hooray!" echoed Nana. "Thank God. Oh, thank God."

"I agree," Damon piped in. "It's time we had a more normal life around here."

Everybody was congratulating me for several minutes until Jannie finally said, "I have to go to *school* now, *Pa-pa.* I wouldn't want to disappoint Mrs. Johnson by being late now, would I? Here's your morning newspaper."

Jannie handed me the *Washington Post,* and my heart jumped a little in my chest. This was a good day indeed. I saw Zachary Taylor's story at the bottom right of the front page. It wasn't the banner headline it deserved to be, but he'd gotten the story on page one.

POTENTIAL SCANDAL OVER UNSOLVED MURDERS IN SOUTHEAST D.C. POSSIBLE RACIAL BIAS SEEN IN POLICE ACTIVITY

"Potential scandal indeed," Nana said, and squeegeed her lower face. "Genocide always is, isn't it?"

Chapter 41

I ENTERED THE STATION HOUSE at around eight, and Chief Pittman's assistant-lackey came scurrying up to me. Old Fred Cook had been a bad detective once, and now he was an equally bad and devious administrator, but he was as smooth a butt-kisser as could be found in the department or anywhere else in Washington.

"The chief of detectives wants to see you in his office posthaste. It's important," Fred told me. "Better move it."

I nodded at him and tried to keep my good mood intact. "Of course it is, he's the chief of detectives. You have any helpful hints for me, Fred? You happen to know what this is about, what I should expect?"

"It's a big deal," said Cook, unhelpful

and happy about it. "That's about all I can tell you, Alex."

He walked away, leaving me hanging. I could feel bile rising in my throat. My good mood had already deserted me.

I walked down the creaking hardwood floors of the hallway to The Jefe's office. I had no idea what to expect, but I sure wasn't prepared for what I found.

I immediately thought about what Damon had said that morning: *It's time we had a normal life around here.*

Sampson was seated inside the chief's office. Rakeem Powell and Jerome Thurman were both in there, too.

"Come in, Dr. Cross." Chief Pittman beckoned with an outstretched hand. "Please come in. We've been waiting for you to arrive."

"What is this?" I said, pulling up a chair next to Sampson's and whispering in his ear.

"Don't know yet, but it's not too good," he said. "The Jefe hasn't said word one to us. Looks like the canary who ate the cat, though."

Pittman came around in front of his desk and leaned his ample buttocks back against it. He seemed particularly full of himself and bullshit this morning. His mousy gray hair was plastered back and looked like a helmet on his bullet head.

"I can tell you what you want to know, Detective Cross," he said. "In fact, I didn't want to tell these other detectives until you got here. As of this morning, detectives Sampson, Thurman, and Powell have been suspended from active duty. They have been working on cases outside the auspices of this department. Evidence is still being gathered about the full extent of these activities and also if any other detectives were involved."

I started to speak up, but Sampson grabbed my arm—hard. "Be cool, Alex."

Pittman looked at the three of them. "Detectives Sampson, Thurman, Powell, you can go. Your union representative has been informed of the situation. You have questions, or issues with my decision, inform your representative."

Sampson's mouth was set hard. He didn't say a word to The Jefe, though. He got up and left the office. Thurman and Powell trailed close behind him. Neither of them spoke to Pittman, either. The three of

222 / JAMES PATTERSON

them were hardworking, dedicated detectives, and I couldn't stand to watch this happen.

I wondered why The Jefe had spared me so far. I also wondered why Shawn Moore wasn't there. The cynical answer was that Pittman wanted to set us against one another, to make us believe that Shawn had spoken against us.

Pittman reached across his desk and picked up a folded copy of the *Washington Post.* "You happen to see this article today? Bottom right?"

He pushed the newspaper toward me. I had to catch the paper to keep it from falling to the floor.

" 'Scandal over unsolved murders in Southeast,' " I said. "Yes, I did. I read it at home."

"I'll bet you did. Mr. Taylor, of the *Post,* quotes unidentified sources in the police department. You have anything to do with the article?" Pittman asked, and stared hard at me.

"Why would I talk to the *Washington Post*?" I asked a question in answer to his. "I told you about the problem in Southeast. I think a repeat killer may be working there. Why go any farther with it than that? Suspending those detectives sure won't help solve the problem. Especially if this sicko is approaching rage, which I believe he is."

"I don't buy this serial-killer story. I don't see any pattern that's consistent. No one else does but you." Pittman shook his head and frowned. He was hot, angry, trying to control himself.

He reached out his hand toward me again. His fingers were like uncooked sausages. He lowered his voice almost to a whisper. "I'd like to fuck you over good, and I will. But for now, it wouldn't be expedient to pull you off the Odenkirk homicide. It wouldn't *look* good, and I suspect it would end up in the *Post,* too. I look forward to your daily reports on the so-called John Doe case. You know, it is time you got some of those unsolved murders off the books. You'll report directly to me on this. I'm going to be all over you, Cross. Any questions?"

I quickly left Chief Pittman's office. Before I hit him.

Chapter 42

SAMPSON, THURMAN, and Rakeem Powell had already left the building by the time I got out of The Jefe's office. I felt as if I could easily go postal. I nearly walked back inside Pittman's office and wiped up the floor with him.

I went to my desk and thought about what to do next, tried to calm myself down before I did anything rash and stupid. I thought about my responsibilities to the people in Southeast, and that helped me. Still, I almost went back after Pittman.

I called Christine and let out some steam. Then, on the spur of the moment, I asked if she could get away for our long weekend, possibly starting on Thursday night. Christine said that she could go. I went and filled out a vacation form and left it on Fred Cook's desk. It was the last thing he and Pittman would expect from me. But I'd already decided the best thing would be to get away from here, cool down, then figure out a plan to move forward.

As I headed out of the building, another detective stopped me. "They're over at Hart's bar," he said. "Sampson said to tell you they reserved a seat for you."

Hart's is a very seedy, very popular gin mill on Second Street. It isn't a cops' bar, which is why some of us like it. It was eleven in the morning, and the barroom was already crowded, lively, even friendly.

"Here he is!" Jerome Thurman saluted me with a half-full beer mug as I walked inside. Half a dozen other detectives and friends were there, too. The word had gotten around fast about the suspensions.

There was a whole lot of laughter and shouting going on. "It's a bachelor's party!" Sampson said, and grinned. "Got you, sugar. With a little help from Nana. You should see the look on your face!"

For the next hour and a half, friends kept arriving at Hart's. By noon the bar was full, and then the regular customers started coming in for their lunch-hour nips. The owner, Mike Hart, was in his glory. I hadn't really thought about having a bachelor's party, but now that I was in the middle of one, I was glad it happened. A lot of men still guard their emotions and feelings, but not so much at a bachelor's party, at least not at a good one thrown by the people closest to you.

This was a good one. The suspensions that had been handed down earlier that morning were mostly forgotten for a few hours. I was congratulated and hugged more times than I could count, and even kissed once or twice. Everybody was calling me "sugar," following Sampson's lead. The "love" word was used, and overused. I was roasted and toasted in sentimental speeches that seemed hilarious at the time. Just about everybody had too much to drink.

By four in the afternoon, Sampson and I were steadying each other, making our way into the blinding daylight on Second Street. Mike Hart himself had called us a cab.

For a brief, clear moment, I was reminded of the purple and blue gypsy cab we were looking for—but then the thought evaporated into the nearly white sunlight.

"Sugar," Sampson whispered against my skull as we were climbing into our cab, "I love you more than life itself. It's true. I love your kids, love your Nana, love your wife-to-be, the lovely Christine. Take us home," he said to the driver. "Alex is getting married."

"And he's the best man," I said to the driver, who smiled.

"Yes I am," said Sampson. "The very best."

Chapter 43

ON THURSDAY NIGHT, Shafer played the Four Horsemen again. He was locked inside his study, but through the early part of the night he could hear the sounds of his family throughout the house. He felt intensely isolated; he was nervous, jittery, and angry for no apparent reason.

While he waited to log on with the other players, he found himself thinking back to his wild car ride through Washington. He relived a particular feeling over and over: the imagined moment of sudden impact with an unmovable structure. He saw it as blinding light, and physical objects, and *himself,* all shattering like glass and then becoming part of the universe again. Even the pain he would feel would be part of the reassembling of matter into other fascinating forms and shapes.

I am suicidal, he finally thought. *It's just a matter of time. I really am Death.*

When it was exactly nine o'clock, he began to type in a message on his computer. The other Horsemen were on-line, waiting for his response to the visit and warning by George Bayer. He didn't want to disappoint them. What they had done had made him even more enthusiastic about playing the game. He wrote:

STRANGELY, DEATH WASN'T SURPRISED WHEN FAMINE APPEARED IN WASHINGTON. OF COURSE HE HAD EVERY RIGHT TO COME. JUST AS DEATH COULD GO TO LONDON, OR SINGAPORE, OR MANILA, OR KINGSTON, AND PERHAPS DEATH WILL PAY ONE OF YOU A VISIT SOON.

THAT'S THE BEAUTY OF THE GAME WE PLAY—ANYTHING CAN HAPPEN.

ULTIMATELY, THE ISSUE IS TRUST, ISN'T IT? DO I TRUST THAT YOU WILL ALLOW ME TO

CONTINUE TO PLAY THE
FANTASY GAME AS I WISH?
AFTER ALL, THAT IS WHAT
MAKES THE GAME
DISTINCTIVE AND ALLURING:
THE FREEDOM WE
EXPERIENCE.

THAT *IS* THE GAME NOW,
ISN'T IT? WE HAVE EVOLVED
INTO SOMETHING NEW. WE
HAVE RAISED THE TABLE
STAKES. SO LET'S HAVE SOME
REAL EXCITEMENT, FELLOW
HORSEMEN. I HAVE A FEW
IDEAS TO TRY OUT ON YOU.
EVERYTHING IS IN THE SPIRIT
OF THE GAME. NO
UNNECESSARY RISKS WILL BE
TAKEN.

LET'S PLAY THE GAME AS IF
OUR LIVES DEPENDED ON IT.

PERHAPS MINE ALREADY
DOES?

AS I TOLD YOU, WE HAVE
TWO NEW PLAYERS. THEY ARE
WASHINGTON DETECTIVES
NAMED ALEX CROSS AND
JOHN SAMPSON. WORTHY

OPPONENTS. I'M WATCHING THEM, BUT I CAN'T HELP WONDERING WHETHER SOON THEY'LL BE WATCHING ME.

LET ME TELL YOU ABOUT A FANTASY SCENARIO THAT I'VE CREATED TO WELCOME THEM TO OUR GAME. I'M SENDING PICTURES NOW—DETECTIVES CROSS AND SAMPSON.

Chapter 44

IT TOOK US A DAY to get organized for
our trip, but everybody seemed to enjoy
the spontaneity, and also the special treat
of our all being together on a vacation for
the first time. And so Damon, Jannie,
Nana, Christine, and I left D.C. in the afternoon and arrived in high spirits at Bermuda
International Airport late on Thursday evening, the twenty-fifth of August.

I definitely wanted to be out of Washington for a few days. The Mr. Smith murder
case had been followed too quickly by the
Jane Doe investigation. I needed a rest. I
had a friend who was part owner of a hotel
in Bermuda, and it wasn't a particularly
long airplane ride. It was perfect for us.

One scene from the airport will always

stick in my mind—Christine's singing "Ja-da, ja-da," with Jannie stuck at her side. I couldn't help thinking that they looked like mother and daughter, and that touched me deeply. They were so affectionate and playful, so natural. It was a mind-photo for me to have and to hold, one of those moments that I knew I'd never forget, even as I watched the two of them dancing and singing as if they'd known each other forever.

We were blessed with extraordinarily good weather for our holiday. It was sunny and blue-skied every day, morning until nightfall, when the sky turned a magical combination of reds, oranges, and purples. The days belonged to all of us, but especially to the kids. We went swimming and snorkeling at Elbow Beach and Horseshoe Bay, and then raced mopeds along the picturesque Middle and Harbour roads.

The nights belonged to Christine and me, and we made the most of them. We hit all the best spots: the Terrace Bar at the Palm Reef, the Gazebo Lounge at the Princess, the Clay House Inn, Once Upon a Table in Hamilton, Horizons in Paget. I loved being with her, and that thought kept

234 / JAMES PATTERSON

drifting through my mind. I felt that what we shared had been strengthened because I had backed off and given her time and space. And I felt whole again. I kept remembering the very first time I had seen her in the schoolyard at Sojourner Truth. *She's the one, Alex.* That thought still played in my head, too.

We sat at the Terrace Bar overlooking the city and harbor of Hamilton. The water was dotted with small islands, white sails, ferries going back and forth to Warwick and Paget. We held hands, and I couldn't stop staring into her eyes, didn't want to.

"Big thoughts?" she finally asked.

"I've been thinking a lot about going into private practice again," I told her. "I think it might be the best thing to do."

She stared into my eyes. "I don't want you to do it for me, Alex. Please don't make me the cause of your leaving your job with the police. I know you love it. Most days you do."

"The Job has been tearing at me lately. Pittman isn't just a difficult boss; I think he's a bad guy. What happened to Sampson and the others is just bullshit. They were working unsolved cases on their own time. I'm tempted to give the story to Zach Taylor at the *Post.* People would riot if they knew the truth. Which is why I *won't* give it to the *Post.*"

She listened and tried to help but she didn't push, and I appreciated that. "It does sound like a terrible, complicated, nasty mess, Alex. I'd like to punch out Pittman, too. He's choosing politics over protecting people. I'm sure you'll know what to do when the time is right."

The next morning, I found her walking in the garden, with tropical flowers strewn in her hair. She looked radiant, even more than usual, and I fell in love all over again.

"There's an old saying I've been hearing since I was a little girl," she told me as I joined her. "If you have only two pennies, buy a loaf of bread with one and a lily with the other."

I kissed her hair, in between the flowers. I kissed her sweet lips, her cheeks, the hollow in her throat.

The kids and I went back to Horseshoe Bay Beach early that afternoon. They couldn't get enough of the deep blue sea, swimming, snorkeling, and building sand castles. And, of course, it was almost time

236 / JAMES PATTERSON

to start school again, so everything about our vacation was extra-special and intense.

Christine took a moped trip into Hamilton to pick up mementos for a few of the teachers at Sojourner Truth. We all waved until she was out of sight on Middle Road. Then back into the water!

Around five o'clock, Damon, Jannie, and I returned to the Belmont Hotel, which sat like a sentinel on lush green hills framed by china-blue skies. All around, everywhere we looked, were pastel-colored cottages with white roofs. Nana was sitting out on the porch, talking to a couple of her new best friends. *Paradise regained,* I thought, and felt something deep and sacred coming back to life inside me.

As I stared out at the cloudless blue sky, I regretted that Christine wasn't there to share it. I actually missed her in just that short a time. I hugged Jannie and Damon, and we were all smiling at the obvious: we loved being here together, and we were so damn fortunate to have one another.

"You miss her," Jannie whispered. It was a statement, not a question. "That's good, Daddy. That's the way it should be, right?"

When Christine still hadn't returned by six o'clock, I struggled between conflicting thoughts of waiting for her at the hotel or driving into Hamilton myself. Maybe she'd had an accident. *Those damn mopeds,* I thought, having found them fun and perfectly safe just the afternoon before.

I spotted a tall, slender woman entering through the front gates of the Belmont, walking against a background of hibiscus and oleander. I sighed with relief, but as I started down the front stairs, I saw that it wasn't Christine.

Christine still hadn't returned, or called the hotel, by six-thirty. Or by seven o'clock.

I finally called the police.

Chapter 45

INSPECTOR PATRICK BUSBY from the Hamilton P.D. arrived at the Belmont Hotel around seven-thirty. He was a small balding man who from a distance looked to be in his late fifties or sixties. As he approached the front porch, though, I could tell he was no more than forty, around the same age as me.

He listened to my story, then said that visitors often lost track of time and of themselves in Bermuda. There were also occasional moped accidents on Middle Road. He promised me that Christine would show up soon, with a mild "road rash" or a "slightly turned ankle."

I wouldn't have any of it. She was always

punctual, and at the very least, she would have called.

I knew that somehow she'd call if she had a minor accident. So the inspector and I rode together between the hotel and Hamilton, and then we toured the streets of the capital city, particularly Front and Reid streets. I was silent and solemn-faced as I stared out of the car, hoping to get a glimpse of Christine shopping on some side street, forgetful of the hour. But we didn't see her anywhere, and she still hadn't called the hotel.

When she still hadn't turned up by nine, Inspector Busby reluctantly agreed that Christine might be missing. He asked a lot of questions that showed me he was a decent cop. He wanted to know if we'd had any kind of argument or disagreement.

"I'm a homicide detective in Washington, D.C.," I finally told him. I'd been holding it back because I didn't want this to get territorial. "I've been involved with high-profile cases involving mass murders in the past. I've known some very bad men. There might be a connection. I hope not, but that could be."

"I see," Busby said. He was such a precise, neat man with his thin pencil mustache. He looked more like a fussy schoolteacher than a cop, more like a psychologist than I did. "Are there any other surprises I should know about, Detective Cross?" he asked.

"No, that's it. But you see why I'm worried, and why I called you. I'm working on a series of nasty murders in Washington right now."

"Yes, I see a reason for your concern now. I will put out a missing-persons report forthwith."

I sighed heavily, then went upstairs and talked to the kids and Nana. I tried my best not to alarm them, but Damon and Jannie started to cry. And then Nana did, too.

We had learned nothing more about Christine or her whereabouts by midnight. Inspector Busby left the hotel at quarter past twelve. He was kind, actually, and considerate enough to give me his home number; he asked me to call right away if I heard from Christine. Then he said my family and I would be in his prayers.

At three, I was still up and pacing my hotel room on the third floor, and doing some praying myself. I had just gotten off the phone with Quantico. The FBI was cross-checking all of my homicide cases to see if anyone I'd investigated had any connection with Bermuda. The Bureau was now concentrating on the current series of unsolved murders in Southeast. I'd faxed them my profile on the Weasel.

I didn't have any logical reason to suspect that the killer might be here in Bermuda, and yet I feared he might be. It was just the kind of feeling that The Jefe had been rejecting about the murders in Southeast.

I understood that the Bureau probably wouldn't get back to me until later in the morning. I was tempted to call friends at Interpol, but I held off. . . . And then I called Interpol, too.

The hotel room was filled with mahogany Queen Anne furniture and wicker, and had dusty-pink carpets. It seemed empty and lonely. I stood like a ghost before the tall, water-stained dormer windows, stared out at the shifting black shapes against the moonlit sky, and remembered how I held Christine in my arms. I felt incredibly helpless and alone without her. I also couldn't believe this had happened.

I hugged myself tightly and became aware of a terrible pain all around my heart. The tightening pain was like a solid column that went from my chest all the way up into my head. I could see her face, her beautiful smile. I remembered dancing with her one night at the Rainbow Room in New York, and dinners at Kinkead's in Washington, and that one special night at her place when we'd laughed and thought maybe we'd made a baby. Was Christine out there somewhere on the island? She had to be. I prayed again that she was safe. She had to be safe. I refused to have any other thought for more than a couple of seconds.

The telephone in the room rang, a short burst, at a little past four in the morning.

My heart was stuck in my throat. My skin crawled, felt as if it were shrinking and no longer fit my body. I rushed across the room and grabbed the phone before the second ring. My hand was trembling.

The strange, muffled voice scared me: "You have e-mail."

I couldn't think straight. I couldn't think at all.

I'd brought my laptop with me on vacation.

Who knows that I have my computer here? Who could know a small detail like that about me? Who's been watching me? Watching us?

I yanked open the closet door, grabbed the computer, hooked it up, and logged on. I scrolled down the e-mail to the last message.

It was short and very concise.

SHE'S SAFE FOR NOW.

WE HAVE HER.

The curt, cold message was worse than anything I could imagine. Each word was branded into my brain, repeating over and over.

"She's safe for now."

"We have her."

Book Three

ELEGY

SAMPSON ARRIVED at the Belmont Hotel the day after Christine disappeared. I hurried down to the small front lobby to meet him. He threw his large arms around me, clasping me tightly but gently, as if he were holding a child in his arms.

"You okay? You holding up?" he asked.

"Not even close," I told him. "I spent half a day checking the e-mail address I got last night. It came from curtain@ mindspring.com. The address was falsified. Nothing is going right."

"We'll get Christine back. We'll find her." He told me what he knew I wanted to hear, but I was sure that he also truly believed it in his heart. Sampson is the most positive human being I've ever met. He won't be denied.

"Thanks for coming. It means a lot to all of us. I can't think straight about anything. I'm really rattled, John. I can't even begin to imagine who could have done this. Maybe the Weasel—I don't know."

"If you *could* think straight now," John said, "I'd be more worried about you than usual. That's why I'm here."

"I kind of knew you'd come."

"Of course you did. I'm Sampson. Occam's razor and all that other deep philosophical shit at work here."

There were a half-dozen guests in the hotel lobby, and all of them looked our way. The hotel staff knew about Christine's disappearance, and I'm sure that the guests at the Belmont knew as well, as did just about everybody else on the small, chatty island.

"The story's on the front page of the local newspaper," Sampson said. "People were reading copies at the airport."

I told him, "Bermuda is small, mostly peaceful and orderly. The disappearance of a tourist, or any kind of violent crime, is unusual here. I don't know how the paper got the story so quickly. The leak must have come out of the police station."

"Local police won't help us. Probably get in the way," Sampson muttered as we walked over to the hotel registration desk. He signed in, then we trudged upstairs to show Nana and the kids that Uncle John was here.

Chapter 47

THE FOLLOWING MORNING, the two of us met for hours with the police in Hamilton. They were professionals, but a kidnapping was a rarity for them. They let us set up in their station house on Front Street. I still couldn't concentrate or focus the way I needed to.

Bermuda is a twenty-one-square-mile island. While the British colony is small, we soon discovered that there are more than twelve hundred roads on the island. Sampson and I split up and covered as much ground as we possibly could. For the next two days we went from six in the morning until ten or eleven at night, without a break. I didn't want to stop, not even to sleep.

We didn't do any better than the locals,

though. No one had seen anything. We'd reached a dead end. Christine had disappeared without a trace.

We were bone-tired. After we finished at the station house on the third night, Sampson and I went for a late swim at Elbow Beach, just down the road from the hotel.

We had learned to swim at the municipal pool in D.C. Nana had insisted that we learn. She was fifty-four at the time, and stubborn. She made up her mind to learn and took lessons with us from the Red Cross. The majority of people in Southeast didn't know how to swim back then, and she felt it was symbolic of the limiting inner-city experience.

So one summer, Sampson and I tackled swimming with Nana at the municipal pool. We went for lessons three mornings a week and usually practiced for an extra hour after that. Nana herself was soon able to swim fifty or more laps. She had stamina, same as now. I rarely get into the water without flashing back to those fine summer days of my youth, when I became a reasonably good swimmer.

Now, Sampson and I floated on the calm surface, out about a hundred yards or so from shore. The sky above was the deepest shade of evening blue, sparkling with countless stars. I could see the curving white line of the beach as it stretched several miles in either direction. Palm and casuarina trees shimmied in the sea breeze.

I felt devastated, totally overwhelmed as I floated on the sea. I kept seeing Christine with my eyes open or closed. I couldn't believe she was gone. I teared up as I thought about what had happened, the unfairness of life sometimes.

"You want to talk about the investigation? My thoughts so far? Little things I learned today? Or give it a rest for the night?" Sampson asked me as we floated peacefully on our backs. "Talk? Or quiet time?"

"Talk, I guess. I can't think about anything else except Christine. I can't think straight. Say whatever you're thinking. Something bothering you in particular?"

"Little thing, but maybe it's important."

I didn't say anything. I just let him go on.

"What puzzles me is the first newspaper stories." Sampson paused and then continued, "Busby says he didn't talk to anybody the first night. Not a single person, he claims. You didn't, either. Story was in the morning edition, though."

"It's a small island, John. I told you that, and you've seen it yourself."

But Sampson kept at it, and I began to think that maybe there was something to it.

"Listen, Alex, only you, Patrick Busby, and whoever took Christine knew. *He* called it in to the paper. The kidnapper did it himself. I talked to the girl at the paper who got the call. She wouldn't say anything yesterday, but she finally told me late today. She thought it was just a concerned citizen calling. I think somebody's playing with your head, Alex. Somebody's running a nasty game on you."

"We have her."

A game? What kind of nasty game? Who were the nasty players? Was one of them the Weasel? Was it possible that he was still here in Bermuda?

Chapter 48

I COULDN'T SLEEP back at the hotel. I still couldn't concentrate or focus, and it was incredibly frustrating. It was as if I were losing my mind.

A *game?* No, this wasn't a game. This was shock and horror. This was a living nightmare beyond anything I had ever experienced. Who could have done this to Christine? Why? Who was the Weasel?

Every time I closed my eyes, tried to sleep, I could see Christine's face, see her waving good-bye that final time on Middle Road, see her walking through the hotel gardens with flowers in her hair.

I could hear Christine's voice all through the night—and then it was morning again.

My guilt over what had happened to her had doubled, tripled.

Sampson and I continued to canvass Middle Road, Harbour Road, South Road. Every person we spoke to in the police and the military believed that Christine didn't simply disappear on the island. Sampson and I heard the same song and dance every day for a week. No shopkeepers or taxi or bus drivers had seen her in Hamilton or St. George, so it was possible that she'd never even arrived in either town that afternoon.

No one, not one witness, remembered seeing her moped on Middle or Harbour roads, so maybe she never even got that far.

Most disturbing of all was that there hadn't been any further communication with me about her since the e-mail on the night she disappeared. An agent at the FBI had investigated the e-mail address and found *it didn't exist.* Whoever had contacted me was a skillful hacker, able to conceal his or her identity. The words I'd read that night were always on my mind.

"She's safe for now."

"We have her."

Who was "we"? And why hadn't there been any further contact? What did they want from me? Did they know they were driving me insane? Was that what they wanted to do? Did the Weasel represent more than one killer? Suddenly that made a lot of sense to me.

Sampson returned to Washington on Sunday, and he took Nana and the kids with him. They didn't want to leave without me, but it was time for them to go. I couldn't make myself leave Bermuda yet. It would have felt as if I were abandoning Christine.

On Sunday night, Patrick Busby showed up at the Belmont Hotel around nine. He asked me to ride with him out past Southampton, about a six-mile drive that he said would take us twenty minutes or more. Bermudians measure distances in straight lines, but all the roads run in wiggles and half-circles, so it always takes longer to travel than you might think.

"What is it, Patrick? What's out in Southampton?" I asked as we rode along Middle Road. My heart was in my throat. He was scaring me with his silence.

"We haven't found Mrs. Johnson. However, a man may have witnessed the abduction. I want you to hear his story. You decide for yourself. You're the big-city detective, not me. You can ask whatever questions you like. Off the record, of course."

The man's name was Perri Graham, and he was staying in a room at the Port Royal Golf Club. We met him at his tiny apartment in the staff quarters. He was tall and painfully thin, with a longish goatee. He clearly wasn't happy to see Inspector Busby or me on his doorstep.

Busby had already told me that Graham was originally from London and now worked as a porter and maintenance man at the semiprivate golf club. He had also lived in New York City and Miami and had a criminal record for selling crack in New York.

"I already told him everything I saw," Perri Graham said defensively as soon as he opened the front door of his room and saw the two of us standing there. "Go away. Let me be. Why would I hold back anything or—"

I cut him off. "My name is Alex Cross. I'm a homicide detective from Washington.

258 / JAMES PATTERSON

The woman you saw was my fiancée, Mr. Graham. May we come in and talk? This will only take a few minutes."

He shook his head back and forth in frustration.

"I'll tell you what I know. *Again,*" he finally said, relenting. "Yeah, come in. But only because you called me Mr. Graham."

"That's all I want. I'm not here to bother you about anything else."

Busby and I walked inside the room, which was little more than an alcove. The tile floors and all the furniture were strewn with wrinkled clothes, mostly underwear.

"A woman I know lives in Hamilton," Graham said in a weary voice. "I went to visit her this Tuesday past. We drank too much wine. Stayed the evening—you know how it is. I got up somehow. Had to be at the club by noon, but I knew I'd be late and get docked some of my pay. Don't have a car or nothin', so I hitched a ride from Hamilton, out South Shore Road. Walked along near Paget, I suppose. Damn hot afternoon, I remember. I went down to the water, cool off if I could.

"I came back up over a knobbly hill, and I witnessed an accident on the roadway. It was maybe a quarter of a mile down the big hill there. You know it?"

I nodded and held my breath as I listened to him. I remembered the stifling heat of that afternoon, everything about it. I could still see Christine driving off on a shiny blue moped, waving and smiling. The memory of her smile, which had always brought me such joy, now put a tight knot in my stomach.

"I saw a white van hit a woman riding a blue moped. I can't be sure, but it almost looked like the van hit her on purpose. Driver, he jumped out of the van right away and helped her up. She didn't look like she was hurt badly. Then he helped her inside the van. Put the moped inside, too. Then he drove off. I thought he was taking her to the hospital. Thought nothing else of it."

"You sure she wasn't badly hurt?" I asked.

"Not sure. But she got right up. She was able to stand all right."

There was a catch in my voice when I spoke again. "And you didn't tell anybody about the accident, not even when you saw the news stories?"

The man shook his head. "Didn't see no

stories. Don't bother with the local news much. Just small-time shit and worthless gossip. But then my girl, she keep talking about it. I didn't want to go to the police, but she made me do it, made me talk to this inspector here."

"You know what kind of van it was?" I asked.

"White van. I think it was maybe a rented one. Clean and new."

"License plate?"

Graham shook his head. "Don't have no idea."

"What did the man in the van look like?" I asked him. "Any little thing you remember is helpful, Mr. Graham. You've already helped a lot."

He shrugged, but I could tell that he was trying to think back to that afternoon. "Nothing special about him. Not as tall as you, but tall. Look like anybody else. Just a black man, like any other."

Chapter 49

IN A SMALL APARTMENT in a suburb of Washington called Mount Rainier, Detective Patsy Hampton lay in bed, restlessly flipping through the pages of the *Post.* She couldn't sleep, but there was nothing unusual about that. She often had trouble sleeping, ever since she was a little girl in Harrisburg, Pennsylvania. Her mother said she must have a guilty conscience about something.

She watched a rerun episode of *ER,* then fetched herself a Stonyfield yogurt with blueberries and logged on to America Online. She had an e-mail from her father, now relocated in Delray Beach, Florida, and one from an old college roommate from the University of Richmond, whom she had never been that close to anyway.

The roommate had just heard from a mutual friend that Patsy was a hotshot police detective in Washington, and what an exciting life she must lead. The roommate wrote that she had four children and lived in a suburb of Charlotte, North Carolina, but added that she was bored with everything in her life. Patsy Hampton would have given anything to have just one child.

She wandered back to the kitchen and got a cold bottle of Evian mineral water. She was aware that her life had become ridiculous. She spent too much time on her job, but also too much time by herself in her apartment, especially on weekends. It wasn't that she couldn't get dates; she was just turned off by men in general lately.

She still fantasized about finding someone compatible, having children. But she was increasingly tired of the depressing and maddening cycle of trying to meet someone interesting. She usually ended up with guys who were either hopelessly boring *or* thirty-something jackasses who still acted like teenagers, though without the charm of youth. *Hopeless, hopeless, hopeless,* she thought as she sent off a cheery lie to her dad in Florida.

The phone rang, and she glanced at her wristwatch—it was twenty past twelve.

She snatched up the receiver. "Hampton speaking."

"It's Chuck, Patsy. Really sorry to call so late. Is it okay? You awake?"

"Sure, no problem, Chucky Cheese. I'm up with the other vampires—yourself included, I guess."

It was kind of late, but she was glad to hear from Chuck Hufstedler, who was a computer geek at the FBI in Washington. The two of them helped each other out sometimes, and she'd recently talked to him about the unsolved D.C. murders, especially the Jane Does. Chuck had told her that he was also in contact with Alex Cross, but Cross had trouble of his own right now. His fiancée had been kidnapped, and Patsy Hampton wondered if it had anything to do with the killings in Southeast.

"I'm wide awake, Chuck. What's up? What's on your big mind?"

He started with a disclaimer that said

volumes about his incredibly low self-es-teem: "Maybe nothing, but maybe some-thing a little interesting on those killings in Southeast, and particularly the two young girls in Shaw. This really comes out of left field, though."

The FBI computer expert had her atten-tion. "That's where this killer lives, Chuck, in *deep* left field. Tell me what you have. I'm wide awake and listening. Talk to me, Chucky Cheese."

Chuck hemmed and hawed. He was al-ways like that, which was too bad because he was basically a really nice guy. "You know anything about RPGs, Patsy?" he asked.

"I know it stands for role-playing games, and let's see, there's a popular one called Dragons and Dungeons, or Dungeons and Dragons—whatever the order."

"It's Dungeons and Dragons, or Ad-vanced Dungeons and Dragons. Confes-sion time, kiddo: I occasionally play an RPG myself, it's called Millennium's End. I play a couple of hours a day, usually. More on weekends."

"New to me. Go on, Chuck." *God,* she

thought, *cyberspace confessions in the middle of the night.*

"Very popular game, even with so-called adults. The characters in Millennium's End work for Black Eagle Security. It's a private organization of troubleshooters who hire out for investigative services around the world. The characters are all good guys, crusaders for good."

"Uh-huh, Chuck. Say six Hail Marys, now make an Act of Contrition, then get to the damn point. It *is* around twelve-thirty, pal."

"Right, I am heartily sorry, and deeply embarrassed, too. Anyway, there's a chat-room on-line that I visited. It's called the Gamester's Chatroom, and it's on AOL. As I speak, there's a fascinating discussion going on about a new kind of game. It's more an *anti*-game, though. All the role-playing games I know are about *good* characters' trying to conquer chaos and evil. The game under discussion has a couple of *evil* characters' *trying to over-come good.* Specifically, Patsy, one of the characters is attacking and murdering women in the Southeast part of D.C. Lots of lurid detail on the murders. These aren't the actual players, but they know about the game. The game itself is probably protected. Thought you should know. The game is called the Four Horsemen."

Patsy Hampton was definitely wide awake now. "I'm on it. Thanks, Chuck. Let's keep this between the two of us for the moment, okay, Chuck?"

"Yeah. Okay."

It took her a couple of minutes to log on to AOL, then get into the Gamester's Chatroom. She didn't participate, just read what the others had to say. This was interesting. She wondered if she had just stumbled onto her first big break in the Jane Doe case.

The others in the room were named Viper, Landlocked, J-Boy, and Lancelot. They chattered on and on about the hottest fantasy games and cutting-edge magazines, which nearly succeeded in putting her to sleep. The Four Horsemen came up twice, but only in passing, as a point of reference. Lancelot was the one who mentioned it. Chuck was right: these probably weren't the actual players, but they knew about the game somehow.

The fantasy nerds were starting to wear

really thin with her by quarter past one. Finally, out of frustration, she typed out a message for the little shitheels. She called herself Sappho.

I CAME IN LATE, BUT HORSEMEN SOUNDS LIKE A NEAT KIND OF REVOLUTIONARY GAME TO ME, LANCELOT. PRETTY AUDACIOUS STUFF, NO?

Lancelot shot back:

NOT REALLY, *SAPPO.* THERE'S A LOT OF IT GOING AROUND LATELY. ANTIHEROES, SICKOS. ESPECIALLY IN VAMPIRE GAME CIRCLES.

Hampton typed:

HAVEN'T I READ ABOUT MURDERS LIKE THESE IN THE NEWSPAPERS? BY THE WAY, IT'S SAPPHO, LIKE THE POET.

Lancelot replied,

YEAH, BUT LOTS OF RPGs USE CURRENT EVENTS. NO BIGGIE, REALLY, *SAPPO.*

Hampton grinned. He was an obnoxious little nerd, but she had him—for the moment, anyway. And she needed him. How much did he know about the Four Horsemen? Could he be a player? She tried to peek at Lancelot's profile, but he had restricted access to it.

YOU'RE FUNNY. ARE YOU A PLAYER, LAUGHALOT, OR JUST AN ART CRITIC?

I DON'T LIKE THE BASIC CONCEPT OF HORSEMEN. ANYWAY, IT'S A PRIVATE GAME. *STRICTLY* PRIVATE. ENCRYPTED.

YOU KNOW ANY OF THE PLAYERS? I MIGHT LIKE TO TRY IT OUT MYSELF?

There was no response to th question. Patsy thought maybe she'd pushed too hard, too fast. Damn! She should have known better. Damn, damn! Come back, Lancelot. Earth to Lancelot.

I REALLY WOULD LIKE TO PLAY THE FOUR HORSEMEN. BUT I'M COOL ABOUT IT. NO BIGGIE. LANCELOT?

Patsy Hampton waited, and then Lancelot left the chatroom. Lancelot was gone.
And so was her connection to somebody
playing a so-called fantasy game about
committing gruesome murders in Washington—murders that had really happened.

Chapter 50

I RETURNED TO WASHINGTON during
the first week of September, and I had
never felt stranger in my own skin. I'd gone
to Bermuda with my family and Christine,
and now I was coming home without her.
Whoever had taken Christine had contacted me only once. I missed her nearly
every moment of every day, and it pained
me to think about where she might still be.

It was an unusually cool and windy day
when I got back to the city. It almost
seemed as if summer had suddenly
changed to the middle of fall, as if I had
been away much longer than I had. I had
been in a fog of unreality in Bermuda, and
it was nearly the same once I was back in

D.C. It had never been this bad before. I was so lost, so unhinged, so battered.

I wondered if Christine and I were part of a madman's elaborate delusion, what profilers call an escalating fantasy. If so, who was this madman, and where was he now? Was it the Weasel? Did I know him from some time in my past? The heartless, spineless bastard had communicated, *"We have her."* And that was it. No further word. Now only silence, which was deafening.

I took a cab from the airport and remembered what had happened to Frank Odenkirk, who had innocently taken a cab one night in August and wound up murdered on Alabama Avenue near Dupont Park. I hadn't thought about the Odenkirk case during the past three weeks. I had rarely even had a thought about the Jane Doe murders while in Bermuda, but I was guiltily reminded of them now. Others had suffered painful losses because of the killer.

I wondered if any progress had been made, and who in the department was running the case, at least the Odenkirk part of it. On the other hand, I didn't feel that I could work on any of the other unsolved murders right now. I felt my place was still in Bermuda, and I nearly headed back as soon as I landed.

Then I could see our house up ahead on Fifth Street. Something strange was happening—there was a huge gathering.

Chapter 51

LOTS OF PEOPLE were standing on the porch and others were clustered in front of the house when the cab arrived. Cars were parked and double-parked all along the street.

I recognized Aunt Tia. My sister-in-law Cilla and Nana were on the porch with the kids. Sampson was there with a girlfriend named Millie, a lawyer from the Justice Department.

Some of them waved as I pulled up, so I knew everything was all right. This wasn't more trouble. But what was this all about?

I saw my niece Naomi and her husband, Seth Taylor, who had come all the way from Durham, North Carolina. Jerome

Thurman, Rakeem Powell, and Shawn Moore were standing on the front lawn.

"Hey, Alex, good to see you," Jerome's deep voice boomed out at me as I passed near him on my way to the porch. I finally set down my travel bag and started shaking hands, giving out hugs, receiving back pats and kisses from all sides.

"We're all here for you," Naomi said. She came over to me and hugged me tightly. "We love you so much. But we'll go away if you don't want us here now."

"No, no. I'm glad you're here, Scootchie," I said, and kissed my niece on both cheeks. A while back, she'd been abducted in Durham, North Carolina. I had been there for her, and so had Sampson. "It's good that you and Seth are here. It's good to see everybody. You can't imagine how good it is."

I hugged relatives and friends, my grandmother, my two beautiful kids, and I realized again how lucky I was to have so many good people in my life. Two teachers from the Sojourner Truth School had also come to the house. They were friends of Christine's, and they started to cry when they came up to me. They wanted to know if any progress had been made and if there was anything they could do.

I told them that we had a witness to the abduction and that we were more hopeful than ever. The teachers were buoyed by the news, which wasn't nearly as good as I made it sound. Nothing more had come of the one eyewitness account of the abduction. No one else had seen the white van that took away Christine.

Jannie cornered me in the backyard around nine o'clock. I had just spent half an hour with Damon in the basement, talking man to man, shadowboxing a little bit.

Damon had told me that he was having trouble remembering Christine's face, exactly what she looked like. I told him that it happened with people and that it was all right. Then we shared a long hug.

Jannie had patiently waited to talk with me.

"My turn?" she asked.

"Absolutely, sweetheart."

Jannie then took my hand and pulled me forward into the house. She quietly led me upstairs—not to her room, but to mine.

"If you get lonely in here tonight, you can come to my room. I *mean* it," she said as she gently shut the door on the two of us. She is so wise and has such a good perspective on so many things. Both she and Damon are such good kids. Nana says they have "sound character," and it is building nicely. So far, so good.

"Thank you, sweetie. I will come to your room if it gets bad in here. You're very thoughtful and nice."

"I am, Daddy. You helped me be this way, and I'm glad of it. Now I have a real serious question for you, Daddy. It's hard, but I have to ask anyway."

"You go ahead," I told her, feeling uncomfortable under her serious little gaze. I wasn't completely focused, and I didn't know if I could handle one of Jannie's hard questions. "I'm listening, sweetheart," I said. "Fire away."

She had let go of my hand, but then she took it up again, held my big hand tightly in both her small ones.

"Daddy, is Christine dead?" she asked me. "You can tell me if she is. Please tell the true truth, though. I want to know."

I almost lost it, sitting on the edge of the bed with Jannie. I'm sure she had no idea how much her question hurt, or how hard it was to answer.

I was hanging over the edge of a dark abyss, just about gone, but I pulled myself together and took a deep, hard breath. Then I tried to answer my little girl's honest question as best I could.

"I don't know yet," I told her. "That's the truth. We're still hoping to find her, sweetie. We found one witness so far."

"But she might be dead, Daddy?"

"Let me tell you the best thing I know about dying," I said to Jannie. "The very best thing that I know. Just about the only thing, in fact."

"You go away, and then you're with Jesus forever," Jannie said. The way she spoke, though, I wasn't sure if she really believed what she was saying. It sounded like one of Nana's "gospel truths," or maybe she'd heard it in church.

"Yes, that can be a great comfort to know, baby. But I was thinking of something else. Maybe it's the same thing, but a different way to look at it."

Her intense little eyes held mine, wouldn't let go. "You can tell me, Daddy.

Please. I want to hear it. I'm very interested in this."

"It's not a bad thing, but it helps me whenever somebody dies. Think about this. We come into life so easily—from somewhere, from the universe, from God. Why should it be any harder when we leave life? We come from a good place. We leave—and go to a good place. Does that make any sense to you, Jannie?"

She nodded and continued to stare deeply into my eyes. "I understand," she whispered. "It's like it's in balance."

She paused a second, thinking it over, then she spoke. "But Daddy, Christine isn't dead. I just know it. She *isn't* dead. She hasn't gone to that good place yet. So don't you lose hope."

Chapter 52

THE CHARACTER and traits of Death were so much like his own, Shafer was thinking as he sped south along I-95. Death wasn't brilliant, but he was always thorough, and he always won in the end.

As the black Jag raced past the exits for various small towns, Shafer wondered if he wanted to be caught now, if he needed to be unmasked, needed to show his true face to everyone. Boo Cassady believed that he was hiding, even from her, but more important, from himself. Maybe she was right. Maybe he did want Lucy and the kids to see who he really was. And the police. But especially the uptight and sanctimonious staff at the embassy.

I am Death—it's who I am. I am a multi-

*ple killer—it's who I am. I am not Geoffrey
Shafer anymore; maybe I never was. But if I
was, it was a long, long time ago.*

Shafer had always had a natural mean
streak, a vengeful, nasty way. He remembered it from his early years traveling with
his family through Europe, then Asia, and
finally back to England. His father had
been in the military and was always a real
"tough guy" around the house. He struck
Shafer and his two brothers often, but not
nearly as often as he hit their mother, who
died of a fall when Shafer was twelve.

Shafer was large as a boy, and he was
one "tough hombre," a real bully. Other
boys feared him, even his brothers,
Charles and George, who believed that
Geoff was "capable of anything." He was.

Nothing in his early days prepared him
for being the man who finally emerged
once he joined MI6. It was there that he
learned he was capable of killing another
human being—and he found that he loved
it. He had discovered his calling, his true
passion in life. He was the ultimate "tough
guy"; he was Death.

He continued traveling south on the in-
terstate highway. Because it was late, traf-

fic was light, mostly high-speeding trucks headed toward Florida, he supposed.

He mentally composed a message to the other fantasy game players.

DEATH GOES TO FREDERICKSBURG, MARYLAND, TONIGHT. A GOOD-LOOKING 37-YEAR-OLD WOMAN LIVES THERE WITH HER MIRROR-IMAGE 15-YEAR-OLD DAUGHTER. THE WOMAN IS DIVORCED, A SMALL-TOWN LAWYER, A PROSECUTOR. THE DAUGHTER IS AN HONOR STUDENT AND A FOOTBALL CHEERLEADER. THE TWO WOMEN WILL BE SLEEPING. DEATH HAS COME TO MARYLAND BECAUSE WASHINGTON IS TOO DANGEROUS NOW. (YES, I TOOK YOUR WARNING TO HEART.) THE D.C. POLICE ARE SEARCHING FOR THE JANE DOE MURDERER. A WELL-THOUGHT-OF DETECTIVE NAMED PATSY HAMPTON IS ON THE CASE, AND

DETECTIVE CROSS HAS
RETURNED FROM BERMUDA.
IT WILL BE INTERESTING TO
SEE IF HIS CHARACTER HAS
CHANGED IN ANY WAY.
CHARACTER IS EVERYTHING,
DON'T YOU AGREE?

I CAN SEE THE CAHILL HOUSE UP
AHEAD. I CAN PICTURE BOTH OF
THE LOVELY CAHILL WOMEN. THEY
LIVE IN A FOUR-BEDROOM RANCH
HOUSE. THE SUBURBAN STREET IS
VIRTUALLY SILENT AT 1:00 A.M. NO
ONE COULD POSSIBLY CONNECT
THESE TWO MURDERS TO THE JANE
DOES. I WISH YOU COULD BE HERE
WITH ME. I WISH YOU COULD FEEL
EXACTLY AS I DO.

Chapter 53

SHAFER PARKED HIS JAG on the shadowy street and felt strangely alone and afraid. He was actually scaring himself. The things he thought and did. No one had a twisted mind like his—no one thought like this. No one had ever had such outlandish fantasies and ideas, and then acted them out.

The other players also had complicated and very sick fantasy lives, of course, but they paled in comparison to his. Famine claimed authorship of a series of psychosexual murders in Thailand and the Philippines. War liked to think of himself as the uncrowned head of the group—he claimed to "influence" the adventures of the others. Conqueror was confined to a

wheelchair and made up stories about using his infirmity to lure his prey close
enough for the kill.

Shafer doubted that any of them actually
had the guts to play the game out in the
real world.

But perhaps they would surprise him.
Maybe each of the others was living out a
homicidal fantasy. Wouldn't that be something?

The Cahill women thought they were so
perfectly safe inside the ranch house, less
than fifty yards away. He could see a green
wooden fence surrounding a stone terrace
and lap swimming pool in the back. The
house had sliding doors to the pool area.
So many possibilities for him to consider.

He might enter the house and murder
both of them execution-style. Then he
would drive directly back to Washington.

The local police and FBI would be totally
baffled. The story might even make net-
work TV. Two women shot and murdered
while they slept, a mother and daughter
whom everybody in their small town admired. No motive for the horrific crime, no
suspects.

He was hard now, and it was difficult to

walk. That was comical to Shafer, his absurd hard-on waddle. His mouth formed a smile.

A dog was howling two or three houses down the street—a small wimpy dog, from the sound of it. Then a larger dog joined in. They sensed death, didn't they? They knew he was here.

Shafer knelt beside a maple tree at the edge of the backyard. He stood in shadows while the moon cast a soft white light across the yard.

He slid the twenty-sided dice out of his pocket, then let them fall on the tufts of lawn. *Here we go. Playing by the rules. Let's see what the night has to offer.* He counted the numerals on the special dice. They appeared fuzzy in the dark.

Shafer couldn't believe what he saw. He wanted to howl like the crazed and bewildered neighborhood dogs.

The dice count was *five.*

Death had to leave! This instant! There could be no murders tonight!

No! He wouldn't do it! To hell with the dice. He wouldn't leave. He couldn't. He was losing all impulse control, wasn't he? Well, so be it. Alea jacta est, he remem-

bered from his schoolboy Latin classes—
Julius Caesar before he crossed the Rubi-
con: "The die is cast."

This was a monumental night. For the
first time, he was breaking the rules. He
was changing the game forever.

He needed to kill someone, and the urge
was everything to him.

He hurried to the house before he
changed his mind. He was nervous. Adrenaline punched through his system. He
used his glass cutter at first, but then just
smashed in a small window with a gloved
hand.

Once inside, he moved quickly down the
darkened hallway. He was sweating—so
unlike him. He entered Deirdre's bedroom.
She was asleep, despite the breaking of
the glass. Her bare arms were thrown up
over her head, the surrender position.

"Lovely," he whispered.

She was wearing white bikini panties
and a matching bra. Her long legs were
spread delicately, expectantly. In her
dreams, she must have known he was
coming. Shafer believed that dreams told
you the truth, and you had better listen.

He was still hard, and so glad he'd chosen to disobey the rules.

"Who the hell are you?" he heard, suddenly. The voice came from behind.

Shafer whirled around.

It was Lindsay, the daughter. She wore nothing but coral-pink underwear, a brassiere and briefs. He calmly raised his gun until it pointed between her eyes.

"Shhh. You don't want to know, Lindsay," he said in the calmest voice, not bothering to disguise his English accent. "But I'll tell you anyway."

He fired the gun.

Chapter 54

FOR THE SECOND TIME in my life I understood what it felt like to be a victim of a terrible crime rather than the detective investigating it. I was disconnected and out of it. I needed to be doing something positive on a case, or get back to volunteer work at St. Anthony's—anything to take my mind off what had happened.

I had to be busy, but I knew I'd lost my ability to concentrate, something that had always come so naturally to me. I came across a pair of shocking murders in Maryland that bothered me for some unspecified reason. I didn't follow up on them. I should have.

I wasn't myself; I was lost. I still spent endless hours thinking about Christine, remembering everything about our time together, seeing her face wherever I went.

Sampson tried to push me. He *did* push me. He and I made the rounds of the streets of Southeast. We put the word out that we were looking for a purple and blue cab, possibly a gypsy. We canvassed door to door in the Shaw neighborhood where Tori Glover and Marion Cardinal had been found. Often we were still going at ten or eleven at night.

I didn't care. I couldn't sleep anyway.

Sampson cared. He was my friend.

"You're supposed to be working the Odenkirk case, right? I'm not supposed to be working at all. The Jefe would be livid. I kind of like that," Sampson said as we trudged along S Street late one evening. Sampson had lived in this neighborhood for years. He knew all the local hangarounds.

"Jamal, you know anything I should know?" he called out to a goateed youth sitting in shadows on a graystone stoop.

"Don't know nothin'. Just relaxin' my mind. Catchin' a cool night breeze. How 'bout yourself?"

Sampson turned back to me. "Damn

290 / JAMES PATTERSON

crack runners working these streets everywhere you look nowadays. Real good place to commit a murder and never get caught. You talk to the police in Bermuda lately?"

I nodded, and my eyes stared at a fixed point up ahead. "Patrick Busby said the story of Christine's disappearance is off the front pages. I don't know if that's good or bad. It's probably bad."

Sampson agreed. "Takes the pressure off them. You going back down there?"

"Not right away. But yeah, I have to go back. I have to find out what happened."

He looked me in the eye. "Are you here with me right now? Are you *here,* sugar?"

"Yeah, I'm here. Most of the time. I'm functioning okay." I pointed up at a nearby redbrick building. "That place would have a view of the front entryway into the girl's building. Any of those windows. Let's get back to work."

Sampson nodded. "I'm here as long as you want to be."

There was something about pounding the streets that appealed to me that night. We talked to everyone in the building that we could find at home, about half the apartments. Nobody had seen a purple and blue cab on the street; nobody had seen Tori or Marion, either. Or so they said.

"You see any connections anywhere?" I asked as we came down the steep stairs of a fourth-floor walk-up. "What do you see? What the hell am I missing?"

"Not a thing, Alex. Nothing to miss. Weasel didn't leave a clue. Never does."

We got back down to the entrance and met up with an elderly man carrying three clear-plastic bags of groceries from the Stop & Shop.

"We're homicide detectives," I said to him. "Two young girls were murdered across the street."

The man nodded. "Tori and Marion. I know 'em. You want to know 'bout that fella watchin' the buildin'? He was sittin' there most the night. Inside a slick, fancy black car," he said. "Mercedes, I think. You think maybe he's the killer?"

Chapter 55

"I BEEN AWAY AWHILE, y'see. Visitin' wit' my two old-bat sisters in North Carolina for a week of good memories, home-cooked food," the elderly man said as we went up to the fourth floor. "That was why I was missed during the earlier time through here by your detectives."

This was old-school police work, I was thinking as I climbed stairs—the kind of work too many detectives try to avoid. The man's name was DeWitt Luke, and he was retired from Bell Atlantic, the huge phone company that services most of the Northeast. He was the fifty-third interview I'd had so far in Shaw.

"Saw him sittin' there around one in the mornin'. Didn't think much of it at first.

Probably waitin' for somebody. Seemed to be mindin' his own business. He was still there at two, though. Sittin' in his car. Seemed kinda strange to me." He paused for a long moment as if trying to remember.

"Then what happened?" I prompted the man.

"Fell asleep. But I got up to pee around three-thirty. He was *still* in that shiny black car. So I watched him closer this time. He was watchin' the other side of the street. Like some kind of damn spy or somethin'. Couldn't tell what he was lookin' at, but he was studyin' somethin' real hard over there. I thought he might be the police. 'Cept his car was too nice."

"You got that right," Sampson said, and barked out a laugh. "No Mercedes in my garage."

"I pulled up a card-table chair behind the darkened window in my apartment. Made sure there were no lights on, so he couldn't see me. By now he'd caught my attention some. Remember the old movie *Rear Window*? I tried to figure out why he might be down there sittin', waitin'. Jealous lover, jealous husband, maybe some kinda night stalker. But he wasn't botherin' anybody far as I could see."

I spoke again. "You never got a better look than that? Man sitting in the car?"

"Around the time I got up to pee, he got out of the car. Opened the door, but the inside light didn't come on. That struck me strange, it bein' such a nice car and all. Fueled my mind even more. I squinted my eyes, get a better look." Another long pause.

"And?"

"He was tall, a blond gentleman. White fella. We don't get too many of them around here at night, or even in the day-time, for that matter."

Chapter 56

DETECTIVE PATSY HAMPTON'S investigation of the Jane Doe murders was starting to show forward movement and positive results. She thought she might have something good in the works. She had confidence in her ability to solve the murders. She knew from experience that she was smarter than everybody else.

It helped to have Chief Pittman and all the department's resources on her side. She had spent the past day and a half with Chuck Hufstedler at the FBI building. She knew she was using Chuck a little, but he didn't seem to mind. He was lonely, and she *did* like his company. She and Chuck were still sitting around at three-thirty in the afternoon when Lancelot entered the

Gamester's Chatroom again. *Laughalot,* she remembered.

"He couldn't resist, could he?" Hampton said to Hufstedler. "Gotcha, you fantasy freak."

Hufstedler looked at her, his thick black eyebrows arched. "Three-thirty in the afternoon, Patsy. What does that say? Tell you what it says to me. *Maybe* he's playing from work. But I bet our Lancelot is a school kid."

"Or he's somebody who likes to play with school kids." She offered a thought that upset her even as she uttered the words.

This time, she didn't try to make contact with Lancelot. She and Chuck just listened in on a stultifying discussion of several role-playing games. In the meantime, he was trying to trace Lancelot.

"He's pretty good at this, a real hacker. He's built a lot of security into his system. Hopefully, we'll get to him anyway."

"I have confidence in you, Cheeseman."

Lancelot stayed in the chatroom past four-thirty. By then it was all over. Chuck had his name and address: Michael Ormson, Hutchins Place, Foxhall.

At a few minutes before five, two dark-blue vans pulled up in front of the Ormson house on the Georgetown Reservoir. Five agents in blue FBI windbreakers and Detective Patsy Hampton surrounded the large, Tudor-style house with an acre or two of front and back lawn and majestic views.

Senior FBI Agent Brigid Dwyer and Hampton proceeded to the front door and found it unlocked. With weapons drawn, they quietly entered the house and discovered Lancelot in the den.

He looked to be around thirteen years old. A baby geek. He was sitting at a computer in his shorts and black socks.

"Hey, what the heck is going on? Hey! What are you doing in my house? I didn't do anything wrong. Who are you guys?" Michael Ormson asked in a high-pitched, peeved, but quivering voice.

He was skinny. His face was covered with acne. His back and shoulders had a rash that looked like eczema. Chuck Hufstedler had been right on target. Lancelot was a teenage geek playing with his fancy computer after school. He wasn't the Weasel, though. This boy *couldn't* be the Weasel.

"Are you Michael Ormson?" Patsy Hampton asked the boy. She had lowered her weapon but hadn't holstered it.

The young boy dropped his head and looked ready to weep. "Oh, God, oh, God," he moaned. "Yes, I'm Michael Ormson. Who are you guys? Are you going to tell my parents?"

Chapter 57

MICHAEL'S FATHER AND MOTHER
were immediately contacted at their jobs at
Georgetown University Hospital and the
U.S. Naval Observatory, respectively. The
Ormsons were currently separated, but
they both made it to Foxhall in less than
ten minutes, even with rush-hour traffic
starting to build. The other two Ormson
children, Laura and Anne Marie, had already come home from high school.

Patsy Hampton convinced the parents
to let her talk to their son at the house. She
told the Ormsons that they could be present, and could interrupt, and even stop the
interview anytime they wished. Otherwise,
she and Agent Dwyer would have to take

Michael to FBI headquarters for the interview.

The Ormsons, Mark and Cindy, agreed to let Michael talk. They were clearly frightened, especially of the FBI personnel, but they seemed to trust Detective Hampton. Most people did, she knew. She was pretty and sincere and had a disarming smile that she used when she needed to.

"I'm interested in the game called the Four Horsemen," Hampton said to the boy. "That's the only reason I'm here, Michael. I need your help."

The teenager dropped his chin to his chest again and then shook his head back and forth. Hampton watched the nervous boy and decided to take a chance with him. She had a hunch that she wanted to play.

"Michael, whatever you think you've done wrong, it's nothing to us. It's *nothing.* We don't care what you've done on your computer. This isn't about you or your family *or* your hacking. There have been some terrible murders in Washington, and there might be a connection to this game called the Four Horsemen. Please help us,

Michael. You're the only one who can. You're the only one."

Mark Ormson, who was a radiologist at Georgetown University Hospital leaned forward on the black leather couch in the den. He looked more frightened now than when he'd gotten home. "I'm beginning to think I better get a lawyer," he said.

Patsy Hampton shook her head and smiled kindly at both parents. "This is *not* about your son, Mr. and Mrs. Ormson. He's not in any trouble with us, I assure you."

She turned back to the teenager. "*Michael,* what do you know about the Four Horsemen? We know you're not one of the players. We know it's a very private game."

The boy looked up. She could tell that he liked her, and maybe trusted her some. "Hardly anything, ma'am. I don't know too much."

Hampton nodded. "This is very important to us, Michael. Someone is killing people in the Southeast part of Washington— *for real,* Michael. This is not a fantasy game. I think you can help us. You can save others from getting murdered."

Michael dropped his head again. He had hardly looked at his mother and father since they arrived. "I'm good with computers. You probably already figured that out."

Detective Hampton kept nodding, giving the boy positive reinforcement. "We know you are, Michael. We had trouble tracing you here. You're *very* good with computers. My friend Chuck Hufstedler at the FBI was really impressed. When all this is over, you can see where he works. You'll like him, and you'll love his equipment."

Michael smiled, showing off large, protruding teeth with braces. "Back at the beginning of summer, probably late in June, this guy came into the Gamester's Chatroom—where you found me."

Patsy Hampton tried to hold eye contact with the boy. She needed him badly; she had a feeling that this was a big break, her biggest so far.

Michael continued to speak softly. "He sort of, like he took over the conversation. Actually, he was pretty much a control freak about it. He kept putting down Highlander, D & D, Millennium, all the hot games that are out now. Wouldn't let anybody else get a word in. Almost seemed like he was high on something.

"He kept hinting about this completely different game he played called the Four Horsemen. It was like he didn't want to tell us about it, but then he would give out bits and pieces anyway, but not much. He wouldn't shut up.

"He said the characters in Dungeons and Dragons, Dune, and Condottiere were predictable and boring—which, I must admit, they are sometimes. Then he said some of the characters in his game were *chaotic evil* instead of *lawful good.* He said they weren't fake heroes like in most RPGs; his characters were more like people in real life. They were basically selfish, didn't really care about others, didn't follow society's rules. He said Horsemen was the ultimate fantasy game. That was all he would tell us about the Four Horsemen, but it was enough. I mean, you could see it was a game for total psychos."

"What was his call name?" Agent Dwyer asked Michael.

"Call name, or his real name?" Michael asked, and offered up a sly, superior smile.

Agent Dwyer and Hampton looked at

each other. *Call name, or his real name?* They turned back to Michael.

"I traced him, just like you traced me. I got through his encryptions. I know his name, and I know where he lives. Even where he works. It's Shafer—Geoffrey Shafer. He works at the British Embassy, on Massachusetts Avenue. He's some kind of information analyst there, according to the embassy's Web site. He's forty-four years old."

Michael Ormson looked sheepishly around the room. He made eye contact with his parents, who finally looked relieved. Then he looked back at Hampton. "Is any of that stuff helpful to you? Did I help?"

"Yes, you did, Laughalot."

Chapter 58

GEOFFREY SHAFER had vowed he would not get high on pharmaceuticals tonight. He'd also decided he was going to keep his fantasies under control, under wraps. He understood precisely what the psychobabbling profilers on the murder cases would be thinking: his fantasy life was escalating, and he was approaching a rage state. And the profilers would be exactly right—which was why he was playing it cool for a while.

He was a skillful cook—skilled at a lot of things, actually. He sometimes put together elaborate meals for his family, and even large dinner parties with friends. When he cooked, he liked to have the family with him in the kitchen; he loved an audience, even his wife and kids.

"Tonight we'll be eating classic Thai," he announced to Lucy and the children as they watched him work. He was feeling a little hyper, and reminded himself not to let things get out of hand at home. Maybe he ought to take some Valium before he began to cook. All he'd taken so far was a little Xanax.

"What sets Thai food apart from other Southeast Asian cuisines are the explicit rules for proportions of ingredients, especially seasonings," he said as he prepared a centerpiece of carved vegetables.

"Thai is a distinctive cuisine, blending Chinese, Indonesian, Indian, Portuguese, Malaysian. Bet you didn't know that, Tricia and Erica."

The little girls laughed, confused—so much like their mother.

He put jasmine blossoms in Lucy's hair. Then a blossom each for the twins. He tried the same with Robert, but his son pulled away, laughing.

"Nothing too hot tonight, darling?" Lucy said. "The children."

"The children, of course, dear. Speaking

of hot, the real heat comes from capsaicin, which is stored in the ribs of these chili peppers. Capsaicin is an irritant and burns whatever it touches, even skin, so it's wise to wear gloves. I'm not wearing gloves, of course, because I'm not wise. Also, I'm a little crazy." He laughed. Everyone did. But Lucy looked worried.

Shafer served the dinner himself, without any help, and he announced the name of each dish both in Thai and in English. *"Plaa meuk yaang,* or roast squid. Delicious." *"Mieng kum,* leaf rolls with 'treasures.' Yummy." *"Plaa yaang kaeng phet,* grilled snapper with red curry sauce. Delectable. A *little* hot, though. Hmmm."

He watched them tentatively sample each course; as they tasted the snapper, tears began to run down their faces. Erica began to choke.

"Daddy, it's too hot!" Robert complained, gulping.

Shafer smiled and nodded blithely. He loved this—the flowing tears, his perfect little family in pain. He savored each exquisite moment of their suffering. He'd managed to turn the dinner into a tantalizing game, after all.

At quarter to nine he kissed Lucy and started off on his "constitutional," as he called his nightly disappearing act. He went out to the Jag and drove a few blocks to Phelps Place, a quiet street without many lights.

He took liberal doses of Thorazine *and* Librium, then injected himself with Toradol. He took another Xanax.

Then he went to his doctor's.

Chapter 59

SHAFER DIDN'T LIKE the arrogant, ass-hole doormen at Boo Cassady's building, and they didn't like him, he decided.

Who needed their approval, anyway? They were shiftless, lazy incompetents, in-capable of doing much more than holding open doors and offering up ingratiating smiles to fat-cat tenants.

"I'm here to see Dr. Cassady," Shafer announced to the familiar black wanker with *Mal* jauntily pinned on his lapel. It was probably there so that he wouldn't forget his own name.

"Right," said Mal.

"Isn't that 'Right, *sir*'?"

"Right, sir. I'll ring up Dr. Cassady. Wait right here, sir."

He could hear Boo through the door-man's staticky phone receiver. She had no doubt left explicit instructions that he be let up immediately. She certainly knew he was coming—they'd talked during the car ride from his house.

"You can go up now, sir," the doorman finally said.

"I'm fucking her brains out, Mal," Shafer said. He waltzed to the elevators with a grin. "You watch that door now. Don't let anyone take it."

Boo was in the hallway to meet him when the elevator cruised to a stop on ten. She was wearing at least five thousand dollars' worth of clothes from Escada. She had a great body, but she looked like a bullfighter or a marching-band leader in the gaudy outfit. No wonder her first two husbands had divorced her. The second husband had been a therapist and treating M.D. Still, she was a good, steady mistress who gave much better than she got. More important, she was able to get him Thora-zine, Librium, Ativan, Xanax. Most of the drugs were samples from drug-company representatives; her husband had left them behind when they'd split. The number of "samples" left by the drug reps amazed Shafer, but she assured him it was common practice. She had other "friends" who were doctors, and she hinted to Shafer that they helped her out in return for an occasional fuck. She could get all the drugs he needed.

Shafer wanted to take her right there in the hall, and he knew Boo would like the spontaneity and the passion that were so clearly missing from her life. Not tonight, though. He had more basic needs: the drugs.

"You don't look too happy to see me, Geoff," she complained. She took his face in her manicured hands. Christ, her long, varnished red nails scared him. "What happened, darling? Something's happened. Tell Boo what it is."

Shafer took her in his arms and held her tightly against his chest. She had large soft breasts, great legs, too. He stroked her frosted blond hair and nuzzled her with his chin. He loved the power he had over her —his goddamned shrink.

"I don't want to talk about it just yet. I'm here with you. I feel much better already."

"What happened, darling? What's

312 / JAMES PATTERSON

wrong? You have to share these things with me."

So he made up a story on the spot, acted it out. Nothing to it. "Lucy claims she knows about us. God, she was paranoid *before* I started to see you. Lucy always threatens to destroy my life. She says she'll leave me. Sue for what fucking little I have. Her father will have me fired, then blackball me in the government *and* in the private sector, which he's perfectly capable of doing. The worst thing is, she's poisoning the children, turning them against me. They use the same belittling phrases that she does: 'colossal failure,' 'underachiever,' 'get a real job, Daddy.' Some days I wonder whether it isn't true."

Boo kissed him lightly on the forehead. "No, no, darling. You're well thought of at the embassy. I know you're a loving dad. You just have a bitchy, mean-spirited, spoiled-rotten wife who gets you down on yourself. Don't let her do it."

He knew what she wanted to hear next, so he told her. "Well, I won't have a bitchy wife for much longer. I swear to God I won't, Boo. I love you dearly, and I'm going to leave Lucy soon."

He looked at her heavily made-up face and watched as tears formed and ruined her look. "I love you, Geoff," she whispered, and Shafer smiled as if he were pleased to hear it.

God, he was so good at this.

Lies.

Fantasies.

Role-playing games.

He unbuttoned the front of her mauve silk blouse, fondled her, then carried her inside to the sofa.

"This is my idea of therapy," he whispered hotly in Boo's ear. "This is all the therapy I need."

Chapter 60

I HAD BEEN UP since before five that morning. I had to call Inspector Patrick Busby in Bermuda. I wanted to talk to him every day, sometimes more than once, but I stopped myself.

It would only make things worse, strain my relations with the local police, and signal that I didn't trust them to handle the investigation properly.

"Patrick, it's Alex Cross calling from Washington. Did I catch you at a good time? Can you talk for a moment now?" I asked. I always tried to sound as upbeat as possible.

I wasn't, of course. I had been up pacing the house, and already had breakfast with Nana. Then I'd waited impatiently until

eight-thirty to call Busby at the station
house in Hamilton. He was an efficient
man, and I knew he was there every morning by eight.

I could picture the thin, wiry policeman
as we talked on the phone. I could see the
tidy cubicle office where he worked. And
superimposed over everything, I could still
see Christine on her moped waving good-
bye to me on that perfectly sunny afternoon.

"I have a few things for you from my
contact at Interpol," I said. I told him about
an abduction of a woman on Jamaica earlier in the summer, and another in Barba-
dos; both were similar, though not identi-
cal, to Christine's disappearance. I didn't
think they were connected, really, but I
wanted to give him something, anything.

Patrick Busby was a thoughtful and patient man; he remained silent until I had finished talking before asking his usual quota
of logical questions. I had observed that he
was flawed as an interrogator because he
was so polite. But at least he hadn't given
up.

"I assume that neither abduction was

ever solved, Alex. How about the women who were taken? Were they found?"

"No, neither woman was seen again. Not a sign of them. They're still missing."

He sighed into the phone receiver. "I hope your news is helpful in some way, Alex. I'll certainly call the other islands and check into it further. Anything else from Interpol or the FBI?"

I wanted to keep him on the line—the lifeline, as I now thought of it. "A few far-flung possibilities in the Far East, Bangkok, the Philippines, Malaysia. Women abducted and murdered, all Jane Does. To be honest, nothing too promising at this point."

I imagined him pursing his thin lips and nodding thoughtfully. "I understand, Alex. Please keep giving me whatever you get from your sources. It's difficult for us to get help outside this small island. My calls for assistance frequently aren't returned. I sincerely wish that I had some good news for you on my end, but I'm afraid I don't.

"Other than Perri Graham, no one saw the man with the van. No one seems to have seen Christine Johnson in Hamilton or St. George, either. It's truly a baffling mystery. I don't believe that she ever got to Hamilton. It's frustrating for us, too. My prayers are with you and your wonderful family and, of course, John Sampson."

I thanked Patrick Busby and hung up the phone. I went upstairs and dressed for work.

I still had nothing really substantial on the murder of Frank Odenkirk, and The Jefe was contacting me daily on e-mail. I certainly knew how the Odenkirk family felt. The media heat about the homicide had died down, though, as it often does. Unfortunately, so had the *Post* stories about the unsolved murders in Southeast.

While I was taking a hot shower, I thought about DeWitt Luke and the mysterious "watcher" on S Street. What was the man in the Mercedes doing out there for so long? Did he have some connection with the murders of Tori Glover and Marion Cardinal? None of this was making complete sense to me. That was the truly maddening thing about the Jane Doe murders and the Weasel. He wasn't like other repeat killers. He wasn't a criminal genius like Gary Soneji, but he was effective. *He gets the job done, doesn't he?*

318 / JAMES PATTERSON

I needed to think more about why someone had been lurking outside Tori Glover's apartment. Was he a private detective? A stalker? Or was he actually the murderer? One possibility hit me. Maybe the man in the car was an accomplice of the killer. Two of them, working together? I'd seen that before in North Carolina.

I turned up the water, made it hotter. I thought it would help me to concentrate better. Steam out the cobwebs in my brain. Bring me back from the dead.

Nana began banging on the pipes from downstairs in the kitchen. "Get down here and go to work, Alex. You're using up all my hot water," she yelled above the noise of the shower.

"Last time I looked, my name was on the water and gas bills," I shouted back.

"It's still my hot water. Always was, always will be," Nana replied.

Chapter 61

EVERY DAY, EVERY NIGHT, I was out on the streets of Southeast, working harder than ever, but with nothing much to show for it. I continued to search for the mysterious purple and blue cab, and for the late-model black Mercedes that DeWitt Luke had seen on S Street.

Sometimes I felt as if I were sleepwalking, but I kept at it, sleepwalking as fast as I could. Everything about the investigation seemed a long shot at best. I received tips and leads every day that had to be followed up; none of them went anywhere, though.

I got home at a little past seven that night, and tired as I was, I still let the kids drag me downstairs for their boxing lesson. Damon was showing me a lot of hand speed, and also some pretty good footwork and power for his age. He's always had good spirit, and I was confident that he wouldn't abuse his burgeoning boxing skills at school.

Jannie was more a student of boxing, though she seemed to recognize the value of being able to defend herself. She was quick at mastering techniques, seeing connections, even if her heart wasn't completely in the sport. She preferred to torture her brother and me with her taunts and wit.

"Alex, telephone," Nana called down from the top of the cellar stairs. I looked at my watch, saw it was twenty to eight.

"Practice your footwork," I told the kids. Then I trudged up the steep stone stairs. "Who is it?"

"Wouldn't say who it was," Nana said as I got up to the kitchen. She was making shrimp and corn fritters, and the room was also filled with the glorious smells of honey-baked apples and gingerbread. It was a late dinner for us—Nana had waited until I got home.

I picked up the phone on the kitchen counter. "Alex Cross."

"I know who you are, Detective Cross." I recognized the voice immediately, though I'd heard it only once before—in the Belmont Hotel, in Bermuda. A chill went right through me, and my hands shook.

"There's a pay phone outside the Budget Drugs on Fourth Street. *She's safe for now. We have her.* But hurry. Hurry! Maybe she's on the pay phone right now! I'm serious. *Hurry!*"

Chapter 62

I EXPLODED out the back kitchen door without saying a word to Nana or the kids. I didn't have time to explain where I was going, or why. Besides, I didn't really know exactly what was happening. Had I just spoken to the Weasel?

Hurry! Maybe she's on the pay phone right now! I'm serious.

I sprinted across Fifth Street, then down a side alley and over to Fourth. I dashed another four blocks south toward the Anacostia River. People on the streets watched me running. I was like a tornado suddenly roaring through Southeast.

I could see the metal frame of a pay phone from more than a block away as I approached Budget Drugs. A young girl was leaning against the graffiti-covered wall of the drugstore, talking on the phone.

I pulled out my detective's shield as I raced the final block toward her.

This particular phone gets a lot of use. Some people in the neighborhood don't have phones in their homes.

"Police. I'm a homicide detective. *Get off the phone!*" I told the girl, who looked nineteen or so. She stared at me as if she couldn't care less that a D.C. policeman was trying to commandeer the phone.

"I'm *using* this phone, mister. Don't care who you are. You can wait your turn like everybody else." She turned away from me. "Probably just calling your honey."

I yanked the receiver away from her, disconnected her call.

"The fuck you think you are!" the girl shouted at me, her face screwed up in anger. "I was talking. The fuck you thinking."

"I'm thinking you better get out of my face. This is a life-and-death situation. Get away from this phone. *Now! Get out of here!*" I could see she had no intention of leaving. "There's been a kidnapping!" I was yelling like a madman.

She finally backed away. She was afraid that I was really crazy, and maybe I was.

I stood there with the phone receiver in my hand, trembling, waiting for the call to come in. I was winded. Sweat covered my body.

I stared up and down Fourth Street.

Nothing obvious or suspicious. I didn't see a purple and blue cab parked anywhere. No one watching me. Somebody definitely knew who I was. He had called me at the Belmont Hotel; he had called me at home.

I could still hear the caller's voice echoing loudly inside my head. I'd been hearing that same deep, wretched voice for weeks.

"She's safe for now."

"We have her."

Those were the words spoken to me six weeks before, in Bermuda. I hadn't heard another word from the caller until now.

My heart was pounding, sounding as if it were amplified in my ears. Adrenaline was rushing like powerful rivers through my bloodstream. I couldn't stand this. The caller had stressed that I *hurry.*

A young man approached the pay phone. He stared at my hand on the receiver. "Wuzup, man? I need to use the phone. The phone? You hear me?"

"Police business." I gave him a hard stare. "Take a walk, please. Go!"

"Don't look like no police business to me," he mumbled.

The man moved away, looking over his shoulder as he retreated down Fourth, frowning, but not stopping to argue with me.

The caller liked to be completely in control, I was thinking as I stood there helpless in front of the busy drugstore. He'd made me wait this long since the Bermuda call, possibly to demonstrate his power. Now he was doing it again. What did he really want, though? Why had he taken Christine? *We* have her, he'd said, and he'd repeated the very same words when he called my house. Was there really a *we?* What kind of group did he represent? What did they want?

I stood at the pay phone for ten minutes, fifteen, twenty. I felt as if I were going mad, but I would stay there all night if I had to. I began to wonder if this was the right phone, but I knew it was. He had been crystal-clear, calm, in control.

For the first time in weeks I allowed myself to truly hope that Christine might be alive. I imagined her face, her deep-brown eyes that showed so much love and warmth. Maybe, just maybe, I would be allowed to talk to her.

I let my anger build toward the unknown caller. But then I cut it off, shut down my emotions, and waited with a cool head.

People came and went, in and out of the drugstore. A few wanted to use the phone. They took one look at me and then moved on in search of another phone.

At five minutes to nine, the phone rang. I lifted the receiver instantly.

"This is Alex Cross," I said.

"Yes, I know who you are. That's already been established. Here's what you should do. *Back all the way off. Just back away. Before you lose everything you care about.* It can happen so easily. In a snap. You're smart enough to understand that, aren't you?"

Then the caller hung up. The line was dead.

I banged the phone with the receiver. I cursed loudly. The manager from the drugstore had come outside and was staring at me.

"I'm going to call the police," he said. "That's a public phone." I didn't bother to tell him I *was* the police.

Chapter 63

WAS IT THE WEASEL who had called? Was I dealing with one killer, or more than one?

If only I had some idea who the caller was and who he meant by *we*. The message scared me just as much as the first one had, maybe even more; but it also gave me hope that Christine might still be alive.

With hope came a jolting surge of pain. If only they would put Christine on the phone. I needed to hear her voice.

What did they want? *"Back all the way off."* Back off from what?

The Odenkirk murder case? The Jane Does? Perhaps even Christine's disappearance? Was Interpol or the FBI getting close to something that had scared them? We weren't close to anything that could solve any of the cases, and I knew timing was critical.

Early Wednesday morning, Sampson and I drove to Eckington. A woman over there knew where a purple and blue cab was garaged. We'd followed up a dozen or so leads like this already, but it didn't matter. Every lead had to be investigated, every single one.

"Cab owner's name is Arthur Marshall," I told Sampson as we walked from my car toward a redbrick garden apartment that had seen better days. "Trouble is, Arthur Marshall seems to be a false identity. Landlady has him working at a Target store. According to Target, he doesn't. Never worked at any Target store. Hasn't been seen around for a while, according to the landlady."

"Maybe we spooked him," Sampson said.

"I hope not, but you may be right."

I glanced around at the lower-middle-class neighborhood as we walked. Overhead, the sky was a bright-blue canvas, nearly empty of clouds. The street was packed with one- and two-story homes. Bright-orange fliers were sticking out from the mailboxes. Every window was a possible lookout for the Weasel. *"Back away,"* he had warned. I couldn't. Not after what he'd done. I knew I was taking a risk, though.

He probably spotted us canvassing the streets. If he was responsible for the Jane Doe murders, he had been working undetected for a long while. He was skillful, good at killing, at not getting caught.

The landlady told us what she knew about Arthur Marshall, which wasn't much more than the information she needed to rent him a one-bedroom apartment and the attached garage. She gave us a set of keys for the place and said we could go look for ourselves.

The second house was similar to the landlady's, except that it was painted Easter-egg blue. Sampson and I entered the garage first.

The purple and blue cab was there.

Arthur Marshall had told the landlady that he owned the cab and operated it as a part-time job. That was a possibility, but it seemed unlikely. The Weasel was close. I could feel it now. Had he known we would find the cab? Probably. Now what? What came next? What was his plan? His fantasy?

"I'm going to have to figure out how to get some techies in here," I told Sampson. "There has to be something in the cab, or maybe upstairs in the apartment. Hair, fibers, prints."

"Hopefully no damn body parts," Sampson said, and grimaced. It was typical cop humor, and so automatic that I didn't give it a second thought. "Body parts are always popping up in these cases, Alex. I don't want to see it. I like feet attached to ankles, heads attached to necks, even if all the parts happen to be dead."

Sampson searched around the front seat of the cab with latex-gloved hands. "Papers in here. Candy and gum wrappers, too. Why not call in a favor from Kyle Craig? Get the FBI boys over here."

"Actually, I talked to Kyle last night," I said. "The Bureau's been involved for some time. He'll help out if we say the word."

Sampson tossed me a pair of gloves,

and I examined the cab's backseat. I saw what could be bloodstains in the fabric of the seat cushion. The stains would be easy enough to check out. John and I finally climbed upstairs into the apartment above the garage. It was dusty, grimy, without much furniture. Eerie and unpleasant on the eyes. It didn't look as if anyone lived there, but if someone did, he was really weird. The landlady had said as much.

The kitchen was mostly empty. An expensive juicer was the only personal indulgence. Not a low-end model—*expensive.* I took out my handkerchief and opened the refrigerator. There was nothing in it but bottled water and some aging fruit. The fruit was rotting, and I hated to think of what else we might find here in the apartment.

"Health nut," Sampson offered.

"Nut, anyway," I said. "There's a sense of animal fear in here. He gets very tense, excited, when he comes to this place."

"Yeah," Sampson said. "I know the feeling."

We entered the bedroom, which was furnished with only a small cot, a couple of stuffed chairs, nothing else. The sense of fear was here, too.

I opened the closet door, and what I saw stopped me dead. There was a pair of khaki pants, a blue chambray shirt, a blue blazer—and something else.

"John, come here," I called. "John!"

"Oh, shit. Do I have to? Not more bodies."

"Just come here. It's him. This is the Weasel's place. I'm sure of it. It's worse than a body."

I opened the closet door wider and let Sampson see what I'd found there.

"Shit," he groaned. "*Goddamn* it, Alex."

Someone had put up pictures. Half a dozen black-and-white photographs were taped to the wall of the closet. It wasn't a killer's shrine; it was meant to be found.

There were pictures of Nana, Damon, Jannie, me, and Christine. Christine almost seemed to be smiling at the camera, that incredible smile of hers, those big, welcoming eyes. The pictures had been taken in Bermuda. Whoever had rented this apartment had taken them. Finally, I had something to link Christine's abduction to the murders in Washington. I knew who had taken her.

"Back off.

"Before you lose everything."

I sensed fear again. It was my own.

Chapter 64

PATSY HAMPTON had decided that she wasn't ready to confide in Chief George Pittman just yet. She didn't want The Jefe interfering or crowding her. Also, she flat out didn't trust or like the bastard.

She still hadn't made up her mind what to do about Alex Cross. Cross was a complication. The more she checked him out, the better he looked. He seemed to be a very good, dedicated detective, and she felt bad about keeping Chuck Hufstedler's information away from him. Chuck had been Cross's source first, but she'd used the techie's crush on her to gain an advantage. She didn't like herself for doing that.

She drove her Jeep to the British Embassy late that afternoon. She had Geoffrey Shafer under limited surveillance—hers. She could get more teams, but that would mean going to Pittman now, and she didn't want anyone to know what she had. She didn't want to be crowded.

She had done her preliminary homework on Shafer. He was in the Security Service, which meant he was British intelligence, operating outside England. Most likely he was a spy working out of the embassy on Massachusetts Avenue. His reputation was okay—good, actually. His current assignment supposedly had to do with the British Government's human-rights program, which meant the assignment was bullshit. He lived in Kalorama, a high-rent district, one he couldn't afford on his salary. So who the hell *was* this Shafer chap?

Hampton sat parked in her vehicle outside the embassy on California Street. She smoked a Marlboro Light and started to think things through. She really ought to talk to Cross about where he was with his investigation. Did he know anything that could help? Maybe he was onto Shafer, too? It was almost criminal for her not to contact Cross and share what she'd gotten from Chucky Cheese.

Pittman's dislike for Cross was well known; he considered him competition. She didn't know Cross that well, but he got too many headlines. Still, she wished she knew what Cross had in his files, and especially whether Geoffrey Shafer had appeared on Cross's radar.

There was too much fricking noise on the fricking street near the British Embassy. Workers were doing construction on the Turkish Chancery across California Street. Hampton already had a headache —her life was one big headache—and she wished they would stop pounding and hammering and battering and sawing. For some reason or other, there was a crowd of people swarming all over the National Mosque today.

At a few minutes past five, Shafer got into his Jaguar in a parking lot outside the glass-walled Rotunda.

She'd seen him twice before. He was in very good shape, and attractive, too, though not a physical type she herself responded to. Shafer sure didn't hang around long after the workday ended. Hampton figured he either had someplace to go or really hated his day job. Possibly both.

She stayed a safe distance behind the black Jag, following it along crowded Massachusetts Avenue. Shafer didn't seem to be heading home, and he wasn't going to Southeast, either.

Where are we going tonight? she wondered as she tailed him. *And what does it have to do with the Four Horsemen? What game are you really playing? What are your fantasies?*

Are you a bad man, a murderer, Geoffrey? You don't look like it, blondie. Such a nice, spiffy car for a scumbag killer.

Chapter 65

AFTER WORK, Geoffrey Shafer joined the clogged artery of rush-hour traffic inching along Massachusetts. Turning out of the embassy, he had spotted the black Jeep behind him.

The tail was still there as he drove down Massachusetts Avenue.

Who's in the Jeep? One of the other players? D.C. police? Detective Alex Cross? They've found the garage in Eckington. Now they've found me. It has to be the bloody police.

He watched the black Jeep as it trailed four cars behind him. There was only one person inside, and it looked like a woman. Could it possibly be Lucy? Had she discovered the truth about him? God, had she finally figured out who and what he was?

He picked up his mobile phone and made a call home. Lucy picked up after a couple of rings.

"Darling, I'm coming home, after all. There's a bit of a lull at the office. We can order in or something—unless you and the children already have plans."

She blathered on in her usual maddening way. She and the twins had been going to catch a movie, *Antz,* but they'd rather stay home with him. They could order from Pizza Hut. It would be fun for a change.

"Yes, what fun," Shafer said, and cringed at the thought. Pizza Hut served indigestible cardboard drenched with very bad tomato soup. He hung up, then took a couple of Vicodin and a Xanax. He thought he could feel cracks slowly opening up in his skull.

He made a dangerous U-turn on Massachusetts Avenue and headed toward home. He passed the Jeep going in the opposite direction and was tempted to wave. A woman driver. Now, who was she?

The pizza got to the house at around

seven, and Shafer opened an expensive bottle of Cabernet. He washed down another Xanax with the wine in the downstairs bathroom. Felt a little confused, fuzzy around the edges. That was all right, he supposed.

Jesus Christ, he couldn't stand being with his family, though; he felt as if he were going to crawl out of his skin. Ever since he was a boy in England he'd had a repetitive fantasy that he was actually a reptile and could shed his own skin. He'd had the dream long before he read any Kafka; he *still* had the disturbing dream.

He rolled three dice in his hand as he sipped his wine, played the game at the dinner table. If the number seventeen came up, he would murder them all tonight. He swore he would do it. First the twins, then Robert, and then Lucy.

She kept prattling on and on about her day. He smiled blithely as she told him about her shopping trip to Bloomingdale's and Bath & Body Works and Bruno Cipriani at the mall. He considered the supreme irony of his taking truckloads of antidepressants and only becoming more depressed. Jesus, he was cycling down again. How low could he go?

"Come, seventeen," he finally said aloud.

"What, darling?" Lucy suddenly asked. "Did you just say something?"

"He's already playing tonight's game," said Robert, and snickered. "Right, Daddy? It's your fantasy game. Am I right?"

"Right, son," Shafer replied, thinking, *Christ, I am mad!*

He let the dice gently fall on the dining table, though. He *would* kill them—if their number came up. The dice rolled over and over, then banked off the greasy pizza box.

"Daddy and his games," Lucy said, and laughed. Erica and Tricia laughed. Robert laughed.

Six, five, one, he counted. *Damn, damn.*

"Are the two of us going to play tonight?" Robert asked.

Shafer forced a smile. "Not tonight, Rob Boy. I'd like to, but I can't. I have to go out again."

Chapter 66

THIS WAS GETTING very interesting. Patsy Hampton watched Shafer leave the large and expensive house in Kalorama at around eight-thirty. He was off on another of his nightly jaunts. The guy was a regular vampire.

She knew that Cross and his friends called the killer the Weasel, and it certainly fit Shafer. There was something uncomfortable about him, something bent.

She followed the black Jag, but he didn't head toward Southeast, which disappointed her. He drove to a trendy supermarket, Sutton on the Run, just off Dupont Circle. Hampton knew the pricey store and called it Why Pay Less.

He parked the sports car illegally, then jogged inside. *Diplomatic immunity.* That pissed her the hell off. What a weasel he was, real Euro-trash.

While he was in the market, Hampton made a command decision. She was pretty sure she was going to talk to Alex Cross. She had thought a lot about it, the pros and cons. Now she figured that she might be endangering lives in Southeast by not sharing at least some of what she knew. If someone died, she wouldn't be able to bear it. Besides, Cross would have gotten the information if she hadn't interceded with Chuck Hufstedler.

Shafer shuffled back out of Sutton on the Run and glanced around crowded Dupont Circle. He had a small bag of overpriced groceries clutched in one arm. Groceries for whom, though? He didn't look in the direction of her Jeep, which was just peeking around the corner.

She followed the black Jag at a safe distance in the light traffic. He got onto Connecticut Avenue. She didn't think he'd spotted her, though he was an MI6 man, so she needed to be careful.

Shafer wasn't far from Embassy Row. He wouldn't be going back to work now, would he? Why the groceries if he was headed to the embassy?

The Jaguar eventually turned into the underground garage of a prewar building in Woodley Park. THE FARRAGUT was engraved on a brass sign in front.

Patsy Hampton waited a few minutes, then pulled into the garage behind the Jag. She needed to look around, check things out if she could.

The garage was public-private, so it wasn't any big deal. She walked over to the attendant in the small kiosk and identified herself.

"The Jag that came in before me, ever see it here before?" she asked.

The man nodded. He was around her age, and she could tell he wanted to impress her if he could. "Sure. I don't know him to talk to, though. Comes here to visit a lady on ten. Dr. Elizabeth Cassady. She's a shrink. I assume he's a patient. He's got a funny look in his eyes," the attendant said, "but so do most people."

"How about me?" Hampton asked.

346 / JAMES PATTERSON

"Nah. Well, maybe a little," the attendant said, and grinned.

Shafer stayed upstairs with Dr. Cassady for nearly two hours. Then he came down and went straight back to the house in Kalorama.

Patsy Hampton followed him, then watched the house for another half hour. She thought that Shafer was probably in for the night. She drove to a nearby diner but didn't go inside right away. She picked up her mobile phone before she had too many second thoughts. She knew Cross's street and got the phone number through information. Was it too late to call? Screw it, she was going through with this.

She was surprised when the phone was picked up on the first ring. She heard a pleasant male voice. Nice. Strong.

"Hello. Alex Cross."

She almost hung up on him. Interesting that he'd intimidated her for a moment. "This is Detective Patsy Hampton. I've been doing some work on the Jane Does. I've been following a man who is a suspect. I think we should talk."

"Where are you, Patsy?" Cross said,

without hesitation. "I'll come to you. Just tell me where."

"I'm at the City Limits diner on Connecticut Avenue."

"I'm on my way," said Cross.

Chapter 67

I WASN'T TOTALLY SURPRISED that Pittman had assigned someone to the Jane Does. Especially after Zach Taylor's article in the *Washington Post*. I was interested in any leads Detective Hampton might have turned up.

I had seen Patsy Hampton around, and she obviously knew who I was. She was supposed to be on a fast track; she was a smart and effective senior homicide detective, though from what I'd heard, she was also a lone wolf. She didn't have any friends in the department, as far as I knew.

She was much prettier than I remembered. She was in very trim, athletic shape, probably early thirties, short blond hair, piercing blue eyes that cut through the diner haze.

She'd put on bright-red lipstick for our meeting, or maybe she wore it all the time. I wondered what was on her mind and what her motives were. I didn't think I could trust her.

"You or me first?" Detective Hampton asked, after we'd ordered coffee. We were seated at a table in the City Limits diner, near a window looking out on Connecticut Avenue.

"I'm afraid I don't know what this is about," I told her.

She sipped her coffee and gave me a look over the cup's rim. She was a strong-willed, confident person. Her eyes told me that much.

"You really didn't know someone else was working the Jane Does?"

I shook my head. "Pittman said that the cases were closed. I took him at his word. He suspended some good detectives for working the cases after hours."

"There's a lot of seriously nasty crap going on in the department. So what's new, though?" she said as she set down her cup. She gave a deep sigh. "I thought I could deal with it by myself. Now I'm not so sure."

"Pittman assigned you to the Jane Does? Personally?"

She nodded, then her blue eyes narrowed. "He assigned me to the Glover and Cardinal murders, and any others I wanted to look into. Gave me free rein."

"And you say you have something?"

"Maybe. I've got a possible suspect. He's involved in a role-playing game that features victims' being murdered, mostly in Southeast. It's all after-the-fact stuff, so he could have read the news stories and then fantasized about them. He works at the British Embassy."

This was a new piece of information, and it surprised me. "How far have you gone with this?"

"Not to Pittman, if that's what you mean. I've done a little discreet checking on the suspect. Trouble is, he seems to be a solid citizen. Very good at his job—supposedly. At least that's the official word from the embassy. Nice family in Kalorama. I've been watching Shafer a little, hoping I'd get lucky. His first name is Geoffrey."

I knew that she was supposed to be a

little bit of a loose cannon, and that she didn't suffer fools gladly. "You're out here alone tonight?" I asked her.

Hampton shrugged. "That's how I usually operate. Partners slow me down. Chief Pittman knows how I like to work. He gave me the green light. All green, all day long."

I knew she was waiting for me to give her something—if I had anything. I decided to play along. "We found a cab that the killer apparently used in Southeast. He kept it in a garage in Eckington."

"Anybody see the suspect in the neighborhood?" She asked the right first question.

"The landlady saw him. I'd like to show her pictures of your guy. Or do you want to do it yourself?"

Her face was impassive. "I'll do it. First thing in the morning. Anything revealing in the apartment?"

I wanted to be straight with her. She'd initiated the meeting, after all. "Photographs of me and my family covered a wall in a closet. They were taken of us in Bermuda. While we were on vacation. He was there watching us all the time."

Hampton's face softened. "I heard your

352 / JAMES PATTERSON

fiancée disappeared in Bermuda. Word gets around."

"There were photographs of Christine, too," I said.

Her blue eyes became sad. I got a quick look behind her tough facade. "I'm really sorry about your loss."

"I haven't given up yet," I told her. "Listen, I don't want any credit for solving these cases; just let me help. He called me at home last night. *Somebody* did. Told me to back off. I assume that he meant this investigation, but I'm not supposed to be on it. If Pittman hears about us—"

Detective Hampton interrupted me. "Let me think about everything you've said. You know that Pittman will totally crucify me if he finds out. You have no idea. Trouble is, I don't trust him." Hampton's gaze was intense and direct. "Don't mention any of this to your buddies, or Sampson. You never know. Just let me sleep on it. I'll try to do the right thing. I'm not such a hardass, really. Just a little weird, you know."

"Aren't we all?" I said, and smiled. Hampton was a tough detective, but I felt okay about her. I took something out of my pocket. A beeper.

"Keep this. If you get in trouble or get another lead, you can beep me anytime. If you find something out, please let me know. I'll do the same. If Shafer's the one, I want to talk to him before we bring him in. This *is* personal for me. You can't imagine how personal."

Hampton continued to make eye contact, studying me. She reminded me of someone I'd known a while back, another complicated woman cop, named Jezzie Flanagan. "I'll think about it. I'll let you know."

"All right. Thanks for calling me in on this."

She stood. "You're not in on it yet. Like I said, I'll let you know." Then she touched my hand. "I really am sorry about your friend."

Chapter 68

WE BOTH KNEW I was in, though. We'd made some kind of deal in the City Limits diner. I just hoped I wasn't being set up by Hampton and Pittman or God knows who else.

Over the next two days, we talked four times. I still wasn't sure that I could trust her, but I didn't have a choice. I had to keep moving forward. She had already visited the landlady who'd rented out the apartment and garage in Eckington. The landlady hadn't recognized the pictures of Shafer. Possibly he'd worn a disguise when he met with her.

If Patsy Hampton was setting me up, she was one of the best liars I'd met, and I've known some good ones. During one of

our calls, she confessed that Chuck Hufstedler had been her source, and that
she'd gotten him to keep the information
from me. I shrugged it off. I didn't have the
time or the energy to be angry at either of
them.

In the meantime, I spent a lot of time at
home. I didn't believe the killer would
come after my family, not when he already
had Christine, but I couldn't tell that for
sure. When I wasn't there, I made sure
Sampson or somebody else was checking
on the house.

On the third night after I met her, Patsy
Hampton and I had a breakthrough of
sorts. She actually invited me to join her on
her stakeout of Shafer's town house in
Kalorama Heights.

He had arrived home from work before
six and remained there until just past nine.
He had a nice-looking expat family—three
children, a wife, a nanny. He lived very
well. Nothing about his life or surroundings
suggested that he might be a killer.

"He seems to go out every night around
this time," Hampton told me as we
watched him walk to a shiny black Jag

parked in a graveled driveway at the side of the house.

"Creature of habit," I said. A *weasel.*

"Creature, anyway," she said. We both smiled. The ice was breaking up a little between us. She admitted that she had checked me out thoroughly. She'd decided that Chief Pittman was the bad guy in all of this, not me.

The Jaguar pulled out of the drive, and we followed Shafer to a night spot in Georgetown. He didn't seem to be aware of us. The problem was that we had to catch him doing something; we had no concrete evidence that he was our killer.

Shafer sat by himself at the bar, and we watched him from the street. Did he perch by the window on purpose? I wondered. Did he know we were watching? Was he playing with us?

I had a bad feeling that he was. This was all some kind of bizarre game to him. He left the bar around a quarter to twelve and returned home just past midnight.

"Bastard." Patsy grimaced and shook her head. Her blond hair was soft and had a nice bounce to it. She definitely reminded me of Jezzie Flanagan, a Secret

Service agent I'd worked with on the kidnapping of two children in Georgetown.

"He's in for the night?" I asked. "What was that all about? He leaves the house to watch the Orioles baseball game at a bar in Georgetown?"

"That's how it's been the last few nights. I think he knows we're out here."

"He's an intelligence officer. He knows surveillance. We also know he likes to play fantasy games. At any rate, he's home for the night, so I'm going home, too, Patsy. I don't like leaving my family alone too long."

"Good night, Alex. Thanks for the help. We'll get him. And maybe we'll find your friend soon."

"I hope so."

On the drive home, I thought a little about Detective Patsy Hampton. She struck me as a lonely person, and I wondered why. She was thoughtful and interesting once you got past her tough facade. I wondered if anyone could ever really get through that facade, though.

There was a light on in our kitchen when I rolled into the driveway. I strolled around to the back door and saw Damon and

Nana in their bathrobes at the stove. Everything seemed all right.

"Am I breaking up a pajama party?" I asked as I eased in through the back door.

"Damon has an upset stomach. I heard him in the kitchen, so I came out to get in his way."

"I'm all right. I just couldn't sleep. I saw you were still out," he said. "It's after midnight."

He looked worried, and also a little sad. Damon had really liked Christine, and he'd told me a couple of times that he was looking forward to having a mom again. He'd already begun to think of her that way. He and Jannie missed Christine a whole lot. Twice now they'd had important women taken away from them.

"I was working a little late, that's all. It's a very complicated case, Damon, but I think I'm making progress," I said. I went to the cabinet and took out two tea bags.

"I'll make you tea," Nana offered.

"I can do it," I said, but she reached for the bags, and I let her take them away from me. It doesn't pay to argue with Nana, especially not in her kitchen.

"You want some tea and milk, big guy?" I asked Damon.

"All right," he said. He pronounced it *Ah-yite,* as they do at the playgrounds and probably even at the Sojourner Truth School.

"You sound like that poor excuse for an NBA point guard Allen Iverson," Nana said to him. She didn't much like street slang, never had. She had started off as an English teacher and never lost her love of books and language. She loved Toni Morrison, Alice Walker, Maya Angelou, and also Oprah Winfrey for bringing their books to a wider audience.

"He's the fastest guard in the league, *Grandma Moses.* Shows what you know about basketball," said Damon. "You probably think Magic Johnson is still playing in the league. And *Wilt Chamberlain.*"

"I like Marbury with the Timberwolves, and Stoudamire with Portland, formerly with Toronto," Nana said, and gave a triumphant little smile. *"Ah-yite?"*

Damon laughed. Nana probably knew more about NBA point guards than either of us. She could always get you if she wanted to.

We sat at the kitchen table and drank tea with milk and too much sugar, and we were mostly quiet, but it was kind of nice. I love family, always have. Everything that I am flows from that. Damon yawned and got up from the table. He went to the sink and rinsed out his cup.

"I can probably sleep now," he reported to us. "Give it a try, anyway."

He came back to the table and gave Nana and me a kiss before he went back upstairs to bed. "You miss her, don't you?" he whispered against my cheek.

"Of course I miss Christine," I said to Damon. "All the time. Every waking minute." I didn't make mention of the fact that I had been out late because I was observing the son of a bitch who might have abducted her. Nor did I say anything about the other detective on surveillance, Patsy Hampton.

When Damon left, Nana put her hand in mine, and we sat like that for a few minutes before I went up to bed.

"I miss her, too," Nana finally said. "I'm praying for you both, Alex."

Chapter 69

THE NEXT EVENING at around six, I took off early from work and went to Damon's choir practice at the Sojourner Truth School. I'd put together a good-sized file on Geoffrey Shafer, but I didn't have anything that concretely linked him to any of the murders. Neither did Patsy Hampton. Maybe he was just a fantasy-game player. Or maybe the Weasel was just being more careful since his taxi had been found.

It tore me up to go to the Truth School, but I had to go. I realized how hard it must be for Damon and Jannie to go there every day. The school brought back too many memories of Christine. It was as if I were suffocating, all the breath being squeezed out of my lungs. At the same time, I was in a cold sweat that coated the back of my neck and my forehead.

A little while after the practice began, Jannie quietly reached over and took my hand. I heard her sigh softly. We were all doing a lot more touching and emoting since Bermuda, and I don't think we have ever been closer as a family.

She and I held hands through most of the choir practice, which included the Welsh folk song "All Through the Night," Bach's "My heart ever faithful, sing praises," and a very special arrangement of the spiritual "O Fix Me."

I kept imagining that Christine would suddenly appear at the school, and once or twice I actually turned back toward the archway that led to her office. Of course, she wasn't there, which filled me with inconsolable sadness and the deepest emptiness. I finally cleared my mind of all thought, just shut down, and let my whole self be the music, the glorious sound of the boys' voices.

After we got home from the choir practice, Patsy Hampton checked in with me from her surveillance post. It was a little past eight. Nana and the kids were putting out cold chicken, slices of pears and apples, cheddar cheese, a salad of endive and Bibb lettuce.

Shafer was still home, and of all things, a children's birthday party was going on there, Patsy reported. "Lots of smiling kids from the neighborhood, plus a rent-a-clown called Silly Billy. Maybe we're on the wrong track here, Alex."

"I don't think so. I think our instincts are right about him."

I told her I would come over at around nine to keep her company; that was the time when Shafer usually left the house.

Just past eight-thirty, the phone in the kitchen rang again as we were digging into the cold, well-spiced, delicious chicken. Nana frowned as I picked up the phone.

I recognized the voice.

"I told you to back off, didn't I? Now you have to pay some consequences for disobeying. It's your fault! There's a pay phone at the old Monkey House at the National Zoo. The zoo closes at eight, but you can get in through the gardening-staff gate. Maybe Christine Johnson is there at the zoo waiting for you. You better get over there quick and find out. Run, Cross, run. Hurry! *We have her.*"

The caller hung up, and I charged upstairs for my Glock. I called Patsy Hampton and told her I'd gotten another call, presumably from the Weasel. I'd be at the National Zoo.

"Shafer's still at his kid's birthday party," she told me. "Of course, he could have called from the house. I can see Silly Billy's truck from where I'm parked."

"Keep in contact with me, Patsy. Phones and beepers. Beeper for *emergencies* only. Be careful with him."

"Okay. I'm fine here, Alex. Silly Billy doesn't pose too much of a threat. Nothing will happen at his house. Go to the zoo, Alex. *You* be careful."

Chapter 70

I WAS AT THE NATIONAL ZOO by ten to nine. I was thinking that the zoo was actually pretty close to Dr. Cassady's apartment at the Farragut. Was it just a co-incidence that I was so close to Shafer's shrink? I didn't believe in coincidences anymore.

I called Patsy Hampton before I left the car, but she didn't pick up this time. I didn't beep her—this wasn't an emergency —not so far.

I knew the zoo from lots of visits with Damon and Jannie, but even better from when I was a boy and Nana used to bring me, and sometimes Sampson, who was nearly six feet tall by the time he was eleven. The main entrance to the zoo was at the corner of Connecticut and Haw-thorne avenues, but the old Monkey House was nearly a mile diagonally across the grounds from there.

No one seemed to be around, but the gardening-staff gate was unlatched, as the caller had said it would be. He knew the zoo, too. More games, I kept thinking. He definitely loved to play.

As I hurried into the park, a steep hori-zon of trees and hills blocked out the lights of the surrounding city. There was only an occasional foot lamp for light, and it was eerie and frightening to be in there alone. Of course, I was sure I *wasn't* alone.

The Monkey House was farther inside the gates than I remembered. I finally lo-cated it in the dark. It looked like an old Victorian railway station. Across a cobble-stoned circle there was a more modern structure that I knew was the Reptile House.

A sign over the twin doors of the old Monkey House read: WARNING: QUARANTINE—DO NOT ENTER! More eeriness. I tried the tall twin doors, but they were securely locked.

On the wall beside the doors I saw a

faded blue and white sign, the international pictograph indicating there was a phone inside. *Is that the phone he wants me to use?*

I shook the doors, which were old and wooden and rattled loudly. Inside I could hear monkeys starting to scream and act out. First the smaller primates: spider monkeys, chimpanzees, gibbons. Then the deeper grunt of a gorilla.

I caught sight of a dim red glow across the cobblestoned circle. Another pay phone was over there.

I hurried across the square. Checked my watch. It was two minutes past nine.

He kept me waiting last time.

I thought about his game playing. Was this all a role-playing game to him? How did he win? Lose?

I worried that I wasn't at the right phone. I didn't see any others, but there was always the one locked inside the old Monkey House.

Is that the phone he wants me to use? I felt frantic and hyper. So many dangerous emotions were building up inside me.

I heard a long, sustained *aaaaahhhh,* like

the sound of a football crowd at the opening kickoff. It startled me until I realized it was the apes in the Monkey House.

Was something wrong in there? *An intruder?* Something or someone near the phone?

I waited another five minutes, and then it dragged on to ten minutes. It was driving me crazy. I almost couldn't bear it any longer, and I thought about beeping Patsy.

Then my beeper went off, and I jumped!

It was Patsy. It had to be an emergency.

I stared at the silent pay phone; I waited a half minute or so. Then I snatched it up.

I called the beeper number and left the number of the pay phone. *I waited some more.*

Patsy didn't call me back.

Neither did the mystery caller.

I was in a sweat.

I had to make a decision now. I was caught in a very bad place. My head was starting to reel.

Suddenly the phone rang. I grabbed at it, almost dropped the receiver. My heart was pounding like a bass drum.

"We have her."

"*Where?*" I yelled into the receiver.

"She's at the Farragut, of course."

The Weasel hung up. He never said she was safe.

Chapter 71

I COULDN'T IMAGINE why Christine would be at the Farragut in Washington, but he'd said she was there. Why would he do that if she wasn't? What was he doing to me? To her?

I ran toward where I thought Cathedral Avenue was located. But it was very dark in the zoo, almost pitch-black. My vision was tunneling, maybe because I was close to being in shock. I couldn't think straight.

My mind in a haze, I tripped over a dark slab of rock, went down on one knee. I cut my hands, tore my pants. Then I was up again, running through thick high bushes that grabbed and ripped at my face and arms.

Animals all around the zoo howled,

moaned, bellowed insanely. They sensed that something was wrong. I could make out the sounds of grizzlies and elephant seals. I realized that I had to be approaching Arctic Circle, but I couldn't remember where it was in relation to the rest of the zoo or the city streets.

Up ahead was a high, Gibraltar-like rock. I clambered up it to try to get my bearings.

Down below I saw a cluster of cages, shuttered gift stores and snack bars, two large veldts. I knew where I was now. I hurriedly climbed back down the rock and started to run again. Christine was at the Farragut. Would I finally find her? Could it actually be happening?

I passed African Alley, then the Cheetah Conservation Station. I came to a vast field with what looked like large haystacks scattered everywhere. I realized that they were bison. I was somewhere near Great Plains Way.

The beeper in my pocket went off again. *Patsy! An emergency! Where is she? Why didn't she call back at the pay-phone number I gave her?*

I was soaked in sweat and almost hyperventilating. Thank God I could now see Cathedral Avenue, then Woodley Road up ahead.

I was a long way from where I'd parked my car, but I was close to the Farragut apartment building.

I ran another hundred yards in the dark, then climbed the stone wall separating the zoo from the city streets. There was blood smeared on my hands, and I didn't know where it had come from. The knee I'd scraped? Scratches from swinging branches? I could hear the loud wail of sirens in the near distance. Was it coming from the Farragut?

I headed there in a sprint. It was a little past ten o'clock. Over an hour had already gone by since the call to my house.

The beeper was buzzing inside my shirt pocket.

Chapter 72

SOMETHING BAD HAD HAPPENED at the Farragut. The burping screams of approaching sirens were getting louder as I raced down Woodley. I was reeling, feeling dizzy. I couldn't focus my mind, and I realized that for one of the few times in recent years, I was close to panic.

Neither the police nor the EMS had arrived at the apartment building yet. I was going to be the first on the scene.

Two doormen and several tenants in bathrobes were clustered in front of the underground-garage entrance. It couldn't be Christine. It just couldn't be. I raced across a quadrant of lawn toward them. Was the Weasel here at the Farragut?

They saw me coming and looked as

frightened as I felt inside. I must have been quite a sight. I remembered that I'd fallen once or twice inside the zoo. I probably looked like a madman, maybe even like a killer. There was blood on my hands and who knew where else.

I reached for my wallet, shook it open to expose my detective's shield.

"Police. What's happened here?" I shouted. "I'm a police detective. My name is Alex Cross."

"Somebody has been murdered, Detective," one of the doormen finally said. "This way. Please."

I followed the doorman down the steeply sloped concrete driveway leading into the garage.

"It's a woman," he said. "I'm pretty sure she's gone. I called nine-one-one."

"Oh, God," I gasped out loud. My stomach clutched. Patsy Hampton's Jeep was tucked back in a corner space. The door of the Jeep was open, and light spilled outside.

I felt terrible fear, pain, and shock as I hurried around the door. Patsy Hampton was sprawled across the front seat. I could tell she was probably dead.

"We have her." This was what the message meant. Jesus God, no. They murdered Patsy Hampton. They told me to back off. For God's sake, no.

Her bare legs were twisted and pinned under the steering wheel. Her upper body was crumpled over at almost a right angle. Patsy's head was thrown back and lay partly off the seat, on the passenger's side. Her blond hair was matted with blood. Her vacant blue eyes stared up at me.

Patsy was wearing a white knit sport shirt. There were deep lacerations around her throat; bright-red blood was still oozing from the wound. She was naked below the waist. I didn't see any other clothes anywhere. She might have been raped.

I suspected that she'd been strangled with some kind of wire, and that she'd been dead for only a few minutes. A rope or garotte had been used in some of the Jane Doe murders. The Weasel liked to use his hands, to work close to his victims, possibly to watch and feel their pain—maybe even while he was sexually assaulting them.

I saw what looked like paint chips

around the deep, ugly neck wounds. Paint chips?

Something else seemed very strange to me: the Jeep's radio had been partly dislodged, but left behind. I didn't understand why the radio had been tampered with, but it didn't seem important right now.

I leaned back out of the Jeep. "Is anyone else hurt? Have you checked?"

The doorman shook his head. "No. I don't think so. I'll go look."

Sirens finally screeched inside the garage. I saw red and blue lights flashing and whirling against the ceiling and walls. Some of the tenants had made it into the garage as well. Why did they have to come and gape at this terrible crime?

A very bad thought flashed in my head. I climbed out of the Jeep, grabbing Patsy's keys out of the ignition. I hurried around to the back. I pushed the release, and the rear door came open. My heart was thundering again. I didn't want to look inside, but when I did, there was nothing. *Jesus, Jesus, Jesus. "We have her!" Is Christine here, too? Where?*

I looked around the garage. Up near the entrance I spotted Geoffrey Shafer's sports car, the black Jaguar. He was here at the Farragut. Patsy must have followed him.

I ran across the garage to the Jag. I felt the hood, then the exhaust pipe. Both were still warm. The car hadn't been in the garage very long. The doors were locked. I couldn't break in. I was all too aware of the search-and-seizure constraints.

I stared inside the Jaguar. In the backseat I could see dress shirts on wire hangers. The hangers were white, and I thought of the chips in Detective Hampton's wounds. Had he strangled her with a hanger? Was Shafer the Weasel? Was he still in the building? What about Christine? Was she here, too?

I said a few words to the patrolmen who'd just arrived, the first on the scene after me. Then I took them with me.

The helpful doorman told me which floor Shafer's therapist's apartment was on. The number was 10D, the penthouse. Like all buildings in D.C., the Farragut was restricted to a height no greater than that of the Capitol dome.

I took the elevator with the two uniformed cops, both in their twenties and both scared shitless, I'd bet. I was close to rage. I knew I had to be careful; I had to act professionally, to control my emotions somehow. If there was an arrest, there would be questions to answer, such as what I was doing here in the first place. Pittman would be on my case in a second.

I talked to the policemen on the way up, more to calm myself than anything else.

"You okay, Detective?" one of them asked me.

"I'm fine. I'm all right. The killer might still be in the building. The victim was a detective, one of our own. She was on surveillance here. The suspect has a relationship with a woman upstairs."

The faces of both young cops tightened. It was bad enough to have seen the murdered woman in her car, but to learn that she was a policewoman, a detective on surveillance, made it worse. Now they were about to confront a cop killer.

We hurried out of the elevator to apartment 10D. I led the way and pressed the bell. I saw what appeared to be drops of blood on the hallway carpet near the door. I noticed the blood on my hands, saw the two cops staring at the blood.

No answer from inside the apartment, so I pounded my fist on the door. Was everyone okay in there? "Police, open up! D.C. police!"

I could hear a woman shouting inside. I had my Glock out, the safety off. I was angry enough to kill Shafer. I didn't know if I could hold myself back.

The uniformed patrolmen took their pistols out of their holsters, too. After just a few seconds I was ready to kick down the door, search-and-seizure constraints or no. I kept seeing Patsy Hampton's face, her dead, vacant eyes, the savage wounds in her crushed throat.

Finally, the door to the apartment slowly opened.

A blond woman was standing there—Dr. Cassady, I assumed. She wore an expensive-looking light-blue suit with lots of gold buttons, but she was barefoot. She looked frightened and angry.

"What do you want?" she demanded. "What the hell is going on here? Do you know what you've done? You've interrupted a therapy session."

Chapter 73

GEOFFREY SHAFER stepped into the doorway and stood a few feet behind his irate therapist. He was tall and imposing and very blond. *He's the Weasel, isn't he?*

"What the hell's the problem here? Who are you, sir, and what do you want?" he asked in a clipped English accent.

"There's been a murder," I said. "I'm Detective Cross." I showed them my badge. I kept looking past Shafer and Dr. Cassady, trying to spot something that would give me probable cause to come inside the apartment. There were lots of plants on the sills and hanging in windows —philodendron, azalea, English ivy. Dhurrie rugs in light pastels, overstuffed furniture.

"No. There's certainly no murderer here," the therapist said. "Leave this instant."

"You should do as the lady says," Shafer said.

Shafer didn't look like a murderer. He was dressed in a navy suit, a white shirt, a moiré tie, a pocket square. Impeccable taste. Completely unruffled and unafraid.

Then I glanced down at his shoes. I almost couldn't believe it. The gods had finally smiled on me.

I pointed my Glock at Shafer. At the Weasel. I went up to him and bent down on one knee. My whole body was trembling. I examined the right leg of his trousers.

"What the *hell* are you doing?" he asked, pulling away from me. "This is completely absurd.

"I'm with the British Embassy," Shafer then stated. "I repeat, I'm with the British Embassy. You have no rights here."

"Officers," I called to the two patrolmen who were still outside the door. I tried to act calm, but I wasn't. "Come here and look. You see this?"

Both patrolmen moved closer to Shafer. They entered the living room.

"Stay out of this apartment!" The therapist raised her voice close to a scream.

"Remove your trousers," I said to Shafer. "You're under arrest."

Shafer lifted his leg and gave a look. He saw a dark stain, Patsy Hampton's blood, smudged on the cuff of his trousers. Fear shot through his eyes, and he lost his cool.

"You put that blood there! You did it," he yelled at me. He pulled out an identification badge. "I am an official at the British Embassy. I don't have to put up with this outrage. I have diplomatic immunity. I will not take off my trousers for you. Call the embassy immediately! *I demand diplomatic immunity.*"

"Get out of here now!" Dr. Cassady yelled loudly. Then she pushed one of the patrolmen.

It was just what Shafer needed. He broke free and ran back through the living room. He rushed into the first room down the hallway, slammed the door, and locked it.

The Weasel was trying to get away. It couldn't happen; I couldn't let it. I got to the door seconds behind him. "Come out of there, Shafer! You're under arrest for the murder of Detective Patsy Hampton.''

Dr. Cassady came screaming down the hall after me.

I heard the toilet flush in the bathroom. No, no, no! I reared back powerfully and kicked in the door.

Shafer was pulling off his trousers, standing on one leg. I tackled him hard, knocked him over, then held him facedown against the tile floor. He screamed curses at me, flailed his arms, bucked his lower body. I pushed his face harder into the floor.

The therapist tried to pull me off Shafer. She was scratching my face, pounding my back with her fists. It took both policemen to restrain her.

"You can't do this to me!" Shafer was yelling at the top of his voice, twisting and turning beneath me, a powerful stallion of a man.

"This is illegal. I have diplomatic immunity!"

I turned to one of the officers.

"Cuff him."

Chapter 74

IT WAS A LONG and very sad night at the Farragut, and I didn't leave until past three. I had never lost a partner before, though I had once come close with Sampson, in North Carolina. I realized that I'd already come to think of Patsy Hampton as a partner, and a friend. At least we had the Weasel in custody.

I slept in the next morning, allowing myself the small luxury of not setting the alarm. Still, I was wide awake by seven. I'd been dreaming about Patsy Hampton, and also about Christine—different, vivid scenes with each of them, the kind of frenetic dreams where you wake up feeling as tired as when you went to bed. I said a prayer for both of them before I finally rolled out of bed. We had the Weasel. Now I had to get the truth out of him.

I slipped on a somewhat worn white satin robe. Muhammad Ali had worn it in his training camp in Manila before the Joe Frazier fight. Sampson had given it to me for my fortieth birthday. He appreciated the fact that while most people would treat the robe as some kind of sacred exhibit in their house, I routinely wear it to breakfast.

I love the old robe, which is unusual for me since I'm not particularly into mementos and souvenirs. Maybe part of it is that I'm supposed to resemble Ali physically, or so people tell me. Maybe I'm a little better looking, but he's definitely the better man.

When I got down to the kitchen, Nana and the kids were sitting at the table watching the small portable TV that she keeps there but doesn't use very often. She prefers to read or chitchat and, of course, cook.

"Ali." Jannie looked up at me and grinned, but then her eyes went back to the TV. "You should watch this, Daddy."

Nana muttered into her cup of tea. "Your British murderer is all over the news this morning. TV and the newspaper, too. 'Diplomatic Immunity May Bar Prosecution of British Embassy Suspect,' 'Spy Linked to Detective Slay.' They already interviewed people in Union Station and on Pennsylvania Avenue. Everybody's mad as a hatter about this diplomatic-immunity disgrace, as they call it. It's just terrible."

"I'm mad. It's not right," Damon said. "Not if he did it. Did he, Dad? Did he do it?"

I nodded. "He did it." I poured milk into my coffee. I wasn't quite ready to deal with Geoffrey Shafer, or the kids, or especially the horrible, senseless murder the night before. "Anything else on the news?"

"The Wizards kicked butt," Damon said with a straight face. "Rod Strickland had a double-double."

"*Shhhh.*" Nana gave us both a mighty look of irritation. "CNN carried stories *from London.* The media there is already comparing this to that unfortunate nanny case in Massachusetts. They say that Geoffrey Shafer is a decorated war hero and that he claims, with good reason, that he was framed by the police. I assume that means you, Alex."

"Yes, it does. Let's watch CNN for a few minutes," I said. Nobody objected, so I switched the channel. A hard knot was forming in my stomach. I didn't like what I was seeing and hearing on TV.

Almost immediately, a reporter came on the screen from London. He introduced himself and then proceeded to give a pompous, thirty-second summary of the previous evening's events.

The reporter looked gravely into the camera. "And now, in a dramatic turn-about, we have learned that the Washington Police Department is investigating a bizarre twist. The senior detective who arrested Geoffrey Shafer might himself be a suspect in the murder case. At least that's what has been reported in the American press."

I shook my head and frowned. "I'm innocent," I said to Nana and the kids. They knew that, of course.

"Until proven guilty," said Jannie, with a little wink.

Chapter 75

THERE WAS A LOUD HUBBUB out in front of the house, and Jannie ran to the living-room window to look. She hurried back to the kitchen with wide eyes, loud-whispering, "It's TV cameras and the newspapers outside. CNN, NBC—lots of them, like that other time, with Gary Soneji. Remember?"

"Of course we remember," said Damon. "Nobody's retarded in this house except you."

"Oh, good Lord, Alex," Nana said, "don't they know decent people are eating breakfast?" She shook her head, rolled her eyes. "The vultures are here again. Maybe I should throw some meat scraps out the front door."

"*You* go talk to them, Jannie," I said, and looked back at the TV. I don't know why I was feeling so cynical, but I was. My remark quieted her down for a half second, but then she figured it was a joke. She pointed a finger at herself. "Gotcha!"

I knew they wouldn't go away, so I took my mug of coffee and headed toward the front door. I walked out into a beautiful fall morning, temperature probably in the low sixties.

Leaves rustled merrily in the elm and maple trees, dappled sunshine fell on the heads of the TV crew and print journalists gathered at the edges of our front lawn.

The vultures.

"Don't be absurd and ridiculous around here," I said, and then calmly sipped my coffee as I stared at the noisy press mob. "Of course I didn't kill Detective Patsy Hampton, or frame anyone for her murder."

Then I turned on my heel and walked back inside without answering a single question from any of them.

Nana and the kids were right behind the big wooden door, listening. "That was pretty good," Nana said, and her eyes sparkled and beamed.

I went upstairs and got dressed for work. "Go to school. *Now!*" I called back to Jannie and Damon. "Get straight A's. Play nicely with your friends. Pay no attention to the craziness everywhere around you."

"Yes, Daddy!"

Chapter 76

ON ACCOUNT OF HIS REQUEST for diplomatic immunity, we weren't allowed to question Geoffrey Shafer about Detective Hampton's murder or anything else. I was incredibly frustrated. We had the Weasel, and we couldn't get to him.

Investigators were lying in wait for me that morning at the station house, and I knew it was going to be a long and excruciating day. I was interviewed by Internal Affairs, by the city's chief counsel, and also by Mike Kersee from the district attorney's office.

Pay no attention to the craziness everywhere around you, I reminded myself over and over, but my own good advice wasn't working too well.

Around three o'clock, the district attorney himself showed up. Ron Coleman is a tall, slender, athletic-looking man; we had worked together many times when he was coming up in the D.A.'s office. I had always found him to be conscientious, well informed, and committed to rationality and sanity. He'd never seemed very political, so it had come as a shock to almost everyone when Mayor Monroe appointed him the D.A. Monroe loves to shock people, though.

Coleman made an announcement: "Mr. Shafer already has an attorney, and he is one of the bright stars of our galaxy. He has retained none other than Jules Halpern. Halpern's probably the one who planted the story that you're a suspect—which you aren't, as far as I know."

I stared at Coleman. I couldn't believe what I'd just heard. "As far as you know? What does that mean, Ron?"

The D.A. shrugged. "We're probably going to go with Cathy Fitzgibbon on our side. I think she's our best litigator. We'll back her up with Lynda Cole and maybe Stephen Apt, who are also top-notch. That's my take on it as of this morning."

I knew all three prosecutors, and they had good reputations, particularly Fitzgibbon. They were on the young side, but nonetheless tireless, smart, dedicated—a lot like Coleman himself.

"You sound like you're preparing for a war, Ron."

He nodded. "As I said, Jules Halpern is Shafer's defense attorney. He rarely loses. In fact, I don't know if he's ever lost a big case like this one. He turns down all the losers, Alex."

I looked directly into Coleman's dark eyes. "We have Patsy Hampton's blood on the killer's clothes. We have blood in the bathroom drain, and I bet we'll have Shafer's fingerprints somewhere in Hampton's car before the end of the day. We may have the wire hanger he used to strangle her. Ron?"

"Yes, Alex. I know what you're going to say. I know your question. It's the same one I have."

"Shafer *has* diplomatic immunity. So why bring in Jules Halpern?"

"That's a very good goddamn question we both came up with. I suspect Halpern's been hired to get us to drop the charges completely."

"We have substantial evidence. He was *washing Patsy Hampton's blood* off himself in the bathroom. There's residue in the sink."

Coleman nodded and shrank back into his easy chair. "I don't understand why Jules Halpern is involved. I'm sure we'll know before too long, though."

"I'm *afraid* we'll know soon," I said.

I decided to leave the station by the back way that night, just in case there was press lying in wait out front on Alabama Avenue. As I stepped outside, a small balding man in a light-green suit popped out from behind the adjacent stone wall.

"That's a good way to get yourself shot," I told him. I was only half kidding.

"Occupational hazard," he lisped. "Don't shoot the messenger, Detective."

He smiled thinly as he handed me a white letter-sized envelope. "Alex Cross, you've hereby been served with a Summons and Complaint. Have a nice night, Detective," he said in his sibilant whine. Then he walked away as surreptitiously as he'd appeared.

I opened the envelope and quickly scanned the letter. I groaned. Now I knew why Jules Halpern had been retained, and what we were up against.

I had been named in a civil suit for "false arrest" and "defamation of the character of Colonel Geoffrey Shafer." The suit was for fifty million dollars.

Chapter 77

THE NEXT MORNING I was summoned to the District of Columbia Law Department offices downtown. This was not good, I decided. The city's chief counsel, James Dowd, and Mike Kersee from the D.A.'s office were already ensconced in red-leather club chairs.

So was Chief of Detectives Pittman, who was putting on quite a show from his front-row seat. "You mean to tell me that because Shafer has diplomatic immunity he can avoid criminal prosecution in criminal court? But he can traipse right into our *civil* court and get protection against false arrest and defamation?"

Kersee nodded and made clucking noises with his tongue and teeth. "Yessirreebob, that's it exactly. Our ambassadors and their staffs enjoy the same kind of immunity in England and everywhere else around the world. No amount of political pressure will get the Brits to waive immunity. Shafer is a war hero from the Falklands. Supposedly he's also pretty well respected inside the Security Service, though lately he seems to have been in some trouble."

"What kind of trouble?" I asked.

"They won't tell us."

Pittman was still badgering the lawyers. "What about that clown from the Baltic Embassy? The one who wiped out the sidewalk café? *He* went to trial."

Mike Kersee shrugged. "He was just a low-level staffer from a low-level country that we could threaten. We can't do that with England."

"Why the hell not?" Pittman frowned and thumped his hand hard against the arm of his chair. "England isn't worth shit anymore."

The phone on Dowd's desk rang, and he raised his hand for quiet. "That's probably Jules Halpern. He said he'd call at ten, and he's an efficient bastard. If it is him, I'll put him on the speaker box. This should be about as interesting as a rectal exam done with a cactus."

Dowd picked up and exchanged pleasantries with the defense attorney for about thirty seconds. Then Halpern cut him off. "I believe we have matters of substance to discuss. My schedule is rather tight today. I'm sure you're hard pressed as well, Mr. Dowd."

"Yes, let's get down to business," Dowd said, raising his thick, curly black eyebrows. "As you know, the police have a qualified privilege to arrest anyone if they have probable cause. You simply don't have a civil case, Counselor—"

Halpern interrupted Dowd before he had finished speaking. "*Not* if that person identifies himself from the outset as having diplomatic immunity, which my client did. Colonel Shafer stood in the doorway of his *therapist's* apartment, waving his British Security Service shield like a stop sign and saying that he had immunity."

Dowd sighed loudly into the phone. "There was blood on his trousers, Counselor. He's a murderer, Counselor, *and* a cop killer. I don't think I need to say any more on the subject. With respect to the alleged defamation, the police also have a qualified privilege to talk to the press when a crime has been committed."

"And I suppose that the chief of detectives' statement in front of reporters—and several hundred million others around the world—isn't slander per se?"

"That's correct, it isn't. There's a qualified privilege with respect to public figures such as your client."

"My client is not a *public* figure, Mr. Dowd. He is a very private individual. He is an intelligence agent. His very livelihood, if not his life, depends on his being able to work undercover."

The chief counsel was already exasperated, possibly because Halpern's responses were so calm, yet always delivered rapid-fire. "All right, Mr. Halpern. So why are you calling us?"

Halpern paused long enough to make Dowd curious. Then he began again. "My client has authorized me to make a very unusual offer. I have strongly advised him against it, but he maintains his right to do so."

Dowd looked startled. I could tell that he

hadn't been expecting any kind of deal offer. Neither had I. What was this about?

"Go ahead, Mr. Halpern," said Dowd. His eyes were wide and alert as they roamed around the room looking at us. "I'm listening."

"I'll bet you are, and all your esteemed colleagues as well."

I leaned forward to hear every word.

Jules Halpern continued with the real reason for his call: "My client wants all possibility of a civil case being brought against him waived."

I rolled my eyes. Halpern wanted to make certain that no one could sue his client in civil court after the criminal court case was concluded. He remembered that O. J. Simpson had been set free in the one court only to be bankrupted in the other.

"Impossible!" said Dowd. "There's no way in hell that will ever happen. No way."

"Listen to me. There *is* a way, or I wouldn't have broached the subject. If this is done, and if he and I can be convinced of a speedy route for a criminal trial, my client will *waive diplomatic immunity.* Yes, you heard me correctly. Geoffrey Shafer wants to prove his innocence in a court of law. He insists on it, in fact."

Dowd was shaking his head in disbelief. So was Mike Kersee. His eyes were glazed with astonishment as he glanced across the room at me.

None of us could believe what we had just heard from the defense attorney.

Geoffrey Shafer wanted to go to trial.

Book Four

TRIAL AND ERRORS

Chapter 78

CONQUEROR HAD WATCHED her work High Street in Kensington for nearly six weeks. She became his obsession, his fantasy woman, his "game piece." He knew everything there was to know about her. He felt—he knew—that he was starting to act like Shafer. They all were, weren't they?

The girl's name was Noreen Anne, and a long time ago—*three years,* to be exact—she had traveled to London from Cork, Ireland, with lovely dreams of being a fashion model on the world stage.

She was seventeen then, nearly five-ten, slender, blond, and with a face that all the boys and even the older men back home told her was destined for magazine covers, or maybe even the cinema.

So what was she doing here on High Street at half past one in the morning? She wondered about it as she forced a coquettish smile and occasionally waved a hand at the leering men in their slowly passing cars that made the rounds of High Street, DeVere Gardens, Exhibition Road.

They'd thought she was pretty, all right —just not pretty enough for British or American magazine covers, and not good enough, not classy enough, to marry or have as a girlfriend.

Well, at least she had a plan, and she thought it was a good one. Noreen Anne had saved nearly two thousand quid since she began to walk the streets. She thought she needed another three thousand or so, and then she would head back to Ireland. She'd start a small beauty shop, because she did know the secrets of beauty, and also a lot about the dreams.

So, here I am in front of the Kensington Palace Hotel in the meantime, she thought. *Freezing my fine bum off.*

"Excuse me, miss," she heard, and

turned with a start. She hadn't heard anyone come up on her.

"I couldn't help noticing you standing
here. You're an extraordinary beauty. But
of course you know that, don't you?"

Noreen Anne felt relief the moment she
saw who it was. This one wouldn't hurt
her, couldn't if he tried. She could hurt *him,*
if it came to that.

He was old, in his late sixties or seventies; he was obscenely fat; and he was
seated in a wheelchair.

And so she went off—with Conqueror.

It was all part of the game.

Chapter 79

THE AMERICANS had promised a speedy route to trial, and the fools had actually delivered.

Five months had passed since the murder of Detective Patsy Hampton. Alex Cross had been shuttling back and forth to Bermuda, but he still had no idea where Christine had disappeared to. Shafer was out of jail but on a very short leash. He hadn't played the game once since Hampton's murder. The game of games had been on hold, and it was driving him mad.

Now Shafer sat in his black Jag in the parking lot directly under the courthouse, feeling hopeful. He was eager to stand trial on the count of Aggravated, Premeditated Murder in the First Degree. The rules of play had been established, and he appreciated that.

The suppression hearing weeks before was still a vivid memory for him. He'd relished every minute of it. The preliminary hearing was held before the jury selection, to determine what evidence would be allowed at the trial; it took place in the spacious chambers of Judge Michael Fescoe. The judge set the rules, so in a way he was the gamemaster. How fabulously droll, how delicious.

Shafer's lawyer, Jules Halpern, argued that Shafer had been in a therapy session at Dr. Cassady's home-office, and therefore had every right to privacy. "That privacy was violated. First, Dr. Cassady refused to let Detective Cross and the other officers come inside. Second, Colonel Shafer showed his identification to the detective. It proved that he was with the British Embassy and had diplomatic immunity. Cross barged into the therapist's office anyway. Consequently, any evidence obtained—if indeed any evidence *was* obtained—is the result of unlawful search."

Judge Fescoe took the rest of the day to consider, then announced his decision the next morning. "As I listened to both sides, it seemed to me that the issues were straightforward and not all that unusual in a murder case. Mr. Shafer does indeed have diplomatic immunity. However, it is my opinion that Detective Cross acted in a reasonable and lawful manner when he went to Dr. Cassady's apartment. He suspected that a grave crime had been committed. Dr. Cassady opened the door, allowing Detective Cross plain view of Mr. Shafer's attire. Colonel Shafer has insisted all along that his diplomatic immunity denied Detective Cross permission to enter the premises.

"I am therefore going to allow the prosecution to use the clothing Colonel Shafer was wearing on the night of the murder, as well as the blood on the carpet outside the apartment door, as evidence.

"The prosecution may also use any evidence found in the parking garage, both in Detective Hampton's car and in Colonel Shafer's," Judge Fescoe continued, and this was the key part of his ruling: "I will *not allow* evidence found once Detective Cross entered the apartment against the stated wishes of both Colonel Shafer and

Dr. Cassady. Any and all evidence discovered during the initial or subsequent searches is suppressed and will not be allowed at the trial."

The prosecution was also told not to make any reference, during the trial, to any other uncharged murders that Shafer was suspected of having committed in Washington. The jury was to understand that Shafer was under investigation only for the murder of Senior Detective Patricia Hampton. Both the prosecution and the defense claimed victory at the end of the suppression hearing.

The stone steps outside the courthouse were swarming with a buzzing, unruly crowd on the morning of the first day. Shafer's "supporters" were wearing UK/OK buttons and waving crisp, new Union Jacks. These wondrous fools made him smile as he clasped both hands high over his head in victory. He enjoyed being a hero immensely.

What a glorious time. Even if he *was* a little high and spacey on a few choice pharmaceuticals.

Both sides were still predicting "slam

dunk" victories. Lawyers were such fabulous bullshitters.

The press was touting the outrageous charade as the "criminal trial of the decade." The media hype, expected and ritualistic, thrilled him anyway. He internalized it as tribute and adulation. His due.

He purposely cut quite a dashing figure; he wanted to make an impression—on the world. He wore a soft-shouldered, tailored gray suit, a striped bespoke shirt from Budd, and black oxfords from Lobb's, St. James's. He was photographed a hundred times in the first few moments alone.

He walked into the courthouse as if in a dream. The most delicious thing of all was that he might lose everything.

Courtroom 4 was on the third floor. It was the largest in the building. Closest to the double set of public doors was a gallery that held around a hundred and forty spectators. Then came the "bar area," where the attorneys' tables were situated. Then the "judge's bench," which took up about a quarter of the room.

The trial began at ten in the morning, and it was all a rattle and hum to him. The lead prosecutor was Assistant U.S. Attorney Catherine Marie Fitzgibbon. He already yearned to murder her, and wondered if he possibly could. He wanted Ms. Fitzgibbon's scalp on his belt. She was just thirty-six, Irish Catholic, single, sexy in her tight-assed way, dedicated to high-minded ideals, like so many others from her island of origin. She favored dark-blue or gray Ann Taylor wardrobes and wore a ubiquitous tiny gold cross on a gold chain. She was known in the D.C. legal community as the Drama Queen. Her melodramatic telling of the gory details was meant to win the sympathy of the jury. A worthy opponent indeed. A worthy prey as well.

Shafer sat at the defendant's table and tried to concentrate. He listened, watched, felt as he hadn't in a long time. He knew they were all watching him. How could they not?

Shafer sat there observing, but his brain was on fire. His esteemed attorney, Jules Halpern, finally began to speak, and he heard his own name. That piqued his interest, all right. He was the star here, wasn't he?

Jules Halpern was little more than five-four, but he cut quite a powerful figure in a court of law. His hair was dyed jet-black and slicked back tightly against his scalp. His suit was from a British tailor, just like Shafer's. Shafer thought, rather uncharitably, he supposed, *Dress British, think Yiddish.* Seated beside Halpern was his daughter, Jane, who was second chair. She was tall and slender, but with her father's black hair and beaked nose.

Jules Halpern certainly had a strong voice for such a slight and small fellow. "My client, Geoffrey Shafer, is a loving husband. He is also a very good father, and happened to be attending a birthday party for two of his children half an hour *before* the murder of Detective Patricia Hampton.

"Colonel Shafer, as you will hear, is a valued and decorated member of the British intelligence community. He is a former soldier with a fine record.

"Colonel Shafer was clearly set up for this murder charge because the Washington police *needed* this terrible crime to be solved. This I will prove to you, and you will have no doubt of it. Mr. Shafer was framed because a particular homicide detective was going through some bad personal times and lost control of the situation.

"Finally—and this is the most essential thing for you to remember—Colonel Shafer *wants* to be here. He isn't here because he has to be; he has diplomatic immunity. Geoffrey Shafer is here to clear his good name."

Shafer nearly stood up in the courtroom and cheered.

Chapter 80

I PURPOSELY, and probably wisely, skipped the first day, then the second and the third day, of the courtroom circus. I didn't want to face the world press, or the public, any more than I had to. I felt like I was on trial, too.

A cold-blooded murderer was on trial, but the investigation continued more feverishly than ever for me. I still had the Jane Does to solve, and the disappearance of Christine, if I could open up any new leads. I wanted to make certain that Shafer would not walk away a free man, and most important, I desperately wanted finally to know the truth about Christine's disappearance. I had to know. My greatest frustration was that because of the diplomatic shenanigans, I had never gotten to question Shafer. I would have given anything for a few hours with him.

I turned the southern end of our attic into a war room. There was an excess of unused space up there, anyway. I moved an old mahogany dining table out from the shadows. I rewired an ancient window fan, which made the attic space almost bearable most days—especially early in the morning and late in the evening, when I did my best work up there—in my hermitage.

I set up my laptop on the table, and I pinned different-colored index cards to the walls, to keep what I considered the most important pieces of the case before me at all times. Inside several bulky and misshapen cardboard boxes, I had all the rest of it: every scrap of evidence on Christine's abduction, and everything I could find on the Jane Does.

The murder cases formed a maddening puzzle created over several years, one that was not given to easy solutions. I was trying to play a complex game against a skillful opponent, but I didn't know the rules of his game, or how it was played. That was Shafer's unfair advantage.

I had found some useful notes in Patsy Hampton's detective logs, and they led me to interview the teenage boy, Michael Ormson, who'd chatted on-line with Shafer about the Four Horsemen. I continued to work closely with Chuck Hufstedler of the FBI. Chuck felt guilty about giving Patsy Hampton the original lead, especially since I'd come to him first. I used his guilt.

Both the Bureau and Interpol were doing an active search of the game on the Internet. I'd visited countless chatrooms myself, but had encountered no one, other than young Ormson, who was aware of the mysterious game. It was only because Shafer had taken a chance and gone into the chatroom that he'd been discovered. I wondered what other chances he'd taken.

Following Shafer's arrest at the Farragut, we did a little search on his Jaguar, and I'd also spent nearly an hour at his home— before his lawyers knew I was there. I spoke to his wife, Lucy, and his son, Robert, who confirmed that he played a game called the Four Horsemen. He had been playing for seven or eight years.

Neither the wife nor the son knew any of the other players, or anything about them.

They didn't believe that Geoffrey Shafer had done anything wrong.

The son called his father the "straight arrow of straight arrows." Lucy Shafer called him a good man, and she seemed to believe it.

I found role-playing game magazines as well as dozens of sets of game dice in Shafer's den, but no other physical evidence relating to his game. Shafer was careful; he covered his tracks well. He was in intelligence, after all. I couldn't imagine him throwing dice to select his victims, but maybe that helped to account for the irregular pattern of the Jane Does.

His attorney Jules Halpern complained loudly and vigorously about the invasion of Shafer's home, and had I uncovered any useful evidence, it would certainly have been suppressed. Unfortunately, I didn't have enough time, and Shafer was too clever to keep anything incriminating in his house, anyway. He'd made one big mistake; he wasn't likely to make another. Was he?

Sometimes, very late at night, as I worked in the attic, I would stop for a while and remember something about Christine. The memories were painful and sad, but also soothing to me. I began to look forward to these times when I could think about her without any interruption. Some nights, I would wander down to the piano in the sun porch and play songs that had been important to us—"Unforgettable," "Moonglow," " 'S Wonderful." I could still remember how she'd looked, especially when I visited at her place—faded jeans, bare feet, T-shirt or maybe her favorite yellow crewneck sweater, a tortoiseshell comb in her long hair that always smelled of shampoo.

I didn't want to feel sorry for myself, but I just couldn't help feeling miserably bad. I was caught in limbo, not knowing one way or the other what had really happened to Christine. I couldn't let her go.

It was paralyzing me, crippling me, making me feel so damn sad and empty. I knew I needed to move on with my life, but I couldn't do it. I needed answers, at least a few of them. *Is Christine part of the game?* I kept wondering. I was obsessed with the game.

Am I part of it?

I believed I was. And in a way, I hoped she was, too. It was my only hope that she might still be alive.

Chapter 81

AND SO I FOUND MYSELF a player in a truly bizarre game that was habit-forming for all the wrong reasons. I began to make up my own rules. I brought in new players. I was in this game to win.

Chuck Hufstedler from the FBI offices in D.C. continued to be helpful. The more I talked to him, the more I realized that he'd had a serious crush on Detective Hampton. His loss, and mine with Christine, united us.

I climbed up to the attic late Friday night after watching *The Mask of Zorro* with Damon, Jannie, Nana, and Rosie the cat. I had a few more facts to check before going to bed.

I booted up the computer, logged on,

and heard the familiar message: *You have mail.* Ever since that night in Bermuda, those words had given me a terrible fright, a chill that tightened my body from head to toe.

Sandy Greenberg from Interpol was replying to one of my e-mails. She and I had worked together on the Mr. Smith case and had become friends. I'd asked her to check on several things for me.

CALL ME ANYTIME TONIGHT, ALEX, AND I MEAN ANYTIME. YOUR IRRITATING DOGGEDNESS MAY HAVE PAID OFF. IT'S VITALLY IMPORTANT THAT YOU CALL. *SANDY.*

I called Sandy in Europe, and she picked up after the second ring. "Alex? I think we've found one of them. It was your bloody idea that worked. Shafer was playing a game with at least one of his old cronies from MI-Six. You were spot on."

"Are you sure it's one of the game players?" I asked her.

"Pretty sure," she shot back. "I'm sitting here now staring at a copy of Dürer's *Four Horsemen,* on my Mac. As you know, the Horsemen are Conqueror, Famine, War,

424 / JAMES PATTERSON

and Death. What a creepy bunch. Anyway, I did what you asked. I talked to some contacts from MI-Six, who found out that Shafer and this one chap regularly keep in touch on the computer. I have all your notes, too, and they're very good. I can't believe how much you figured out from back there in the colonies. You're a very sick puppy, too."

"Thanks," I said. I let Sandy ramble on for a few minutes. A while back I'd recognized that she was a lonely person, and that even though she sometimes put up a cantankerous front, she craved company.

"The name this chap uses in the game is Conqueror. Conqueror lives in Dorking, Surrey, in England," Sandy told me. "His name is Oliver Highsmith, and he's retired from MI-Six. Alex, he was running several agents in Asia at the same time Shafer was there. Shafer worked under him. It's eight in the morning over here. *Why don't you call the bastard?*" Sandy suggested. "Or send him an e-mail. I have an address for him, Alex."

I started to wonder about the other players in the Four Horsemen game. Were there really four of them, or was that just the name of the game? Who were these players? How was the game actually played? Did all, or indeed any, of them act out their fantasies in real life?

My message to Conqueror was simple and straightforward and not too threatening, I hoped. I didn't see how he could resist answering me.

DEAR MR. HIGHSMITH,
I AM A HOMICIDE DETECTIVE
IN WASHINGTON, D.C.,
LOOKING FOR INFORMATION
ABOUT COLONEL GEOFFREY
SHAFER PERTAINING TO THE
FOUR HORSEMEN. I
UNDERSTAND THAT SHAFER
WORKED FOR YOU IN ASIA.
TIME IS OF THE ESSENCE. I
NEED YOUR HELP. PLEASE
CONTACT DETECTIVE ALEX
CROSS.

Chapter 82

I WAS SURPRISED when a message came right back. Oliver Highsmith—Conqueror—must have been on-line when my e-mail went through.

DETECTIVE CROSS. I AM WELL AWARE OF YOU, SINCE THE ONGOING MURDER TRIAL IS A RATHER BIG STORY IN ENGLAND, AND IN THE REST OF EUROPE, FOR THAT MATTER. I HAVE KNOWN G.S. FOR A DOZEN YEARS OR MORE. HE DID WORK UNDER ME, BRIEFLY. HE IS MORE AN ACQUAINTANCE THAN A CLOSE FRIEND, SO I HAVE NO EXPERTISE OR BIAS ABOUT

HIS GUILT OR INNOCENCE. I
HOPE IT'S THE LATTER, OF
COURSE.

NOW, AS TO YOUR
QUESTION ABOUT THE FOUR
HORSEMEN. THE GAME—AND
IT *IS* A FANTASY GAME,
DETECTIVE—IS HIGHLY
UNUSUAL IN THAT ALL OF THE
PLAYERS ASSUME THE ROLE
OF GAMEMASTER. THAT IS TO
SAY, EACH OF US CONTROLS
HIS OWN FATE, HIS OWN
STORY. G.S.'S STORY IS EVEN
MORE DARING AND UNUSUAL.
HIS CHARACTER, THE RIDER
ON THE PALE HORSE—DEATH
—IS DEEPLY FLAWED. ONE
MIGHT EVEN SAY EVIL. THE
CHARACTER IS SOMEWHAT
LIKE THE PERSON ON TRIAL
IN WASHINGTON, OR SO IT
SEEMS TO ME.

HOWEVER, I MUST MAKE A
FEW IMPORTANT POINTS. THE
APPEARANCE OF ANY MURDER
FANTASIES IN OUR GAME
ALWAYS OCCURRED DAYS

AFTER REPORTS OF MURDERS
IN THE NEWSPAPERS. BELIEVE
ME, THIS WAS THOROUGHLY
CHECKED BY US ONCE G.S.
WAS ACCUSED. IT WAS EVEN
BROUGHT TO THE ATTENTION
OF INSPECTOR JONES AT THE
SECURITY SERVICE IN
LONDON, SO I'M SURPRISED
YOU WEREN'T INFORMED
BEFORE NOW. THE SERVICE
HAVE BEEN TO SEE ME ABOUT
G.S. AND WERE COMPLETELY
SATISFIED, I ASSUME, SINCE
THEY HAVEN'T BEEN BACK.
   ALSO, THE OTHER PLAYERS
—WHO HAVE THEMSELVES
BEEN CHECKED OUT BY
SECURITY—ARE ALL
REPRESENTED BY POSITIVE
CHARACTERS IN THE GAME.
AND AS I'VE SAID, AS
POWERFULLY INVOLVING AS
HORSEMEN IS, IT IS
NEVERTHELESS ONLY A GAME.
BY THE WAY, DID YOU KNOW
THAT BY SOME SCHOLARLY
ACCOUNTS THERE IS A FIFTH

HORSEMAN? *MIGHT THAT BE YOU, DR. CROSS?*

FYI—THE CONTACT AT THE SERVICE IS MR. ANDREW JONES. I TRUST HE WILL VOUCH FOR THE VERACITY OF MY STATEMENTS. IF YOU WISH TO CONVERSE FURTHER, DO SO AT YOUR OWN RISK. I AM 67 YEARS OF AGE, RETIRED FROM INTELLIGENCE (AS I LIKE TO PUT IT), AND A RATHER FAMOUS WINDBAG. I WISH YOU MUCH LUCK IN YOUR SEARCH FOR TRUTH AND JUSTICE. I MISS THE CHASE MYSELF.

CONQUEROR

I read the message, then reread it. *"Much luck in your search?"* Was that as loaded a line as it sounded?

And was I now a player—the fifth Horseman?

Chapter 83

I WENT TO COURT EVERY DAY the following week, and like so many other people, I got hooked on the trial. Jules Halpern was the most impressive orator I had ever watched in a courtroom, but Catherine Fitzgibbon was effective as well. The verdict would depend on whom the jury believed more. It was all theater, a game. I remembered that as a kid I used to regularly watch a courtroom drama with Nana, called *The Defenders.* Every show began with a deep-voiced narrator's saying something to the effect of, "The American justice system is far from perfect, but it is still the very best justice system in the world."

That may be true, but as I sat in the

courtroom in Washington, I couldn't help thinking that the murder trial, the judge, the jury, the lawyers, and all the rules were just another elaborate game, and that Geoffrey Shafer was already planning his next foray, savoring every move that the prosecution made against him.

He was still in control of the game board. He was the gamemaster. He knew it, and so did I.

I watched Jules Halpern conduct smooth examinations that were designed to give the impression that his monstrous, psychopathic client was as innocent as a newborn baby. Actually, it was easy to drift off during the lengthy cross-examinations. I never really missed anything, though, since all the important points were repeated over and over, ad nauseam.

"Alex Cross . . ."

I heard my name mentioned and refocused my attention on Jules Halpern. He produced a blown-up photograph that had appeared in the *Post* on the day after the murder. The photo had been taken by another tenant at the Farragut and sold to the newspaper.

Halpern leaned in close to the witness

on the stand, a man named Carmine Lopes, a night doorman at the apartment building where Patsy Hampton had been murdered.

"Mr. Lopes, I show you Defendant's Exhibit J, a photograph of my client and Detective Alex Cross. It was taken in the tenth-floor hallway soon after the discovery of Detective Hampton's body."

The blowup was large enough for me to see most of the detail from where I was sitting in the fourth row. The photo had always been a shocker to me.

In it, Shafer looked as if he had just stepped out of the pages of *GQ*. In comparison, my clothes were tattered and dirty. I had just come off my crazy marathon run from the zoo, and I had been down in the garage with poor Patsy's body. My fists were clenched tightly, and I seemed to be roaring out anger at Shafer. Pictures *do* lie. We know that. The photograph was highly inflammatory, and I felt it could instill prejudice in the minds of the jurors.

"Is this a fair representation of how the two men looked at ten-thirty that evening?" Halpern asked the doorman.

"Yes, sir. It's very fair. That's how I re-member it."

Jules Halpern nodded as if he were re-ceiving vital information for the first time. "Would you now describe, *in your own words,* what Detective Cross looked like at that time?" he asked.

The doorman hesitated and seemed slightly confused by the question. I wasn't. I knew where Halpern was going now.

"Was he dirty?" Halpern jumped in and asked the simplest possible question.

"Er, dirty . . . sure. He was a mess."

"And was he sweaty?" the defense law-yer asked.

"Sweaty . . . yeah. We all were. From being down in the garage, I guess. It was a real hot night."

"Nose running?"

"Yes, sir."

"Were Detective Cross's clothes ripped, Mr. Lopes?"

"Yes, they were. Ripped and dirty."

Jules Halpern looked at the jury first, then at his witness. "Were Detective Cross's clothes bloodstained?"

"Yes . . . they sure were. That's what I noticed first, the blood."

"Was the blood anywhere else, Mr. Lopes?"

"On his hands. You couldn't miss it. I sure didn't."

"And Mr. Shafer, how did Mr. Shafer look?"

"He was clean, not mussed at all. He seemed pretty calm and collected."

"Did you see any blood on Mr. Shafer?"

"No, sir. No blood."

Halpern nodded, then faced the jury. "Mr. Lopes, which of the two men looked more like someone who might have just committed a murder?"

"Detective Cross," the doorman said without hesitation.

"Objection!" the district attorney screamed, but not before the damage was done.

Chapter 84

THAT AFTERNOON, the defense was scheduled to call Chief of Detectives George Pittman. The assistant district attorney, Catherine Fitzgibbon, knew that Pittman was on the docket, and she asked me to meet her for lunch. "If you have an appetite before Pittman goes on," she added.

Catherine was smart, and she was thorough. She had put away nearly as many bad guys as Jules Halpern had set free. We got together over sandwiches at a crowded deli near the courthouse. Neither of us was thrilled about Pittman's upcoming appearance. My reputation as a detective was being ruined by the defense, and

436 / JAMES PATTERSON

it was a hard thing to watch and do nothing.

She bit down into a hefty Reuben sandwich that squirted mustard onto her forefinger and thumb. Catherine smiled. "Sloppy, but worth it. You and Pittman are really at odds, right? More like you hate each other's guts?"

"It's serious dislike, and it's mutual," I told her. "He's tried to do me in a couple of times. He thinks I'm a threat to his career."

Catherine was attacking her sandwich. "*Hmmm,* there's a thought. Would you be a better chief of detectives?"

"Wouldn't run, wouldn't serve if elected. I wouldn't be good cooped up in an office playing political Ping-Pong."

Catherine laughed. She's one of those people who can find humor almost anywhere. "This is just fricking great, Alex. The defense is calling the chief of detectives as one of *its* goddamn witnesses. He's listed as hostile, but I don't think he is."

Catherine and I finished off the rest of her sandwich. "Well, let's find out what Mr.

Halpern has up his sleeve today," she said.

At the start of the afternoon session, Jules Halpern did a careful and thorough setup of Pittman's credentials, which sounded reasonably impressive in the abstract. Undergrad at George Washington, then law school at American; twenty-four years on the police force, with medals for bravery and citations from three different mayors.

"Chief Pittman, how would you describe Detective Cross's record in the department?" asked Halpern.

I cringed in my seat. Felt my brow wrinkle, my eyes narrow. *Here we go,* I thought.

"Detective Cross has been involved in some high-profile cases that the department has solved," he said, and left it at that. Not exactly praise, but at least he hadn't gone on the attack.

Halpern nodded sagely. "What, if anything, has changed his performance recently?"

Pittman looked my way, then answered. "A woman he was seeing disappeared while they were on a trip together in Bermuda. Since that time, he's been distracted and distant, quick to anger, not himself."

Suddenly I wanted to speak up in the courtroom. Pittman didn't know the first thing about Christine and me.

"Chief Pittman, was Detective Cross ever a suspect in the disappearance of his girlfriend, Mrs. Christine Johnson?"

Pittman nodded. "That's standard police procedure. I'm sure he was questioned."

"But his behavior on the job has changed since her disappearance?"

"Yes. His concentration isn't the same. He's missed days of work. It's all a matter of record."

"Has Detective Cross been asked to seek professional help?"

"Yes."

"Did you ask him to seek help yourself?"

"I did. He and I have worked together for a number of years. He was under stress."

"He's under a *lot* of stress? Is that fair to say?"

"Yes. He hadn't closed a single case recently."

Halpern nodded. "A couple of weeks

before the Hampton homicide, you suspended some detectives he was friendly with."

Pittman's look was somber. "Unfortunately, I did."

"Why did you suspend the detectives?"

"The detectives were investigating cases outside the auspices of the department."

"Is it fair to say they were making up their own rules, acting like vigilantes?"

Catherine Fitzgibbon rose to her feet and objected, but Judge Fescoe allowed the question.

Pittman answered, "I don't know about that. *Vigilantes* is a strong word. But they were working without proper supervision. The case is still under investigation."

"Was Detective Cross part of the group that was making up its own rules to solve homicides?"

"I'm not certain. But he was spoken to about the matter. I didn't believe he could handle a suspension at that time. I warned him and let it slide. I shouldn't have," said Pittman.

"No further questions."

None needed, I thought.

Chapter 85

THAT NIGHT, after he left the court-house, Shafer was flying high. He thought that he was winning the game. He was manic as hell, and it felt both good and bad. He was parked in the dark garage under Boo Cassady's building. Most manics aren't really aware of it when they're exhibiting signs of a manic episode, but Shafer knew. His "spirals" didn't come out of nowhere; they built and built.

The irony and the danger of being back in her building weren't lost on him. Scene of the crime, and all that rot. He wanted to go to Southeast tonight, but that was too risky. He couldn't hunt—not now. He had something else in mind: the next few moves in his game.

It was unusual, though not unheard-of, for the defendant in a first-degree homicide trial to be out roaming the streets, but that had been one of the prerequisites of his dropping his immunity. What choice did the prosecution have? None at all. If the D.A. hadn't agreed, he had a free pass to keep him out of jail.

Shafer followed a tenant he'd seen several times into the lift from the garage and took it to Boo's apartment. He rang the doorbell. Waited. Heard her padding across the parquet floor. Yes, Act One of tonight's performance was about to begin.

He knew she was watching him through the door's peephole, just as he had watched Alex Cross through it on the night Patsy Hampton got her just deserts. He had seen Boo a few times after his release, but then he'd cut her off.

When he'd stopped seeing her, she lost it. Boo had called him at work, then at home, and constantly on his car phone, until he changed the bloody number. At her worst, she reminded him of the nutcase Glenn Close had played in the movie *Fatal Attraction*.

He wondered if he could still push her

buttons. She was a fairly bright woman, and that was a large part of her problem. She thought far too much, double- and triple-think. Most men, especially dull-witted Americans, didn't like that, which made her even crazier.

He put his face against the door, felt its cool wood on his cheek. He started his act.

"I've been petrified to see you, Boo. You don't know what it's been like. One slipup, anything they can use against me, and I'm finished. And what makes it worse is that I'm innocent. You know that. I talked to you the whole time from my house to yours that night. You know I didn't kill that detective. Elizabeth? Boo? Please say something. At least curse at me. Let the anger out . . . Doctor?"

There was no answer. He rather liked that. It made him respect her more than he had. What the hell, she was more screwed up than he was.

"You know exactly what I'm going through. You're the only one who understands my episodes. I need you, Boo. You know I'm manic-depressive, bipolar, whatever the hell you shrinks want to call my condition. Boo?"

Then Shafer actually started to cry, which nearly made him laugh. He uttered loud, wrenching sobs. He crouched on his haunches and held his head. He knew he was a far better actor than so many of the high-priced fakers he saw in the movies.

The door to the apartment slowly opened. "Boo-hoo," she whispered. "Is poor Geoff in pain? What a shame."

What a bitch, he thought, but he had to see her. She was testifying soon. He needed her tonight, and he needed her help in the courtroom.

"Hello, Boo," he whispered back.

Chapter 86

ACT TWO of the evening's performance.

She stared at him with huge dark-brown eyes that looked like amber beads, the kind she bought at her swanky shops. She'd lost weight, but that made her sexier to him, more desperate. She wore navy walking shorts and an elegant pink silk T-shirt—but she also wore her pain.

"You hurt me like no one ever has before," she whispered.

He held himself under control, playacting, a truly award-winning performance. "I'm fighting for my life. I swear, all I think about is killing myself. Haven't you heard anything I've said? Besides, do you want your picture all over the tabloids again?

Don't you see? That's why I've been staying away from you."

She laughed bitterly, haughtily. "It's going to happen anyway when I testify. The photographers will be everywhere I go."

Shafer shut his eyes. "Well, that will be your chance to hurt me back, darling."

She shook her head and frowned. "You know I wouldn't do that. Oh, Geoff, why didn't you at least call? You're such a bastard."

Shafer hung his head, the repentant bad boy. "You know how close I was to the edge before all this happened. Now it's worse. Do you expect me to act like a responsible adult?"

She gave a wry smile. He saw a book on the hallway table behind her: *Man and His Symbols.* Carl Jung. How fitting. "No, I suppose not, Geoff. What do you want? Drugs?"

"I need you. I want to hold you, Boo. That's all."

That night, she gave him what he wanted. They made love like animals on the gray velvet love seat she used for her clients, then on the JFK-style rocking chair where she always sat during sessions. He took her body—and her soul.

Then she gave him drugs—antidepressants, painkillers, most of her samples. Boo was still able to get the samples from her ex, a psychiatrist. Shafer didn't know what *their* relationship was, and frankly, he didn't care. He swallowed some Librium and shot up Vicodin at her place.

Then he took Boo again, both of them naked and sweating and frenzied on the kitchen counter. *The butcher block,* he thought.

He left her place around eleven. He realized he was feeling worse than before he'd gone there. But he knew what he was going to do. He'd known before he went to Boo's. It would explode their little minds. Everyone's. The press. The jury.

Now for Act Three.

Chapter 87

AT A LITTLE PAST MIDNIGHT, I got an emergency call that blew off the top of my head. Within minutes I had the old Porsche up close to ninety on Rock Creek Parkway, the siren screaming at the night, or maybe at Geoffrey Shafer.

I arrived in Kalorama at 12:25. EMS ambulances, squad cars, TV news trucks were parked all over the street.

Several neighbors of the Shafers' were up and had come outside their large, expensive houses to observe the nightmare scene. They couldn't believe this was happening in their upscale enclave.

The chatter and buzz of several police radios filled the night air. A news helicopter was already hovering overhead. A truck marked CNN arrived and parked right behind me.

I joined a detective named Malcolm Ainsley on the front lawn. We knew each other from other homicide scenes, even a few parties. Suddenly, the front door of the Shafer house opened.

Two EMTs were carrying a stretcher outside. Dozens of cameras were flashing.

"It's Shafer," Ainsley told me. "Son of a bitch tried to kill himself, Alex. Slit his wrist and took a lot of drugs. There were open prescription packets everywhere. Must've had second thoughts, though. Called for help."

I had enough information about Shafer from the discovery interviews preceding the trial, and from my own working profile on him, to begin to make some very educated guesses about what might have happened. My first thought was that he suffered from some kind of bipolar disorder that caused both manic and depressive episodes. A second possibility was cyclohymia, which can manifest itself in numerous hypomanic episodes as well as depressive symptoms. Its associated symptoms could include inflated self-esteem, a decreased need for sleep, excessive involvement in "pleasurable" activities, and an increase in goal-directed activity—in Shafer's case, maybe, an intensified effort to win his game.

I moved forward as if I were floating in a very bad dream, the worst I could imagine. I recognized one of the EMS techies, Nina Disesa. I'd worked with her a few times before in Georgetown.

"We got to the bastard just in time," Nina said, and narrowed her dark eyes. "Too bad, huh?"

"Serious attempt?" I asked her.

Nina shrugged. "Hard to tell for sure. He hacked up his wrist pretty good. Just the left one, though. Then the drugs, *lots* of drugs—doctors' samples."

I shook my head in utter disbelief. "But he definitely called out for help?"

"According to the wife and son, they heard him call out from his den, 'Daddy needs help. Daddy is dying. Daddy is sick.' "

"Well, he got *that* part right. Daddy is incredibly sick. Daddy is a monumental sicko."

I went over to the red and white ambulance. News cameras were still flashing all over the street. My mind was unhinged, reeling. *Everything is a game to him. The victims in Southeast, Patsy Hampton, Christine. Now this. He's even playing with his own life.*

"His pulse is still strong," I heard as I got close to the ambulance. I could see one of the EMT workers checking the EKG inside the van. I could even hear beeps from the machine.

Then I saw Shafer's face. His hair was drenched with perspiration, and his face was as pale as a sheet of white paper. He stared into my eyes, trying to focus. Then he recognized me.

"You did this to me," he said, mustering strength, suddenly trying to sit up on the stretcher. "You ruined my life for your career. You did this! You're responsible! Oh, God, oh, God. My poor family! Why is this happening to us?"

The TV cameras were rolling film, and they got his entire Academy Award–quality performance. Just as Geoffrey Shafer knew they would.

Chapter 88

THE TRIAL had to be recessed due to Shafer's suicide attempt. The courtroom shenanigans probably wouldn't resume until the following week.

Meanwhile, the media had another feeding frenzy, including banner headlines in the *Washington Post,* the *New York Times, USA Today.* At least it gave me time to work on a few more angles. Shafer was good—God, he was good at this.

I had been talking with Sandy Greenberg nearly every night. She was helping me collect information on the other game players. She had even gone and talked with Conqueror. She said she doubted that Oliver Highsmith was a killer. He was late-sixties, seriously overweight, and wheelchair-bound.

Sandy called the house at seven that night. She's a good friend. Obviously, she was burning the midnight oil for me. I took the call in the sanctuary of my attic office.

"Andrew Jones of the Security Service will see you," she announced in her usual perky and aggressive manner. "Isn't that great news? I'll tell you: *it is.* Actually, he's eager to meet with you, Alex. He didn't say it to me directly, but I don't think he's too keen on Colonel Shafer. Wouldn't say why. Even more fortuitous, he's in Washington. He's a top man. He matters in the intelligence arena. He's very good, Alex, a straight shooter."

I thanked Sandy and then immediately called Jones at his hotel. He answered the call in his room. "Yes. Hello. It's Andrew Jones. Who is this, please?"

"It's Detective Alex Cross of the Washington police. I just got off the line with Sandy Greenberg. How are you?"

"Good, very good. Well, hell, not really. I've had better weeks, months. Actually, I stayed here in my room hoping that you'd call. Would you like to meet, Alex? Is there someplace where we wouldn't stand out too much?"

I suggested a bar on M Street in half an hour, and I arrived there a minute or two early. I recognized Jones from his description on the phone: "Broad, beefy, red-faced. Just your average ex-rugby type—though I never bloody played, don't even watch the drivel. Oh, yes, flaming red hair and matching mustache. That should help, no?"

It did. We sat in a dark booth in back and got to know each other. For the next forty-five minutes, Jones filled me in on several important things, not the least of which was politics and decorum within the English intelligence and police communities; Lucy Shafer's father's good name and standing in the army, and the concern for his reputation; and the desire of the government to avoid an even dicier scandal than the current mess.

"Alex, if it were true that one of our agents committed cold-blooded murders while posted abroad, and that British intelligence knew nothing about it, the scandal would be a true horror and a major embarrassment. But if MI-Six *knew anything* about what Colonel Shafer is suspected of doing! Well, it's absolutely unthinkable."

"Did it?" I asked him. "Is this situation unthinkable?"

"I won't answer that, Alex—you know I can't. But I am prepared to help you if I possibly can."

"Why?" I asked, then, "Why now? We needed your help on this before the trial began."

"Fair question, good question. We're prepared to help because you now have information that could cause us a hell of a lot of trouble. You're privy to the *unthinkable.*"

I said nothing. I thought I knew what he was alluding to, though.

"You've discovered a fantasy game called the Four Horsemen. There are four players, including Shafer. We know you've already contacted Oliver Highsmith. What you probably don't know yet, but will find out eventually, is that all the players are former or current agents. That is to say, Geoffrey Shafer might be just the beginning of our problems."

"All four of them are murderers?" I asked.

Andrew Jones didn't answer; he didn't have to.

Chapter 89

"WE THINK that the 'game' originated in Bangkok, where three of the four players were posted in 'ninety-one. The fourth, Highsmith, was a mentor to George Bayer, who is Famine in the Four Horsemen. Highsmith has always worked out of London."

"Tell me about Highsmith," I said.

"As I said, he's always been in the main office, London. He was a high-level analyst, then he actually ran several agents. He's a very bright chap, well thought of."

"He claimed that the Four Horsemen was just a harmless fantasy game."

"It may be for him, Alex. He may be telling the truth. He's been in a wheelchair since 'eighty-five. Automobile accident.

His wife had just left him, and he cracked. He's an enormous fellow, about three hundred pounds. I doubt that he's getting about and murdering young women in the scuffier neighborhoods of London. That's what you believe Shafer was doing here in Washington? The Jane Doe murders?"

Jones was right, and I didn't deny it. "We know he was involved in several murders, and I think we were close to catching him. He was picking up his victims in a gypsy taxicab. We found the cab. Yes, we knew about him, Andrew."

Jones tented his thick fingers, pursed his lips. "You think Shafer knew how close you and Detective Hampton were getting?"

"He may have known, but there was also a lot of pressure on him. He made some mistakes that led us to an apartment he rented."

Jones nodded. He seemed to know a great deal about Shafer, which told me he'd been watching him, too. Had he been watching me as well?

"How do you think the other game players might react to Shafer's being so out of control?" I asked.

"I'm fairly sure they felt threatened. Who wouldn't? He was a risk to all of them. He still is." Jones continued, "So, we have Shafer, who's probably been committing murders here in Washington, acting out his fantasies in real life. And Highsmith, who probably couldn't do that, but could be a sort of controller. Then there's a man named James Whitehead, in Jamaica, but there have been no murders of the Jane Doe variety on that island or any other one nearby. We've checked thoroughly. And there's George Bayer in the Far East."

"What about Bayer? I assume you've investigated him, too."

"Of course. There's nothing specific in his record, but there was an incident, a possible connection, to follow up on. Last year in Bangkok, two girls who worked in a strip bar in Pat Pong disappeared. They just vanished into the noisy, teeming streets. The girls were sixteen and eighteen, respectively, bar dancers and prostitutes. Alex, they were found nailed together in the missionary position, wearing only garters and stockings. Even in jolly old Bangkok, that caused quite a stir. Sound distressingly similar to the two girls who were killed in Eckington?"

I nodded. "So we have at least two unsolved Jane Does in Bangkok. Has anyone actually questioned Bayer?"

"At this point, no, but he's being watched. Remember the politics, the fear of a scandal that I mentioned earlier? There's an ongoing investigation of Bayer and the others, but to some extent our hands are tied."

"*My* hands aren't tied," I said to Jones. "That's what you wanted me to say, isn't it? What you expected? It's why you met with me tonight?"

Jones turned very serious. "It's how the world works, I'm afraid. Let's do this together from here on. If you help us . . . I promise to do what I can to find out what happened to Christine Johnson."

Chapter 90

THE TRIAL RESUMED sooner than expected—the following Wednesday, in fact. There was speculation in the press about how serious Shafer's self-inflicted wounds had been. None of the public's perverse interest in the case seemed to have been lost.

It seemed impossible to predict the outcome, a fact of life I tried not to let get me down too much. Both Shafer and I were present in the packed courtroom that first morning back. Shafer looked pale, weak—an object of sympathy, perhaps. I certainly couldn't take my eyes off him.

Things got stranger and stranger. At least they did for me. Sergeant Walter Jamieson was called that morning. Jamieson had been at the Police Academy when I attended it. He had taught me my craft, and he was still there, teaching others. I couldn't imagine why he would be called as a witness in Patsy Hampton's murder case.

Jules Halpern approached the witness with a heavy-looking hardback book open in his hands.

"I read to you from the textbook *Preserving the Crime Scene: A Detective's Primer,* which you wrote twenty years ago and which you still use in your classes: 'It is *imperative* that the detective not disturb the crime scene until backup can be brought in to corroborate charges effected by the detective to unearth evidence, lest those charges be misconstrued to be those of the perpetration. Gloves *must* be worn at all times at a crime scene.' Did you write that, Sergeant Jamieson?"

"Yes, I did. Most certainly. Twenty years ago, as you said."

"Still stand by it?" Halpern asked.

"Yes, of course. A lot of things have changed, but not that."

"And you heard earlier testimony that Detective Cross wore gloves both inside Detective Hampton's car and at the Cassady apartment?"

"Yes, I heard the testimony. I also read the grand-jury transcripts."

Halpern turned on the overhead projector in the courtroom. "I direct your attention to prints number one-seventy-six and two-eleven provided by the D.A.'s office. You see the ones denominated?"

"Numbers one-seventy-six and two-eleven. I see them."

"Now, the prints are denominated 'Detective Hampton Belt Buckle: ID: Alex Cross/Right Thumb' and 'Left Side Dashboard: ID: Alex Cross/Left Forefinger.' What does that mean? Can you explain the markings to us?"

"It means that Alex Cross's prints were found on Detective Hampton's belt as well as on the dashboard of her car."

Jules Halpern paused for a full ten seconds before he went on. "And may we not therefore conclude, Sergeant Jamieson, that Detective Cross himself may be our murderer and rapist?"

"Objection!" Catherine Fitzgibbon stood up and shouted.

"Withdrawn," said the defense attorney. "I'm finished here."

Chapter 91

LAWYERS FOR BOTH the prosecution and the defense continued to appear regularly on Larry King and other TV shows, and to boast that their cases were "slam dunks." If you listened to the lawyers, neither side could lose.

In the courtroom, Jules Halpern had the fierce look and body language of someone brimming with confidence and determination. He was riding the case hard. He looked like a jockey whipping his Thoroughbred to victory.

The bailiff stood and announced, "The defense calls Mr. William Payaz."

I didn't recognize the name. Now what? Now *who?*

There was no immediate response in the courtroom.

No one came forward.

Heads craned around the room. Still, no one responded. Who was the mystery witness?

The bailiff repeated, a little louder, "Mr. Payaz. Mr. William Payaz."

The double doors in the back of the room suddenly opened, and a circus-style clown walked in. The gallery began to whisper loudly, and a few people laughed. What a world we lived in; what a circus, indeed.

The clown took the stand, and both the prosecution and the defense were immediately called forward for a sidebar by Judge Fescoe. A heated discussion ensued that none of the rest of us could hear. The clown issue was apparently resolved in favor of the defense. After being sworn in, the clown was asked his name for the record.

With his white-gloved right hand raised, he said, "Billy."

The bailiff asked, "Last name, please?"

The clown said, "First name, Silly. Last name, Billy. Silly Billy. I had it legally changed," he turned and confided to the judge.

Jules Halpern then took over, and he treated the clown with respect and seriousness. First, he asked him to state his credentials, which the clown did, politely. Then Halpern asked, "And what brings you here today?"

"I did a party for Mr. Shafer out in Kalorama on the fateful and terrible night of the murder. It was his twins' fifth birthday. I did a party when they were four as well. I brought a video along. Want to see?" he said, speaking as if he were addressing a crowd of three-year-olds.

"Of course," said Jules Halpern.

"Objection!" Catherine Fitzgibbon called out loudly.

The video was admitted over the prosecution's objections and after yet another lengthy sidebar. The newspapers had claimed that Judge Fescoe was intimidated by Jules Halpern, which seemed the case.

The tape began with an arresting close-up of a painting of a clown's face. As the camera pulled back, everyone in the courtroom could see it was the sign on Silly

Billy's van, which was parked in front of a handsome redbrick town house with a glass conservatory linked to the main building. The Shafer house.

The next scene showed Silly Billy ringing the front bell and apparently surprising the Shafer children at the door.

Once again, the prosecution objected to the videotape. There was another sidebar. The lawyers returned to their seats, and the tape resumed.

The other children at the birthday party then ran to the door. The clown handed out toys from a sack slung over his shoulder—teddy bears, dolls, shiny red fire trucks.

Silly Billy then performed magic tricks and gags on the sun porch, which looked out onto the backyard. The yard was very pretty, with potted orange trees, white climbing roses, a jasmine vine, lush green grass.

"Wait! I hear something outside!" he turned and said into the camera. He ran and disappeared from sight.

The kids all followed. The tension of surprise and imminent fun showed in the children's eyes.

A cream-colored pony appeared, cantering slowly around the corner of the house. Silly Billy was riding the pony.

But when the clown dismounted, the kids discovered that the clown was actually Geoffrey Shafer! All the kids went wild, but especially the Shafer twins. They ran and hugged their daddy, who seemed the perfect father.

There were heartwarming candid shots of the children eating frosted cake and playing party games. There were more shots of Shafer laughing and playing with several of the children. I suspected that Jules Halpern had supervised the final editing of the tape. It was very convincing.

The adult guests at the party, all dressed up and looking sophisticated, gave glowing testimonials. They said that Geoffrey Shafer and his wife were outstanding parents. No longer in his clown costume but in a smart navy suit, Shafer modestly deflected the tributes. He had changed into the same clothes he wore when he was apprehended at the Farragut.

The tape ended with the smiling and quite beautiful twins telling the camera that they loved their mommy and daddy for making their "dream come true." The lights came up. The judge granted a brief recess.

I felt incredibly angry that the video had been shown. It made Shafer out to be a wonderful father—and such a *victim.*

The jury was all smiles, and so was Jules Halpern. He had argued masterfully that the tape was crucial to establishing Geoffrey Shafer's state of mind shortly before Patsy Hampton's murder. Halpern was so skillful an orator that he'd actually made the outrageous request to show the video sound logical. At any rate, it was moot now.

Shafer himself was smiling broadly, as were his wife and son. It suddenly occurred to me that Shafer had been riding a pale horse at the party for his children. He was Death, from the Four Horsemen.

It was all theater and games to him, his entire life.

Chapter 92

SOMETIMES I WANTED to shut my eyes tight and not have to watch another moment of the trial. I wanted things to be the way they'd been before the Weasel.

Catherine Fitzgibbon was doing a very good job with each witness, but the judge seemed to be favoring the defense whenever possible. It had begun at the critical suppression hearing, and it continued now.

Lucy Shafer took the witness stand early that afternoon. The warm, homespun videotaped images of the Shafer family were still fresh in the minds of the jurors.

I had been trying to understand Lucy Shafer's odd and perplexing relationship with her husband since the first time I met her, on the night of Patsy Hampton's murder. What kind of woman could live with an unrepentant monster like Shafer and not know it? Could this woman be that much in denial? Or was there something else that motivated her, somehow held her captive to Shafer? I had seen all kinds of marital relationships in my therapy practice, but nothing like this.

Jane Halpern conducted the questioning, and looked every bit as confident and winning as her father. She was tall and slender, with wiry black hair tied in a bow with a dark-crimson ribbon. She was twenty-eight, just four years out of Yale Law School, but seemed older and wiser.

"Mrs. Shafer, how long have you and your husband known each other?"

Lucy Shafer spoke in a gentle but clear voice. "I've known Geoffrey for most of my adult life, actually. My father was his commanding officer in the army. I believe I was just fourteen when I first met Geoff. He was nine years older. We married when I was nineteen, after my second year at Cambridge. Once, when I was studying for exams, he showed up at university in full military dress—polished saber, medals, shiny black leather riding boots—right in the middle of the library. I was studying in a sweatshirt or some such awful getup, and I don't think I'd washed my hair in days. Geoff told me it didn't matter. He didn't care a bit about appearances. He said he loved me and always would. I must tell you, he's kept that promise."

"Very nice," Jane Halpern said, seemingly utterly charmed, as if she'd never heard the story before. "And has he remained romantic?"

"Oh, yes, even more so. Scarcely a week goes by when Geoff doesn't bring me flowers, or perhaps a beautiful Hermès scarf, which I collect. And then there are our 'ouch' excursions."

Jane Halpern wrinkled her nose, and her dark-brown eyes twinkled. "What are 'ouch' excursions?" she asked with the exuberant curiosity of a morning TV-show host.

"Geoff will take me to New York, or maybe Paris, or back to London, and I get to shop for clothes until he says 'ouch.' He's very generous, that way."

"A good husband, then?"

"The best you could imagine. Very hard-working, but not so much that he forgets about his family. The children adore him."

"Yes, we could tell that from this morning's film, Mrs. Shafer. Was the party an unusual occasion?"

"No. Geoffrey's always throwing parties. He's very joyful, full of life, full of fun and surprises. He's a sensitive, very creative man."

I looked from Lucy Shafer to the jury box. She had the jurors in a spell, and they couldn't take their eyes off her. She was also credible. Even I had the sense that she genuinely loved her husband, and more important, that she believed *he* loved *her.*

Jane Halpern milked the testimony for all it was worth. I couldn't blame her. Lucy Shafer was attractive and seemed nice, kind, and obviously was very much in love with her husband and adored her children, but she didn't appear to be a fool. Just someone who had found exactly the man she wanted and valued him deeply. That man was Geoffrey Shafer.

It was the indelible image the jurors took away with them at the end of the day.

And it was an amazing lie, spun by a master.

Chapter 93

I TALKED THINGS OVER with Andrew Jones when I got home after court that afternoon. I'd tried to contact Oliver Highsmith again, but so far hadn't gotten any response. Also, there was nothing new to link Shafer to the Jane Doe murders in Washington. Shafer didn't seem to have murdered anyone, at least locally, in the past several months.

After a dinner of chicken pot pie, salad, and rhubarb pie, Nana gave the kids the night off from their chore of doing the dishes. She asked me to stay and help, to be her "partner in grime," as we used to call it.

"Just like the good old days, same as it ever was," I said as I splashed soap and water onto silver and dishes in the porcelain sink that's as old as the house.

Nana dried the kitchenware as quickly as I got it to her. Her fingers were still as nimble as her mind. "I like to think we're older *and* wiser," she chirped.

"I don't know. I'm still the one getting dishwater hands."

"I haven't told you something, and I should have," Nana said, going serious on me.

"Okay," I said, and stopped splashing water and soap bubbles around in the sink. "Shoot."

"What I wanted to say is that I'm proud of the way you've been able to handle the terrible things that have happened. Your strength and your patience have given me inspiration. And I'm not easily inspired, especially by the likes of you. I know it has had the same effect on Damon and Jannie. They don't miss a thing."

I leaned over the sink. I was feeling in a confessional mood. "It's the worst stretch of my life, the hardest thing I've ever had to do. It's even worse than when Maria died, Nana, if that's possible. At least back then I knew for sure she was dead. I could let myself grieve. I could finally let her go and breathe again."

Nana came around the sink and took me in her arms, which always surprised me with their strength.

She looked me squarely in the eyes, just like she always has since I was around nine years old. She said, "Let yourself grieve for her, Alex. Let her go."

Chapter 94

GEOFFREY SHAFER had an attractive, loving wife, and that incongruous and monstrously unfair fact bothered me a lot. I couldn't understand it as a psychologist or as a detective.

The clever testimony of Lucy Shafer continued early the following morning and lasted just over an hour. Jane Halpern wanted the jury to hear more about Lucy's wonderful husband.

Finally, it was Catherine Fitzgibbon's turn. In her own way, she was as tough, and maybe as formidable, as Jules Halpern.

"Mrs. Shafer, we've all been listening to you intently, and it all sounds very charming and idyllic, but I'm troubled and confused by something. Here's what troubles me: your husband tried to commit suicide eight days ago. Your husband tried to kill himself. So maybe he isn't quite what he seems to be. Maybe he isn't so well balanced and sane. Maybe you're mistaken about who he really is."

Lucy Shafer stared directly into the prosecuting attorney's eyes. "In the past few months, my husband has seen his life, his career, and his good name falsely put in jeopardy. My husband couldn't believe that these horrible charges were made against him. This whole Kafkaesque ordeal drove him, quite literally, to despair. You have no idea what it means to lose your good name."

Catherine Fitzgibbon smiled and then quipped, "Sure I do. Of course I do. Haven't you read the *National Enquirer* lately?" That got a laugh from the courtroom audience, even the jury members. I could tell that they liked Catherine. So did I.

She continued, "Isn't it true that your husband has been treated for 'despair' for many years? He's seeing a psychologist,

Mrs. Shafer. He suffers from manic depression, or bipolar disorder, correct?"

Lucy shook her head. "He's had a midlife crisis. That's all it is. It's nothing unusual for men his age."

"I see. And were you able to help him with his crisis?"

"Of course I was. Although not with respect to his work. So much of what he does is classified and top-secret. You must understand that."

"I must," the prosecutor said, then quickly went on, "So your husband has a great many secrets he keeps from you?"

Lucy frowned, and her eyes shot darts at the wily prosecutor. "In his *work,* yes."

"You knew that he was seeing Dr. Cassady? Boo Cassady?"

"Yes, of course I did. We often talked about it."

"How often did he see her? Do you know? Did he tell you that? Or was it *top-secret?*"

Jane Halpern shouted, "Objection!"

"Sustained. Ms. Fitzgibbon," warned Judge Fescoe, with an arched brow.

"Sorry, Your Honor. Sorry, Lucy. All

right, then. How often did your husband see Boo Cassady?"

"He saw her as much as necessary, I suppose. I believe her name is *Elizabeth.*"

"Once a week? Twice? Every day?" Fitzgibbon pressed on, without missing a beat.

"I think once a week. Usually it was once a week."

"But the doormen at the Farragut testified that they saw your husband much more than that. Three or four times a week, on average."

Lucy Shafer shook her head wearily and glared at Fitzgibbon. "I trust Geoffrey completely. I don't keep a leash on him. I certainly wouldn't *count* his therapy sessions."

"Did you mind that Dr. Cassady—*Elizabeth*—was such an attractive woman?"

"No. Don't be absurd."

Fitzgibbon looked genuinely surprised. "Why is that absurd? I don't think it is. I think *I'd* mind if my husband was seeing an attractive woman at her home-office two, three, four times a week."

Fitzgibbon moved swiftly. "Didn't it

bother you that Boo Cassady was a surrogate *sex* therapist for your husband?"

Lucy Shafer hesitated, seemed surprised, and glanced quickly at her husband. *She hadn't known.* It was impossible not to feel sorry for her.

Jane Halpern quickly rose from her seat. "Objection! Your Honor, there is no foundation that my client was seeing a sex surrogate."

Lucy Shafer visibly pulled herself together on the witness stand. She was clearly stronger than she looked. Was she a game player, too? Could she be one of the players? Or did she and her husband play a completely different kind of game?

She spoke. "I'd like to answer the question. Madam Prosecutor, my husband, Geoffrey, has been such a good husband, such a good father, that even if he felt it necessary to see a sex therapist, and did *not* want to tell me about it because of the hurt or shame he felt, I would understand."

"And if he committed *cold-blooded murder*—and did not want to tell you?" the prosecutor asked, then turned to the jury.

Chapter 95

ELIZABETH "BOO" CASSADY was in her late thirties, slender and very attractive, with lustrous brown hair that she had worn long since she was a young girl. She was a regular shopper at Neiman Marcus, Saks, Nordstrom, Bloomingdale's, and various chic specialty shops around Washington. It showed.

She had gotten the nickname Boo as an infant because she always laughed and laughed whenever she heard the sound of somebody playing peek-a-boo with her. She soon learned to do it herself, muttering "*boo, boo, boo, boo.*" In school, right through college, she kept the name, friends said, because she could be a little scary at times.

For her important day in court she'd chosen a single-breasted pantsuit, beautifully cut, very soft and flowy. Her outfit was an eye-pleasing mix of coffee and cashmere cream. She looked like a professional person, and a successful one.

Jules Halpern asked her to state her name and occupation for the record. He was amiable but businesslike, a little cooler than he had been with other witnesses.

"Dr. Elizabeth Cassady. I'm a psychotherapist," she replied evenly.

"Dr. Cassady, how do you know Colonel Shafer?"

"He's a patient of mine, and has been for over a year. He sees me at my office at twelve-oh-eight Woodley Avenue once or twice a week. We increased the frequency of the sessions recently, after Mr. Shafer's attempted suicide."

Halpern nodded. "What time are the sessions?"

"Usually early evening. They can vary according to Mr. Shafer's work schedule."

"Dr. Cassady, I direct your attention to the evening of the murder of Detective

Hampton. Did Geoffrey Shafer have a therapy session with you that night?"

"Yes, he did. At nine P.M., from nine until ten. I think he may have arrived a little earlier that night. But the session was scheduled for nine."

"Could he have arrived as early as eight-thirty?"

"No. That isn't possible. We were talking to each other on cell phones from the time he left his house in Kalorama until he arrived at my building. He was feeling a great deal of guilt about his latest dark mood's coming too close to his daughters' birthday party."

"I see. Was there any break in your conversation with Colonel Shafer?"

"Yes. But it was a very short one."

Halpern kept the pace brisk. "How much time passed between the time the two of you stopped talking on the cell phone and his arrival at your office?"

"Two or three minutes—five at the most. While he parked and came upstairs. No more than that."

"When he arrived at your office, did Geoffrey Shafer seem unsettled in any way?"

486 / JAMES PATTERSON

"No, not at all. He appeared relatively cheerful, actually. He had just hosted a successful birthday party for the twins. He felt it had gone very well, and he dotes on his children."

"Was he out of breath, tense, or perspiring?" Halpern asked.

"No. As I said, he was calm and looked quite fine. I remember it very clearly. And after the intrusion by the police, I made careful *notes* to keep everything accurate and fresh," she said, then glanced at the prosecution table.

"So you made notes for the sake of accuracy?"

"Yes, I did."

"Dr. Cassady, did you notice any blood anywhere on Colonel Shafer's clothing?"

"No, I did not."

"I see. You saw no blood on Shafer. And when Detective Cross arrived, did you see any blood on him?"

"Yes, I saw dark stains or streaks of blood on his shirt and suit coat. Also on his hands."

Jules Halpern paused to let everything sink in with the jury. Then he asked a final question: "Did Colonel Shafer look as if he had just murdered someone?"

"No, certainly not."

"I have nothing further," said the defense attorney.

Daniel Weston did the cross-exam for the prosecution. He was twenty-nine years old, bright, quick-witted, a rising star—and known to be a ruthless hatchet man in the prosecutor's office.

Dan Weston was also good-looking, blond, and rugged. He got physically close to Boo Cassady. They made a fetching couple, which was precisely the visual idea he wanted to communicate.

"Ms. Cassady, you weren't Mr. Shafer's *psychiatrist,* were you?"

She frowned slightly, but then managed a weak smile. "No, a psychiatrist has to be a medical doctor. You know that, I'm sure."

"And you are not a medical doctor?"

She shook her head. "I am not. I have a doctorate in sociology. You know that, too."

"Are you a *psychologist?*" Weston asked.

"A psychologist usually has a graduate degree in psychology, sometimes a Ph.D."

"Do you have a graduate degree in psychology?"

"No. I'm a psychotherapist."

"I see. Where did you train to be a psychotherapist?"

"American University. I graduated with a Ph.D. in Social Work."

Daniel Weston kept coming at Cassady. There was hardly a beat between answer and question. "This 'psychotherapy office' of yours at the Farragut, what sort of furnishings does it have?"

"A couch, desk, lamp. It's basically very spare. Lots of plants, though. My patients find the atmosphere functional but also relaxing."

"No box of tissues by the couch? I thought that was a must," Weston said with a wry smile.

The witness was clearly annoyed now, and maybe even shaken. "I take my work very seriously, Mr. Weston. So do my patients."

"Was Geoffrey Shafer referred to you by someone?"

"Actually, we met at the National Gallery

. . . at the Picasso erotic-drawings exhibit. That's been covered in depth by the press."

Weston nodded, and a thin smile crossed his lips. "Ah, I see. Are your sessions with Geoffrey Shafer erotic? Do you ever discuss sex?"

Jules Halpern rose quickly—a regular Jules-in-the-box. "Objection! Doctor-patient privilege. It's confidential."

The young prosecutor shrugged and flipped back his blond curls with his hand. "I'll withdraw the question. No problem. Are you a sexual surrogate?"

"No, I am not. As I stated earlier, I am a psychotherapist."

"On the evening of the murder of Detective Hampton, did you and Geoffrey Shafer discuss—"

Jules Halpern quickly rose again. "Objection. If the prosecution is inquiring into the patient's privileged disclosures—"

Weston raised both arms in frustration. He smiled at the jurors, hoping they felt the same way. "All right, all right. Let me see. I'll take this out of the so-called doctor-patient realm and ask you, quite simply, if you, Ms. Cassady, a woman, have had sexual relations with Geoffrey Shafer, a man?''

Elizabeth "Boo" Cassady hung her head and stared down at her lap.

Daniel Weston smiled, even as Jules Halpern objected to the question and was upheld by Judge Fescoe. Weston felt that he had made his point.

Chapter 96

"CALL DETECTIVE ALEX CROSS."

I took a deep breath, composed my mind, body, and soul, then walked up the wide center aisle of the courtroom to testify. Everyone in the room was watching me, but the only person I really saw was Geoffrey Shafer. The Weasel. He was still playing the part of the wronged innocent man, and I wanted to bring him down. I wanted to cross-examine him myself, to ask the real questions that needed to be asked, to tell the jury about all the suppressed evidence, to bring justice down on him with all its crushing force.

It was a hard thing to have worked honestly for so many years and now to be accused of being a rogue cop, someone who had tampered with evidence and perhaps worse. It was ironic, but now maybe I would have the opportunity to set the record straight, to clear my name.

Jules Halpern smiled cordially at me as I sat down in the witness stand. He established eye contact, quickly looked over at the jury, then turned back to me. His dark eyes radiated intelligence, and it seemed an incredible waste that he was working for Shafer.

"I want to start by saying that it is an honor to meet you, Detective Cross. For years I, like most of the jurors, I'm sure, have read in the Washington papers about the murder cases you have helped solve. We admire your past record."

I nodded and even managed a grudging smile of my own. "Thank you. I hope you'll admire my present and future record as well," I said.

"Let's hope so, Detective," Halpern said. He moved on. We parried for half an hour or so before he asked, "You suffered a terrible personal tragedy a short time before the arrest of Colonel Shafer—could you tell us about it?"

I fought the urge to reach out and grab

the polite-sounding, insidious little man by the neck. I leaned closer to the mike, struggled for control.

"Someone dear to me was kidnapped while we were in Bermuda on vacation. She's still missing. I haven't given up hope that she'll be found. I pray every day that she's still alive."

Halpern clucked sympathetically. He was good, much like his client. "I really am sorry. Did the department give you adequate time off?"

"They were understanding and helpful," I said, feeling my jaw stiffen with resentment. I hated that Halpern was using what had happened to Christine to unsettle me.

"Detective, were you officially back on active duty at the time of Detective Hampton's murder?"

"Yes, I went back on full-time duty about a week before the murder."

"Was it requested that you stay off active duty for a while longer?"

"It was left up to me. The chief of detectives did question my ability to resume my duties, but he made it my choice."

Halpern nodded thoughtfully. "He felt

your head might be elsewhere? Who could blame you if it was?"

"I was upset, I still am, but I've been able to work. It's been good for me. The right thing to do."

There were several more questions about my state of mind, and then Halpern asked, "When you found out that Detective Hampton had been murdered, how upset were you?"

"I did my job. It was a bad homicide scene." *Your client is a butcher. Do you really want to get him off? Do you realize what you're doing?*

"Your fingerprints were on Detective Hampton's belt and on the dashboard of her car. Her blood was on your clothes."

I paused for several seconds before I spoke again. Then I tried to explain. "There was a huge, jagged tear in Detective Hampton's jugular vein. Blood was everywhere in the car, and even on the cement floor of the garage. I tried to help Detective Hampton until I was certain she was dead. That's why my fingerprints were in the car and Detective Hampton's blood was on my clothes."

"You tracked blood upstairs?"

"No, I did not. I checked my shoes carefully before I left the garage. I checked *twice*. I checked because I *didn't* want to track any blood up into the building."

"But you were upset, you admit that much. A police officer had been murdered. You forgot to put on gloves when you first searched the scene. There was blood on your clothes. How can you possibly be so sure?"

I stared directly into his eyes and tried to be as calm as he was. "I know exactly what happened that night. I know who killed Patsy Hampton in cold blood."

He raised his voice suddenly. "No, you do not, sir. That's the point. *You do not.* In frisking Colonel Geoffrey Shafer, isn't it fair to say that you were in physical contact with him?"

"Yes."

"And isn't it possible blood from *your* clothes got onto *his?* Isn't it even likely?"

I wouldn't give him an inch. I couldn't. "No, it isn't possible. That blood was on Geoffrey Shafer's trousers *before* I arrived."

Halpern moved away from me. He wanted me to sweat. He walked over to the jury box, occasionally looking back at me. He asked several more questions about the crime scene, and then said, "But Dr. Cassady didn't see any blood. And the two other officers didn't see any blood, either—*not until after you came into contact with Colonel Shafer.* Colonel Shafer was on the phone for three to five minutes before he met with his therapist. He went straight there from his children's birthday party. *You have no evidence, Detective Cross!* Except what you brought into Dr. Cassady's apartment yourself. You have absolutely no evidence, Detective! You arrested the wrong man! You framed an innocent man!"

Jules Halpern threw up his hands in disgust. "I have absolutely no further questions."

Chapter 97

I TOOK A BACK WAY out of the courthouse. I usually did that anyway, but on
this day it was essential. I had to avoid the
crowds and the press, and I needed to
have a private moment to recover from my
time on the witness stand.

I'd just had my ass pretty well kicked by
an expert asskicker. Tomorrow, Cathy Fitzgibbon would try to undo some of the
damage in cross-exam.

I was in no hurry as I walked down a
back stairway that was used by maintenance and cleaning people in the building,
and also served as a fire escape.

It was becoming clear to me that there
was a chance Geoffrey Shafer would be
acquitted. His lawyers were the best, and

we'd lost important evidence at the suppression hearing.

And I *had* made a bad mistake at the homicide scene, when, in my rush to help Patsy Hampton, I'd neglected to put on gloves.

It was an honest mistake, but it probably created doubt in the minds of the jurors. I'd had more blood on me than Shafer. That was true. Shafer might actually get away with murder, and I couldn't stand the thought. I felt like yelling as I descended the twisting flights of stairs.

And that's exactly what I did. I yelled at the top of my voice, and it felt so damn good to get it out. Relief flowed through my body, however temporary it might be.

At the bottom of the concrete stairs was the basement of the courthouse. I headed down a long, dark hallway toward the rear lot where the Porsche was parked. I was still lost in my thoughts, but calmer after hollering my fool head off in the stairwell.

There was a sharp bend in the hallway near the exit to the parking lot. I came around the turn and saw him. I couldn't believe it. The Weasel was right there.

He was the first to speak. "What a surprise, Dr. Cross. Sneaking away from the madding—or is it 'maddening'?— crowd. Tail between your legs today? Don't fret, you did all right upstairs. Was that you yelling in the halls? Primal screams are the best, aren't they?"

"What the hell do you want, Shafer?" I asked him. "We're not supposed to meet or talk like this."

He shrugged his broad shoulders, wiped his blond hair away from his eyes. "You think I care about rules? I don't give a shit about rules. *What do I want?* My good name restored. I want my family not to have to go through any more of this. I want it all."

"Then you shouldn't have killed all those people. Especially Patsy Hampton."

Shafer smiled. "You're very sure of yourself, aren't you? You don't back down. I admire that, to a degree. I played the game of being a hero once myself. In the army. It's interesting for a while."

"But it's much more interesting to be a raving lunatic murderer," I said.

"See? You just don't back down from

your bullheaded opinions. I love it. You're wonderful."

"It's not opinion, Shafer. You know it, and so do I."

"Then prove it, Cross. Win your pitiful, sodding case, will you? Beat me fair and square in a court of law. I even gave you a home-court advantage."

I started to walk toward him; I couldn't help myself. He stood his ground.

"This is all an insane game to you. I've met assholes like you before, Shafer. I've beaten better. I'll beat you."

He laughed in my face. "I sincerely doubt it."

I walked right past him in the narrow tunnel.

He pushed me—*hard,* from behind. He was a big man, and even stronger than he looked.

I stumbled, almost went over onto the stone floor. I wasn't expecting the outburst of anger from him. He held it in so well in court, but it was close to the surface. The madness that *was* Geoffrey Shafer. The violence.

"Then go ahead, beat me. See if you can," he yelled at the top of his voice.

"Beat me right here, right now. I don't think you can, Cross. I know you can't."

Shafer took a quick step toward me. He was agile and athletic, not just strong. We were almost the same size—six-two or -three, two hundred pounds. I remembered that he'd been an army officer, then MI6. He still looked to be in excellent shape.

Shafer pushed me again with both hands. He made a loud grunting noise. "If you've beaten better, then I should be a pushover. Isn't that so? I'm just a *pushover.*"

I almost threw a punch; I wanted to. I ached to take him down, to wipe the smug, superior look off his face.

Instead, I grabbed him hard. I slammed Shafer up against the stone tunnel wall and held him there.

"Not now. Not here," I said in a hoarse, raw whisper. "I'm not going to hit you, Shafer. What? Have you run to the newspapers and TV? But I am going to bring you down. Soon."

He came out with a crazy laugh. "You are fucking hilarious, do you know that? You're a *scream.* I love it."

I walked away from Shafer in the dark

tunnel. It was the hardest thing I'd ever had to do. I wanted to beat the answers out of him, get a confession. I wanted to know about Christine. I had so many questions, but I knew he wouldn't answer them. He was here to bait me, to *play.*

"You're losing . . . everything," he said to my back.

I think I could have killed Geoffrey Shafer on the spot.

I almost turned, but I didn't. I opened the creaking door and went outside instead. Sunlight streamed into my eyes, half blinding me for a dizzying moment. Shading my face with an arm, I climbed the stone stairs to the parking area, where I got another unwanted surprise.

A dozen grim-faced members of the press, including some well-known reporters, were gathered in the back parking lot. Someone had alerted them; someone had tipped them off that I was coming out this way.

I looked back at the gray metal door, but Geoffrey Shafer didn't come out behind me. He had retreated and disappeared back into the basement.

"Detective Cross," I heard a reporter call

my name. "You're losing this case. You know that, don't you?"

Yes, I knew. I was losing everything. I just didn't know what I could do to stop it.

Chapter 98

THE FOLLOWING DAY was taken up with my cross-examination by Catherine Fitzgibbon. Catherine did a good job of redressing some of the harm done by Jules Halpern, but not all of it. Halpern consistently broke up her rhythm with his objections. Like so many recent high-profile trials, this one was maddening. It should have been easy to convict and put away Geoffrey Shafer, but that wasn't the case.

Two days later, we got our best chance to win, and Shafer himself gave it to us, almost as if he were daring us. We now realized that he was even crazier than we'd thought. The game was his life; nothing else seemed to matter.

Shafer agreed to take the stand. I think I

was the only one in the courtroom who wasn't completely surprised that he was testifying, that he was playing the game right in front of us.

Catherine Fitzgibbon was almost certain that Jules Halpern had advised, begged, and warned him not to do it, but there Shafer was anyway, striding toward the witness stand, looking as if he had been called up there to be ceremoniously knighted by the queen.

He couldn't resist the stage, could he? He looked every bit as confident and in control as he had the night I arrested him for Patsy Hampton's murder. He was dressed in a navy-blue double-breasted suit, white shirt, and gold tie. Not a single blond hair was out of place, nor was there any hint of the anger that was boiling just under the surface of his meticulously groomed exterior.

Jules Halpern addressed him in conversational tones, but I was sure that he felt uneasy about this unnecessary gamble.

"Colonel Shafer, first, I want to thank you for coming to the witness stand. This is completely voluntary on your part. From the very beginning, you've stated that you wanted to come here to clear your name."

Shafer smiled politely and then cut off his lawyer with a raised hand. The lawyers on both sides of the bar exchanged looks. What was happening? What was he going to do?

I leaned way forward in my seat. It struck me that Jules Halpern might actually *know* that his client was guilty. If so, he wouldn't be able to cross-examine him. Legally, he couldn't ask questions that disguised the real facts as he knew them.

This was the only way Shafer could have his moment in the sun: a soliloquy. Once called to the stand, Shafer could give a speech. It was unusual but absolutely legal —and if Halpern knew that his client was guilty, it was the only way Shafer could take the stand and not be incriminated by his own attorney.

Shafer had the floor. "If you will please excuse me, Mr. Halpern, I believe I can talk to these good people myself. I really can manage. You see, I don't need a lot of expert help to tell the simple truth."

Jules Halpern stepped back, nodded sagely, and tried to keep his poise. What else could he do under the circumstances? If he hadn't known before that his client was an egomaniac or insane, he surely knew it now.

Shafer looked toward the jury. "It has been stated here in court that I am with British intelligence, and that I was MI-Six, a spy. I'm afraid that I am actually a rather unglamorous agent—Double-or-Nothing, if you will."

The light, well-aimed jab at himself drew laughter in the courtroom.

"I am a simple bureaucrat, like so many others who toil away their days and nights in Washington. I follow well-established procedures at the embassy. I get approvals for virtually everything I do. My homelife is simple and orderly as well. My wife and I have been married nearly sixteen years. We love each other dearly. We're devoted to our three children.

"So I want to apologize to my wife and children. I am so frightfully sorry for this hellish ordeal they've had to go through. To my son, Rob, and the twins, Tricia and Erica, I'm so sorry. If I'd had any idea what a circus this would become, I would have insisted on maintaining diplomatic immunity rather than trying to clear my name, our name, *their* name.

"While I'm making heartfelt apologies, I'll make one to all of you for being a bit of a bore right now. It's just that when you're accused of murder, something so heinous, so unthinkable, you want desperately to get it off your chest. You want to tell the truth more than anything else in the world. So that's what I'm doing today.

"You've heard the evidence—and there simply isn't any. You've heard character witnesses. And now you've heard from me. I did not kill Detective Patsy Hampton. I think you all know that, but I wanted to say it to you myself. Thank you for listening," he said, and bowed slightly in his seat.

Shafer was brief, but he was poised and articulate and, unfortunately, very believable. He always held eye contact with the jury members. His words weren't nearly as important as the way he delivered them.

Catherine Fitzgibbon came forward to do the cross-examination. She was careful with Shafer at first; she knew he had the jury on his side for the moment. She waited until near the end of her cross-exam to go after Shafer where he might be most vulnerable.

"Your statement was very nice, Mr. Shafer. Now, as you sit before this jury, you claim that your relationship with Dr. Cassady was strictly professional, that you did not have a sexual relationship with her, correct? Remember, you are under oath."

"Yes, absolutely. She was, and hopefully will continue to be, my therapist."

"Notwithstanding the fact that she admits to having a sexual relationship with you?"

Shafer held his hand out toward Jules Halpern, signaling for him not to object. "I believe that the court record will show that she did *not* admit to such."

Fitzgibbon frowned. "I don't follow? Why do *you* think she didn't answer counsel?"

Shafer shot back, "That's so obvious: because she didn't care to *dignify* such a question."

"And when she hung her head, sir, and looked down at her lap? She was nodding assent."

Shafer now looked at the jury and shook his head in amazement. "You misread her completely. You missed the point again, Counselor. Allow me to illustrate, if I may. As King Charles said before being beheaded, 'Give me my cloak lest they think I tremble from fear.' Dr. Elizabeth Cassady was deeply embarrassed by your associate's crude suggestion, and so was my family, and so am I."

Geoffrey Shafer looked at the prosecutor with steely eyes. He then acknowledged the jury again. "And so am I."

Chapter 99

THE TRIAL was almost over, and now came the really hard part: waiting for the verdict. That Tuesday, the jurors retired to the jury room to commence their deliberations in the murder trial of Geoffrey Shafer. For the first time, I allowed myself to actually think the unthinkable—that Shafer might be set free.

Sampson and I sat in the rear row of the courtroom and watched the twelve members depart: eight men and four women. John had come to court several times, calling it the "best and sleaziest show this side of the Oval Office," but I knew he was there to give me support.

"The son of a bitch is guilty; he's mad as little Davey Berkowitz," Sampson said as he watched Shafer. "But he has a lot of good actors on his side: doting wife, doting mistress, well-paid lawyers, Silly Billy. He could get away with it."

"It happens," I agreed. "Juries are hard to read. And getting harder."

I watched as Shafer courteously shook hands with the members of his defense team. Jules and Jane Halpern both had forced smiles on their faces. *They know, don't they? Their client is the Weasel, a mass murderer.*

"Geoffrey Shafer has the ability to make people believe in him when he needs to. He's the best actor I've seen," I said.

Then John left and I snuck out the back way again. This time neither Shafer nor the press was lying in wait downstairs or in the rear parking lot.

In the lot, I heard a woman's voice, and I stopped moving. *I thought it was Christine.* A dozen or so people were walking to their cars, seemingly unaware of me. I felt fevered and hot as I checked them all. None of them was her. Where had the voice come from?

I took a ride in the old Porsche and listened to George Benson on the CD player. I remembered the police report about Shafer's thrill-seeking ride that ended near Dupont Circle. It seemed a strangely appealing prospect. I took my own advice not to try to guess how the jury would decide the case. It could go either way.

I let myself think about Christine, and I choked up. It was too much. Tears began to stream down my cheeks. I had to pull over.

I took a deep breath, then another. The pain in my chest was still as fresh as it had been the day she disappeared in Bermuda. She had tried to stay away from me, but I wouldn't let her. I was responsible for what had happened to her.

I drove around Washington, riding in gently aimless circles. I finally reached home more than two and a half hours after leaving the courthouse.

Nana came running out of the house. She must have seen me pull into the driveway. She'd obviously been waiting for me.

I leaned out of the driver's-side window. The deejay was still talking congenially on Public Radio.

"What is it, old woman? What's the matter now?" I asked Nana.

"Ms. Fitzgibbon called you, Alex. The jury is coming back. They have a verdict."

Chapter 100

I WAS APPREHENSIVE as could be. But I was also curious beyond anything I could remember.

I backed out of the driveway and sped downtown. I got back to the courthouse in less than fifteen minutes. The crowd on E Street was even larger and more unruly than it had been at the height of the trial. At least a half-dozen Union Jacks waved in the wind; contrasting with them were American flags, including some painted across bare chests and faces.

I had to push and literally inch my way through the crush of people up close to the courthouse steps. I ignored every question from the press. I tried to avoid anyone with a camera in hand, or the hungry look of a reporter.

I entered the packed courtroom just before the jury filed back inside. "You almost missed it," I said to myself.

Judge Fescoe spoke to the crowd as soon as everyone was seated. "There will be no demonstrations when this verdict is read. If any demonstrations occur, marshals will clear this room immediately," he instructed in a soft but clear voice.

I stood a few rows behind the prosecution team and tried to find a regular breathing pattern. It was inconceivable that Geoffrey Shafer could be set free; there was no doubt in my mind that he'd murdered several people—not just Patsy Hampton, but at least some of the Jane Does as well. He was a wanton pattern killer, one of the worst, and had been getting away with it for years. I realized now that Shafer might be the most outrageous and daring of all the killers I'd faced. He played his game with the pedal pressed to the floor. He absolutely refused to lose.

"Mr. Foreman, do you have a verdict for us?" Judge Fescoe asked in somber tones.

Raymond Horton, the foreman, replied, "Your Honor, we have a verdict."

I glanced over at Shafer; he appeared confident. As he had since the trial began, he was dressed today in a tailored suit, white shirt, and tie. He had no conscience whatsoever; he had no fear of anything that might happen to him. Maybe that was a partial explanation for why he'd run free for so long.

Judge Fescoe looked unusually stern. "Very well. Will the defendant please rise?"

Geoffrey Shafer stood at the defense table, and his longish blond hair gleamed under the bright overhead lighting. He towered over Jules Halpern and his daughter, Jane. Shafer held his hands behind him, as if he were cuffed. I wondered if he might have a pair of twenty-sided dice clasped in them, the kind I had seen in his study.

Judge Fescoe addressed the foreman again. "As to count one of the indictment, Aggravated, Premeditated Murder in the First Degree, how do you find?"

The foreman, "*Not guilty,* Your Honor."

I felt as if my head had suddenly spun off. The audience packed into the small room went completely wild. The press rushed to the bar. The judge had promised to clear the room, but he was already retreating to his chambers.

I saw Shafer walk toward the press, but then he quickly passed them by. What was he doing now? He noticed a man in the crowd and nodded stiffly in his direction. Who was that?

Then Shafer continued toward where I was, in the fourth row. I wanted to vault over the chairs after him. I wanted him so bad, and I knew I had just lost my chance to do it the right way.

"Detective Cross," he said in his usual supercilious manner. "Detective Cross, there's something I want to say. I've been holding it in for months."

The press closed in; the scene was becoming smothering and claustrophobic. Cameras flashed on all sides. Now that the trial had ended, there was nothing to prevent picture-taking inside the courtroom. Shafer was aware of the rare photo opportunity; of course he was. He spoke again, so that everyone gathered around us could hear. It was suddenly quiet where we stood, a pocket of silence and foreboding expectation.

"You killed her," he said, and stared deeply into my eyes, almost to the back of my skull. *"You killed her."*

I went numb. My legs were suddenly weak. I knew he didn't mean Patsy Hampton.

He meant Christine.

She was dead.

Geoffrey Shafer had killed her. He had taken everything from me, just as he'd warned me he would.

He had won.

Chapter 101

SHAFER WAS A FREE MAN, and he was enjoying the bloody hell out of it. He'd wagered his life. He had gambled, and he had won big-time. *Big-time!* He had never felt anything quite like this exhilarating moment following the verdict.

Shafer accompanied Lucy and the children to a by-invitation-only press conference held in the pompous, high-ceilinged grand-jury room. He posed for countless photos with his family. All of them hugged him again and again, and Lucy couldn't stop crying like the brain-dead, hopelessly spoiled and crazy child she was. If some people thought *he* was a drug abuser, they'd be shocked by Lucy's intake. Christ, that was how he'd first learned about the amazing world of pharmaceuticals.

He finally punched his arm into the air and held it there as a mocking sign of victory. Cameras flashed everywhere in the room. They couldn't get enough of him. There were nearly a hundred reporters wedged into the room. The women reporters loved him most of all. He was a legitimate media star now, wasn't he? He was a hero again.

A few gate-crashing agents of fame and fortune pressed their cards at him, promising obscene amounts of money for his story. He didn't need any of their tawdry offers. Months before, he had picked out a powerful New York and Hollywood agent.

Christ, he was free as a bird! He was absolutely flying now. After the press conference, claiming concern for their safety, he sent his wife and children ahead without him.

He stayed behind in the court law library and firmed up book-deal details with Jules Halpern and representatives from the Bertelsmann Group, now the most powerful book-publishing conglomerate in the world. He had assured them that they would get his story, but of course they weren't going to get anything close to the truth. Wasn't that the way with the so-called tell-all, bare-all nonfiction published these days? The Bertelsmann people knew this, and still they'd paid him dearly.

After the meeting, he took the slow-riding lift down to the court's indoor car park. He was still feeling incredibly high, which could be dangerous. A set of twenty-sided dice was burning a hole in the pocket of his suit trousers.

He desperately wanted to play the game. Now! The Four Horsemen. Or better yet, Solipsis—*his* version of the game. He wouldn't give in to that urge, though, not yet. It was too dangerous, even for him.

Since the beginning of the trial, he had been parking the Jaguar in the same spot; he *did* have his patterns, after all. He'd never bothered to put coins in the meter, not once. Every day there was a pile of five-dollar tickets under the windshield wiper.

Today was no exception.

He grabbed the absurd parking tickets off the windshield and crumpled them into a ball in his fist. Then he dropped the wad of paper onto the oil-stained concrete floor.

"I have diplomatic immunity," he said aloud, and smiled as he climbed into his Jag.

Book Five
_____

ENDGAME

SHAFER COULDN'T BELIEVE IT. He had made a very serious and perhaps irreversible mistake. The result wasn't what he had expected, and now his whole world seemed to be falling apart. At times he thought it couldn't have been any worse had he gone to prison for the cold-blooded murder of Patsy Hampton.

Shafer knew that he wasn't just being paranoid or mad. Several of the pathetic wankers inside the embassy watched him every bloody time he stepped out of his office. They seemed to resent and openly despise him, especially the women. Who had turned them against him? Somebody surely was responsible.

He was the white, English O. J. Simpson. A weird, off-color joke to them. Guilty though proven innocent.

So Shafer mostly stayed inside his office with the door closed, sometimes locked. He performed his few remaining duties with a growing sense of irritation and frustration, and a sense of the absurd. It was driving him mad to be trapped like this, to be a pathetic spectacle for the embassy staff.

He idly played with his computer and waited for the game of the Four Horsemen to resume, but the other players had cut him off. They insisted that it was too dangerous to play, even to communicate, and *not one of them* understood why this was the perfect time to play.

Shafer stared out onto Massachusetts Avenue for interminably long stretches during the day. He listened to call-in talk shows on the radio. He was getting angrier and angrier. He needed to play.

Someone was knocking on the door of his office. He turned his head sharply and felt a spike of pain in the back of his neck. The phone had begun to ring. He picked up and heard the temp he'd been assigned. Ms. Wynne Hamerman was on the intercom.

"Mr. Andrew Jones is here to see you," she said.

Andrew Jones? Shafer was shocked. Jones was a hot-shit director from the Security Service in London. Shafer hadn't known he was in Washington. What the hell was this visit about? Andrew Jones was a high-level, very tough prick who wouldn't just drop by for tea and biscuits. *Mustn't keep him waiting too long.*

Jones was standing there, and he looked impatient, almost furious. What was this about? His steely blue eyes were cold and hard; his face was as rigid as that of an English soldier posted in Belfast. In contrast, his brilliant red hair and mustache made him look benign, almost jolly. He was called Andrew the Red back in London.

"Let's go inside your office, shall we? Shut the door behind you," Jones said in a low but commanding voice.

Shafer was just getting past his initial surprise, but he was also starting to lose it. Who did this pompous asshole think he was to come barging into his office like this? By what right was he here? How dare he? The toad! The glorified lackey from London.

"You can sit down, Shafer," Jones said. Another imperious command. "I'll be brief and to the point."

"Of course," Shafer answered. He remained standing. "Please do be brief and get to the point. I'm sure we're both busy."

Jones lit up a cigarette, took a long puff, then let the smoke out slowly.

"That's illegal here in Washington," Shafer goaded him.

"You'll receive orders to return to England in thirty days' time," said Jones as he continued to puff on his cigarette. "You're an embarrassment here in Washington, as you will be in London. Of course, over there the tabloids have re-created you as a martyr of the brutal and inefficient American police and judicial systems. They like to think of this as 'D.C. Confidential,' more evidence of wholesale corruption and naïveté in the States. Which we both know, in this case, is complete crap."

Shafer sneered. "How dare you come in here and talk to me like this, Jones? I was framed for a heinous crime I didn't commit. I was acquitted by an American jury. Have you forgotten that?"

Jones frowned and stared him down. "Only because crucial evidence wasn't allowed in the trial. The blood on your trousers? That poor woman's blood in the bathroom drain at your mistress's?" He blew smoke out the side of his mouth. "We know everything, you pathetic fool. We know you're a stone-cold killing freak. So you'll *go* back to London and stay there —until we catch you at something. Which we will, Shafer. We'll make something up if we have to.

"I feel sick to my stomach just being in the same room with you. Legally, you've escaped punishment this time, but we're watching you so very closely now. We will get you somewhere, and someday soon."

Shafer looked amused. He couldn't hold back a smile. He knew he shouldn't, but he couldn't resist the play. "You can try, you insufferable, sanctimonious shit. You can certainly try. But get in line. And now, if you please, I have work to do."

Andrew Jones shook his head. "Well, actually, you *don't* have any work to do,

Shafer. But I am happy to leave. The stench in here is absolutely overpowering. When was the last time you bathed?" He laughed contemptuously. "Christ, you've completely lost it."

Chapter 103

THAT AFTERNOON, I met with Jones and three of his agents at the Willard Hotel, near the White House. I had called the meeting. Sampson was there, too. He'd been reinstated in the department, but that didn't stop him from doing what had originally gotten him into trouble.

"I believe he's crazy," Jones said of Shafer. "He smells like a commode at boot camp. He's definitely going down for the count. What's your take on his mental state?"

I knew Geoffrey Shafer inside and out by now. I'd read about his family: his brothers, his long-suffering mother, his domineering father. Their travels from military base to military base until he was twelve. "Here's what I think. It started with a serious bipolar disorder, what used to be called manic depression. He had it when he was a kid. Now he's strung out on pharmaceutical drugs: Xanax, Benadryl, Haldol, Ativan, Valium, Librium, several others. It's quite a cocktail. Available from local doctors for the right price. I'm surprised he can function at all. But he survives. He doesn't go down. He always wins."

"I told Geoff he has to leave Washington. How do you think he'll take it?" Jones asked me. "I swear his office smelled as if a dead body had been festering there for a couple of days."

"Actually, his disorder can involve an accompanying odor, but it's usually steely, like metal—very pungent, sticks to your nostrils. He probably isn't bathing. But his instincts for playing the game, for winning and surviving, are amazing," I said. "He won't stop."

"What's happening with the other players?" Sampson inquired. "The so-called Horsemen?"

"They claim that the game is over, and that it was only a fantasy game for them," Jones told him. "Oliver Highsmith stays in touch, mostly to keep tabs on us, I'm sure. He's actually a scary bastard in his own right. Says he's saddened by the murder of Detective Hampton. He's still not a hundred percent sure that Shafer is the killer. Urges me to keep my mind open on that one."

"Is your mind open on it?" I asked, looking around the room at the others.

Jones didn't hesitate. "I have no doubt that Geoffrey Shafer is a multiple murderer. We've seen enough and heard enough from you. He is quite possibly a homicidal maniac beyond anything we've ever known. And I also have no doubt that eventually he's going down."

I nodded my head. "I agree," I said, "with everything you just said. But especially the homicidal-maniac part."

Chapter 104

SHAFER WAS talking to himself again that night. He couldn't help it, and the more he tried to stop, the worse it became; the more he fretted, the more he talked to himself.

"They can all bugger off—Jones, Cross, Lucy and the kids, Boo Cassady, the other spineless players. Screw them all. There was a reason behind the Four Horsemen. It wasn't just a game. There was more to it than simple horseplay."

The house at Kalorama was empty, much too quiet at night. It was huge and ridiculous as only an American house can be. The "original" architectural detail, the double living room, the six fireplaces, the long-ago dead flowers from Aster florist, the unread books in gold and brown leather bindings, Lucy's marmite. It was driving him up the twelve-foot-high walls.

He spent the next hour or so trying to convince himself that he wasn't crazy— more specifically, that he wasn't an addict. Recently, he'd added another doctor in Maryland to his sources for the drugs. Unfortunately, the illegal prescriptions cost him a fortune. He couldn't keep it up forever. The Lithium and Haldol were to control his mood swings, which were very real. The Thorazine was for acute anxiety, which was fucking bloody real as well. The Narcan had also been prescribed for his mood swings. The multiple injections of Loradol were for something else, some pain from he couldn't remember when. He knew there were good reasons, too, for the Xanax, the Compazine, the Benadryl.

Lucy had already fled home to London, and she'd taken the traitorous children with her. They'd left exactly one week after the trial ended. Her father was the real cause. He'd come to Washington and spoken to Lucy for less than an hour, and she'd packed up and left like the Goody Two-shoes she'd always been. Before she departed, Lucy had the nerve to tell Shafer she'd stood by him for the sake of the children and her father, but now her "duty" was over. She didn't believe he was a murderer, as her father did, but she knew he was an adulterer, and that, she couldn't take for one moment longer.

God, how he despised his little wifey. Before Lucy left, *he* made it clear to *her* that the real reason she'd performed her "duty" was so he wouldn't reveal her unsavory drug habit to the press, which he *would* have done and still might do, anyway.

At eleven o'clock he had to go out for a drive, his nightly "constitutional." He was feeling unbearably jittery and claustrophobic. He wondered if he could control himself for another night, another minute. His skin was crawling, and he had dozens of irritating little tics. He couldn't stop tapping his goddamn foot!

The dice were burning a bloody hole in his trouser pocket. His mind was racing in a dozen haphazard directions, all of them very bad. He wanted to, needed to, kill somebody. It had been this way with him for a long time, and that had been his dirty little secret. The other Horsemen knew the story; they even knew how it had begun. Shafer had been a decent English soldier, but ultimately too ambitious to remain in the army. He had transferred into MI6 with the help of Lucy's father. He thought there would be more room for advancement in MI6.

His first posting was Bangkok, which was where he met James Whitehead, George Bayer, and eventually Oliver High-smith. Whitehead and Bayer spent several weeks working on Shafer, recruiting him for a specialized job: he would be an assassin, their own personal hit man for the worst sort of wet work. Over the next two years, he did three sanctions in Asia, and found that he truly loved the feeling of power that killing gave him. Oliver High-smith, who ran both Bayer and Whitehead from London, once told him to depersonalize the act, to think of it as a game, and that was what he did. He had never stopped being an assassin.

Shafer turned on the CD in the Jag. *Loud,* to drown out the multiple voices raging in his head. The old-age-home rockers

Jimmy Page and Robert Plant began a duet inside the cockpit of his car.

He backed out of the drive and headed down Tracy Place. He gunned the car and had it up close to sixty in the block between his house and Twenty-fourth Street. *Time for another suicidal drive?* he wondered.

Red lights flashed on the side of Twenty-fourth Street. Shafer cursed as a D.C. police patrol car eased down the street toward him. *Goddamn it!*

He pulled the Jag over to the curb and waited. His brain was screaming. "Assholes. Bloody impertinent assholes! And you're an asshole, too!" he told himself in a loud whisper. "Show some self-control, Geoff. Get yourself under control. Shape up. Right now!"

The Metro patrol car pulled up behind him, almost door to door. He could see two cops lurking inside.

One of them got out slowly and walked over to the Jag's driver's-side window. The cop swaggered like a hot-shit all-American cinema hero. Shafer wanted to blow him away. Knew he could do it. He had a hot semiautomatic under the seat. He touched the grip, and God, it felt good.

"License and registration, sir," the cop said, looking unbearably smug. A distorted voice inside Shafer's head screeched, *Shoot him now. It will blow everybody's mind if you kill another policeman.*

He handed over the requested identification, though, and managed a wanker's sheepish grin. "We're out of Pampers at home. Trip to the Seven-Eleven was in order. I know I was going too fast, and I'm sorry, Officer. Blame it on baby-brain. You have any kids?"

The patrolman didn't say a word; not an ounce of civility in the prick. He wrote out a speeding ticket. Took his sweet time about it.

"There you go, Mr. Shafer." The patrol officer handed him the speeding ticket and said, "Oh, and by the way, we're watching you, shithead. We're all over you, man. You didn't get away with murdering Patsy Hampton. You just *think* you did."

A set of car lights blinked on and off, on and off, on the side street where the patrol car had been sitting a few moments earlier.

Shafer stared, squinted back into the

darkness. He recognized the car, a black Porsche.

Cross was there, watching. Alex Cross wouldn't go away.

Chapter 105

ANDREW JONES sat next to me in the quiet, semi-darkened cockpit of the Porsche. We'd been working closely together for almost two weeks. Jones and the Security Service were intent on stopping Shafer before he committed another murder. They were also tracking War, Famine, and Conqueror.

We watched silently as Geoffrey Shafer slowly turned the Jaguar around and drove back toward his house.

"He saw us. He knows my car," I said. "Good."

I couldn't see Shafer's face in the darkness, but I could almost feel the heat rising from the top of his head. I knew he was crazed. The words "homicidal maniac" kept drifting through my mind. Jones and I were looking at one, and he was still running free. He'd already gotten away with one murder—*several* murders.

"Alex, aren't you concerned about possibly putting him into a rage state?" Jones asked as the Jaguar eased to a stop in front of the Georgian-style house. There were no lights on in the driveway area, so we wouldn't be able to see Geoffrey Shafer for the next few seconds. We couldn't tell if he'd gone inside.

"He's already in a rage state. He's lost his job, his wife, the children, the game he lives for. Worst of all, his freedom to come and go has been curtailed. Shafer doesn't like having limitations put on him, hates to be boxed in. He can't stand to lose."

"So you think he'll do something rash."

"Not rash, he's too clever. But he'll make a move. It's how the game is played."

"And then we'll mess with his head yet again?"

"Yes, we will. Absolutely."

Late that night, as I was driving home, I decided to stop at St. Anthony's. The church is unusual in this day and age in that it's open at night. Monsignor John Kelliher believes that's the way it should be, and he's willing to live with the vandalism and the petty theft. Mostly, though, the people in the neighborhood watch over St. Anthony's.

A couple of worshipers were inside the candlelit church when I entered, around midnight. There are usually a few "parishioners" inside. Homeless people aren't allowed to sleep there, but they wander in and out all through the night.

I sat watching the familiar red votive lamps flicker and blink. I sucked in the thick smell of incense from Benediction. I stared up at the large gold-plated crucifix and the beautiful stained-glass windows that I've loved since I was a boy.

I lit a candle for Christine, and I hoped that somehow, someway, she might still be alive. It didn't seem likely. My memory of her was fading a little bit, and I hated that. A column of pain went from my stomach to my chest, making it hard for me to breathe. It has been this way since the night she'd disappeared, almost a year ago.

And then, for the first time, I admitted to myself that she was gone. I would never see her again. The thought caught like a shard of glass in my throat. Tears welled in my eyes. "I love you," I whispered to no one. "I love you so much, and I miss you terribly."

I said a few more prayers, then I finally rose from the long wooden pew and silently made my way toward the doors of the vestibule. I didn't see the woman crouching in a side row. She startled me with a sudden movement.

I recognized her from the soup kitchen. Her name was Magnolia. That was all I knew about her, just an odd first name, maybe a made-up one. She called out to me in a loud voice, "Hey, Peanut Butter Man, now you know what it's like."

Chapter 106

JONES AND SANDY GREENBERG from Interpol had helped get the other three Horsemen under surveillance. The net being cast was large, as the catch could be if we succeeded.

The huge potential scandal in England was being carefully watched and monitored by the Security Service. If four English agents turned out to be murderers involved in a bizarre "game," the fallout would be widespread and devastating for the intelligence community.

Shafer dutifully went to the embassy on Wednesday and Thursday. He arrived just before nine and left promptly at five. Once inside, he stayed out of sight in his small office, not even venturing out for lunch. He spent hours on America Online, which we monitored.

Both days, he wore the same gray slacks and a double-breasted blue blazer. His clothes were uncharacteristically wrinkled and unkempt. His thick blond hair was combed back; it looked dirty and greasy, and resisted the high winds flowing through Washington. He looked pale, seemed nervous and fidgety.

Was he going to crash?

After dinner on Friday night, Nana and I sat out in back of the house on Fifth Street. We were spending more time together than we had in years. I knew she was concerned about me, and I let her help as much as she wanted. For both our sakes.

Jannie and Damon were washing the dishes inside and managing not to squabble too much. Damon washed while Jannie dried. Damon's tape deck played the beautiful score from the movie *Beloved.*

"Most families have a dishwasher and drier these days," Nana said, after she'd taken a sip of her tea. "Slavery has ended in America, Alex. Did you happen to hear about that?"

"We have a dishwasher and drier, too.

Sounds like they're in good working order. Low maintenance, low cost. Hard to beat."

Nana clucked. "See how long it lasts."

"If you want a dishwasher, we can buy one—or are you just practicing the fine art of being argumentative before you launch into something more deserving of your talents? As I remember, you are a fan of Demosthenes and Cicero."

She nudged me with her elbow. "Wiseapple," she said. "Think you're so smart."

I shook my head. "Not really, Nana. That's never been one of my big problems."

"No, I suppose not. You're right, you don't have a big head about yourself." Nana stared into my eyes. I could almost feel her peering into my soul. She has an ability to look very deeply into things that really matter. "You ever going to stop blaming yourself?" she asked me. "You look just terrible."

"Thank you. Are you ever going to stop nagging me?" I asked, smiling at her. Nana could always bring me out of the doldrums, in her own special way.

She nodded her small head. "Of course I

will. I'll stop one day. Nobody lives forever, Grannyson."

I laughed. "You probably will, though. Live longer than me or the kids."

Nana showed lots of teeth—her own, too. "I *do* feel pretty good, considering everything," she said. "You're still chasing him, aren't you? That's what you're doing nights. You and John Sampson, that Englishman Andrew Jones."

I sighed. "Yeah, I am. And we're going to get him. There may be four men involved in a series of murders. Here and in Asia, Jamaica, London."

She beckoned to me with a bent, crabbed forefinger. "Come closer now."

I grinned at her. She's such a soft touch, really, such a sweetie, but such a hard-ass, too. "You want me to sit down on your lap, old woman? You sure about that?"

"Good Lord, no. Don't sit on me, Alex. Just lean over and show some respect for my age and wisdom. Give me a big hug while you're at it."

I did as I was told, and I noticed there wasn't any fuss or clatter coming from the kitchen anymore.

I glanced at the screen door and saw

that my two little busybodies were watching, their faces pressed against the mesh wire. I waved them away from the door, and their faces disappeared.

"I want you to be so very, very careful," Nana whispered as I held her gently. "But I want you to get him somehow, someway. That man is the worst of all of them. Geoffrey Shafer is the worst, Alex, the most evil."

Chapter 107

THE GAME had never really ended, but it had changed tremendously since the trial in Washington.

It was five-thirty in the evening in London, and Conqueror was waiting at his computer. He was both anxious and feverishly excited about what was happening: the Four Horsemen was starting up again.

It was 1:30 A.M. in Manila, in the Philippines. Famine was ready for a message, and a new beginning to the game he loved.

And War awaited news of the Four Horsemen at his large house on the island of Jamaica. He, too, was obsessed with how it would end and whether he would be the winner.

It was twelve-thirty in Washington. Geoffrey Shafer was driving fast to the White Flint Mall, from the embassy. He had a lot to accomplish that afternoon. He was revved and manic.

He sped up Massachusetts Avenue, past the British Embassy and the vice president's house. He wondered if he was being followed and supposed it was possible. Alex Cross and the other police were out there, just waiting to get him. He hadn't spotted them yet, which only meant that they were getting serious now.

He made a quick right, hit a traffic circle, and shot onto Nebraska Avenue, heading toward American University. He snaked around back roads near the university, then got on Wisconsin and sped toward the mall.

He entered Bloomingdale's and found the department store sparsely peopled—a little depressing, actually. Good; he despised the American shopping scene anyway. It reminded him of Lucy and her brood. He walked at a leisurely pace through the men's clothing section. He picked up a few overpriced Ralph Lauren Polo sport shirts, then two pairs of dark trousers.

He draped a black Giorgio Armani suit over his arm and took the bundle into the changing rooms. At a security desk inside, he handed the clothes to an attendant on duty, posted there to curtail shoplifters, no doubt.

"Changed my mind," he said.

"That's not a problem, sir."

Shafer then jogged down a narrow corridor that led to a rear exit. He sprinted toward the glass doors and burst through them into a parking lot in back. He saw signs for Bruno Cipriani and Lord & Taylor and knew he was headed in the right direction.

A Ford Taurus was parked there near the F pole. Shafer jumped inside, started it, and drove up the Rockville Pike to Montrose Crossing, a little over a mile away.

He didn't think anyone was following him now. He passed Montrose and went north to the Federal Plaza shopping center. Once there, he entered the Cyber Exchange, which sold new and used software and lots of computers.

His eyes darted left and right until he saw exactly what he needed.

"I'd like to try out the new iMac," he told the salesperson who approached him.

"Be my guest. You need any assistance, holler," the salesperson said. "It's easy."

"Yes, I think I'm fine. I'll call if I get stuck. I'm pretty sure I'm going to buy the iMac, though."

"Excellent choice."

"Yes. Excellent, excellent."

The lazy clerk left him alone, and Shafer immediately booted up. The display model was connected on-line. He felt a rush of manic excitement, but also a tinge of sadness as he typed in his message to the other players. He'd thought this through and knew what had to be said, what had to be done.

GREETINGS AND SALUTATIONS. THIS GLORIOUS AND UNPRECEDENTED ADVENTURE OF EIGHT YEARS, THE FOUR HORSEMEN, IS NEARLY AT AN END NOW. YOU HAVE STATED YOUR CASE VERY LOGICALLY, AND I ACCEPT THE REGRETTABLE CONCLUSION YOU'VE REACHED. THE GAME HAS

BECOME TOO DANGEROUS. SO I PROPOSE THAT WE CREATE AN UNFORGETTABLE ENDING. I BELIEVE THAT A FACE-TO-FACE MEETING IS A FITTING END. IT'S THE ONLY CONCLUSION THAT I CAN ACCEPT.

THIS WAS INEVITABLE, I SUPPOSE, AND WE HAVE DISCUSSED IT MANY TIMES BEFORE. YOU KNOW WHERE THE GAME ENDS. I PROPOSE THAT WE START PLAY ON THURSDAY. TRUST ME, I WILL BE THERE FOR THE GRAND FINALE. IF NECESSARY, I CAN BEGIN THE GAME WITHOUT YOU. DON'T MAKE ME DO THAT. . . . *DEATH.*

Chapter 108

AT NINE O'CLOCK on Monday morning, Shafer joined the monotonous, stomach-turning line of workaday morons stuck in traffic going in the direction of Embassy Row. He had the intoxicating thought that he would never again have to work after today. Everything in his life was about to change. He couldn't go back.

His heart was pounding as he stopped and waited at the green light on Massachusetts Avenue near the embassy. Car horns beeped behind him, and he was reminded of his suicide run a year ago. Those were the days, damn it. Then he blasted through on the red. He ran. He had rehearsed his escape. This was for keeps.

He saw two blocks of clear roadway

ahead, and he floored the gas pedal. The Jaguar leaped forward with raw, phallic power, as it were. The sports car rocketed toward the puzzle of side streets around American University.

Ten minutes later he was turning in to the White Flint Mall at fifty, gunning the Jag up to fifty-five, sixty, sixty-five as he sped across the mostly empty lot. He was sure no one had followed him.

He drove toward a large Borders Books & Music store, turned right, then zoomed up a narrow side lane between buildings.

There were five exits out of the mall that he knew of. He accelerated again, tires squealing.

The surrounding neighborhood was a warren of narrow streets. Still no one was behind him, not a single car.

He knew of a little-used one-way entrance onto the Rockville Pike. He got on the road, heading out against the barrage of traffic streaming to work in the city. He hadn't spotted any cars speeding behind him inside the mall, or on the side streets, or on the pike.

They probably had only one car, or at most two, on him in the morning. That made the most sense to Shafer. Neither the Washington Metro police nor the Security Service would approve a larger surveillance detail to follow him. He didn't think they would, anyway.

He'd probably lost them. He whooped loudly and started blaring the Jag's horn at all the pathetic suckers and fools stuck in the oncoming lanes, headed for work. He'd been waiting nearly eight years for this.

It was finally here.

Endgame.

Chapter 109

"WE'VE STILL GOT HIM?" I asked Jones, nervously looking around at the half-dozen agents working in the crisis room inside the British Embassy. The room was filled with state-of-the-art electrical equipment, including half a dozen video monitors.

"Still got him. He won't get away that easily, Alex. Besides, we think we know where he and the others are going now."

We had a tiny, sophisticated homing device on the Jaguar, but there was a reasonable chance that Shafer would discover it. So far, he hadn't. And now he was running in the Jag, running with the bait— at least that was what we *thought* was happening.

The Horsemen were all on the move. Oliver Highsmith had been followed from his home in Surrey to Gatwick Airport, outside London. Agents at the airport made sure that Conqueror got on the British Air flight to New York, then called Washington to report he was en route.

A couple of hours later, an agent phoned from the Philippines. George Bayer was at Ninoy Aquino Airport in Manila. Famine had purchased a ticket to Jamaica, with a stopover in New York.

We already knew that James Whitehead had retired to Jamaica, and that he was on the island now. War was waiting for the others to arrive.

"I'm trying to get a fixed pattern for the Four Horsemen game, but there are several points of view at work. That's what they like about the game, what makes it so addictive," I said to Jones as we waited for more information to come in.

"We know that at least three of them have been playing the game since they were stationed in Thailand, in 'ninety-one. Around that time, bar girls and prostitutes began to disappear in Bangkok. The local police didn't spend much time on the investigations. Girls in Pat Pong had disappeared before. The police have somewhat the same attitude here in Washington with respect to the Jane Doe killings. These girls didn't mean much. They were written off. Murders and disappearances in Southeast certainly aren't investigated like ones in Georgetown or on Capitol Hill. It's one of Washington's dirty little secrets."

Jones lit a new cigarette off the butt of his last one. He puffed, then said, "It might be just Shafer who's involved in the actual murders, Alex. Either that or the others are much more careful than he is."

I shrugged my shoulders. I didn't think so, but I didn't have enough concrete evidence to argue my case effectively with Jones, who was himself no slouch as a detective.

"The end of the Four Horsemen is coming, right? Can they really end their little fantasy game?" Sampson asked.

"It sure looks like they're getting together," I said. "Four former British agents, four grown men who love to play

diabolical games. In my opinion, four murderers."

"Possibly." Andrew Jones finally admitted that the unthinkable could be true:
"Alex, I'm afraid you could be right."

Chapter 110

JAMAICA MUST HAVE BEEN chosen because it was relatively private, and because James Whitehead owned a large beach house there. But perhaps there were other angles attached to the game of the Four Horsemen. I hoped that we would know soon enough.

Oliver Highsmith and George Bayer arrived on the island within minutes of each other. They met at the baggage claim inside Donald Sangster Airport, then drove for about an hour to the posh Jamaica Inn in Ocho Rios.

We were on the move, too. Sampson and I had gotten there on an early-morning flight from D.C. The weather was glorious. Blue skies, warm breezes. We heard strains of English and Jamaican Creole at the airport, reggae and ska. The rustle of the banana trees as the sea breeze rushed through them was like a soft chorus.

The hotel in Ocho Rios was very private and old-fashioned, just forty-five rooms overlooking the sea. We arrived there simultaneously with four English teams. There were also two teams of detectives from Kingston.

The English High Commission office in Kingston had been alerted about our presence and our purpose here. Full cooperation had been promised. Everyone was committed to bringing down all four game players, whatever the consequences, and I was very impressed with the English group, and also with the local detectives.

We waited for Geoffrey Shafer. Sampson and I were strategically positioned to watch the narrow, shaded road that led to the hotel. We were on a lush hillside between the hotel and the sparkling blue Caribbean sea. Andrew Jones and another agent were in a second car hidden near the hotel's rear entrance. Six of Jones's agents were posing as porters and maintenance workers at the hotel. The Jamaican detectives were also posted on the grounds.

We'd had no news about Shafer. He had finally lost us. But we believed he would join the others. Jones complained that there weren't enough of us to stop Shafer if he was coming after the others. I agreed; if Shafer was playing kamikaze, there would be no adequate defense.

So we waited and waited. Continual updates came in over the car's short-wave radio. The messages didn't stop all afternoon. They were a kind of electronic heartbeat for our surveillance detail.

"Oliver Highsmith is still in his room. Doesn't want to be disturbed, apparently. . . ."

"Bayer is in his room as well. Subject was spotted on the terrace about ten minutes ago, checking out the beach with binoculars. . . ."

"Bayer has left his room. He's taking a dip in the deep blue sea. Subject is in a red-striped swimming costume. Difficult to miss. Makes the job easier. Not on the eyes, though. . . ."

"Black Mercedes arriving at the front

gate. Driver's tall and blond. Could be Geoffrey Shafer. You see him, Alex?"

I reported immediately, "The blond man isn't Shafer. Repeat, it isn't Shafer. Too young, probably American. Young wife and two children tagging along. False alarm. It isn't Shafer."

The radio reports continued.

"Highsmith has just ordered up from room service. Two English breakfasts in the middle of the day. One of our people will take it up to him. . . ."

"Bayer is back from his swim. He's well tanned. Little guy, but muscular. Tried to hit on some ladies. Struck out."

Finally, at around six o'clock, I made another report. "James Whitehead just drove up in a green Range Rover! He's coming inside the hotel. War is here."

Only one more game player to go.

We waited. Death had yet to arrive.

Chapter 111

SHAFER was in no particular hurry to flash the checkered flag. He took his sweet time thinking through each possible scenario. He had spotted the coast of Jamaica on the horizon several hours before. He had originally flown to Puerto Rico, then sailed from there in a chartered boat. He wanted to be able to leave either by air or by sea.

Now he calmly waited for nightfall, drifting in his boat with the cooling trade winds. It was the famous "blue hour" on the sea, just past sunset, extraordinarily serene and beautiful. Also magical and slightly unreal. He had finished five hundred more push-ups on the deck of the boat, and he wasn't even winded. He could see half a dozen large cruise ships anchored near Ocho Rios. All around him were scores of smaller boats like his own.

He remembered reading somewhere that the island of Jamaica had once been the personal property of Christopher Columbus. It pleased him to think there had been a time when a man could take whatever he wanted, and often did. His body was tight and hard, and he was bronze from the three days of sun during his trip. His hair was bleached even blonder than usual. He'd had the drugs under control for almost a week now. It had been an act of will, and he'd risen to the challenge. He wanted to win.

Shafer felt like a god. No, he *was* a god. He controlled every move in his own life and in the lives of several others. There were surprises left, he thought as he slowly sprayed his body with cooling streams of water. There were surprises for everybody who still chose to be in the game.

His game.

His plan.

His ending.

Because this wasn't just a game; it never had been. The other players had to know that by now. They understood what they had done, and why there had to be payback. It was what the Four Horsemen had been all about from the beginning: *Endgame is payback, and payback is mine . . . or theirs? Who knows for sure?*

His father had taught him and his brothers to sail, probably the only useful thing he'd ever done for Shafer. He actually could find peace on the sea. It was the real reason he'd come to Jamaica by boat.

At eight o'clock he swam to shore, passing several of the smaller sailboats and a few motorboats. He found the physical exertion a neat antidote to his anxiety and nerves. He was a strong swimmer and diver, and good at most other sports as well.

The night air was peaceful and calm and fragrant. The sea was flat. Not a ripple disturbed the surface. Well, there would be plenty of ripples soon.

A car was waiting for him just off the coast road, a black Ford Mustang, glossy and shiny in the moonlight.

He smiled when he saw it. The game was progressing beautifully.

Famine was there to meet him.

No, Famine was there for another reason, wasn't he?

George Bayer was waiting on shore to kill him.

Chapter 112

"GEORGE BAYER isn't in his room. He's not with Oliver Highsmith or James White-head, either. Damn it to hell! He's loose."

The alarming message went out over the two-way radio. Sampson and I had been watching the south side of the hotel for close to eight hours, and we were sure George Bayer hadn't come our way.

We heard Andrew Jones's concerned voice on the radio. "Remember that all of the Four Horsemen are agents, like ourselves. They're capable and deadly. Let's find Bayer right away, and be extra alert for Geoffrey Shafer. Shafer is the most dangerous player—at least we *think* he is."

Sampson and I hurried out of our rented sedan. We had our guns out, but they seemed inappropriate at the beautiful and serene resort. I remembered feeling the same way nearly a year before, in Bermuda.

"Bayer didn't come this way," Sampson said. I knew he was concerned that Jones's people had lost Famine. *We* wouldn't have made that mistake, but we were seen as backup, not the primary team.

The two of us quickly walked up a nearby hill that gave us a perspective on the manicured lawns rolling down toward the hotel's private beach. It was getting dark, but the grounds near the hotel were relatively well lit. A couple in bathing suits and robes slowly walked toward us. They were holding hands, oblivious to the danger. No George Bayer, though. And no Shafer.

"How do they end this thing?" Sampson asked. "How do you think the game ends?"

"I don't think any of them knows for sure. They probably have game plans, but anything can happen now. It all depends on Shafer, if he follows the rules. I think he's beyond that, and the other players know it."

We hurried along, running close to the hotel buildings. We were getting nervous and concerned looks from the hotel guests we passed on the narrow, winding sidewalk.

"They're all killers. Even Jones finally admits that. They killed as agents, and then they didn't want to stop. They liked it. Now maybe they plan to kill one another. Winner takes all."

"And Geoffrey Shafer hates to lose," said Sampson.

"Shafer doesn't ever lose. We've seen that already. *That's* his pattern, John. It's what we missed from the start."

"He doesn't get away this time, sugar. No matter what, Shafer doesn't walk."

I didn't answer Sampson.

Chapter 113

SHAFER wasn't even breathing hard as he made it to the white-sand shoreline. George Bayer stepped out of the black Ford Mustang, and Shafer watched for a weapon to appear. He continued to walk forward, playing the game of games for the highest stakes of all: his life.

"You bloody *swam?*" Bayer asked, his voice jovial yet taunting.

"Well, actually, it's a fantastic night for it," Shafer said, and casually shook water off his body. He waited for Bayer to move on him. He observed the way he tensed and untensed his right hand. Watched the slight forward slant of his shoulders.

Shafer took off a waterproof backpack and pulled out fresh, dry clothes and

576 / JAMES PATTERSON

shoes. Now he had access to his weapons. "Let me guess. Oliver suggested that you all gang up on me," he said. "Three against one."

Bayer smiled slyly. "Of course. That had to be considered as an option. But we rejected it because it wasn't consistent with our characters in the game."

Shafer shook his hair, let the water drip off. As he dressed, he turned halfway away from Bayer. He smiled to himself. God, he loved this—the game of life and death against another Horseman, a master player. He admired Bayer's calmness and his ability to be so smooth.

"His playing is so bloody predictable. He was the same way as an agent and analyst. George, they sent you because they thought I'd never suspect you'd try to take me out by yourself. You're the first play. It's so obvious, though. A terrible waste of a player."

Bayer frowned slightly but still didn't lose his cool, didn't let on what he felt. He thought that was the safest attitude, but it told Shafer his suspicion was true: Famine was here to kill him. He was sure of it.

George Bayer's cool demeanor had given him away.

"No, nothing like that," Bayer said. "We're going to play according to the rules tonight. The rules are important to us. It's to be a board game, a contest of strategy and wits. I'm just here to pick you up, according to plan. We'll meet face to face at the hotel."

"And we'll abide by the throw of the dice?" Shafer asked.

"Yes, of course, Geoff." Bayer held out his hand and showed him three twenty-sided dice.

Shafer couldn't hold back a sharp laugh. This was so good, so rich. "So what did the dice say, George? How do I lose? How do I die? A knife? A pistol? A drug overdose makes a great deal of sense to me."

Bayer couldn't help himself. He laughed. Shafer was such a cocky bastard, such a good killer, a wonderful psychopathic personality. "Well, yes, it might have occurred to us, but we played it completely straight. As I said, they're waiting at the hotel for us. Let's go."

Shafer turned his back to Bayer for an

instant. Then he pushed hard off his right foot. He sprang at Bayer.

But Bayer was more than ready for him. He threw a short, hard punch that struck Shafer's cheek, rattled and maybe even loosened a few teeth. The right side of Shafer's head went completely numb.

"Good one, George. Good stuff!"

Then Shafer head-butted Bayer with all of his strength. He heard the crunch of bone against bone, saw an explosion of dizzying white before his eyes. That got his adrenaline flowing.

The dice went flying from Bayer's hand as he reached for a gun, or some other weapon. It was tucked in the back of his waistband.

Shafer clutched Bayer's right arm, twisted with all of his strength, and broke it at the elbow. Bayer shrieked in pain.

"You can't beat me! Nobody has, nobody can!" Shafer screamed at the top of his voice.

He grabbed George Bayer's throat and squeezed with superhuman strength. Bayer gagged and turned the brightest red, as if all the blood in his body had rushed to his head. George was stronger than he appeared, but Shafer was speeding on adrenaline and years of pure hatred. He outweighed Bayer by twenty pounds, all of it muscle.

"*Noooo.* Listen to me." George Bayer wheezed and gasped. "Not like this. Not here."

"*Yes, George. Yes, yes.* The game is on. The game that you bastards started. Tally-ho, old chap. *You* did this to me. You made me what I am: Death."

He heard a loud, crisp snap, and George Bayer went limp against him. He let his body fall to the sand.

"One down," said Shafer, and finally allowed himself a deep, satisfying breath. He snatched up the fallen dice, shook them once, then hurled them into the sea. "I don't use the dice anymore," he said.

Chapter 114

HE FELT SO DAMN GOOD. So fine. God, how he had missed this! The mainline of adrenaline, the incomparable thrill. He knew it was likely that the Jamaica Inn was being watched by the police, so he parked the Mustang at the nearby Plantation Inn.

He walked at a quickening pace through the crowded Bougainvillea Terrace. Drinks were being served while the wretched song "Yellowbird" played loudly. He had a nasty fantasy about shooting up the terrace, killing several dickhead tourists, so he got away from the crowded area immediately for everybody's sake—but mostly for his own.

He strolled the beach, and it calmed him. It was quiet, restful, the strains of calypso music gently weaving through the night air. The stretch between the two hotels was eye-catching, with plenty of spotlights, sand the color of champagne, thatched umbrellas placed at even intervals. A very nice playing field.

He knew where Oliver Highsmith was staying: in the famous White Suite, where Winston Churchill and David Niven and Ian Fleming had slept once upon a time. Highsmith loved his creature comforts almost as much as he loved the game.

Shafer despised the other Horsemen, in part because he wasn't of their snobbish social class. Lucy's father had gotten him into MI6; the other players had gone to the right universities. But there was another, more powerful reason for his hatred: they had dared to use him, to feel superior and throw it in his face.

He entered through a white picket-fence gate at the property line of the Jamaica Inn. He broke into a soft jog. He wanted to run, to sweat. He was feeling manic again. Playing the game had made him too excited.

Shafer held his head for a moment. He wanted to laugh and scream at the top of his lungs. He leaned against a wooden post on the path leading up from the beach, and tried to catch his breath. He knew he was crashing, and it couldn't have happened at a worse time.

"Everything all right, sir?" a hotel waiter stopped to ask him.

"Oh, couldn't be better," Shafer said, waving the man away. "I'm in heaven, can't you tell?"

He started walking toward the White Suite again. He realized that he was feeling the same way he had that morning last year when he nearly crashed his car in Washington. He was in serious trouble again. He could lose the game right now, lose everything. That required a change of strategy, didn't it? He had to be more daring, even more aggressive. He had to act, not think too much. The odds against him were still two to one.

At the far end of the courtyard, he spotted a man and a woman in evening clothes. They were loitering near a white stucco portico strewn with flowers. He decided they were Jones's people. They had staked out the hotel, after all. They were here for him, and he was honored.

The man glanced his way, and Shafer abruptly lowered his head. There was nothing they could do to stop or detain him. He'd committed no crime they could prove. He wasn't wanted by the police. No, he was a free man.

So Shafer walked toward them at a leisurely pace, as if he hadn't seen them. He whistled "Yellowbird."

He looked up when he was a few yards away from the pair. "I'm the one you're waiting for. I'm Geoffrey Shafer. Welcome to the game."

He pulled out his Smith & Wesson nine-millimeter semiautomatic and fired twice.

The woman cried out and grabbed the left side of her chest. Bright-red blood was already staining her sea-green dress. Her eyes showed confusion and shock before rolling back into her forehead.

The male agent had a dark hole where his left eye had been. Shafer knew the man was dead even before his head struck the courtyard floor with a loud, satisfying smack.

He hadn't lost anything over the years. Shafer hurried toward the White Suite and Conqueror.

The gunshots certainly would have been heard. They wouldn't expect him to run straight into the trap they'd set. But here he was.

Two maids were pushing a squeaking cleanup cart out of the White Suite. Had they just turned down Conqueror's bed? Left the fat man a box of chocolate mints to nibble?

"Get the hell out of here!" he yelled, and raised his gun. "Go on, now! Run for your lives!" The Jamaican maids took off as if they had just seen the devil himself, and later they would tell their children they had.

Shafer burst in the front door of the suite, and there was Oliver Highsmith free-wheeling his chair across the freshly scrubbed floor.

"Oliver, it's you," Shafer said. "I do believe I've caught the dreaded Covent Garden killer. You did those killings, didn't you? Fancy that. Game's over, Oliver."

At the same time, Shafer thought, *Watch him closely. Be careful with Conqueror.*

Oliver Highsmith stopped moving, then slowly but rather nimbly turned his wheelchair to face Shafer. A face-to-face meeting. This was good. The best. Highsmith had controlled Bayer and Whitehead from London when they were all agents. The original game, the Four Horsemen, had been his idea, a diversion as he eased into retirement. "Our silly little fantasy game," he always called it.

He studied Shafer, cold-eyed and measuring. He was bright—an egghead, but a genius, or so Bayer and Whitehead claimed.

"My dear fellow, we're your friends. The only ones you have now. We understand your problem. Let's talk things through, Geoffrey."

Shafer laughed at the fat man's pathetic lies, his superior and condescending attitude, his nerve. "That's not what Georgie Bayer told me. Why, he said you were going to murder me! Hell of a way to treat a friend."

Highsmith didn't blink, didn't falter. "We're not alone here, Geoff. They're at the hotel. The Security Service team is on the grounds. They must have followed you."

"And *you,* and *Bayer,* and *Whitehead!* I know all that, Oliver. I met a couple of crackerjack agents down the hall. Shot 'em dead. That's why I have to hurry up, can't tarry. The game's on a clock now. Lots of ways to lose."

"We have to talk, Geoff."

"Talk, talk, talk." Shafer shook his head, frowned, then barked out a laugh. "No, there's nothing for us to talk about. Talk is such an overrated bore. I learned to kill in the field, and I like it much more than talking. No, I actually love it to death."

"You *are* mad," Highsmith exclaimed, his grayish-blue eyes widening with fear. Finally, he understood who Shafer was; he wasn't intellectualizing anymore. He felt it in his gut.

"No, actually, I'm not insane. I know precisely what I'm doing—always have, always will. I know the difference between good and evil. Anyway, look who's talking: the Rider on the White Horse."

Shafer moved swiftly toward Highsmith. "This isn't much of a fight—just the way I was taught to perform in Asia. You're going to die, Oliver. Isn't that a stunning thought? Still think this is a bloody fantasy game?"

Suddenly Highsmith jumped to his feet. Shafer wasn't surprised; he knew he couldn't have committed the murders in

London from a wheelchair. Highsmith was close to six feet, and obese, but surprisingly quick for his size. His arms and hands were massive.

Shafer was faster. He struck Highsmith with the butt of his gun, and Conqueror went crashing down on one knee. Shafer bludgeoned him a second time, then a third, and Highsmith dropped flat on the floor. He groaned loudly and slobbered blood and spit. Shafer kicked the small of his back, kicked a knee, kicked his face.

Then he bent and put the gun barrel against Highsmith's broad forehead. He could hear the distant sound of running footsteps' slapping down the hall. Too bad —they were coming for him. *Hurry, hurry.*

"They're too late," he said to Conqueror. "No one can save you. Except me, Conqueror. What's the play? Counsel me. Should I save the whale?"

"Please, Geoff, no. You can't just kill me. We can still help each other."

"I'd love to stretch this out, but I really have to dash. I'm throwing the dice. In *my mind.* Oh, bad news, Oliver. The jig is up. You just lost the game."

He inserted the barrel of his gun into

Highsmith's pulpy right ear, and fired. The gunshot blew Conqueror's gray matter all over the room. Shafer's only regret was that he hadn't been able to torture Oliver Highsmith for a much, much longer time than he had.

Then Shafer was running away, and suddenly he was struck with a realization that actually surprised him: he had something to live for. This was a wonderful, wonderful game.

I want to live.

Chapter 115

SAMPSON AND I sprinted toward the secluded wing of the hotel where Oliver Highsmith had his suite. There had been gunshots, but we couldn't be everywhere at once. We'd heard the pistol reports all the way on the other side of the Jamaica Inn.

I wasn't prepared for the bloody massacre scene we found. Two English agents were down in the courtyard. I'd worked with them both, just as I'd worked side by side with Patsy Hampton.

Jones and another agent, in addition to a team of local detectives, were already crowded into Highsmith's suite. The room was abuzz. Everything had turned to chaos and carnage in a burst of homicidal madness.

"Shafer went through two of my people to get here," Jones said in an angry voice strained with tension and sadness. He was smoking a cigarette. "He came in shooting, took down Laura and Gwynn. Highsmith is dead, too. We haven't found George Bayer yet."

I knelt and quickly checked the damage to Oliver Highsmith's skull. It wasn't subtle. He'd been shot at point-blank range, and the wound was massive. I knew from Jones that Shafer had resented the senior man's intelligence, and now he'd blown out his brains. "I told you he liked to kill. He has to do this, Andrew. He can't stop.

"Whitehead!" I said. "The end of the game."

Chapter 116

WE DROVE FASTER than the narrow, twisting road safely allowed, barreling toward James Whitehead's home. It wasn't far.

We passed a road sign that read Mallard's Beach—San Antonio.

Sampson and I were quiet, lost in our own thoughts. I kept thinking of Christine, couldn't stop the images from coming. *"We have her."* Was that still true?

I didn't know, and only Shafer, or possibly Whitehead, could give me the answer. I wanted to keep both of them alive if I could. Everything about the island, the exotic smells and sights, reminded me of

Christine. I tried, but I couldn't imagine a good conclusion to any of this.

We headed toward the beach and soon were skimming past private houses and a few very large estates, some with long, winding driveways that stretched a hundred yards or more from the road to the main house.

In the distance I could see the glow of other house lights, and I figured we had to be close to James Whitehead's. Was War still alive? Or had Shafer already come and gone?

Jones's voice came in spits over the radio: "This is his place, Alex. Glass and stone house up ahead. I don't see anybody."

We pulled in near the crushed-seashell driveway leading to the house. It was dark, pitch-black and satiny. There were no lights on anywhere on the property.

We jumped out of our cars. There were eight of us in all, including one team of detectives from Kingston, Kenyon and Anthony, both of whom were acting nervous.

I didn't blame them. I felt exactly the same way. The Weasel was on a rampage, and we already knew he was suicidal.

Geoffrey Shafer was a homicidal-suicidal maniac.

Sampson and I ran through a small garden that had a pool and cabana area on one side and an expanse of lawn and the sea on the other.

We could see Jones's people beginning to fan out across the grounds. *Shafer came into the hotel with guns blazing,* I thought. *He doesn't seem to care whether or not he survives. But I do. I need to question him. I have to know what he knows. I need all the answers.*

"What about this prick Whitehead?" Sampson asked as we hurried toward the house.

It was dark near the water, a good place for Shafer to attack from. Dark shadows stretched out from every tree and bush.

"I don't know, John. He was at the hotel briefly. He's a player, so he's after Shafer, too. This is it: *Endgame.* One of them wins the game now.

"He's here," I whispered. "I know it."

I could definitely sense Geoffrey Shafer's presence; I was sure of it. And the fact that I *knew* scared me almost as much as he himself did.

Shots sounded from the darkened house.

My heart sank, and I had the most disturbing and contradictory thought: *Please don't let Geoffrey Shafer be dead.*

Chapter 117

ONE MORE TARGET, one last oppo-
nent, and then it would be over. Eight glorious years of play, eight years of revenge,
eight years of hatred. He couldn't bear to
lose the game. He'd shown Bayer and
Highsmith a thing or two; now he'd demonstrate to James Whitehead which of
them was truly "superior."

Shafer had noisily crashed through thick
foliage, then waded waist deep into a foul-
smelling swamp. The water was distressingly tepid, and the oily green scum on the
surface was an inch or two thick.

He tried not to think about the swamp,
or the insects and snakes that might infest
it. He'd waded into far worse waters during
his days and nights in Asia. He kept his

eyes set on James Whitehead's expensive beach house. One more to go, just one more Horseman.

He'd been to the villa before, knew it well. Beyond the swamp was another patch of thick foliage, and then a chain-link fence and Whitehead's manicured yard. He figured that Whitehead wouldn't expect him to come through the swamp. War was cleverer than the others, though. He'd been committing murders in the Caribbean for years, and not even a blip had shown up to suggest a pattern to the police. War had also helped him in the matter of Christine Johnson, and that had gone perfectly. It was a mystery, inside a mystery, all inside a complex game.

Shafer lost track of everything real for a moment or two—where he was, who he was, what he had to do.

Now, *that* was scary—a little mental breakdown at the worst possible time. Ironically, it was Whitehead who had first gotten him dependent on uppers and downers in Asia.

Shafer began to slosh across the fetid swamp, hoping the water wouldn't be over his head. It wasn't. He came out and climbed over the chain-link fence on the far side. He started across the back lawn.

He had the most powerful obsession about destroying James Whitehead. He wanted to torture him—but where would he find the time? Whitehead had been his first handler in Thailand, and then in the Philippines. More than anyone, Whitehead had made Shafer into a killer. Whitehead was the one he held responsible.

The house was still dark, but Shafer believed War was in there.

Suddenly a gun fired from the house. *War* indeed.

Shafer began to zig and zag like an infantryman thoroughly trained in combat. His heart was thundering. Reality came in odd stop-and-go movements. He wondered if Whitehead had a nightscope on his gun. And how good a shot he was.

Whether he'd ever been in combat.

Was he frightened? Or was he excited by the action?

He figured that the doors to the house were locked and that War was crouched low, hiding inside, waiting to take a shot without too much exposure. He had never done his own dirty work, though; none of them had—not Whitehead, not Bayer, not Highsmith. They had used Death, and now he'd come for them. If they hadn't agreed to meet in Jamaica, he would have come after them one at a time.

Shafer broke into a full sprint toward the house. Gunshots exploded from inside. Bullets whizzed past him. He hadn't been hit. Because he was so good? Or because War wasn't?

Shafer threw both arms up in front of his face. This was it. He dived through the large picture window in the loggia.

Glass exploded everywhere as the window blew into a thousand small pieces. He was inside!

War was here, close by. Where was his enemy? How good was James Whitehead? His mind was filled with important questions. A dog was barking somewhere in the house.

Shafer tumbled across the tile floor and hit the leg of a heavy table, but came up firing anyway. *Nothing.* No one was in the room.

He heard voices outside, in front. The police were here! Always trying to spoil his fun.

Then he saw War trying to run. Tall, gangly, with longish black hair. War had blinked first. He was heading toward the front door, looking for help from the police, of all people.

"You can't make it, Whitehead. Stop! I won't let you get out! Stay in the game."

Whitehead apparently realized he couldn't get out the front door. He turned toward a stairway, and Shafer followed, only a few steps behind. War turned sharply and fired again.

Shafer flicked his hand at a wall switch, and the hall lights flashed on.

"Death has come for you! It's your time. Look at me! Look at Death!" he screamed.

Whitehead kept moving, and Shafer calmly shot him in the buttocks. The wound was large, gaping, and Whitehead screamed like a stuck pig. He whirled and fell halfway down the stairs. His face slammed against the metal railing as he fell.

He finally lay writhing at the foot of the stairs, where Shafer shot him again, this time between the legs. War screamed again. Then he began to moan and to sob.

Shafer stood over him, triumphant, his

heart bursting. "You think sanctions are a game? Is this still a game to you?" he asked in the softest voice. *"I believe it's great fun, but do you?"*

Whitehead was sobbing as he tried to speak. "No, Geoffrey. It's not a game. Please stop. That's enough."

Shafer began to smile. He showed his enormous teeth. "Oh, you're so wrong. It's lovely! It is the most amazing mind game you could imagine. You should feel what I feel right now, the power over life and death."

He had a thought, and it changed everything, changed the game for him and Whitehead. This switch was so much better than what he'd originally planned.

"I've decided to let you live—not very well, but you *will* live."

He fired the semiautomatic again, this time into the base of Whitehead's spine.

"You will never forget me, and the game will continue for the rest of your life. Play well. I know *I* shall."

Chapter 118

THE MOMENT WE HEARD the gunshots, we ran toward the main house. I
raced ahead of the others. I had to get to
Shafer before they did. I had to take him
myself. I had to talk to him, to know the
truth once and for all.

I saw Shafer slip out a side door of the
house. Whitehead must be dead. Shafer
had won the game.

He was running toward the sea, moving
fast and purposefully. He disappeared behind a small sand dune shaped like a tur-
tle. Where was he going? What was next
for him?

Then I saw him again. He was kicking off
his shoes and getting out of his trousers.
What was he doing?

I heard Sampson come running up behind me. "Don't kill him, John! Not unless we have to," I yelled.

"I know! I know!" he called.

I plunged ahead.

Shafer turned and fired off a shot at me. The distance was too great for any real accuracy with a handgun, but still, he was a good shot, and he came pretty close. He knew how to use a gun, and not just from a few feet away.

I glanced over and saw that Sampson was kicking off his sneakers, pulling away his pants. I did the same with my sweats and T-shirt.

I pointed out to sea. "He must have a boat out there. One of those."

We saw Shafer striding into the low waves of the Caribbean, heading into a cone of light made by the moon.

He did a shallow dive and started to swim in a smooth-looking crawl stroke.

Sampson and I were down to our underwear, nothing very pretty. We both made shallow dives into the sea.

Shafer was a very strong swimmer and was already pulling ahead of us. He swam with his face in the water, lifting it out sideways after several strokes to catch a breath.

His blond hair was slicked back and shone in the moonlight. One of the boats bobbing out there had to be his. But which one?

I kept a single thought in my head: stretch and kick, stretch and kick. I felt as if I were gathering strength from somewhere inside. I had to catch Shafer—I had to know the truth about what he'd done to Christine.

Stretch and kick, stretch and kick.

Sampson was laboring behind me, and then he started to fall even farther back.

"Go," I called to him. "Go back for help. I'll be all right. Get somebody out there to check those boats."

"He swims like a fish," Sampson shouted back.

"Go. I'll be fine. Hold my own."

Up ahead I could still see Shafer's head and the tops of his shoulders glistening in the creamy white moonlight. He was stroking evenly, powerfully.

I kept going, never looking back to shore, not wanting to know how far I had come already. I refused to be tired, to give up, to lose.

I swam harder, trying to gain some sea on Shafer. The boats were still a good way away. He was still going strong, though. No sign of tiring.

I played a mind game of my own. I stopped looking to see where he was. I concentrated only on my own stroke. There was nothing but the stroke; the stroke was the whole universe.

My body was feeling more in sync with the water, and I was buoyed as it got deeper. My stroke was getting stronger and smoother.

I finally looked. He was starting to struggle. Or maybe that was just what I *wanted* to see. Anyway, it gave me a second wind, added strength.

What if I actually caught him out here? Then what? We'd fight to the death?

I couldn't let him get to his boat before me. He'd have guns on board. I needed to beat him there. I had to win this time. Which boat was his?

I swam harder. I told myself that I was in good shape, too. And I was. I'd been to the gym every day for almost a year—ever since Christine disappeared.

I looked up again and was shocked at what I saw.

Shafer was there! Only a few yards away. A few more strokes. Had he lost it? Or was he waiting for me, gathering strength?

The closest boat was no more than a hundred, a hundred and fifty yards away.

"Cramp!" he called out. "Bad one!" Then Shafer went under.

Chapter 119

I DIDN'T KNOW what to think or exactly what to do next. The pain on Shafer's face looked real; he looked afraid. But he was also a good actor.

I felt something underneath me! He grabbed hard between my legs. I yelled and managed to twist away, though he'd hurt me.

Then we were grabbing at each other, struggling like underwater wrestlers. Suddenly, he pulled me under with him. He was strong. His long arms were like powerful vises, and he held me tightly.

We went down, and I started to feel the coldest, most serious fear of my life. I didn't want to drown. Shafer was winning. He always found a way.

Shafer stared into my eyes. His eyes were incredibly intense and manic and crazed. His mouth was closed, but it was twisted and evil-looking. He had me; he would win again.

I pushed forward as hard as I could. When I felt him straining against me, I reversed directions. I kicked out with my leg and caught Shafer under the jaw, maybe in the throat. I hit him with all of my strength, and he began to sink.

His long blond hair floated up around his face. His arms and legs went limp.

He began to sink, and I followed him. It was even darker under the surface. I grabbed one of his arms.

I barely caught him. His weight was pulling me with him, toward the bottom. I couldn't let him go. I had to know the truth about Christine. I couldn't go on with my life unless I knew.

I had no idea how deep the water was here. Shafer's eyes had been wide open, and so had his mouth; his lungs must be filling with water by now.

I wondered if I'd broken his neck with my kick. Was he dead, or just unconscious? I took some satisfaction in the idea that I might've broken the Weasel's neck.

Then it really didn't matter. Nothing did. I had no more breath. My chest felt as if it would collapse. There was a fire spreading wildly inside me. Then a severe ringing started in both ears. I was dizzy and starting to lose consciousness.

I let Shafer go, let him sink to the bottom. I didn't have a choice. I couldn't think about him anymore. I had to get to the surface. I couldn't hold my breath any longer.

I swam frantically up, pulled at the water, kicked with all my might. I didn't think I could make it; it was too far to the surface.

I had no more breath.

Then I saw Sampson's face looming above me. Close, very close. It gave me strength.

His head was framed against a few stars and the blue-black of the sky. "Sugar," he called as I finally came up for air.

He held me up, let me get my breath, my precious breath. We both treaded water for a while. My mind was reeling.

I let my eyes explore the surface for some sign of Shafer. My vision was blurred, but I didn't see him. I was certain he'd drowned.

Sampson and I slowly paddled back to shore.

I hadn't gotten what I needed out there. I hadn't been able to learn the truth from Shafer before he drowned.

Once or twice I glanced back to make sure that Shafer wasn't following us, that he was gone. There was no sign of him. There was only the sound of our own tired strokes cutting into the tide.

Chapter 120

IT TOOK TWO MORE exhausting days and nights to finish with the local police investigation, but it was good to keep focused and busy. I no longer had any hope of finding Christine, or even discovering what had happened to her.

I knew it was remotely possible that Shafer hadn't taken Christine, that it had been some other madman from my past, but I didn't give that possibility more than a passing thought. I couldn't go there. It was too crazy an idea, even for me.

I'd been unable to grieve from the start, but now the monstrous finality of Christine's fate struck me with all of its brutal force. I felt as if my insides had been hollowed out. The constant, dull ache I had known for so long now became a sharp stab of pain that pierced my heart every waking moment. I couldn't sleep, yet I felt as if I were never fully awake.

Sampson knew what was happening to me. There was nothing he could say, but he made comforting small talk, anyway.

Nana called me at the hotel, and I knew it was Sampson's doing, though both of them denied it. Jannie and Damon got on the phone, and they were both sweet and kind and full of life and hopefulness. They even put Rosie the cat on for a friendly long-distance meow. They didn't mention Christine, but I knew she was always in their thoughts.

On our final night on the island, Sampson and I had dinner with Jones. We had become friendly with him, and he finally told me some facts he had previously withheld for Security reasons. He wanted me to have some closure; he felt I deserved that much.

Back in 1989, after joining MI6, Shafer had been recruited by James Whitehead. Whitehead in turn reported to Oliver Highsmith, as did George Bayer. Shafer performed at least four "sanctions" in Asia

over the next three years. It was suspected, but never proved, that he, Whitehead, and Bayer had also murdered prostitutes in Manila and Bangkok. These
murders were obviously the precursors to
the Jane Does, and to the game itself. All in
all, it had been one of the worst scandals
in the history of the Security Service. And it
had effectively been covered up. That was
how Jones wanted to keep it, and I had no
worthwhile objection. There were already
more than enough unfortunate stories to
keep people cynical about their govern-
ments.

Our dinner broke up at around eleven,
and Jones and I promised to keep in
touch. There was one bit of disturbing
news, though no one wanted to overstate
the significance of it: Geoffrey Shafer's
body still hadn't been found. Somehow
that seemed a fitting end.

Sampson and I were due to catch the
first flight to Washington on Tuesday morning. It was scheduled to leave at ten past
nine.

That morning, the skies were swirling
with black clouds. Heavy rain pounded on
our car's roof all the way from the hotel to

the Donald Sangster Airport. Schoolchildren ran along the side of the road, shielding themselves from the rain with flopping banana-tree leaves.

The downpour caught us good as we tried to dash out from under the cover of the tin overhang outside the rent-a-car depot. The rain was cool, though, and it felt good on my face and head and on the shirt plastered to my back.

"It'll be real good to be home," Sampson said as we finally made it to a shelter under the metal roof painted a bright yellow.

"I'm ready to go," I agreed. "I miss Damon and Jannie and Nana. I miss being home."

"They'll find the body," Sampson said. "Shafer's."

"I knew who you meant."

The rain hammered the airport's roof without mercy, and I was thinking how much I hated to fly on days like this—but it would be good to be home, to be able to end this nightmare. It had invaded my soul, taken over my life. In a way I supposed it was as much a "game" as any that Shafer had played. The murder case had obsessed me for over a year, and that was enough.

Christine had asked me to give it up. Nana had asked, too, but I hadn't listened. Maybe I hadn't been able to see my life and actions as clearly then as I did now. I was the Dragonslayer, and all that meant, the good and the bad. In the end, I held myself responsible for Christine's kidnapping and murder.

Sampson and I walked past the colorful concession stands without any real interest, barely a passing nod. Street hawkers, called higglers, were selling wooden jewelry and other carvings, but also Jamaican coffee and cocoa.

Each of us carried a black duffel bag. We didn't exactly look like vacationers, I was thinking. We still looked like policemen.

I heard a voice calling loudly from behind, and I turned back to look at the commotion coming up from the rear.

It was one of the Jamaican detectives, John Anthony, shouting out my name in the noisy terminal, running our way. He was several steps ahead of Andrew Jones, who looked powerfully dismayed.

Jones and Anthony at the airport? What

in God's name was happening now? What could possibly have gone wrong?

"The *Weasel?*" I said, and it came out like a curse.

Sampson and I stopped to let them catch up with us. I almost didn't want to hear what they had to tell us.

"You have to come back with us, Alex. Come with me," Jones said, slightly out of breath. "It's about Christine Johnson. Something's turned up. Come."

"What is it? What's happened?" I asked Jones, and then turned to Detective Anthony when the Englishman was slow in answering.

Anthony hesitated, but then he said, "We don't know for sure. It could be nothing at all. Someone claims to have seen her, though. She may be here in Jamaica, after all. Come with us."

I couldn't believe what he had just told me. I felt Sampson's arm wrap tightly around me, but everything else seemed unreal, as in a dream.

It wasn't over yet.

Chapter 121

ON THE ROAD out of the airport, Andrew Jones and Detective Anthony filled us in on what they knew. I could tell they were trying not to build up my hopes too much. I'd been in the same untenable situation many times, but not as a victim of a crime.

"Last night we caught a small-time local thief breaking into a house in Ocho Rios," Anthony said as he drove, the four of us packed tightly in his Toyota. "He said he had information to trade. We told him we would hear what he had to say, and then we would decide. He revealed that an American woman had been kept in the hills east of Ocho Rios, near the town of Euarton. There's an outlaw group lives up there sometimes.

"I learned about it only this morning. I called Andrew, and we hurried to the airport. The man says she was called Beatitude. No other name was used. I contacted your hotel, but you had already left for the airport. So we came out here to get you."

"Thank you," I finally said, realizing I had probably been told as much as they knew.

Sampson spoke up. "So why does this helpful thief appear now, after all this time?"

"He said there was a shooting a few nights ago that changed everything. Once the white men died, the woman wasn't important anymore. Those were his words."

"You know these men?" I asked Detective Anthony.

"Men, women, children. Yes, I've dealt with them before. They smoke a lot of ganja. Practice their hybrid religion, worship the Emperor Haile Selassie, y'know. A few of them are small-time thieves. Mostly, we let them be."

Everyone in the car grew quiet as we hurried along the coast road toward Runaway Bay and Ocho Rios. The storm had passed quickly, and suddenly the island's hellified sun was blazing again. Sugarcane workers with machetes on their hips were tramping back into the fields.

Past the village of Runaway Bay, Detective Anthony turned off the main road and headed up into the hills on Route A1. The trees and bushes here were a thick jungle. The road eventually became a tunnel boring through vines and branches. Anthony had to turn on the headlights.

I felt as if I were drifting through a mist, watching everything as if in a dream. I understood that I was trying to protect myself, but I also knew it wasn't working.

Who was Beatitude? I couldn't make myself believe that Christine was alive, but at least there was a chance, and I clung to that. I had given up weeks before. Now I allowed myself to remember how much I loved her, how much I missed her. I choked hard and turned my face toward the window. I went deep inside myself.

Suddenly, bright light shone in my eyes. The car had exited the brush after two or three miles that had seemed much longer on the twisting road. We were entering lush hills that looked something like the American South back in the fifties and sixties—

maybe Georgia or Alabama. Children in dated clothes played in front of small run-down houses. Their elders sat on uneven, slanted porches and watched the occasional car drive past.

Everything looked and felt so surrealistic. I couldn't focus.

We turned onto a skinny dirt road with a thick, high corridor of grass running between deep tire ruts. This had to be the place. My heart was pumping loudly and sounded like a tin drum being pounded in a tunnel. I felt every bump in the road like a hard punch.

Beatitude? Who is the woman they're holding? Can it possibly be Christine?

Sampson checked the load in his Glock. I heard the mechanism slide and *click* and glanced his way.

"They won't be happy to see us, but you won't need the gun," Anthony turned and said. "They probably know we're coming. They watch the local roads. Christine Johnson might not be here now, if she was ever here at all. But I knew you would want to see for yourself."

I didn't say anything. I couldn't. My mouth felt incredibly dry, and my mind was a blank. We were still involved with the Four Horsemen, weren't we? Was this Shafer's play? Had he known we'd eventually find this place in the hills? Had he set a final trap for us?

We arrived at an old green house with tattered white cloth over the windows and a burlap bag for a front door. Four men immediately came outside, all of them sporting dreadlocks.

They walked toward us, their mouths set hard, their eyes blazing with distrust. Sampson and I were used to the look from the streets of Washington.

Two of the men carried heavy field machetes. The other two wore floppy shirts, and I knew they were armed beneath the loose-fitting clothes.

"Galang. Go back, mon," one of them shouted loudly at us. "Nah woman here."

Chapter 122

"NO!"

Detective Anthony got out of the car with both hands held high. Sampson, Jones, and I followed his lead.

We could hear the beat of traditional drums coming from the woods directly behind the main house. A pair of lounging dogs raised their lazy heads to look at us and barked a few times. My heart was thundering faster now.

I didn't like the way this was going down.

Another one of the men called to us, "I and I would like you to leave."

I recognized the figure of speech: the double pronoun represented the speaker and God, who live together in each person.

"Patrick Moss is in jail. I'm Detective Anthony, from Kingston. This is Detective Sampson, Detective Cross, and Mr. Jones. You have an American woman here. You call her Beatitude."

Beatitude? Could it be Christine?

A man wielding a machete in one hand glared and spoke to Anthony. "Galang bout yuh business. Lef me nuh. Nah woman here. Nah woman."

"This *is* my business, and we *won't* leave you alone," I said, surprising the man with my understanding of his dialect. But I know Rastaman from D.C.

"Nah woman here. Nah American," the man repeated angrily, looking directly at me.

Andrew Jones spoke up. "We want the American woman, then we'll leave. Your friend Patrick Moss will be home by tonight. You can deal with him in your own way."

"Nah American woman here." The original speaker spat defiantly on the ground. "Turn around, go back."

"You know James Whitehead? You know Shafer?" Jones asked.

They didn't deny it. I doubted we'd get any more from them than that.

"I love her," I told them. "I can't leave. Her name is Christine."

My mouth was still dry, and I couldn't breathe very well. "She was kidnapped a year ago. We know she was brought here."

Sampson took out his Glock and held it loosely at his side. He stared at the four men, who continued to glare back at us. I touched the handle of my gun, still in its holster. I didn't want a gunfight.

"We can cause you a whole lot of trouble," Sampson said in a low, rumbling voice. "You won't believe how much trouble is coming your way."

Finally, I just walked forward on a worn path back through the tall grass. I passed by the men, lightly brushing against one of them.

No one tried to stop me. I could smell ganja and sweat on their work clothes. Tension was building up inside me.

Sampson followed me, no more than a step or two behind. "I'm watching them," he said. "Nobody's doing anything yet."

"Doesn't matter," I said. "I have to see if she's here."

Chapter 123

AN OLDER WOMAN with long and wildly frazzled gray and white hair stepped out of the front door as I reached the scarred, un-painted steps. Her eyes were ringed with redness.

"Come with me." She sighed. "Come along. You nah need no weapon."

For the first time in many months, I al-lowed myself to feel the tiniest flash of hope, though I didn't have any reason to, other than the rumor that a woman was being kept here against her will.

Beatitude? Something to do with bless-edness and happiness? Could it be Chris-tine?

The old woman walked unsteadily around the house and through light bushes, trees, and ferns out back. About sixty or seventy yards into the thickening woods, she came to half a dozen small shacks, where she stopped. The shacks were made of wood, bamboo, and corrugated metal.

She walked forward again and stopped at the next-to-last shack in the group.

She took out a key attached to a leather strap around her wrist, inserted it in the door lock, and jiggled it.

She pushed the door forward, and it creaked loudly on a rusty hinge.

I looked inside and saw a plain, neat, and clean room. Someone had written *The Lord Is My Shepherd* in black paint on the wall.

No one was there.

No Beatitude.

No Christine.

I let my eyes fall shut. Desperation enveloped me.

My eyes slowly opened. I didn't understand why I had been led to this empty room, this old shack in the woods. My heart was ripped in two again. Was it some kind of trap?

The Weasel? Shafer? Was he here?

Someone stepped out from behind a small folding screen in one corner of the room. I felt as if I were in free fall, and a small gasp came out of my mouth.

I didn't know what I had been expecting, but it wasn't this. Sampson put out his hand to steady me. I was barely aware of his touch.

Christine slowly stepped into the shafts of sunlight coming from the single window in the shack. I had thought I would never see her again.

She was much thinner, and her hair was braided and longer than I'd ever seen it. But she had the same wise, beautiful brown eyes. Neither of us was able to speak at first. It was the most extraordinary moment of my life.

I had gone cold all over, and everything was moving in slow motion. It seemed supernaturally quiet in the small room.

Christine was holding a light-yellow blanket, and I could see a baby's head just peeking above the crown of the covers. I walked forward even though my legs were trembling and threatening to buckle. I could hear the baby softly cooing in the nest of blankets.

"Oh, Christine, Christine," I finally managed.

Tears welled in her eyes, and then in mine. We both stepped forward, and then I was awkwardly holding her. The little baby gazed up peacefully into both our faces.

"This is our baby, and he probably saved my life. He takes after you," Christine said. Then we kissed gently, and it was so sweet and tender. We held on for dear, dear life. We melted into each other. Neither of us could believe this was actually happening.

"I call him Alex. You were always right here," Christine told me. "You were always with me."

Epilogue

LONDON BRIDGES, FALLING

HIS NAME was Frederick Neuman, and he liked to think of himself as a citizen of the European community rather than of any single country, but if anyone asked, he claimed to be German. His head was shaved close, and it made him look severe, but also more impressive, he thought—an amazing accomplishment in itself.

He would be remembered as "quite tall, thin and bald," or as an "interesting *artiste* type," and several people *did* see him that week in Chelsea in London. *I want to be remembered. That's important.*

He shopped, or at least window-shopped, on the King's Road and in Sloane Street.

He went to the cinema in Kensington High Street.

And the Waterstone's bookshop.

Nights, he would have a pint or two at the King's Head. He mostly kept to himself at the pub.

He had a master plan. Another game was beginning.

He saw Lucy and the twins at Safeway one afternoon. He watched them from across rows of baked beans, then followed them down the aisles filled with shoppers. No harm, no foul—no problem for anybody.

He couldn't resist the challenge, though. The dice started to play in his head. They rattled the number he wanted to hear.

He kept walking closer and closer to the family, careful to keep his face slightly averted, just in case, but still watching Lucy out of the corner of his eye, watching the twins, who were perhaps more dangerous.

Lucy was examining some wild Scottish salmon. She finally noticed him, he was sure, but she didn't recognize him—obviously. Neither did the twins. Dumb, silly little girls—mirrors of their mother.

The game was on again—so delicious. He'd been away from it for a while. He had the book money, his advance from the trial tell-all, which he kept in Switzerland. He had bummed around the Caribbean after his escape by boat from Jamaica. He'd gone to San Juan and been tempted to act up there. Then on to Europe—first to Rome, Milan, Paris, Frankfurt, and Dublin, and finally home to London. He'd strayed only a couple of times on the whole trip. He was such a careful boy now.

It felt just like old times as he got oh-so-close to Lucy in the shopping aisle. Jesus, his physical tics were back. He was tapping his foot nervously and shaking out his hands.

He'd have thought she'd notice that, but she was such a vacuous blond cow, such a cipher, such a waste of his time; even now, as he got closer and closer, only a foot or two away, she still didn't recognize him.

"Oh Loo-cy . . . it's Ricky," he said, and grinned and grinned. "It's me, *darling*."

Swish. Swish. He swiped at her twice, back and forth, as they passed like strangers in the aisle at Safeway. The blows barely crisscrossed Lucy's throat, but they cut it inches deep.

She dropped to her bony knees, both hands clutching her neck as if she were strangling herself. And then she saw who it was, and her blue eyes bulged with shock and pain and finally with what seemed to be a terrible sadness.

"Geoffrey," she managed in a gurgling voice, as blood bubbled from her open mouth.

Her last word on Earth. His name.

Beautiful for Shafer to hear—the recognition he craved—revenge for all of them. He turned away, forced himself to, before he did the twins as well.

He was never seen again in the Chelsea neighborhood, but everyone would remember him for as long as they lived.

God, would they remember.

That tall bald monster.

The one in all-black clothes, the inhuman freak.

The heartless killer who had committed so many horrible murders that even *he* had lost count.

Geoffrey Shafer.

Death.

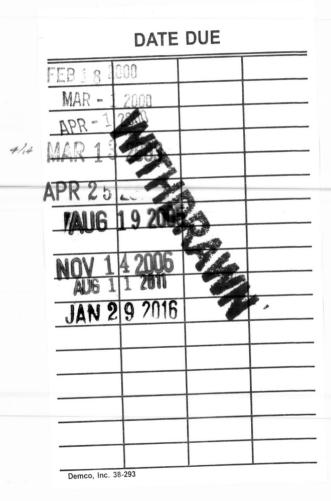